ESCAPE CLAUSE

David Berardelli

ESCAPE CLAUSE

GRAVESTONE PRESS

PART I
The First Day

CHAPTER ONE

The neon lights flashing *Pleasure Palace* splashed onto the hectic crowd bullying its way through the front doors.

Hank Lee parked his Caddie in the crowded front lot. He followed the thinning line up to the door, paid the cover charge, and squeezed past the well-dressed steroid freaks guarding the door.

Hank never came to strip joints. In his view, tossing hard-earned cash at a bunch of half-naked females he wasn't allowed to touch was expensive and plain stupid. But he wasn't here to touch or even look at half-naked women. He was here to find a man--someone who hadn't exactly been using the brain cells he'd been born with.

Amos Miller, a surveyor with Anderson & Associates, one of Orlando's major architectural firms, had been in trouble before, and women and alcohol were usually the cause of it. As Executive Field Administrator for A&A, Hank supervised the crews working the construction site. His duties dealt with overseeing the surveying operation and making sure things ran smoothly for the life of the project. During the last few weeks, Amos had been making things difficult. Broken up over his young wife leaving him, he was hitting the bottle more than usual and had been thrown in the drunk tank twice during the last two weeks, which made it difficult for him to show up for work.

Like most rough, hard-living men, Amos could attract women, but had no luck keeping them. His clever lines and clowning-around tactics were effective in the beginning, but not sufficient to sustain a lasting relationship. And it didn't help that he consistently attracted women who weren't looking to make a lasting commitment.

Judging by what Hank had learned from the other surveyors, finding Amos and sobering him up would not be easy. His latest wife, April, was more than thirty years his junior, flirted constantly, and had supported herself quite well dancing naked when she met Amos here, at Jennifer's. Hank figured this was the most logical place to begin his search. Whether she'd gone back to her former trade was anyone's guess. But it might be a good starting point.

Inside, the big room exploded with spectacular neon. It took him a little while to acclimate his eyes to the flashing multicolored glare. While he waited for his vision to return, he considered his options. The only way to help Amos was to convince him April wasn't worth this aggravation. All women were the same when the lights were out. Why would any man put himself through hell for one particular woman, when there were so many others to choose from?

It was a sexist, chauvinistic attitude--one Hank didn't believe at all, but it was the only thing he could come up with that might penetrate the thick skull of a hard-drinking construction worker. But, no matter what he might say to Amos, he doubted any well-meaning words of wisdom or sexist generalities would work. Love could be tough and unforgiving under the best of conditions. It was ten times worse when you messed it up. Hank knew trying to pound sense into a lovesick man pushing sixty was going to be like banging the man's head against a brick wall.

Looking around, Hank spotted a couple middle-aged guys in loud Hawaiian shirts ogling the gal gyrating on the nearest dance platforms. A scantily clad roving waitress came up to him and asked if he'd like a drink. He ordered Jack's on ice and continued looking for Amos. Finally, he found him perched on a barstool in front of a dance platform at the far end of the main room, his bald head pulled back far enough to pop a disk in his neck. A bottle of Budweiser sat on the counter in front of him. He was no prize package--that was evident--but he was oblivious to everything except the near-naked strawberry blonde dancing on the sparkling pedestal in front of him.

Hank sat down beside Amos and could tell by the older man's glazed expression that the only thing that could get Amos off his stool would be a baseball bat to the back of his head. Amos was a hopeless addict, and the dancing blonde before him was the drug that had him by the balls.

"Amos."

No response.

Hank tapped the man on the shoulder.

Startled, Amos yanked himself out of his trance. "H-Hank?" He squinted. "I didn't know you came

7

here."

"I don't."

Amos blinked and turned back to the blonde.

Hank hoisted the drink as soon as it was placed in front of him. Thankfully it was strong. "That April?"

"Yeah. Ain't she sweet?"

"I'm developing a serious zit just watching her."

She gyrated her hips and jiggled her small round breasts. Ignoring Amos, she smiled down at Hank. That was all he needed right now--another man's ex coming on to him. He turned away from her and faced Amos. "I'll make this short and sweet," he said. "Dragon Lady wants your ass. I told her you'd straighten out."

Amos glanced at him, dazed.

"You need a break, and I'm gonna give you one. If you fuck it up, it's my ass too."

Amos turned back to April dancing before him.

Hank sighed peevishly. He had better things to do with his time than hassle with a drunken, lovesick old man. But he knew what Amos was going through, and he really did want to give him one more chance to clean up his act and save his job. The last thing Amos needed was the company manager, Colleen Moore, swooping down on him with her razor-sharp talons. For Hank, getting through the month without throttling Colleen had become a personal challenge. The image of his hands closing around her swanlike neck and squeezing until her beautiful face turned blue made his mouth water. He took another gulp of his drink, avoiding the water ring on the bar near his elbow.

8

Colleen had been running Anderson & Associates the last three years and genuinely loved her role as the Stone Bitch. The office workers referred to her as Cat Woman. The construction crew called her Dragon Lady. The A&A execs didn't care what she was called, because she always seemed to know what she was doing.

Colleen projected an image of competence and professionalism--two important qualities the project manager of a major architectural firm desperately needed. The company, a subsidiary of Division Development Association, based out of Columbus, Ohio, kept offices in half a dozen states. Anderson & Associates specialized in high-rises and had been making a killing in the Orlando area for more than twenty years.

Colleen viewed Amos Miller as a fly in the ointment and would not tolerate such 'avoidable irritations.' She took her work seriously and considered the project her own personal creation. Anything compromising the work drove her into a rage. Hank had been called into her office half a dozen times the past two days to discuss Miller's fate.

"Fire him," she'd told him that morning. "He's compromising my project. At this rate, we'll lose our next contract. We're talking Disney for the second quarter of next year. *Disney*, for God's sake." The famous name had flowed softly and reverently from her pouty collagen lips, as if in solemn prayer. "We all know how they feel about slipshod operations. They want two mega complexes, and they don't care about price.

Between nine and ten figures has already been mentioned. We're talking *billions*. I refuse to let one drunken loser screw us out of such a huge contract."

Hank couldn't understand why Colleen had singled out Amos. Construction crews were a wild, horny bunch. Everyone knew that. "All those guys drink," he told her. "Take a peek in some of the local bars tonight and you'll see quite a few familiar faces."

"I don't care how much they drink, as long as they do their job while they're on the site. Miller's not doing his job. He's jeopardizing the project."

"How can one man jeopardize a huge contract like this one?"

"The publicity, Lee. If Disney suspects we tolerate drunks, that'll be it. They'll take their gold elsewhere."

"He's going through hell. Give him a break."

"Everyone's got problems. We've all learned to deal with them. Miller's old enough to be my father. Why should he get any more consideration than the rest of us?"

"I know what he's going through." Hank had been through similar circumstances himself. He wasn't about to let her kick a man while he was down.

"Drunks are trash. Believe me. I lived with one. You're my field man. Handle it."

Now things were clear. This had become personal. "So you want Amos nailed to the cross because you had a bad experience with a drunk?"

Colleen's large, dark, almond eyes blazed. "Get him to deliver. He was a good surveyor once. Talk to him. Tell him his ass is on the line."

"He won't listen."

"What makes you say that?"

Hank turned to her large square window. The sun was high and bright, the heavy tint barely able to keep down the powerful glare. In spite of the wide-open view, he felt trapped. Confined. "He's been screwed. When a guy's been screwed, he doesn't listen."

"Nobody ever said life was fair."

He sighed. The situation with Amos was just like what he had endured several years earlier, when Heidi drained his checking and savings accounts before walking out. Those were dark, unforgiving days. The bottle thundered into the picture, numbing things and blurring them just enough to help him sleep through the nightmares. He'd desperately wanted someone to help him out of the gutter and tell him things would get better. Someone had--at least she'd tried. But, like Amos, Hank hadn't been able to listen. His self-pity had automatically drowned out everything--and everyone--around him.

"I just think we could all use a break," he'd said to his reflection in the window.

"Talk to him, Lee," Colleen had ordered. "People with engineering and teaching degrees are working at Burger King for a lot less than we're paying Miller."

Now, as Hank sat finishing his drink, he knew it would be much easier to strangle Colleen Moore than give an ultimatum to Amos Miller, whose guts had been ripped out by a selfish young woman.

Amos poured some beer down his gullet and set the bottle shakily on the counter. "April ... she ... don't want me, Hank. Told me yesterday. Wants somebody that makes the big bucks. Somebody younger, wears a suit, drives a nice car." He frowned at Hank. "Somebody with thick, bushy *hair*." Amos reached up and touched his own bare scalp.

"Weren't you bald when she met you?" Hank knew, the moment he said it, how ridiculous that sounded.

"She saw you the other day when she picked me up at the site. Asked who you were, then said I ought to shave once in a while." He shrugged. "I shaved. Then she moved out."

"Listen, Amos..."

"She was planning all along to move out, but was scared to tell me. Thinks I'll do something drastic. I came over tonight to tell her it's okay, I understand. Soon as she's done with her number."

"How long were you two married?"

"Two years."

Hank shrugged. "You'll find someone else." He couldn't believe how much he sounded like Bing Crosby in an old Father O'Malley movie. But Colleen hadn't given him much choice.

"I dunno..."

"Hell, you've still got some juice left. Women are everywhere nowadays. The ratio's at least three to one here in Florida. It may be higher now, women starting up companies and all. You can find someone better. Trust me."

"Not like her. She can go all night long, make

you think you died and went to heaven."

"A lot of women can do that."

Amos shook his head.

"Give someone else a try. Maybe shop around in a better place."

"Like where?"

Hank couldn't believe how few brain cells this man was using. "Someplace where a girl has to wear clothes and doesn't have to show anyone how close she shaves her mound."

Amos just sighed and had more beer.

Hank couldn't blame Amos. This was no different from when Heidi decided she needed a drastic change in her lifestyle.

Hank dropped a crumpled ten on the counter and stood up. "You gonna be all right?"

"Yeah."

"Be at work tomorrow morning, then. Eight o'clock."

"Sure thing."

Hank pushed through the crowd and squeezed past the bouncers at the door. As he pulled in some fresh evening air, he hoped the residual thumping in his head from the loud music would go away.

Amos's beat-up white Nissan pickup sat just six spaces down from Hank's Caddie. A sticker that said *Surveyors Get it Done Right!* showed prominently on the rear bumper.

Hank edged down the gravel aisle. *If he doesn't show in fifteen minutes, I'll go back in and haul his ass outside.* He sincerely hoped he wouldn't have to go back in. Paying a cover charge twice to rescue a grown man who should know better was ridiculous.

He slid behind the wheel of the Caddie, sat back, and pulled down the knot of his tie. His scalp began to itch. It always did when something wasn't quite right. In Saudi, it itched constantly. Since he'd come home, that quirk had saved his bacon a couple of times, prevented him from embarrassing himself several times, and kept him out of trouble most of the time. But even though it always rang true, it still worried him.

CHAPTER TWO

Seated at her vanity, Sally Bascomb carefully applied mascara.

These days it took a little longer to get it right. It also took a steadier hand--not to mention a tad more makeup.

She first noticed the crow's feet about a year ago, spotting them one morning when the sun peeked in through the bathroom blinds while she brushed her teeth. Back then, she had to squint and move close to the mirror to see them. But lately squinting proved unnecessary. Now she could see them clearly, even five feet from the mirror, without the sun shining on her face. The little buggers had decided to dig deeper and widen, as if getting ready to build an interstate bypass around her eyes.

Sighing, she inspected her handiwork. Not exactly breathtakingly fresh, but still good enough to turn her husband's head--if only he'd look her way. She couldn't imagine how much longer this semblance of self-confidence would stay with her. It was a miracle she had any left at all, thanks to the mood swings Warren had been demonstrating lately.

She couldn't help thinking it was her fault. She tried telling herself during the last couple of months that nothing was wrong. Business pressures were responsible for Warren's foul temper and lack of interest in her. Long hours, deadlines, dealing with uncooperative people all over the world could easily take a toll. But each day brought about new fears.

15

The evidence proved frighteningly clear. Warren spent longer hours at the office and less time at home. Their conversations invariably turned into heated arguments. Worse, they hadn't had sex more than five times in the last twelve months.

Forcing herself back to more practical matters, she pushed a comb through her heavy blond mane, thanking God it was still thick and full. If she let it fall freely, with stray curls touching her cheeks, she could hardly notice the crow's feet.

But despite her hair, her youthful appearance and her slim, taut figure, some things refused to cooperate – such as that unwanted monster she'd been dreading for years. That horrid beast that would arrive, in spite of her efforts, in just three years. The dreaded Four-O. Every woman's mortal enemy.

Back when she'd dropped out of college to work as a swimsuit model for J.C. Penny's, she was twenty-one, whippet-thin, and didn't have to worry about wrinkles or sags or what an added pound would do to her perfect figure. Everything looked good on her. Heads turned wherever she went. Forty was so far away, she didn't even give it a second thought. Little did she know how quickly that freedom from worry would fly away.

Now she was struggling not to lose ground. But Bally could only do so much. Three weekly sessions of aerobics, combined with twenty minutes of sheer torture using their sadistic weight machines, would send anyone scrambling for the nearest plastic surgeon. And if that wasn't enough, she took brisk walks around the block each night after supper to burn off any unwanted calories. Her regimen kept her weight down and made everything tight and firm. It also stopped her hips from spreading and the wattle from pulling her chin loose. Those who didn't know her, guessed her at around thirty. But when her husband spent so much time with rich, important men walking around with gorgeous, slender women half their age hanging on their arms, she realized just how demanding and unforgiving the battlefield actually was.

She wondered if her physical changes could be the main reason for Warren's attitude change ... why, after nearly seven years of marriage, he no longer seemed interested. Things could be worse, but a girl didn't think of stuff like that when her husband stayed away more and tended to her less.

That episode three days ago continued eating away at her. Muriel had, as usual, planned supper for seven and was having a terrible time keeping the Porterhouse steaks from becoming desiccated chunks of charcoal. Warren's explanation for his two-hour tardiness--*corporate nonsense*--was tossed casually over his shoulder as he headed straight for the wet bar. While he fixed his drink, Sally waited for more of an explanation. When he didn't provide any, she did her best to fill in the blanks. Last-minute meetings. Conference calls. A crisis at one of the overseas plants. Labor conflicts. Management difficulties. Union troubles. Stockholder problems. Any one of dozens of possibilities could have sufficed, but he didn't bother to elaborate.

As founder and CEO of Bas-Com, Inc., the Orlando-based software conglomerate, Warren had his plate full. He'd single-handedly started up the works and was directly involved in every aspect of the business. He would not tolerate anything happening without his knowledge. Working close to eighty hours each week had never been much of a challenge.

As his wife, Sally realized this. She also considered the pressures her husband encountered during the average workday. She could sympathize with him, support him, and certainly didn't want to make the situation worse by demanding explanations when she knew how busy and difficult his schedule was. So she'd stood there silently while he made his drink, patiently hoping he'd glance her way, notice her pleasant smile, and soften. But he'd merely gulped his drink and wandered off to his study.

Her father had acted similarly while she was growing up--coming home, saying little, fixing a drink, then plopping in his favorite armchair to read the paper while Mom finished fixing supper. Growing up this way had primed her for this sort of lifestyle. Although she'd had only a few relationships before Warren--most of them casual, with one serious affair that ended horribly--she'd known men all her life and was familiar with their attitudes and moods. But even though she was nearly thirty when she married Warren, she still wasn't prepared for her husband's sudden change in behavior.

She feared he might be going through a crisis. After all, he'd turned fifty last August. As far as she knew, he hadn't experienced that silly midlife male thing. But since he was over forty when they'd met, and had recently been divorced, he might have suffered one earlier.

Thoughts of another woman briefly entered her mind. While part of her knew that could be a definite possibility, her more practical side dismissed it. Unless Warren was having a clandestine relationship in his office, he simply didn't have the time. And he wasn't the sort of man who sneaked around.

For Warren, a divorce meant inconvenience and a hefty outlay of money. He'd been divorced three times before. Each time had cost him more than a million dollars, plus stocks and other perks. Warren was worth half a billion dollars. Though he could easily afford such costs, the inconvenience of divorce proceedings and court appearances meant much more aggravation than handing over large sums of money.

Divorce meant something much worse to Sally. Though their pre-nup would leave her in terrific shape financially, she'd be forced to face the rest of her life alone--just another divorced, middle-aged woman whose best days were behind her. The image made her cringe.

She'd never wanted money to become a major factor in her future. She hadn't even known Warren was rich when she first met him. She'd wanted only love and companionship. If the money was there, fine. If not, it didn't matter, as long as love dominated the picture.

She'd met Warren on the rebound from a passionate relationship with a terrific guy with too

19

much baggage, who couldn't forget what his ex-wife had done to him. Although their union had resulted in the greatest relationship and the best sex she'd ever known, Sally could not compete with a memory. And after enduring the agony of watching the man she loved crawl back to his former love, Sally forced herself out of the picture.

But that was another matter. In another life. A life she no longer thought about--not much, anyway.

She knew things would be even worse if she'd been able to bear children. With Warren, this had never been an issue. He had two grown offspring from a previous marriage and had expressed no interest in bringing anyone else into the world. This was good because she'd never wanted kids either. As a former child whose parents frequently fought, watching her parents silently avoiding one another was not something she fondly remembered.

With one last glance in the mirror, Sally declared herself presentable. Maybe not as ravishing as she was just a few years ago, but certainly attractive and pleasant enough to greet her husband with a warm smile and a tender kiss.

Sally hurried off to the kitchen to see how Muriel was coming along with supper.

CHAPTER THREE

Standing between two pine trees, Bill Landry directed the thick stream onto a giant mound of fire ants. *There ya go, you little bastards. Run or get pissed on...*

When nothing was going right, he wanted to kick ass whenever he could. Pissing on anything--even a bunch of stupid fire ants--made you feel better, giving the illusion you were getting even. Sometimes that was the only thing that really mattered.

The ants scurried away, finding sanctuary beneath some dead leaves and a pile of pine needles. They'd come back. Ants always did--they didn't know any better.

Still nothing going on at the estate. There hadn't been any traffic at all during the last hour, which wasn't unusual in a place like that. The ritzier the neighborhood, the quieter it was. Bankers and investors relaxed in their leather-lined studies, sipping imported brandies while their brats were away at Harvard or Yale, getting drunk and high between exams. *Keep everything nice and quiet to relieve the stress of handling millions of bucks each day. When you're a fat cat, you don't want any fuss going on near your multi-million-dollar pad. That's what mega-taxes are for. Something bugs you, you just picked up the cell, and the rent-a-cops magically appear.*

Heading back, Bill tossed his spent smoke onto the pile on the sandy ground beside the rented pickup truck. He reached into his shirt pocket and coaxed out another Marlboro from the crumpled pack. *Only six left. Shit.* He couldn't remember if he had a fresh pack in his duffel bag. Right now, he could barely remember his own name. *William, Bill, Billy, Landry* ... none of those familiar monikers fit him at the moment. *Sucker* felt more like it. Or just plain *Idiot.*

He climbed back into the pickup and slammed the door, rocking the truck, but Tommy Schiller didn't notice--he was still slouched in the passenger seat, glassy-eyed and stupid from that shit-smelling Colombian weed he'd pulled out of his shirt pocket ten minutes earlier. *Schiller and his stash. Why can't he stick to the coke? At least it doesn't stink.* He would never understand how anyone could smoke something tasting that bad. It seemed like everyone they worked with went for that shit-- especially the programmers and half the program analysts.

Might as well suck on fresh dog shit. Tastes and smells like it--and it'll even turn your brain into dog shit. Schiller's brain was already mush--why coax things along? At least beer tasted better--and right now he felt like he needed one, or two, maybe even three. He'd had two a couple hours ago, but it wasn't enough to get him through this. Beer was about the only thing that relaxed him these days. Beer and two or three shots of Wild Turkey. Schiller, however, didn't go for beer or whiskey. His vices ran more expensive--a line of snort was required to put all his worries to rest. Snort and one or two of his pills.

But who gave a shit anyway? Like it or not, Schiller was his partner in this evil deed--even when the dumb-ass sat there, playing with his hair, twirling a thick red clump of it around his skinny index finger as he tore off another piece of thumbnail from his other hand still holding that smoldering, stinking roach.

Dragging his hands down his sweaty face, Bill couldn't ignore the constant chewing noise--sounded like some rat in a wall. He glared over at Schiller. "Do you *have* to do that shit?"

Schiller lowered his hand. "What shit?"

"Eating your fingernails like that."

Schiller shrugged. "It's the only way I know to eat them."

Bill hated it when Schiller chewed his fingernails--hated it even worse when he found jagged slivers on the dash, or on the console, or on his seat. He felt like decking him or shoving him outside onto the pavement. Dumb-ass kids could get away with stuff like that, not a programmer pushing thirty, for Christ's sake. It just wasn't dignified behavior for a competent adult ... not that Schiller was all that competent. "Why the hell do you have to do it at all? It's gross."

Schiller shrugged, stuck his thumb back in his mouth, and started chomping again.

"Next time we stop at a 7-Eleven, I'm gonna buy you some Life Savers. Or gum."

"Life Savers don't last very long."

"They will if you suck on them instead of chewing them up."

"Rather just eat them. And gum ... I just swallow

23

it as soon as it loses its flavor. Don't chew it anymore."

Landry huffed impatiently, wanting to ask why he didn't just spit out old gum like a normal person, but he didn't bother. Schiller wasn't normal, and asking would be a waste of time. Anyway, it wasn't worth getting mad over. *The asshole to get mad at isn't even home yet.*

Bill sat back and glared at Warren Bascomb's estate, straight ahead and up the hill beyond the clearing, bigger than shit behind the stone entrance at the end of the grassy knoll. *Like some egotistical monument to his conniving greatness. Or maybe he's just overcompensating for some personal shortcoming.* Bill grinned briefly as he continued to eye the huge estate looming not far away, imagining the same chain of events he and Schiller had witnessed the last three nights. At eight o'clock, the streetlamps at the corner would automatically flicker on. At eight-fifteen, the floods fronting the estate would splash the lawn, shrubbery, and wrought-iron gate with a hazy golden glow. At eight-thirty, the spotlight behind the church would douse the expansive lot with a thin blanket of bright yellow, its frayed edges stopping just a few yards from the wooded area that partially concealed the truck in which he and Schiller now sat.

A quick glance in the side mirror told him no one was wandering about in the church parking lot. Even if someone was out there, they wouldn't spot the pickup. The woods partially concealed them, and it was getting dark. He checked the dash clock again. Just a few minutes past seven. A typical evening in Central Florida in mid-May. The scent of honeysuckle hung heavily in the air. Gulls squawked not too far away. Toward the west, the hazy orange sun lightly brushed the tips of the palms.

A quiet night, to be sure, but it didn't help Bill breathe any easier. He wished he was anywhere else but right here, right now, waiting to do what he was supposed to do. But he couldn't be anywhere else, no matter how bad he wanted to be--couldn't just click his heels together and appear somewhere else. That only happened in fairy tales and old movies. If his and Schiller's lives hadn't been going down the shitter, they could be somewhere else ... the fishing camp, maybe, or sitting on the beach, watching the babes parade around in their skimpy bikinis. That would mean their lives were still somewhat stable. It might even mean their futures still held a glimmer of hope. But they had a job to do, and it *had* to be done. Destiny dictated it--*Bascomb* dictated it--and there was no way he and Schiller could get out of it. They were screwed, and they both knew it.

He scanned the estate driveway once again, looking for the flash of headlights that would get this freak-show started. He wasn't ashamed to admit he was nervous. More nervous, even, than he'd been that day Bascomb escorted him and Schiller into the empty conference room and threatened them with Federal time and other scary shit. That was the day he came dangerously close to pissing his pants.

Schiller, on the other hand, was ready for the rubber room. And who could blame him? Bill glanced over at the skinny runt. He wasn't exactly the world's calmest human, and tonight was no walk in the park. This kind of waiting would make anyone but a seasoned professional crawl out of their skin. But it would come to an end soon. Another hour, maybe, and then it would be over--if they were lucky.

Time sure trudges along like a dying snail when you're waiting for shit to happen, but it makes healthy tracks when you're having the time of your life. "Feels like we've been here all night," he said.

Schiller coughed wetly and tossed the smoldering black sliver of his spent roach through the open window. Watching Schiller dig through his pockets, Bill pushed more foulness out through the window opening, into the warm evening air, determined to let the air-conditioning take care of it once they got on the move. "You're not gonna smoke another one of those shit sticks, are you?"

Schiller found his regular cigarettes and lit one. "It's too soon to see Salvador Dali again. Otherwise, you'd end up doing this by yourself."

Bill lit another of his own cigarettes and sat back. Whenever Schiller was jamming with Salvador Dali, the skinny runt turned into a post. You could nail a sign to his forehead that said *OUT TO LUNCH,* and the dope-head wouldn't even notice. "What was Dali doing the last time you zapped yourself into his little playroom?"

"Squatting over a canvas, using the ends of his stash to paint something."

"Weird."

Schiller shrugged. "Sucker was *born* weird. But he sure made cool pictures."

Bill shook his head. *Weirdoes stick together.*

Schiller sucked down some smoke and stared straight ahead. "Sure is taking his sweet time."

"CEOs don't exactly have regular hours. That's why no one ever knows where he is."

"And why we've been out here three straight days now."

Three days and still no show. Almost like the bastard was deliberately making this thing drag on. "Didn't expect it to be easy, did we?" Bill said.

"I don't know what I expected, Billy..."

"We're in too deep now."

"Way too deep."

"Our own damned fault."

"Yeah, for getting caught."

Bill shook his head. "I still can't figure how that happened."

"Bad karma."

"Don't go all whacky-religious on me, now..." He hated when Schiller brought up that kind of shit.

Schiller shrugged. "No other reason for it. Not when everyone else was pulling something too, and we were the ones to get caught."

"Everything just seemed to turn around and go all funny." He sighed, mulling over Schiller's mention of karma, and the childhood images shot past. *You sow what you reap.* They'd taught him that in catechism class. *Do unto others. An eye for an eye. Vengeance is mine.* The Bible was chock-full of good shit like that. Funny, though. He'd never thought much about any of that back then. All he'd cared about was skipping catechism class with the rest of the guys, without the folks finding out.

"We've always been on Bascomb's bad side," Schiller said. "Take that backup program I created for him two years ago. It was just as efficient and workable as anything anyone else coulda done. But not for him--no siree. He wanted a whole new configuration. Didn't want the competition to get it. That's all I heard that weekend. The fucking competition. Jeez ... every ten minutes he was pulling up every bit of Spyware and Malware he could find. Dude's fucking paranoid."

"He treated me the same when I created that website for him." Bill pushed out some foul memories along with the cigarette smoke. "Bastard trashed it and told me to design a new one. Gave me *four damned hours* to do it." He wiped the back of his neck. The anger was getting him really hot. "Coulda made a grand, maybe more, from anyone else. Damn."

"And you killed yourself designing the new one."

"I didn't have a choice."

"Like tonight?"

Bill tried to read his friend's expression in the darkness of the cab. He hadn't liked the way Schiller had said that. "What're you getting at?"

"Not a fucking thing."

"You sure?"

Schiller pushed out another cloud of cigarette smoke between his pursed lips. The plume scattered against the dark windshield in gray slivers, like a wavy starburst. "I'd give anything to get out of this."

"Can't."

"Yeah. He made things pretty clear."

"Spelled everything right out."

Penetrating the woods straight ahead, headlights splashed the road, slowing as the vehicle moved steadily toward the estate.

Schiller gulped audibly. "That him, Billy?"

Bill Landry stiffened, and his pulse raced. "You got it."

CHAPTER FOUR

A trickle of ice tapped Sally between the shoulder blades as Warren passed through the dimly lit archway.

He approached the wet bar with that cold, hooded look in his dark eyes. *Another bad day, obviously. Probably something to do with the recent drop in Venture stock.*

Venture was worth several million, and was a major extension of Bas-Com. Its collapse would be disastrous. It was only natural Warren's nerves would be on edge. But she didn't know much of the details, because Warren clammed up whenever she tried discussing it. She couldn't remember his behavior shifting so much until the Venture problems, but could she blame Venture for *all* his stress?

She was determined not to let Warren's demeanor intimidate her. He was her husband--not the enemy. They should be rationalizing their differences and problems and sharing their thoughts and concerns. Discussing the market and its ups and downs would probably help manage the ups and downs of their marriage, considering how closely Warren's mood mimicked his company's stock performance.

Understanding the workings of big money had always been difficult for Sally. Growing up in a middle-class household--her father constantly working, her mother home, tending the house--had made her appreciate hard work and the meager rewards associated with it. Struggling had always been second nature to her. She'd gone to college on a partial scholarship, waitressing to pay her bills until she decided to try modeling. The modeling paid top-dollar, but her career was incredibly short, and she soon found herself waitressing again, tending bar on the side, and working as a receptionist to pay the bills. But at least it was honest, straightforward work. For Sally, sitting at a console and watching your profits and holdings jump around like a drunken mosquito was no different from watching a foreign movie without subtitles.

"How was your day?" she asked softly.

"A killer." He raised the glass to his lips and eased some of the strong mixture into his mouth.

She saw that filmy curtain of indifference sway between them again. She couldn't let the conversation drop completely. Being a major stockholder of Bas-Com, she needed to be involved in some way. She didn't want to insult her husband by not showing interest. "I'm sorry to hear that."

"*That* certainly means a lot." He downed the rest of the drink and reached for the vodka bottle.

Sally's forehead grew warmer. Warren only drank this much when he was really upset. "Do you want to talk about it?"

"What else would you like to know?" He replaced the vermouth bottle on the white laced doily.

"Whatever you'd like to tell me."

"I'm really not in a talking mood right now."

She was obviously going about this the wrong

31

way. She should let this go. She already had some idea what happened--why not leave it at that?

Muriel. My one true ally.

"I'll check on dinner." She tried to pass. "The roast should be just about--"

"I ate earlier."

She froze. Her concern had quickly morphed into something else. The tapping at the base of her skull grew hot. "Why ... didn't you call?"

"Didn't think of it."

She took in a breath and forced down the heat trying to climb up her throat. "It would have been nice if you had."

He just shrugged.

"So you decided to eat at the office and not give me a heads-up?"

"Things were crazy. It's done, so forget it. You're hungry. Eat."

"Maybe I'll have something later." She was too upset to think about supper right now.

"If you're not hungry, why all the fuss?"

"I *was* hungry..."

"And I'm supposed to feel guilty for having a bear of a workday? For wolfing down a quick sandwich during an overseas conference call and not asking your permission first?"

"Warren..." Further talk would be fruitless. "Let's not fight, okay?"

"I wasn't the one who started this." His glare grew cold, almost evil. Sally could actually feel the burning within him as he reached for the vodka bottle once again.

"Why are you drinking so much?"

"I'm thirsty. Enough said?"

"I don't understand you sometimes."

He sighed tiredly. "I run a corporation. There are things you can't possibly–"

"I know. It's always the corporation. Your excuse for everything."

"You don't seem to mind the lifestyle it's given you when you take your classic car out to the mall, buy five grand worth of clothes–"

"I *never* spend that much." She had no idea where he'd gotten his information. She hadn't spent that much in clothes all year. "And the car was a birthday present. Why are you bringing *that* up?"

"With all the damned questions, you're starting to sound like the jerks I have to deal with at work."

"So, now I'm a jerk because I try to talk to you? Thank you *so* much."

"How am I supposed to feel? You stand there, tossing your silly questions at me, and don't like the answers you're getting."

"I guess I'm not supposed to ask *any* questions."

"You can, as long as they're reasonable."

"How am I supposed to know if they're reasonable?"

"You're fairly intelligent. Who knows? You might get lucky." He swallowed more of his drink.

It was time to end this. "I don't want to do this. I wanted to have a nice supper with you–"

"I know, I know. I should have stopped right in the middle of that conference call. How silly of me."

The heat radiating from him made her shiver. Where in heaven's name was it coming from?

"Why are you so angry?"

"I don't know. Why *am* I?"

She shrugged. "I'm beginning to think you don't want me around anymore."

"Maybe I just want a little peace and quiet after ten hours of knocking heads together."

She strongly suspected there was much more to this than his craving for peace and quiet. But this wasn't the time to get into it. "Warren, let's start over, please?"

"Go take your walk."

"I usually take my walk after supper."

"Then have your supper and take your walk. Or take your walk, *then* come back and have your supper. Do whatever the hell you please." He sighed once again. "I have people bugging me all day long. When I come home, I'd like to know that the bugging has ended for a while."

"Maybe you need some time to yourself," she said quietly.

His silence told her what she'd feared all along. It wasn't the business or the corporation. It wasn't even the stress. It was her. *I'm a stranger. In my own house.*

Without another word, he disappeared through the dining room doorway.

I need to get away. This place is suffocating me...

No walking again tonight. She was much too upset. In her present state, she was liable to walk all the way to Altamonte before her nerves settled down and made her aware of where she was.

Her keys and purse sat in the Mustang. She'd left them there when she'd come home from the grocery. Tears filled her eyes as she pulled open the back door and disappeared into the muggy night.

**

"What's going on in there?" The heavy sense of dread slid down Tommy's back, like cold molasses.

"You in a hurry?" Billy said, leaning back in his seat.

"Just wondering what's happening."

"Getting your panties in a wad won't help."

That was all well and good, Billy saying that, but Tommy hated when things didn't feel right. At least in programming you could work things out, figure what went wrong by stepping it out and tracking down the ABEND. Everything blended, formed a pattern. When it fucked up, you just started all over.

He felt much more comfortable with the programs he'd designed, things progressing in steps, falling on top of one another like a stack of well-placed dominos, one job kicking off the next, over and over, until it all ended normally. This situation wasn't exactly a program, but it still should happen like that, since he and Billy had it all worked out.

Bascomb and his old lady would eat supper. They'd talk. *How was your day, dear? Fine, precious, made two mil today. Really? That's nice.* Then coffee and maybe a drink later on. Maybe even a little nookie if Bascomb wanted to celebrate making that two million. Then he'd retire to his study to finish up some work, as planned, while the missus went out for her evening stroll.

So why did Tommy have this hugantic lump in the back of his throat he couldn't force down? He looked over at Billy, who stayed silent. *Fuck him.*

35

Apparently he'd decided things were going just fine. He was smoking his cigarette, all mellow and comfortable in his seat, waiting patiently.

Tommy couldn't let the shakes take over. He needed some snort but knew Billy wouldn't approve. Any other time, he'd tell Billy where to stick it. But not now. No siree. Without Billy, he was about as fucked as a body could possibly be.

Billy flicked his smoke out the window and sat up. "We probably have half an hour or so until the old lady shows."

Tommy couldn't understand Billy sometimes. He seemed all calm and collected, as if this waiting game were no worse than standing in line at the local 7-Eleven to buy a six-pack of Bud.

"Another half-hour," Tommy said under his breath. *Half an hour here, half an hour there. We're pros, we can handle anything. We should put a fucking sign on the door of the truck and advertise ... Kidnappers-R-Us.*

"What's wrong?" Billy asked.

"Nothing."

"You're acting like you just sat down on a pile of fire ants."

"I got this lump in my throat."

"Force it down."

"It won't go down."

"Why not?"

"'Cause something's wrong, and I can't figure out what it is."

"You're in too much of a damned hurry, that's all."

"Last two nights, she's due for her walk but

36

doesn't show. Dammit, Billy, she knows we're out here!"

Billy let loose with a heavy sigh. "You're full of shit."

"Jeez ... we haven't seen a sign of her in three days. Something's wrong. I can feel it." Tommy's gut started up its grinding noises again. Like that time he'd had too many *jalapeños* in his lunch at Taco Bell.

"She'll show." Billy had pulled his seat back up. He actually looked worried, which made Tommy feel a little better. He didn't want to be the only one crapping his drawers.

***

Ten minutes after Hank left the Pleasure Palace and sat waiting in his car, Amos staggered outside.

He'd obviously sucked down another beer or two. He shuffled, his tennis shoes, kicking up gravel. Then he stumbled, nearly falling on his ass.

Sighing, Hank pushed open the Caddie door.

Amos had dropped his keys. He got down awkwardly and crawled on all fours on the gravel, searching. He didn't notice when Hank squatted beside him.

"Looking for something, or are you planning to take a catnap under your truck?"

"You're real funny," Amos snarled, not laughing. His sudden belligerence suggested April had probably pressed another button.

"I try. Need some help with your keys?"

"I can find 'em, dammit." Amos groped blindly underneath the pickup.

The keys sat near the front tire. Hank scooped

them up and straightened. "I really shouldn't be giving these to you."

"Saying I'm too drunk to drive my ass home?" Amos snatched them up and straightened so abruptly, he nearly fell backward.

"That about covers it."

Amos's face crinkled. His small dark eyes glistened in the haze of the streetlight. "You're an asshole, Hank Lee. Anyone ever tell you that?"

"Once or twice. And now you, apparently."

"Well, I mean it."

"I can tell you're sincere."

"Fuck you. Fuck you and your twelve-hundred-dollar suits, your thick brown hair, and your uppity attitude. And that goddamn expensive heap you haul your uppity ass around in. And another thing. Your stupid smart-ass jokes just ain't cuttin' it tonight."

"Actually, this suit went for seven-fifty on the spring clearance rack. I can't take credit for the hair--it's the Italian on my mother's side, so I'm told. I bought the Caddie when it was a year old. The attitude comes from dealing with nasty people. As for the bad jokes?" He shrugged. "Just something I picked up from the Marines. Guess it's an acquired taste."

Without warning, Amos threw a clumsy roundhouse punch, missing Hank's jaw by two feet. Groaning, Amos collapsed onto the rough gravel.

I really don't need this... After wasting much of his workday arguing with Colleen Moore, Hank considered this a totally unsatisfying end to the evening. But since he was already here, he figured he might as well save Amos the indignity of being hauled off by the OPD and tossed into the drunk tank.

Squatting, he grabbed Amos under the arms and propped him up against the side of the truck. He dragged him toward the back, lowered the tailgate, and laid him down on the bed. Once he got back to his Caddie, he started it up and coasted toward Amos's truck. He got out, opened the back door, pulled Amos from the pickup bed, dragged him over, and pushed him into the back of his car.

Tired and disgusted, Hank slid behind the wheel and pulled away.

CHAPTER FIVE

Being stuck outdoors, watching through a truck windshield as this crappy evening turned even darker was bad enough, but with the shakes rippling through his body, everything got worse.

Tommy felt nervous and jumpy all over, even without all sorts of bugs flying around--mosquitoes, gnats, flies. He'd never liked the outdoors. When something wasn't biting him, it was buzzing around his ears. He swatted at a shrill hum hovering near his nose.

He felt much better sitting at the computer in an air-conditioned room. That was his domain, where he reigned supreme. His own personal realm. He could work miracles from his computer. The warm rush of power flowed heavily through him. Life made sense. He seldom got the shakes in his own domain. But when the shakes came, he had to do something fast.

Best thing for that was to take a quick jaunt down the hall and maybe have a smoke in the parking lot. Valium also hit the spot--if he was lucky enough to have some with him. But he tried staying away from those bad boys when he was working. He couldn't very well run a program when his fingers couldn't feel the keyboard.

It didn't take very much to calm him. Just one of the tiny caplets he always brought with him for emergencies--like right now, just to take the edge off. He glanced over at Billy as he made a move for his trouser pocket.

"You'd better not be digging for one of those damned downers," Billy warned with a glare.

"I'm getting the shakes."

"Just wait."

"Jeez, Billy, you know how I get."

"We *can't* screw this up. Anyone finds out what we're up to, we're toast."

"Just one'll calm me down."

Billy shook his head.

"How come you're not losing it?" It baffled Tommy how Billy could be so unaffected. "You're in this, too."

"Am I?"

Billy could be such a butthole. "Yeah, Billy, you are. But you're acting like you don't even care."

"Maybe I'm just holding it together because someone has to, and I know you won't."

"Jeez ... sometimes you seem like you're not even here in the first place."

Billy sighed. "I zone out a lot."

Tommy rubbed his hands together to stave off the trembles. "I'd like to zone out too..."

"Yeah. With those fucking meds you always carry around."

"I can't just close my eyes and forget everything like you do."

"Try."

"I can't."

"Then quit worrying so much. We'll get through this."

"I just keep wondering what went wrong, Billy. Maybe you screwed something up, triggered some kind of hidden security app when you created that

41

dummy account and dumped those junk shares into it."

"You saying it's *my* fault we're in this mess?"

Tommy shrugged. "It should've worked..."

"Damned straight. More than a dozen other boneheads at Venture were doing the same thing."

Tommy nodded fitfully. It was a sound idea. Made sense too, since the stock was about to be unloaded anyway. "So how'd we end up getting pinched for it? Are we the only ones Bascomb dragged in and threatened with felony charges?"

"I dunno. Just lucky, I guess."

"Shoulda bought a Lotto ticket, too."

"Maybe your nasty little habit of selling coke on company property got Bascomb's attention," Billy suggested. "And he was already keeping an eye on us."

Tommy hated when Billy brought that up. "I'm not the only one who does that, either."

"You were the one he caught. Red-handed."

Tommy lit a cigarette with shaky fingers.

"And because of that, Bascomb was scoping *both* of us."

Tommy puffed away, hoping the nicotine would relax him for now.

A hundred yards straight ahead, the automatic lights came on, turning the estate into a miniature White House. Trimmed shrubbery and flower gardens surrounded the mansion. The stone fountain on the front lawn splashed a shower of multicolored spotlighted water into the small pond.

The artificial tranquility was interrupted by the glare of headlights highlighting the woods in front

42

of them. A vehicle sped down the paved drive, pulling out quickly.

"That's ... her Mustang," Billy said.

"Shouldn't she still be eating supper?" This made no sense. "What're we supposed to do now?" Tommy shrieked.

"Calm down." Billy started up the truck but kept the lights off. "Looks like she's not taking her walk again tonight."

"If that's her."

"It's her. Bascomb wouldn't be caught dead driving an old Stang. Even a classic."

"Why not? It's a really cool ride."

"Bascomb's a lot of things, but he's not cool."

Tommy felt the shakes trying to flare up again. This was not good at all. Everything was supposed to be so fucking quick and easy. They were to wait until Bascomb's wife circled the block on her nightly walk. Only for the past few nights, she hadn't taken her damned walk, so they couldn't very well snatch her from the sidewalk and push her into the back of the truck. Following her in a moving vehicle so they could somehow nab her was never part of the plan. "She's getting away. What are we supposed to do?"

"We're gonna follow her, dumb-ass, and cut her off somehow before she gets on the main highway."

"*Follow* her? I dunno, Billy..."

Billy stomped on the gas pedal, and the truck lurched forward. "What choice do we have? We gotta do this, or Bascomb'll come down on us ... *hard*."

"I don't like this ... it doesn't feel right."

43

"When did it ever?"

**

Her pulse fluttering wildly, Sally pulled into northbound traffic.

This can't be happening. I'm imagining all this. All I have to do is rub my eyes and wake up. Everything will go away, like a bad dream. I'll be in bed with Warren lying beside me, filling the bedroom with his terrible snoring.

But she knew better. She wasn't dreaming, she was behind the wheel of her car, heading for the GreeneWay. She'd left the comfort of her home because she needed fresh air--to think, to get away.

As a teenager, she'd frequently taken long walks at night whenever something was bothering her. Luckily, she and her family lived in a fairly nice neighborhood with very little crime, so she wasn't afraid to go off by herself. The darkness and night air refreshed her mind, got rid of all the bad stuff clouding her thoughts, and helped her to see things much clearer. With a new perspective, she could understand the things she'd had trouble grasping. And the relative quiet--without all the arguing of her parents--helped calm her nerves. Getting away had always seemed to work in the past, but would it do anything for her now?

No. I'm a grown woman, with grown-up problems. Things aren't that simple anymore.

Her husband had treated her horribly, worse than he'd ever done before. He belittled her, dismissed her, made her feel guilty for being there in the first place ... for being his wife, for being alive.

What the hell is going on? What's happened

between us?

Tears streamed down her face, and she swiped them away with the back of her hand. She barely watched the road as she tried to think back, assessing their relationship.

When she'd first met Warren in that bamboo shack on Miami Beach, she'd only been bartending there for a few weeks. The bright sun, palm trees, and white sand gave her new life a mystical, endless-vacation ambience – quite a change from the emotionally traumatic night she'd fled Orlando. Forgetting the man who'd betrayed her love felt almost impossible at first. But making drinks for people and listening to their problems made her own dark memories pale in comparison.

Warren came strolling in that sunny afternoon, wearing sandals, a straw hat, Bermuda shorts, and the loudest, baggiest Hawaiian shirt she'd ever seen. He plopped down on a stool and flashed her that signature shark smile of his and told her one of the lamest old bar jokes in the world. She'd laughed, more out of professional politeness than real humor. Psyched up by his small success, he told her another bad joke, and then another, until she was genuinely laughing.

She remembered how good it felt to laugh and burst out with a little half-laugh right there in the car. But it sounded more like a sob than a giggle. She shook her head and wiped her eyes, trying to watch the road better after someone swerved in front of her. But it took only a second for her to think back to her first days with Warren, such a welcome relief after the awful split that nearly

45

broke her.

Warren had come to Miami to attend a software convention. After that first afternoon, he returned to the bar the next day, and the next, and she realized he was quite witty and smoothly charming, with self-confidence that screamed for attention – her attention. For the first time in a very long time, she began to feel good about herself again. She needed that – craved it – and didn't want it to stop. When the convention ended, he stuck around. For the next several weeks, he treated her like a princess, taking her everywhere to show her a good time, and aggressively wooed her by showering her with gifts and compliments. He clearly wanted her. She was flattered. But more important, she needed someone to want her after the betrayal and disappointment she'd been through recently. It was easy to let herself believe Warren's repeated and surprising professions of love. She gave herself permission to move past the hurt of an affair gone bad, and Warren had been ready to replace that regret with a shiny new relationship full of promise. Gradually the pain in her heart lessened. After a while, she no longer thought much about it. It didn't fully disappear, of course. But that didn't matter, because she had no illusions that it ever would.

She'd agreed to marry Warren without really getting to know him or allowing herself to think things through – without admitting the fact that she just wanted her life of lonely despair to be over after the ugly breakup still haunting her dreams. But if she'd been thinking clearly then, she would have realized as soon as Warren shoved a prenup in her face, life with him wasn't going to be all wine and roses. That's when she realized how much money Warren really had, and how eager his attorney was to protect his assets for him, even when he didn't seem to be able to think with the right head.

The one thing she did right was to have her friend Paul George look over the prenuptial contract. She'd known Paul and his wife Cheryl since college and treasured their enduring friendship. Paul now had a thriving law practice, and only when he was satisfied with the terms, did he give her the go-ahead to marry the man he clearly stated wasn't right for her and didn't deserve her. Clearly having more professional knowledge of Warren than she did, he pointed out she'd be Warren's fourth wife in a long string of affairs and broken marriages. He warned her Warren had the reputation of a habitual womanizer and was easily swayed by any pretty face and shapely figure flashing in his face.

But Sally didn't listen. Still stinging from the loss of a love that had meant everything to her, she was desperate to move on. A love like that only comes once in a lifetime – if at all – and she'd lost hope of ever finding another man like the one who'd got away, stolen back by his ex-wife. In that frame of mind, she didn't want to admit she was marrying Warren as a consolation prize, and that Warren, in turn, treated her more like a contest grand prize he'd won, and not an individual he actually loved and cherished. She focused instead on the fact that they had fun together, and he professed his love to her constantly, as if that would help close the deal. Although the sex wasn't stupendous for her, he always came away satisfied, glowing about his performance. At the time, she believed pleasant companionship with benefits was enough. After all, what else was there out there for her? The best was already taken.

So, she married Warren, and moved right back to Orlando, the one place she didn't want to be. But she didn't worry so much, knowing she'd be running with a different crowd now. It would be highly unlikely she'd ever see the one man she used to love, and the ex-wife who'd managed to coax him back into bed with her. Sally still found herself wondering if he'd remarried the beautiful, snarky bitch. And, if so, were they still together?

Shaking her head, Sally focused on the road ahead as the overhead streetlights showered everything with a soft, hazy glow. It didn't matter what her old flame was doing, or who he was with now. Sally had moved on, and she had a marriage of her own to worry about.

But what kind of marriage did she really have? As soon as the wedding was over, so was the honeymoon, it seemed. She fell into the routine of the dutiful but neglected wife, and Warren dropped all pretense of trying to impress her or indulge her. Oh, sure, he took her on lots of trips to exotic places, but he showed her off like the arm candy she knew she was. He still told her how much he loved her, but he also slighted her and neglected her and made her feel bad on a regular basis – not something a man would do to a woman he truly cared about.

She couldn't count the number of times he'd come home, abrupt and uncommunicative, and head straight for the wet bar. Sometimes he'd get short with her when she didn't have enough sense to keep her mouth shut and give him time to cool off. After a drink or two, he usually calmed down and apologized, using the now-familiar excuse of business stress to gloss over his rudeness. Lately, however, he was never in a good mood. He stormed in, had his drinks, and didn't even bother to apologize for being late, or missing dinner, or inconveniencing her and taking her for granted. He'd either ignore her completely, or snap at her if she pushed the issue. But he'd never stood there, belittling her like he did tonight. What was different? What had gone so wrong at work that—

Work's not the reason, she told herself honestly. The look in his eyes tonight said it all.

She started to sob but gulped and held her breath until she thought her lungs would explode.

I won't fall apart over this. It's stupid, and I don't deserve any of it. It's not my fault!

Finally, she exhaled and then sucked in a shaky breath.

Wake up! This has been going on ever since we got married. Now it's worse and getting way out of hand. What's next? Physical abuse? A little slap across the cheek to settle the old lady down? How much longer am I going to let him do this to me before I face the truth? I'm better than this. I don't have to put with his crap! I know it, and he knows it. So, why is he treating me like dirt?

The answer came to her instantly.

He doesn't care – and maybe never truly did. He used to want me, even if I was just decoration, but now he's made it clear. He simply doesn't want me anymore.

Her next realization ripped through her, coming from some hidden place, and lunging at her like a caged animal finally let loose after too much confinement.

Do I want him? Do I really want to stick around and put up with his abuse? I'm not getting anything out of this arrangement, and it's clear things aren't going to improve. I've just been going through the motions, hoping we'd forge a strong and lasting union.

The obvious answer came out quick and vicious.

You know what you must do, Sal.

New tears streamed down her face, but she didn't bother wiping them away. She bit her lip and let out a breath she hadn't realized she was holding.

He doesn't love me. And I was just a stupid, gullible fool to tell myself he ever loved me. After four marriages, his reputation, and the way he treats me, it's clear he isn't capable of love. And him saying, 'I love you,' is just meaningless words coming out of his mouth like a habitual chant – not that I've heard those words lately. There's only one thing I can do.

Leave.

She bit back more tears and shook her head as she mindlessly guided her barreling Mustang between the lines in the road. Leaving meant running away. Again. Leaving meant admitting failure in love. Again. She sucked in a deep breath and let it out slowly.

Just calm down and try to think this through.

Warren would be drunk by now. He'd been drinking by the time he'd stepped into the alcove. And he'd had three more before she even left the house. He usually fell asleep when he'd had too much to drink. Sometimes he crashed in his study. She could probably sneak back home without him noticing. If he was in the study, retreating to their bedroom would not be a problem. But what if he was sleeping in their bed? He could even be sitting on the couch, waiting for her to come back so he could continue his tirade.

No. Returning right now wouldn't be very bright. What am I going to do now? Think ... think!

Finding another place for the night seemed much more sensible. And she needed to talk to somebody. *Paul.*

He knew her situation better than anyone, having reviewed and modified her prenuptial contract with Warren to guarantee she got the best possible deal in a worst-case scenario. Well, things were getting pretty close to worst-case, in her estimation. She needed some solid advice about what to do next. Paul was not only her personal legal counsel, but he was also always there whenever she needed a friendly ear. Although it was a bit late to be asking such a favor, she knew he and Cheryl wouldn't mind putting her up for the night. All she had to do was let them know what was going on.

She opened the console and reached for the cell phone.

It wasn't there.

My God. What did I–

Then she remembered. It was probably still hanging from the strap of its small black leather case on the coat tree in the hall. She'd passed it on her way out of the house, not even noticing or thinking about it in her storm of anger. At the time, she was focused on getting away from Warren and breathing in some fresh air. Using the car for her escape was an afterthought. The keys remained in the ignition, with her clutch purse on the passenger seat. She always kept them there. With the usual half a dozen twenties and a credit card or two inside it, most of the time it was all she needed. But this was an emergency.

She cursed herself for leaving her phone behind. She'd just have to find a phone somewhere to call Paul and Cheryl. They probably wouldn't even mind if she just showed up unannounced, although she never liked doing things that way. Best do it properly and call first.

She just needed a place to crash and some friendly faces to help her through this. She was tired of trying to deal with it alone. With a good talk about all her options, and then hopefully a good night's sleep, she'd be able to see things much clearer in the morning. Then maybe when she did go back home, she could sit down with Warren and talk things out to find out what was really bothering him, instead of imagining the worst.

She pulled onto 417 and headed north toward Altamonte, where Paul and his wife Nancy lived. It was getting late, but that was no problem. Paul always worked late.

Sally punched the gas pedal, staying in the slow lane even when approaching seventy-five miles an hour. Since it was well past rush hour, there was less traffic than usual. She kept it at seventy-five for the next few miles to cover more distance and hoped the rest of the night would be an improvement over the last half-hour.

It couldn't possibly get any worse...

***

With Amos snoring loudly in the back seat, Hank took the Caddie east on Colonial.

After talking to Colleen Moore that day, Hank had found out from Personnel that Amos lived in a small one-bedroom garden apartment off East Colonial, a couple of miles from the 417 exit.

The apartment complex was obviously one that hadn't had been earmarked by the City for a facelift during the last few years. Since it clearly catered to minorities, it would be placed on low priority. Such developments were usually torn down, bulldozed and replaced. The people who owned and operated them knew this. As a result, very few resources were spent on improvements. Consequently, the dirty brick buildings all needed roof repair. The front doors cried out for a fresh coat of paint. The tiny lawns fronting each building hadn't seen a mower recently. Junked cars, some sitting on blocks, filled many of the parking spaces. A trio of slender, dark-haired young men strolled shirtless down the crumbling walk, smoking cigarettes and chattering away in Spanish.

Hank parked, got out, and circled around the back to nudge Amos awake. Supporting him around the waist, he half-dragged him to the building.

One bare light bulb fastened to a cheap sconce screwed into the wall added frayed strands of orange haze to the hall. The area smelled of garbage and booze. Using Amos's keys, Hank opened the door and pulled him inside.

The apartment was small, sparsely decorated, and smelled of cigarettes, stale beer, and burnt onions. Hank dropped Amos onto the worn green couch and sat heavily in a battered armchair. He pushed a big-knuckled hand through his hair and cursed himself for being pulled into this mess.

What the hell was he doing here, anyway? He was a Field Administrator--not a nursemaid for an over-the-hill surveyor who couldn't control his hormones.

Still, Hank believed everyone needed a second chance. That statement usually rang true, but was it realistic? He'd already given Amos a chance by not firing him. To show his gratitude, the idiot had tried rearranging Hank's face.

Hank knew he shouldn't take that seriously. Amos hadn't even been aware of what he was doing at the time. The only thing moving around in the man's thick skull was the glistening image of April strutting around in her pasties and G-string.

Amos rubbed his temples and grunted into a sitting position. When his eyes finally focused, he noticed Hank. "What the hell did I do *this* time?"

"You tried to deck me."

"*Jesus*. Sorry, Hank. Did I ... *hurt* you?"

"You might have, if you'd have gotten a little closer."

54

"Thank God." Amos rubbed his eyes. "Hope you know I was really fucked up."

"I'm glad you cleared it up. I wondered."

"You coulda beat the living shit outa me."

About time the idiot began seeing things clearly. "I hate to say this, Amos, but you *need* someone to do that for you."

"Too late. April already did one helluva job."

"April's just being female."

"She does that really well, too."

"All the more reason to get her out of your blood."

"Ain't that easy."

"My ex-wife was a hot number too. Just as sexy as April." Hank didn't want to share his memories with anyone, but nothing else seemed to work for Amos, and he didn't want to stay here any longer than he had to. "But like all beautiful women, she was high-maintenance. She wanted me around her all the time and didn't like it when I spent too much time working. She wanted me to take her places and show her off. She'd make all kinds of plans and arrangements without asking me, then throw a tantrum if I couldn't make it or take her where she wanted to go. She never seemed content unless she was out among people, showing everyone how beautiful she was. In public, she was a totally different person who didn't even seem to notice that I was there with her. But in private, she made me feel like the greatest guy in the world. I was on a constant roller-coaster ride with that woman. She was so good at what she did, I had no idea I was even on a ride at the time."

The sourness in his throat from the memories came back. Hank feared it would always be just one breath away. He breathed out carefully. "That's the way it was with me, Amos. And from where I stand, that's the way it is with you." He shrugged. "Face it. She doesn't want you anymore."

Amos suddenly appeared older and smaller. Hank hated himself for blasting him.

"I know." Amos looked down at his feet. "Christ, I see it every time I look in the mirror. I was too old for her when we got married. Guess our hormones were in overdrive."

"Then why let some bimbo who doesn't—"

"She's *not* a bimbo." Amos's face tightened.

"You've got a good job, Amos. If you straighten up, you might be able to stay with A&A another couple of years. There's a huge project in the works for next year--who knows what'll follow? But Colleen Moore's after your ass, and when she goes after someone, he's as good as dead."

"Ain't afraid of her."

"You'd better be."

Amos blinked. "You saying she's got *you* scared?"

"Scared isn't the right word. I don't trust her, and I watch every damned thing I say to her. The big boys listen to her. She looks good and dresses well, so quite naturally the investors want her around. She's got degrees in management and business. That makes her even more attractive. And when a bright, educated, hot-looking female is running a company, it makes everyone look good. That's it in a nutshell."

"She fucks around. *That's* why she's boss."

"Makes no difference. If you straighten up, she'll forget about you and go after someone else. Got it?"

"Yeah."

Hank stood and instantly felt the fatigue drifting back in warm waves. "Got a way to pick up your truck at the club?"

"One of the guys'll take me in tomorrow. I can get a ride back out there during lunch."

"Good plan. But do yourself one huge favor while you're there."

"What's that?"

"Don't go inside."

***

Billy slowed down at the yellow light and stopped at the big four-way intersection. "Don't wanna get too close." He stared at the heavy columns of headlights straight ahead. "We saw where she got on. We won't let her get far."

Tommy didn't think too much of Billy's statement. How could anybody keep an eye on a vehicle in this much traffic without getting close? "What happens if we lose her?"

Billy opened his window a crack to let some smoke out. "We won't. That car's a classic, and it really stands out. How many others like that do you see—"

Across the street, three messy-looking dudes in tee shirts and baggy jeans came out of a liquor store, all three carrying brown bags. "I'm not talking about the car, Billy."

Billy closed the window and glanced at him. "Go on. Spit it out."

57

"She's a looker. Beautiful ladies always attract attention. She probably can't go anywhere without being noticed. All kinds of horny assholes out there."

"Women like her have to deal with all sorts of bastards all their lives. Don't worry about her. She can handle herself."

Billy still wasn't getting it. "Maybe so. But we don't know where she's going. We might not be able to get close enough if we wait too long. And we sure don't want anyone spotting us."

Billy shrugged. "We saw where she went. We'll figure something out."

"Won't matter much if we can't keep an eye on her."

"We'll be all right. What can go wrong?"

What can go wrong? Tommy stared at Billy. *Lots of things.* Lots of things had already gone wrong--which explained why they were in this mess in the first place. He sure hoped Billy knew what he was doing...

He also hoped the damned light would change soon. Sally Bascomb's classic Mustang could easily turn off one of the dozens of exits on that stretch. Then they'd have to scrap their plan *again*.

He slouched lower in the seat. He couldn't handle this much longer. He'd definitely need a seriously large batch of Valium. "This light's too fucking long. Someone needs to fix it. We've been sitting here five minutes, now. Five minutes could mean five miles on that road."

Billy sighed with audible irritation. "No one can average sixty in all this traffic."

"She could still make some distance in five minutes."

"You're gonna worry yourself right into the rubber room."

Billy's suggestion made him less tense, somehow. Traffic, crowds, and too much noise had always made him jumpy. "Least it's quiet in there."

"They'll give you meds, too. You'll be in heaven."

"You know something, Billy? You're the worst best friend a guy ever had."

"How would you know? You never had a friend before."

"People are assholes. Who wants an asshole for a friend?"

Billy snorted. "Hell, *I've* got one."

"Funny, Billy. Very funny."

***

A one-story gray blockhouse sat sandwiched between an auto body shop and a deserted strip mall a few blocks from Amos Miller's apartment complex on East Colonial.

The sign *TILLIE'S TAVERN* hung over the porch, swaying in the waft from heavy eastbound traffic.

Hank parked next to a black SUV in the small gravel lot. He got out and pulled in some warm, exhaust-laden air. A mosquito flitted around but didn't prove troublesome. Not even mosquitoes wanted to be near heavy traffic.

The dark air-conditioned room boasted three people--the barmaid, and an elderly couple sitting at a table near the front window, probably the owners of the SUV. Hank went to the far end of the bar and lowered his tired butt onto a stool.

The barmaid, a tall, skinny platinum blonde in her late forties, approached him. Her black velvet vest covered much of her long-sleeved white shirt. She wore black slacks and smelled of ginger. A black leather belt with a huge gold Western buckle encircled her tiny waist. She took his order and rushed off.

One minute later, she slid a Jack's on ice carefully in front of him. The strong drink sent a warm buzz throughout his tense limbs. Just what he needed.

He turned on his stool and rested his tense back against the padded counter, thinking once again of Amos Miller. Some guys just didn't have the sense God gave a slug. But it wasn't totally Amos's fault. Men his age frequently turned to young babes when women their own age no longer showed any interest. Wasn't much else a sexually active man pushing retirement age could do, other than find a hooker or face lonely frustration.

Hank had dealt with women most of his business career. Things were much clearer now than when he'd first entered the corporate arena. Women in their twenties presented a dynamite package--great bodies, faces, personalities. They flirted shamelessly and could stir up any man with very little effort. It didn't take a rocket scientist to realize they had the world by the balls. But by the time a woman slipped past thirty, gravity had already begun its destructive process. Wrinkles and loose flesh pulled her face downward, making her self-conscious and insecure. As a result, she flirted less and was more concerned with facelifts, Botox, and collagen. She'd already lost most of her softness by the time she reached her forties. Battling men, gravity, and younger women for another decade had taken its toll. Her priorities changed, turning pleasure from the carnal to the material. Why settle for a horny Neanderthal when you could find much more personal satisfaction in a sauna, jewelry outlet, or clothing store?

Hank finished his drink just as the barmaid strolled by, buffing a glass with a soft white cloth and asking casually, "Another drink?"

"How could you tell?"

"You're wearing that look."

"What look?"

"The one that says you need another drink."

"You're really good."

She winked. "Now you sound like one of my exes."

"Which one?"

"They were all pretty bright."

"Then why are they exes?"

She shrugged. "They just weren't quite bright enough."

***

Bascomb's old lady pulled off the main drag, then turned onto East Colonial.

Goddammit! Bill Landry waited for his chance and followed suit, getting behind a tour bus, which slowed them down until the next light, when the bus went through.

Schiller stuck a partially-chewed-up fingernail

between his teeth and sucked on it. Even though Landry wanted to chew on something himself, this wasn't the time to lose it. If he showed any panic at all, Schiller would turn into a basket case. "Don't get tense," he said. "We're right behind her."

Schiller squirmed in the seat. "I can't see her. Can you see her, Billy? I sure as hell can't."

"She's a couple of vehicles in front of that tour bus."

"She pulled off. How could she pull off and still be in front of that bus?"

"She hasn't gained that much distance."

"How d'ya know?"

"I just know."

"This is bad, Billy. She gets into six lanes of heavy traffic and you tell me not to get tense. Tell me why this isn't bad."

"Like I said, we have her in sight."

"Look at this traffic. Doesn't anyone stay home anymore? Whatever happened to having dinner, cracking open a beer, and sitting in front of the tube to watch some TV?"

"This is Florida. Nobody stays home."

"That stupid tour bus better turn off. It's blocking our view. How can we watch her if some asshole cuts behind her and blocks our view? Jeez ... we're gonna lose her!"

Landry wanted to slap the shit out of the little jerk. "Calm down."

Schiller ran a hand briskly through his hair. "What if she pulls into the Mall to do some shopping? All she has to do is flash some thigh. We'll need tickets to see her again."

"Why the hell would she want to shop at this time of night?"

"I don't know. I don't even know why she's here instead of back at the mansion, eating dinner."

"We won't lose her. She's easy to spot. She's got that hot body. And she always wears jeans."

"That makes it even worse."

He was getting tired of Schiller's whining. But he knew what his friend meant. Though they hadn't seen her tonight, he'd bet his left nut she had on a pair of designer jeans so tight, you could see every dimple and cleft on that fine ass. Sally Bascomb was a babe. She carried around some mileage, probably even squirted out a kid or two, some time back ... but she was still one helluva fox. Everyone at Venture had seen that picture in Bascomb's office--her posing in front of their pool in a two-piece so flimsy, you wondered what in holy hell kept the damned thing from popping.

A damned shame what she saw in Bascomb, anyway. The big jerk was fifty, smelled of cigars, and hauled around an extra forty pounds in his five-thousand-dollar tailored Baroni suit. Of course, everybody knew what the hottest babes went for. It was on TV, the news, and in the tabloids. Dammit, it was everywhere. Only a blind hermit wouldn't know what hot babes were after--athletes, rock stars, politicians, attorneys, doctors, not to mention CEOs. Women wanted cold, hard cash and the power that went with it. It didn't matter what their sugar daddy looked like, or how nasty he was. Money didn't talk, it screamed.

Yeah. It screamed, all right. Look what we're

doing for it...

He felt the rage coming back. Bascomb and his money, his luck, and his empire. And, of course, the hot, arrogant gold-digger driving around town in that damned classic Mustang GT. They both deserved to lose it all. Both Bascomb *and* his bitch. Their money, their lives. It only seemed right. Fair. Just. Almost a balance in the universe. In fact—

Schiller suddenly gasped and stiffened in his seat. "She's turning *off*, Billy!"

CHAPTER SIX

The three steakhouses across the six-lane highway were packed.

At the corner, McDonald's swarmed with crowds of people inside, with a long line barely moving at the takeout window. The Japanese restaurant adjacent to it and the seafood buffet across the street also handled a capacity crowd.

Sally had no desire to hunt for a parking place. She didn't want to squeeze through anxious hordes of hungry people to search for a phone inside. In her present state, she preferred being by herself. She realized how impossible such a feat was in a place like Orlando, but she was determined. If she could hear herself think, she'd feel much more at ease.

As she sat at the red light, she scanned the area straight ahead. Tune-up places. More restaurants. An oil-change place. A small block building, probably a bar & grill, sat quietly not far from the main drag. It didn't look crowded at all. Just two cars parked out in front. It also had a payphone near the end of the building. Life was good.

The light changed. She squeezed through the intersection, eased into the turn lane, crossed the small lot, then parked at the far corner of the building and slid out of the Mustang.

The phone reeked of cigarettes, machine oil, and something sour. She wiped the receiver carefully with the bottom of her shirt and tried not to think about what it had touched. Using the quarters she'd collected from her console, she dialed the number.

One ring, two rings. The answering machine kicked in with the prerecorded message, *"You have reached the private office of Paul George, Attorney-at-law. I'm not at my desk at the moment. If you'll leave your message..."*

Her watch said 8:40. This made no sense. Paul usually didn't leave his office until well after nine.

He was probably in the john or sneaking out for a quick bite.

She hung up and decided to wait ten minutes. If he were in the john, ten minutes would be plenty of time. It might not be enough time to grab a sandwich, but oh well...

Heavy traffic roared past. Someone honked. Someone yelled something. A van passed, its speakers thumping loudly.

Five minutes. Ten.

Sally redialed the number. The answering machine again. *Darn.* Her cell phone had Paul's unlisted home number programmed into it. If only she'd brought it with her...

She wanted to slam down the receiver. Not very ladylike, but it might be the most satisfying thing she could do now. In fact, she might feel really good if she could just let go and–

Keep your cool. Go inside and have a drink. Then you can try Paul again.

She could use a drink anyway. Maybe it would settle her nerves. And since the bar didn't appear to be crowded, she wouldn't have to worry about anyone bothering her.

She gently replaced the receiver, collected her change, then trotted up the front steps.

66

Hank Lee stared longingly at the pool table on the other side of the dimly lit room.

In different circumstances, he'd be playing by himself to unwind. He hadn't played in a while--hadn't done a *lot* of things in a while, for that matter. Working for A&A kept him too busy for most-leisure time pursuits. But he wasn't complaining. He'd been with A&A several years. They treated him well. Why shitcan it just because he couldn't see eye-to-eye with his bitch of a boss? Nowadays a person had to hold onto a job that paid well and offered good benefits--they were hard to come by.

On the other hand, moving on might make him feel better about himself, and things in general. Financially he was in good shape, with a sizeable savings account and a checking account that would last him several months if he decided to walk off the job. He didn't think he'd have too much trouble finding work elsewhere, even in the current economy. Over the years, he'd formed a few friendships that might also serve as valuable contacts.

The front door opened, bringing in a woman, the sounds of heavy traffic, and a trail of exhaust fumes. The woman closed the door and stood in the dark entranceway, possibly debating whether she wanted to come in. After a few moments, she ran a hand through her hair and chose a stool at the other end of the bar, just inside the door. She faced the bar, her heavy blond mane obscuring her face. The barmaid walked over and started talking to her, blocking his view entirely. But even in the semi-darkness he could make out a few important details. The gal stood about five-six and probably weighed around one-twenty, all of it well-proportioned. She had a really nice figure and wore her jeans tight. Judging by the sparkles on her fingers, she was married to a doctor or some other highly paid professional who didn't mind spending money on this woman.

Hank felt the warm glow of familiarity invade his thoughts. And his scalp itched.

The babe fiddled with her small bag and mumbled something he could not hear. Then she ran both hands through her hair, obviously upset. He'd seen that gesture before, many times--performed by a woman he'd upset ... many years ago. He squinted, trying to get a better look at her. *No ... couldn't be.*

The barmaid went to the glass shelf and picked up a bottle.

Hank smirked, convincing himself the mystery woman was upset with Hubby Doc, who was probably giving her a rough time. Or maybe the guy she was sleeping with on the sly--their pool attendant, gardener, or mechanic--was giving her grief. He found himself wondering why so many women, especially the good-looking, well-off brand, were always upset and frustrated.

Colleen Moore was a perfect example. If anyone needed laid, it was Colleen. But whoever chose to try it would be taking his life in his hands. It would be much safer and infinitely more gratifying to entertain oneself with a pictorial issue of *Captured*

Cunts or *Bound Babes.*

Hank finished his drink and dropped some bills on the counter. *Time to call it a night.* If Amos didn't show up at the site, the next morning would probably be rough. Colleen would blame Hank and hold it over him, just because he'd asked for some leniency with Amos. *Best enjoy a good night's sleep, just in case.*

He got up from his stool and stretched. The blonde had disappeared in the john. Hank wanted to ask if they knew one another, but since she'd vanished so quickly, he didn't have the chance. Anyway, she was obviously having a rough time, and she'd probably mistake his sincere question as a come-on. After dealing with Colleen Moore and Amos Miller, Hank didn't need more bullshit, especially from a rich blonde with *way* too much sparkle on her fingers.

***

Nervously waiting in the dimly lit parking lot of the auto body shop next door, Tommy and Billy silently watched Tillie's front door.

Tommy lowered his hand and spat out a nail shard. "Why a bar, Billy?"

"No idea. And for Chrissakes, watch where you spit out those damned things."

"Why would she leave right after her husband comes home, and head for a bar?"

"Go in and ask her."

"Nothing's making sense tonight, Billy. Nothing at all."

Billy rubbed his eyes. "I'm about to scrub this mess."

Tommy glanced at Billy. In the dark, he couldn't see his expression. "We can't do that ... can we?"

"You know we can't."

"Then why'd you—"

"Because I'm frustrated, dammit."

Billy was right. This was frustrating, and it made no sense. They were following a woman all over the city, and it didn't look like they were going to get any closer to her than they were right now. But they had to. They had no choice.

"We can't go in there," Billy said. "We can't scrub this damned thing, and we can't go in there."

"Why not sneak over there and stay by her car when she comes out?" Tommy suggested. "It's dark enough. And no one'll see us over there."

"What about all this traffic? What if a cop spots us when we're shoving her into the truck? That's another thing. What'll we do with the truck? Park it next to the Stang? She'll spot it as soon as she comes out of the bar. And we sure as hell can't carry her all the way from there to here. What if someone pulls up just as we're carrying her to the truck? What do we say? She's a party girl? Can't hold her liquor? The world's dumbest schmuck would see through that."

Tommy hadn't thought of any of that. He just didn't want to go through this again. He didn't want to go through any of it again.

A big, dark-haired guy came out of the bar and moved toward the Cadillac, then stopped and stared at Sally Bascomb's Mustang. The hair on the back of Tommy's neck bristled. What if the big jerk tried picking up Bascomb's old lady when she came

70

outside? What if she decided to take him up on it? He might've already hit on her and got lucky. She might've asked him to follow her when she came out. So where was she? Why hadn't she come out?

Their plan would be *so* shot to shit if she came back out and joined up with him. Then they'd have to scrub this whole thing like Billy said, and do it again tomorrow night. *No. Not again. I can't possibly do this again...*

The big guy opened the door of the Cadillac and got carefully behind the wheel. He did it the way all big guys did--butt first, then a careful squeeze to get that big chest in there without whacking it on the steering wheel. The door closed.

Tommy could feel the shakes coming back. The big guy wasn't pulling out.

***

After patting her flushed cheeks with cold water from the tap, Sally took a long look at the troubled face staring back at her in the smudged bathroom mirror.

The small, dark room was depressing. The single, small-watt light bulb dangling from a frayed cord a few feet from the cracked plaster ceiling provided a shredded veil of orange light, enabling her to see the sadness in her own eyes.

What was she doing here? She should be home, enjoying dinner and appreciating the efforts Muriel had made to prepare the roast. With a wineglass in her hand, she should be looking into her husband's eyes and feeling the strong connection only a happily married couple can experience.

It should be no different from the family dinners

she remembered as a child. Dad would sit down at the table and discuss his day while he ate. Mom would listen carefully, as any dutiful wife would, even contributing to the conversation when asked. There was always some frustration in Dad's voice, some anger, but the meal went on as scheduled, and any other family business was also discussed during this same time.

Sally's memories of her family were not always warm, not always kind. Dad was obstinate, distant, and moody. Mom was obsessive, short-tempered, and sometimes cruel. But even with their shortcomings, her parents were always there for her. And even though they were two different people with different moods, ideals, and opinions, frequently arguing and fighting with each other, anyone could see they belonged with one another.

Not so with her and Warren. In the seven years they'd been together, Sally had never sensed the same deep connection with Warren that she'd seen with her own parents, or even other couples. Warren possessed many of the same qualities her father had. Perhaps this was why she'd been attracted to him in the first place. But with these qualities came other things shared amongst only the select few associated with big money and power. Warren possessed his own thick, invisible barrier, and could safely place it around him in a heartbeat. He used it when he was irritated … or annoyed … or frustrated. He used it when something was troubling him and he didn't want to communicate with anyone. The bigger the problem, the heavier and thicker the barrier. It was no doubt a necessary aid in the world of big business, one that would help him concentrate in times of stress. But it was also one quality that could seriously damage a relationship. As it was doing now.

Enough of this. This is a rest room, for pity's sake. Sally blotted her wet cheeks gently with a paper towel, then went back out and hurried to the front door.

"How 'bout your drink?" The barmaid's voice snapped her back to reality. She glanced at the counter where the drink sat, right where she'd left it. She just didn't want to waste the time. She had to contact Paul. She'd try one more time before getting back in the Mustang. She really needed to get to a place where she could calm down and sort things out.

Briefly she wondered if the barmaid had a phone she could use. She didn't see one on the counter, or on the woman's belt. Just as well. Sally felt very, very isolated. Conversation with a stranger, or any other sort of intrusion, would make the situation worse. She didn't even like the barmaid questioning her about the drink. She'd feel strange about making a call with a stranger standing around, listening. Paul might ask questions she wouldn't want to answer in front of an audience.

The payphone outside would suffice.

Sally found a twenty and dropped it on the counter. "Sorry, I really don't have the time for a drink right now."

The barmaid studied the bill, as if trying to figure out what it was. "This is too much. Lemme give you some change–"

73

"Don't worry about it. And thanks."

Sally fled outside. Under the haze of the streetlamp, she fed quarters into the payphone and punched in Paul's number again. She held her breath. Moments later, the answering machine came on, echoing the same spiel as before. She slammed the phone down, then stomped back over to the Mustang and got in. She'd just have to get back on 417 and drive there unannounced. Red Bug Road was less than ten minutes away. It wouldn't be that late when she reached Paul's. She was reasonably sure Nancy wouldn't mind.

A soft voice in the back of her head told her to drive back home. *Warren's your husband. You need to talk to him. That's what Mom would do. Just find something to do or say that will make the hatred vanish from his eyes.*

But I'm nothing like Mom. And Warren is nothing like Dad.

Even though her parents argued much of the time, Sally was sure they did so because they cared about each other. If they hadn't, they wouldn't have bothered to make a fuss.

Warren argued because he was stressed, angry, fed up, and who knew what else. And she had become his convenient target to vent all his wrath. He scared her, and she didn't want to share space with him--at least not tonight. And the way she was feeling, not for a very long time to come, either. It just felt very wrong, living with someone you feared and no longer trusted.

How about a motel? That might not be such a bad idea. She'd see if Paul was home. If not, she'd find the closest motel and sack out there for the night.

***

A vintage green GT-350 sat at the end of the building, looking both gorgeous and sweet.

Hank had always wanted one of those babies. Probably belonged to the blonde. No doubt a birthday present from Hubby. A chick like her would have to own a fancy set of wheels.

He wanted to walk over there for a closer look but didn't want to cause problems. If she came out and saw him checking out her car, she might get the wrong idea. A babe looking like her probably had strange guys approaching her all the time. But that didn't mean she liked it.

Hank slid behind the wheel of the Caddie. The urge to take a nap hit him as soon as he relaxed in the comfortable leather seat. It had been a long day. The trip home would only take about twenty minutes. After two strong drinks in the last hour, he would be especially careful, even though he wasn't feeling tipsy, just tired. With ten years' practice social drinking and his size and body weight to absorb and process the alcohol in his bloodstream, he was far from drunk. Nevertheless, the OPD had been cracking down on drunk drivers and would think nothing of nailing some poor schnook on his way home.

He switched on the ignition, put it in reverse, and stopped. The blonde came out of the bar and trotted over to the payphone on the other side of the Mustang. She set her small black bag on the metal shelf, found change, and fed the phone. She dialed, leaned against the frame, and waited. Her back was to him. All he could see was that fine ass filling those jeans.

Hank had been a connoisseur of women's asses for years. He'd been watching them and studying them since puberty and never tired of it. One thing he learned early on was that no two were exactly alike. Right now, his itching scalp told him something was very familiar about this woman...

She suddenly slammed the phone in its cradle, picked up her bag, flung open the door of the Mustang, and jumped in.

Someone obviously wasn't where he or she was supposed to be. He'd bet money that in her present mood, the GT would become her next immediate casualty. She'd start it up, slam it in reverse, and spit gravel, tearing out of there. Probably without paying much attention to anything else.

The Mustang roared loudly, drowning out the passing traffic. It jerked out of its space, stopped abruptly, and swerved around Hank's car, missing it by inches. It tore out of the lot and crossed the busy highway without the slightest pause.

Hank, you certainly know women...

***

Lucky for them, Sally Bascomb wasn't interested in the big guy sitting in the Cadillac.

After trying the payphone at the end of the building one more time, she slammed down the receiver and jumped into the Mustang. "Then why's the big guy just sitting there in the Cadillac?" Tommy asked.

"Fucker probably got a healthy peek at those

76

jeans."

This didn't make sense. "They came out of the same place, Billy. Wouldn't he have seen her inside? It's not that big, and it's not exactly packed, you know."

"I've been in there before. They keep it pretty dark because it's a good pick-up place--especially on the weekends. They've got candles on the tables, a couple of overhead bar lights so the barmaid can find what she's looking for, and a few lights toward the back, if you wanna use the pool table." Billy shrugged. "He might not have seen her go in."

"I guess it's possible."

"Quit worrying."

Easier said than done. The big jerk could really mess things up. All he had to do was walk over and ask Sally Bascomb for directions. Or tell her how hot she looked in those jeans.

As far back as Tommy could remember, people were always getting in the way when you didn't want them to. They were either where you didn't want them to be or looking at something you didn't want anyone to see. Or *not* looking when you really wanted them to.

Billy could be right. Maybe the big jerk *was* salivating over those jeans. Hopefully he'd snap out of it pretty soon. He'd remember he had a wife, maybe even kids waiting for him at home. But Tommy still couldn't help worrying. He'd seen it all before. A dynamite chick struts past a couple of horny guys, and their hormones go all kinds of crazy, fucking up their heads.

"He's weirding me out. He puts the move on her,

77

our plan's shot."

"You're right," Billy said. "He's not budging."

The Mustang roared to life. The guy in the Cadillac stayed where he was. *Good deal. Stay there. Don't move.*

The Mustang's taillights came on. It backed up quickly. The Cadillac's lights also came on. *Big fat bummer. He's gonna follow her. Dammit. That big jerk's gonna follow her.*

"Hope you're thinking of something quick, Billy," Tommy said, a giant sourball sliding up his throat.

Without a word, Billy slammed the truck into gear.

***

Hank slipped into reverse and pushed down on the gas pedal.

He turned the Caddie around and headed out of the small parking lot. A loud roar and a sudden movement to his left made him hit the brakes. A white Dodge four-door pickup shot out of the lot of the auto body shop next door, cutting him off in a heavy spray of gravel as it crossed the highway and plunged into the eastbound stream of traffic.

Hank sat there for a few minutes, his neck hot, his hands forming a death grip on the wheel. After a few deep breaths, the heat enveloping him dissipated. He pried his right hand loose, reached up, and wiped his forehead. It took him a few moments to regain his composure.

First and foremost, he wanted to make it home without dying. And, of course, without becoming involved in a traffic accident. OPD would smell his breath and give him the breathalyzer test. Then they'd cuff him and haul him in, no questions asked. Better take his time on his way back to his apartment. Then he could sack out and try to get a little shuteye before facing Colleen in the morning.

After one last deep breath, he urged the Caddie carefully over the curb ramp and looked both ways. When he saw his chance, he pulled out. Less than a mile later, the image slowly materializing in his consciousness flashed into his brain.

He didn't know if the jeans or the thick blond hair had done it. Or maybe it was the familiar way she moved. The way her hips shifted, the strides she took. It could even have been the shock of the bastard in the Dodge pickup that pumped adrenalin into his system and triggered the light in his brain. Whatever it was, the image flared brightly before he reached the next intersection.

Sally? Was that you?

CHAPTER SEVEN

Heading north on the GreeneWay, Sally kept it at a steady 75.

She was relieved traffic wasn't so heavy. At least she could make some time before she got onto Red Bug, which was usually awful during the evening rush hour. In just a few minutes she'd be pulling into Paul's drive. Part of her wanted Paul to be home so she could vent. But another part wanted him to be gone so she could find a motel room and spend the night by herself, contemplating her future.

She did need to spend some time thinking things out. She couldn't continue putting up with Warren's abusive moods. The fact that his attitude toward her had been getting progressively worse scared her. If things continued their normal course, physical abuse was bound to follow. She couldn't possibly tolerate that kind of behavior.

Paul knew about Warren long before Sally had gotten involved with the man. In addition to his many business associates, Paul knew all sorts of executives and corporate heads, due to his business dealings. Paul also dabbled in the market when he wasn't handling clients. When Sally first informed Paul of her plans to marry Warren, Paul insisted on drafting a detailed pre-nuptial agreement that would benefit Sally in the event of a divorce or separation. At the time, Sally had considered Paul overly cautious but respected his efforts, knowing Paul was more knowledgeable about such matters and was only looking out for her best interests.

The basis of the agreement entitled Sally to a settlement of five million dollars if the marriage was dissolved mutually, after a period of seven years. Unless Sally had been proven unfaithful or certifiably mentally incompetent, the sum remained unchanged.

Warren, of course, had initially balked to the arrangement, saying it was unfair and excessive. His figure remained in the one-million range, which he said would enable Sally to leave the marriage without financial worries. However, after consulting with his own attorney, Bill Wright, who totally accepted Paul George's legal terms, Warren reluctantly agreed.

Little did she know how accurate Paul had been about Warren--how obsessed and ruthless her husband was about making money. He was so self-absorbed in his financial pursuits that he frequently locked her out of his world, inviting her in only when he wanted her temporary assistance.

Paul had also been accurate about Warren's moods. Like all successful men, Warren suffered frequent bursts of temper. It didn't surprise Paul when she told him about the abuse directed at her during Warren's regular bouts of drinking.

Now, as she shot past the Aloma Boulevard exit, she wondered why she'd withstood it so long. Was it the money? The prestige? The comfort and security of living in a mansion? Or was it her unshakable illusion that no matter how difficult her husband was to live with, it was her responsibility to deal with it, and hold on. Was this illusion brought on by images of her own parents? Of Mom remaining by Dad's side until he died of a heart attack at sixty-one? No matter how frequently they fought or argued, they remained together. Dad was never physically abusive, but his hurtful insults tossed at everyone were expected to be ignored, since it was just the badness of the workday making its way out of his system. And once they just rode it out, Dad would be fine and dandy once again.

Wasn't that what she'd originally thought when she first left the house and got into the Mustang? That Warren would be fine once he sacked out on the couch and had some sleep? Or was this the result of something else? Something much worse?

Maybe it was her fear of growing old, her somewhat superstitious fear that once a woman hit thirty, her chances of finding true love dropped like a rock tossed down an empty well.

True love. She'd experienced it only once before. And since she knew she'd never experience it again, she had to cling to the fact that no matter how difficult and incorrigible Warren was, their marriage was the closest thing to true love she would ever find. And each time that bleak image surfaced, her heart sank. It was heart-wrenching, but it was true. And like it or not–

The Mustang faltered going up the next hill. Fear thrashed through her as she gripped the wheel and eased up on the gas. *What else can happen tonight?*

Her pulse hammering, she shifted her attention to the brightly lit dashboard. It took her only seconds to focus on the gas gauge. *Oh my God.* The needle had settled on the wrong side of red.

The message slammed into her overwrought

brain like a jolt of electricity. *Empty. My dear sweet Lord.*

Her stomach squeezed up her throat, choking her. *"I don't believe this..."*

Her left hand reluctantly released the wheel. Her index finger had gone completely numb. It seemed to belong to someone else. She watched uneasily as her manicured nail vigorously tapped the display, shocking her each time as she tried coaxing the gauge back to the other side of red. The part of her brain that refused to look at things logically, that still believed in magic and miracles, told her this silly effort might actually persuade the needle to move back a quarter of an inch. Even an eighth would help her make it over the next hill. Then she could coast down the winding grade that would take her close enough to the next exit, where she might be able to find a payphone.

The Mustang coughed once--a pitiful groan of ultimate defeat--then died. Holding back hot tears, she directed the car off the shoulder. Her teeth chattered. The vehicle continued moving until it stopped on its own. *Please ... just a few more feet,* she prayed, hoping it would find one last burst of strength and keep going. After encountering a tiny upgrade, it stopped dead in its tracks.

This can't be happening! Her tired brain hallucinated, conjuring up every conceivable type of horror that could be in store for a hapless woman stranded on a busy highway at night--alone, without a cell phone.

Close your eyes. When you open them again, you'll be turning off and zipping right on through the E-Pass lane. She closed them and took a few deep breaths. *There. Feels better already, right?*

Swallowing the lump in her throat, she opened her eyes ... and found herself still sitting in her dead car off the shoulder, trembling. The tears gathered, streaming down her hot cheeks.

***

Straight ahead, the Mustang slowed down at the bottom of the hill, pulled off, and eased to a stop.

His nerves quivering, Bill Landry eased up on the gas, bringing the truck down to fifty, then thirty, before edging onto the shoulder and killing the lights.

"What's happening, Billy?" Schiller squawked. "Why'd she pull off?"

Bill was wondering the same thing. Why in hell would the woman suddenly pull over on such a dangerous stretch at night? No woman in her right mind would stop on this road deliberately--it was scary at night, with folks doing ninety, dodging each other as if it were some stupid game. Half of them were tourists not knowing where the hell they were going but wanting to get there fast anyway. The others lived south, working in the Altamonte area, Sanford, or Lake Mary, and using 417 because it was the fastest way of getting back and forth to work.

The Mustang had slowed and coasted to a stop off the road, with no show of brake lights. That meant the car had quit on its own, rather than Sally Bascomb stopping it for some reason. He guessed since the lights had gone off suddenly, she'd shut them off after the car crawled to a stop. She either had gas or engine trouble. No surprise there. The Stang was a honey of a classic, but at over forty, and no older set of wheels could be kept cherry unless the owner had a top-notch mechanic who didn't mind shacking up with the damned thing. Bill stroked his beard, wondering what to do next.

"Billy?"

"Maybe she ran outa gas."

"How could a lady like her run out of gas?"

He rolled his eyes and huffed. Schiller obviously spent too much time cuddling with computers to know anything about flesh-and-blood females-- except maybe the hookers on South Orange Blossom Trail on Friday nights after cashing his check at the Credit Union. "My ex did stupid things like that all the time. Never checked for gas--never even knew where the hell the oil gauge was. Every time I turned around, she was calling me, all hysterical. 'Bring some gas,'" he mimicked in a snarly, high-pitched tone. "'I'm stuck out here, all alone, and it's getting dark.'"

But even as he said it, he knew Trudi didn't belong in the same class as this woman. Sally Bascomb may have run out of gas, but she was still a damned sight classier than Bill's selfish, slutty ex. Ten times more high maintenance, too. But all classy chicks were super high maintenance. And who could blame them? If she was gonna let some rich asshole lead her around and jump her bones whenever he pleased, the bitch might as well milk the jerk for all he was worth.

"She hasn't budged." Schiller stared straight down the hill.

Bill glanced at the stream of headlights approaching in his rearview mirror. "Once there's a hole, I'll just creep down the hill. She's out of gas, she'll have to make a decision shortly."

"She'll probably call, get someone out here."

Sometimes it was a real chore, figuring out what was going on under that messy red mop. "With what?"

"Probably has a cell phone."

He took a breath. "Tell me something. If she has a cell phone, why'd she try to use that payphone at Tillie's?"

"Jeez. Guess I forgot. She obviously doesn't have her phone with her."

"Or maybe it doesn't work."

"Think she'll walk?"

"Doesn't have much choice. Without a cell, she'll have to leave the car. If she heads back to Aloma, she'll have to walk back up the hill."

"Past our truck?" Schiller began chewing a nail.

"I don't think she'll backtrack."

"Aloma's only half as far as Red Bug."

"She's probably too upset to think clearly. She's alone. It's nighttime. She's miles from anything. And she doesn't have a phone. Anybody would lose it right off."

"But if she doesn't head this way, then how will we approach her?"

"Just like we planned all along." Maybe their luck was finally changing. "This might even work better."

"How?"

"Everyone's breaking their necks getting to

86

wherever they're headed, so there won't be a problem with eyewitnesses. And since she's scared, she'll be desperate enough to accept help-- especially if we follow the original plan."

Schiller went silent.

Bill lit a cigarette. "Get ready. Just in case we have to move fast."

Groping in the dark, Schiller grabbed the leather satchel behind his seat. Working by feel, he zipped it open. His hands must have gone useless. The zipper opened and shut again and again.

"You need help?"

"I'm fine. Just ... fine." Schiller finally got it open. Using the tiny light above the visor mirror, he applied the whiskers they'd bought at the costume store on Orange Avenue. After a few minor adjustments, he turned to Bill.

Schiller with a beard was hilarious. It was like putting fake whiskers on your redheaded female cousin. But Bill was too nervous to laugh. Maybe it would work.

He pulled in a giant lungful of smoke and sat back. "Now we wait."

***

Sally was smart enough to realize that when something terrible happened, the first reaction was to tell yourself you're imagining it.

It's a dream, a nightmare, and you have nothing to fear because it's simply not real. Just close your eyes and count slowly to ten. And when you open them again, the nightmare will be gone.

She knew it was stupid, but she tried lying to herself anyway, just in case it might actually work.

87

After slowly counting to ten, she anxiously opened her wet eyes and found herself locked in the same dark horror. This mirrored the time she was lost in the woods years ago, when the family had gone to visit Aunt Margaret's farm out in the country. Sally was around eight or nine at the time. Her aunt's place was situated several miles down a dirt road out in the middle of nowhere. It was the first time Sally, having been born and raised in the city, had even seen the woods. Her past experience was limited to what she'd seen in movies and TV shows.

While everyone sat on Aunt Margaret's back porch, chattering away, Sally, wanting to explore, ventured through the twisted paths in the pine forest about a hundred yards behind the old two-and-a-half-story farmhouse. The freshness and wide-openness was intoxicating, the air sweet--nothing like the confining sourness of the city. She had never felt so free. Her journey took her down hills and across streams, until the greenery grew so thick with trees, vines, and wild brush, she could barely continue on.

When the quiet of her surroundings registered a feeling of intense isolation, a strange tingling started in her limbs. She suddenly realized she had no idea where she was. She'd lost all sense of direction. Everywhere she turned looked the same. She couldn't even recognize the path that had brought her to where she was. The woods, so wide-open and fresh just moments earlier, now engulfed her, making it hard to breathe. The wide-open fresh air, suddenly replaced by brush, pine needles, tall trees, and hanging vines, had abandoned her.

By this time, the tingling had taken over, edging her toward full-blown hysteria. She broke into a frantic run, tripping over deadfalls and ripping the new skirt Mom had bought her for their visit. Her fears of wild animals and other unknown threats made her nightmare bigger, more frightening. Her feeling of isolation grew. Reality had scampered into the brush like a frightened rabbit. She fought hard to regain her senses, her equilibrium. How long ago had she left Aunt Margaret's house? Was it days? Weeks? Or just hours? She forced herself to think rationally. *Take deep breaths. Focus. Close your eyes. Count to ten.*

When she opened her eyes again, she expected to see Aunt Margaret's house just beyond the clearing. But she didn't. No house, no clearing. Instead, a touch of reality, of reason, had trickled its way into her frightened mind. *I haven't been here for days or weeks. Less than an hour, most likely. And I'm probably much closer to the house than I even realize.*

But when the sun sank low in the sky, warning her of the approaching night, she panicked again. Her imagination took over, wrapping her mind in a tight, suffocating veil of cold hysteria. The beasts would leave their dens. Under the heavy cloak of darkness, they'd hunt for fresh food. And they'd smell her.

She turned away from the sinking sun and trudged through the thick brush, hoping she'd somehow find her way back to the house. The day grew darker, causing her to hasten her steps. *Keep moving. Never stop again. And don't panic.*

Whatever you do, don't panic. Put as much distance between you and your fears--as well as the monsters living in the woods.

She'd never forget the warmth radiating through her when her father appeared just beyond the clearing, nor the invigorating wash of release rushing down her limbs when she jumped eagerly into his arms.

But even though her imagination had matured over the years, replacing her little-girl fantasies and fears, the news media and her own personal observations had taught her that monsters did indeed exist. They filled prisons, occupied key positions in Government, manipulated the stock market, and headed major countries. They populated law enforcement, childcare, religion, and education. Monsters existed everywhere.

The fear that had frightened her so much as a child had, after all these years, returned very quickly. It had metamorphosed into a dark strip of concrete overrun by fast-moving metallic creatures oozing foul odors. Their speed was like an elixir, their power intoxicating. And with the steel and plastic and tinted glass covering them, anonymity protected them as they roared past.

Nice, unassuming people became Freddie Kruger when they slipped behind the wheel of an automobile. They turned deaf, dumb and blind in their quest to reach their destinations. And they could, in an instant, turn their frustrations into a horrible nightmare of road-rage. This setting provided the perfect opportunity for mindless violence. It was just as isolated as the woods, with civilization miles away.

Stop it! she told herself. *Keep the panic at bay. Don't let it take hold.*

Sally rested her head against the seat and willed herself to think rationally.

***

The sight at the crest of the hill made Hank shake his head in utter amazement.

A white Dodge four-door truck sat off the road.

Was it the same truck that had cut him off in Tillie's parking lot? Maybe, maybe not. There were a lot of white Dodge four-door pickups on the roads these days. But he wouldn't be at all surprised if it was the same truck. Some people were just too stupid to live. The things they did baffled the imagination. A moron gets behind the wheel, cuts others off in a mad frenzy to get onto the main road, drives like an idiot for three miles ... then pulls over.

Hank thought he had seen it all after returning from Saudi. Naïve of him, for sure, but at twenty, he was too young to have seen enough examples of genuine stupidity to think that was the worst of it. After coming home, he'd seen things just as stupid and ridiculous. He didn't know if it was because he was getting older or less tolerant; but it was becoming more and more difficult to turn a blind eye. *Idiots have taken over the planet and are tearing it to pieces.*

Hank zoomed on by, passing several vehicles. A couple of sports cars instantly crept up behind him as he soared down the hill. He punched it to the floor, kicking the Caddie up to ninety before easing into the slow lane. He kept an eye on the followers in case they planned on cutting him off. They merely zipped on past, both doing well over a hundred, and were gone in seconds.

Hank glanced back in his rearview mirror again, wondering what the driver was doing in the pickup. Possibly hoisting a bottle or preparing a line of snort. The lights were off. He probably intended to have his own private party. Or maybe he was too drunk to drive responsibly and decided to sleep it off. Of course, that type of thinking was unduly optimistic. A responsible drunk was a contradiction in terms.

Sally immediately crept back into his thoughts. That chapter of his life ended seven years ago. Sally had ended it herself by simply walking out. No word, no phone call--nothing. And he never heard from her again.

Judging by how well they'd gotten along with one another and enjoyed each other's company, he often wondered why it had ended so suddenly. So silently. Like the final heartbeat of a dying bird. Or the period at the end of a sentence.

It was a love that had never been given the chance to grow, to become something wonderful. He was confident that if it had been given the chance, it would have turned into a once-in-a-lifetime thing that romance novelists write about. But it hadn't. As much as Heidi had hurt him by divorcing him, Sally had hurt him even worse by leaving just when their love had begun to grow.

She should've given him some sort of explanation--a reason why she no longer wanted him. He knew he was being a jerk at the time, but

Heidi had practically destroyed him, and he was still vulnerable and confused. Sally knew he was still on the mend when they first met.

He'd tried his best to fight the loneliness Heidi had caused when she'd walked out. At first, the bottle had worked wonders. But when he realized he was slowly killing himself, he tried keeping busy by working extra hours. It kept his mind busy and forced him to spend less time by himself. For a while, he thought he'd made progress. When he met Sally, it became obvious that, with her help, he could survive and even continue the rest of his life. Sally had made him feel like a man again. Desired. Irresistible. Strong. As they saw more of one another, the painful flashes of Heidi toned down considerably, even vanished for brief periods.

Only a few months later, with the exception of an occasional nightmare, he considered himself cured. Because of Sally, he'd reached the point where he could go for days without Heidi even entering his thoughts.

But he'd obviously been deceiving himself about his new relationship. Sally had apparently grown tired of playing nursemaid and decided to look elsewhere for a partner with less bruises and scars.

If that had truly been her at the bar, she'd done extremely well for herself. The rocks on her fingers looked genuine. And the GT-350 was a rare classic. Even though the barroom--and the night--was too dark to reveal enough detail, he could tell she still looked terrific.

Maybe she *was* having a rough night. *So what?* A lot of folks were probably also having a rough night tonight.

CHAPTER EIGHT

Sally shivered in the darkness of the car while the heavy flow of headlights zipped up the hill, so frighteningly close.

What should I do? Get out and look for a call box? Or just stay here and wait for someone to stop?

What if someone *did* stop? What if he was a rapist or serial killer, or someone who wouldn't turn down the opportunity of stealing a classic car? What were the chances of a genuinely *good* person stopping to help?

Staying put suddenly seemed dangerous. Finding a call box might be a much better solution. There would probably be one over the next hill, not far from the Red Bug exit.

She didn't know anyone who'd ever used one. Even if she found one that hadn't been spray-painted or vandalized with Super Glue, walking along the highway would make her vulnerable. She'd be out there on foot, helpless, and highly visible in her tight-fitting jeans. She'd often wondered if cell phones were originally invented because so many people were being run over, shot, or kidnapped trying to use a call box.

The thought of leaving the security of her car sent chills scurrying down her back. One thing was certain: nothing positive would happen while she remained here, feeling sorry for herself.

Picking up her clutch took two tries. She just couldn't manage to make her trembling fingers work. When she finally got hold of her handbag, she rechecked the contents--two credit cards, driver's license, and some twenties. Suppose she was caught and robbed? She had no pepper spray. The tiny canister remained with her main purse and cell phone still hanging on the coat tree back at the house. Deciding what to take with her and what to leave behind in the car, she removed the bills--sixty bucks and a couple of ones--and dropped the clutch on the floor. She'd had more than eighty but had left that twenty with the barmaid back at Tillie's.

Her rings caught on the denim material of her jeans when she stuffed the bills in a hip pocket. The gems were worth money--a criminal would have to be blind not to see them. Besides, they'd get in her way. They always did. She never liked wearing so much jewelry. She'd only worn the rings because she'd been getting ready for dinner, and Warren liked seeing her wear them. He'd said they made her look 'regal.' Yeah, she felt like a royal ass right now, letting Warren rattle her so badly that she walked out without her purse and phone. She yanked the rings off one by one, snatched the clutch off the floor, and shoved the rings inside.

What if something horrible happened and she needed something to use as a bribe for assistance in case the twenties weren't enough? Which ring would be the most valuable? Which one wouldn't she care about losing? The answer came surprisingly quick. She snapped open the clutch, removed her wedding ring, and slipped it back on. Its value had suddenly shifted from sentimental to practical. Her last argument with Warren no doubt had much to do with this decision.

She sat back and took a deep breath to clear her mind. The situation was dismal, but if she could keep her head on straight, she might be able to devise a workable plan. It wouldn't be long before someone spotted the Mustang and pulled over for a closer look. From what she'd read, classic cars were high on the auto theft list. Any car thief would jump at the chance to steal it. It wouldn't be very bright-- or safe--to be present if this occurred. But would leaving her credit cards and rings in the car be any smarter? She thought for a second and decided she'd rather let a car thief have them than be accosted by someone who would be tempted to cause her harm trying to get at them.

She looked outside the car to take stock of her surroundings and figure out the best way to proceed. A four-foot-high chain-link fence separated the woods from the grass about two hundred feet from the highway. Scaling it would give her access to the woods.

The woods. Escaping it as a child, then finding refuge in it as an adult. The irony nearly brought a smile to her lips.

She took another deep breath to consider her options. Aloma was closer than Red Bug. If she backtracked and reached the tollbooth, she could hide in the bushes and screen the traffic slipping through. She could approach someone who looked reasonably safe--a middle-aged couple, perhaps-- and ask them to call the police.

She took one last deep breath and clumsily grabbed the door handle. Her heart skipped a beat as a pack of vehicles roared by. Her hand shook. The pack quickly disappeared beyond the next hill. *Do it. Now. Before another pack tears down the hill.*

Holding her breath, she pushed open the door, jumped out, pushed down the door-lock, slammed the door shut, and quickly circled the front of the Mustang. Without losing a step, she disappeared into the darkness.

***

At the bottom of the hill, a vertical sliver of light glinted on the driver's side, turning black instantly.

Bill Landry waited until the next car passed, then switched on the ignition. "Show time," he said, his voice coming from some strange place. "That was probably her getting out. I have a feeling she's headed for the woods."

"Why would she chance it in the woods instead of trying to hitch a ride?" Schiller asked.

"Would *you* try that on this stretch? Especially if you were a hot blonde in tight jeans?"

"I just don't know why she'd try the woods, Billy. All sorts of *critters* living there."

"She probably figures she'll stand a better chance." Critters versus perverts or psycho killers. A critter would hurt its prey only if it was cornered. The same couldn't be said for perverts or psycho killers. "I can't say as I blame her."

Bill waited for a gap, then pulled out.

Schiller began playing with his whiskers. "So we go on just like we planned?"

A sickening feeling took over as Bill raced the truck down the winding hill. They hardly had any time. Amongst the trees, she could probably outmaneuver them and hide. That would be it, their plan shot all to hell.

"This'll be trickier," he said. "But if we're friendly, we'll earn her trust. Especially now, since she's vulnerable. It might be easier than if she was back in her own neighborhood, taking her walk."

"You really think so?"

"She's scared shitless. A friendly face might calm her down. She might also lower her guard."

"Billy?"

"Yeah?"

"She's not the only one who's scared shitless."

***

Running through thick grass in the dark in unfamiliar territory is dangerous.

It's also very stupid. It takes courage, stamina, genuine hysteria, and complete disregard for your health and safety.

Sally wasn't thinking about any of that. She was determined to reach the fence. She didn't even care about tripping, or getting snagged or cut on the fence, or even encountering wild dogs or other scary things living in the woods. She didn't want anything distracting her. She wasn't even worried about how she could maneuver through the trees. Reaching the woods and staying hidden had become her primary objective.

A truck slowed, coming down the hill.

Oh my God...

Her face hot, she broke into a sprint, her legs pumping more furiously than ever. The grass was unnaturally thick. The landscaping people the GreeneWay contracted obviously hadn't brought out their mowers recently. Straight ahead, the fence appeared just thirty yards away. Even in the dark, she could distinguish the glint of its slender horizontal outline in front of the trees.

Behind her, the truck slowed to a stop.

Twenty yards to go.

The slamming of a door made her eardrums ring.

My God, they've seen me ... don't turn around.

She was relieved the aerobics had automatically kicked in. She wouldn't have a chance otherwise.

The trees drew closer. *Forty feet ... thirty.*

Despite the panic welling up within her, she forced her attention on the tree line. If she kept moving in a straight line she wouldn't have to worry about tilting her body, throwing herself off-balance and stumbling.

Twenty-five feet. Twenty.

A loud male voice penetrated the passing traffic behind her. "Mrs. Bascomb!"

Had she gone crazy? Had someone *really* called her? How could anyone know it was her?

Her imagination had taken over. What she'd heard sounded like her name because she wanted it to. The little girl in her *wanted* someone to help, to come to her rescue. Someone who knew her, who wasn't dangerous.

She hadn't *really* heard her name, had she? How could anyone spot her in the dark when her back faced the road? It was a fairly dark night, and the moon wasn't full. She was nearly a hundred yards away, running like mad, her hair all over the place.

It was the panic--the fear--running wild. But it sure did *sound* like her name...

The Mustang. Whoever called her might be familiar with the car. It was possible, wasn't it? She knew a lot of people. Someone might have recognized it. How many GT-350s were out there, anyway? Someone who knew her or Warren may have recognized it. Even in the darkness its sleekness stood out. Anyone could tell it was a classic.

"*Sally Bascomb?*"

There. Her first *and* last name. Someone knew it was her. Maybe her streak of bad luck had changed after all...

***

Just a few feet from the chain-link fence, Sally Bascomb stopped running and whirled around.

She stood shaking, her wide-open eyes watching his every move. Tommy realized he was shaking just as much. Good thing the strong breeze roared past, making his skin tingle. At least it would conceal some of his fears.

This was all up to him. He had to get her to relax, convince her everything was okay and that he was here to help. He had to be extra careful. If he made the wrong move or said the wrong thing, she'd scale that fence in a heartbeat. But if he did everything right, he and Billy would be rich.

Brazil. That's where all this was supposed to end from the beginning. Fly down there, buy a place near the beach, and find a couple of hot sex slaves. Big tits, long black hair--and you didn't even have to learn the language. Brazilian babes lusted after rich Americans. As Billy told him many times, "You give them the green, they'll give you the

101

pink." And the one person who could make it all happen stood just a few yards away.

"Mrs. Bascomb?"

She still watched him while trying to catch her breath. Hauling ass like that is tough, even when you're in good shape, like she was.

"It's me!" she shouted over the passing traffic. "Who are *you*?"

Play it cool, now. He and Billy had gone over this hundreds of times before. Everything would be all right as long as no one else stopped to see what was happening. Tommy kept the flashlight aimed at the grass in front of his feet so as not to frighten her. He raised it, the light showing his own face, to help gain her trust. "I'm Johnny." He moved a little closer--nonchalantly, as if they'd just met in the street, talking like old friends. "Johnny O'Brien."

He'd picked the name specifically. O'Brien was one of Bascomb's corporate attorneys at Venture. O'Brien had a fair complexion and always wore a beard. She no doubt had seen him and might even remember. O'Brien liked showing off in front of women.

The bad thing was, Tommy didn't resemble O'Brien. But as Billy had reassured him, time and time again, it was hard to distinguish specific features at night--especially on guys with beards.

"We met at the software convention on International Drive last year," Tommy told Sally Bascomb, trying to make it sound real, natural.

She pushed back a thick wad of her hair that had fallen over her face. Her hair sure looked nice. He hoped she wouldn't mess with it too much, just let it do what it wanted. The breeze might push it forward again.

"You remember me? From last year?" She approached him cautiously. Her expression was guarded. Her eyes were wide-open and focused, her body tense. This was not going to be easy at all.

"I work for your husband, and—"

"Which company?"

"Venture."

She blinked, then said, "I ... don't remember you, but I meet a lot of people." She sighed, making the valley between her breasts deepen. Tommy quickly forgot what he was doing. Then she smiled--a little at first, then all the way. "You don't know how happy I am to see a friendly face. Especially since you know my husband. It's *scary* out here."

"What happened?" He forced himself to look at her eyes. It was damned difficult. Her boobs sure did look terrific, even though they were covered. "Car break down?"

She shook her head. "Ran out of gas."

Tommy lowered the flashlight. His heart thumped so loudly, he could hear it. He knew what was going to happen. He also knew he had to think past this. Billy had told him to forget the unpleasantness and concentrate on the end result. *Think Brazil.* Billy had said that when he thought he was losing it, just think of those Brazilian babes, and that would put his head back on right. He took a deep breath and forced a smile. "How can I help?"

"You can give me a ride to the nearest phone, if you don't mind." She moved toward the parked vehicles. "Unless you've got a cell phone in your truck. Which convention was it, by the way?"

He stiffened. *This lady's smart.*

"It was ... at the Marriott."

For a moment he thought she'd also stiffened, but figured she'd just stepped in a dip in the ground. "I don't remember going to *that* one, but I might have just forgotten."

Good deal. She'd forgotten. Cool. No problem. Almost there. "I forget a lot, too," he said.

His heart pumped even louder as they drew closer to the pickup. Billy was crouched between the vehicles, his knockout packet ready. *Just a few more seconds. Almost there. Brazil. Babes galore.* Tommy forced himself not to faint or throw up.

She moved slightly in front of him, obviously in a hurry to get to safety. *Good deal. No problem.* She really knew how to move, swaying those hips. Sure had a nice figure. The way her hair danced from the wind blowing down the hill gave him a warm feeling. A whiff of her sandalwood perfume mixed in with her sweat brushed his face.

Without meaning to, he envisioned her in the truck, all bundled up, unable to see or speak, not knowing what was going on or where they'd take her--or what would happen afterward. Tommy began shivering.

This is wrong. Everything about this is wrong. Cops are everywhere--even in Brazil--so why are we doing this? I dunno. I remember the Brazil thing, but forget everything else...

"Forget a *lot*," he said, the cool night air tickling his face.

She turned, watching him closely. "You okay?"

104

He gave her his best grin. His face sure felt funny, the muscles tight in some places, loose in others. He knew it must have looked that way, too. His face was probably just about as fucked up as it could possibly be. Sally Bascomb's wide-open eyes told him she'd just seen something that scared the living shit out of her. She began backing up.

***

As they approached the vehicles, the skinny bearded guy who said he was Johnny O'Brien started acting weird.

He seemed agitated, sweating, and shaking. She told herself maybe he was just the nervous type. But when he wiped his wet forehead and shivered, even though it was in the seventies, her limbs turned into blocks of ice.

She knew she hadn't gone to the convention at the Marriott. Warren wanted her to go, but she'd begged off. She spent too much time dressing up so she could smile on cue and talk to people she didn't know about things that didn't even interest her. It made her feel cheap, on display. Meeting people was all right, but not when it meant having to show off, or act the part of someone she wasn't.

Johnny O'Brien. She finally remembered him, and the realization slammed her. Johnny wore specially cut suits, drank Tanqueray gin, collected wood carvings from all over the world, and smoked expensive Italian cigars. He was also six feet tall-- much taller than this guy. A sour bubble filled her throat. "Wh-What did you say your name was?" she asked, her heart in her mouth.

"Tommy," he said quickly, then his face froze.

The lull in the traffic created a sudden bubble of heavy silence that engulfed them. "I ... thought you said *Johnny...*"

This guy wasn't Johnny O'Brien. And he wasn't about to help her at all. Something terribly *bad* was happening. Her instincts kicked in. *Run. The woods. Now! Run harder than you've ever run in your life...*

She spun around but had time only to take a single step. A dark shape emerging from the darkness rushed toward her just as she twisted around. In that same instant, she was pinned helplessly. The person who'd snuck up behind her was taller, bigger. He picked her up easily, grabbing her around the waist with one arm. With his other hand he shoved something over her face. A sweet/sour antiseptic smell moved with lightning speed toward her eyes. Despite the fumes smothering her, her panic increased. She lashed out with her arms and legs.

As she faltered and her eyes rolled, she heard the roaring traffic zoom past, no one slowing. No one cared, or maybe no one could see them. She vaguely remembered they were behind the truck, secluded. Hidden.

Her wrists were hastily grabbed and held – possibly by the first guy. His hands were cold, but they held her fast. A warm cloud of blackness floated in front of her, making everything hazy. Her heart, deafeningly loud in her ears, sounded like someone banging a bass drum in a large empty room. She got her left hand free and groped at the cool wetness over her face. Her strength dissolved in seconds, followed by the panic evaporating, and a strange sense of peace filled the darkness. Her hand slipped away and fell quietly to her side as the blackness overtook her.

PART II
The Second Day

CHAPTER NINE

Groggy and stiff, Hank Lee awoke just before seven.

Was it remnants of the whiskey applying the pressure to the back of his head? His confrontation with Colleen Moore was more likely the culprit. Or that nasty business with Amos Miller. Probably a combination, plus the incident with the jerk in the Dodge pickup.

He grabbed the aspirin bottle from the kitchen cabinet, choked down three, then spent the next twenty minutes in the shower, letting the warm spray massage his throbbing head.

He didn't want to face Colleen with a hangover. The best way to avoid a morning confrontation was to drive directly to the site. He'd go there on the pretext of checking on Amos. He could bullshit with some of the contractors and spend at least some of the morning with more amiable human beings. Construction workers were a rough bunch, but much better company than white collars. He'd discovered that as a kid working construction the summer months to pay for college. You always knew where you stood. With white collars, you never knew whose hand held the knife pointed at your back.

Colleen seldom went to the site. Dirt, sweat,

rough-talking men, and fresh air didn't exactly turn her crank. She usually only showed up in the field for a groundbreaker. She always rushed home afterward--no doubt to shower and send her classy threads off to the dry cleaners.

Hank finished his coffee. His thoughts had drifted back to the previous night as he trudged down the hall to brush his teeth and finish dressing. He was certain that was Sally Burns at Tillie's. The image of those rocks on her fingers made his jaw muscles tighten. They looked pricey, too--the kind a wealthy man gives a woman. *His* woman.

Past history, Henry. Finish dressing. Comb your hair. Concentrate on work, the site, avoiding Colleen. You've got your own life, remember?

He couldn't concentrate--not at first. Images of Sally kept drifting into his mind. He couldn't stop remembering how sweet she was--how unassuming and considerate. She never acted like a pampered, self-centered woman--what anyone would expect from a gorgeous babe who used to be a swimsuit model. She never cared about her hair being messed up when they were walking along the beach or driving with the windows down. She occasionally wore her food--especially when they shared a pizza. And he always had to personally wipe the tomato sauce off her chin.

Whenever they were together, she was always more concerned about him than herself. She always wanted him to talk about himself. She asked questions and made him the center of attention. And whenever he asked her questions, she was always reluctant to talk about herself. It wasn't that she was

109

evasive; she just seemed to be uncomfortable talking about herself. He'd only found out about her being a model later in their relationship, when he'd asked her if she'd graduated college.

She was the perfect woman, but he was too damned stupid and too wrapped up in his own problems to realize it. But just like his problems, their relationship had died and become part of his past.

It was a sunny morning--not a cloud in the sky. The squawking of gulls echoed from the lake behind the complex. Hank fired up the Caddie and backed out of his space. As the pounding in his head diminished, he pulled out onto the main highway and was approaching the GreeneWay entrance ramp in just ten minutes.

The sight less than a mile past the Red Bug exit made his scalp itch. The GT-350 sat off the road, facing north. Was he imagining things?

It was definitely the same car he'd seen at Tillie's. It sat at the bottom of the same hill where the Dodge pickup had been sitting. Possibly the same truck that had cut him off at the bar.

He turned off at the next exit, pulled back onto the GreeneWay, shot through the E-Pass lane, and took the ramp south, heading onto the Aloma exit. The crest of the hill soon came into view. As he guided the Caddie down the slope, he eased off the gas, veered off onto the shoulder, and coasted the rest of the way down, stopping the Caddie five yards or so from the rear bumper of the Mustang.

He stared at it nearly a minute, pulling in some bad vibes, then got out of the car. The loud, irritating roar of a motorcycle increased as it swept down the hill, slowing before pulling over, then stopping behind the Caddie.

***

The pickup sat among some scrub oaks down a dirt path two miles east of Semoran Boulevard, in one of the few undeveloped areas still standing. The early morning sun twinkled through the branches of the trees.

Bill Landry stayed close to the back of the truck, trying to get the kinks out. The big vehicle had a bed liner, but even the foam pads they'd put under the sleeping bags couldn't make it feel any better than a concrete slab. Schiller hadn't helped, either, tossing and turning, moaning and mumbling.

Schiller had been wandering around the last half-hour, disappearing in the trees, coming back a few minutes later, mumbling some more, then disappearing again. Schiller would be right at home in a psycho ward. He didn't even need a nail trim, since he'd already nibbled them all down to the quick. Just give him a buzz cut, a gown, and a magazine so he could entertain himself poking out people's eyes in the pictures.

Schiller sucked down the last of his cigarette and dropped the glowing butt on the sand at his feet. "Wish I was back at the console, crashing jobs."

Bill wanted to kill the jerk for almost blowing it last night. Bascomb's old lady would've gotten away if she'd had a few more seconds. Good thing Bill had counted on his friend freaking--which was why he gave her the juice when he did. He'd wanted to wait till she was getting in the truck. But at least

111

they were behind the vehicles, so no one could see what they were doing.

He glared at Schiller. "*Now* what's your problem?"

"Didn't realize what we were doing till ... till we actually did it. Makes me wanna puke. That lady in there–"

"Keep your voice down." He shot a quick glance at the truck.

"Why? So she can't hear us? What if she does? She's not gonna be able to *tell* anyone, is she? That's the plan, isn't it?"

"Everything'll go down fine. Just you watch."

"That's just *it*, Billy. I don't *want* to watch. I don't *want* to do anything to her. I–"

"Shut up. You think I want to do this more than you do?" But the plan had already been put into action, and there was no turning back. Now it was time to face the consequences. "We've got a job to do, and it has to be done. Stop your whining. You're acting like a frightened ten-year-old."

"I *feel* like a frightened ten-year-old."

"Face facts. We *can't* go back. We *can't* set her free. Put that in your head and keep it there. It's the program."

Schiller found a fresh cigarette from the crumpled pack in his shirt pocket. He lit it with shaky hands, scattering smoke everywhere.

"Think of the bottom line here," Bill said. "It'll give you all the motivation we need."

Schiller didn't reply. He stared at the truck.

"What's wrong now?"

"She's so ... *quiet* in there..."

112

"It's not like she can *say* anything, even if she wanted to."

"Billy ... you sure you didn't give her too much of that stuff?"

"Positive. I researched it online."

Schiller swallowed audibly. "I ... just think she should be awake by now. It's been what? Eight? Nine hours? What if she's dead? What if you gave her too much? What if–"

"Tommy, will you shut the hell up? She's okay. Trust me." He fumbled for his own cigarettes.

"We ... need to find out."

"I know."

"So ... are you gonna check and see if she's okay?"

Bill shook his head as he lit up and sucked smoke from his cigarette to settle his nerves. "Yeah, I'm gonna go check on her. Just see that you keep your mouth shut."

Schiller's hands trembled as he shrugged and puffed rabidly on his cigarette. "Okay, Billy. Okay."

***

Sally opened her eyes to the complete darkness.

Nausea swept through her. Ripples of heat slid heavily down her limbs. Her head was hot. Something pressed against her temples. She tried opening her mouth, but something pressed against her lips stopped her. *Tape*?

She made a feeble attempt to pull it from her lips, grunting when her arms would not move. They were partially numb and felt like they were pulled behind her back and held together at the wrists. She tried again, pulling harder, cringing when jolts of

113

pain danced up her arms. *More tape, apparently.* But at least she was able to wiggle her aching fingers.

She tried moving her legs and quickly found that her ankles were also immobile.

The darkness registered coldly. So did the heat pressing against her temples. A soft cloth had been wrapped around her head and fastened tightly. *My dear sweet Lord...*

Her mind wanted to shut off, go blank, reset itself, and switch back on when everything returned to a familiar setting, possibly in the back yard beside the pool, or maybe in aerobics class.

Her pulse, amplified within the confines of the blindfold, thumped loudly. *Think, Sal. Force yourself. Go back to the beginning. Get a handle on this.* She forced herself to concentrate. *The Mustang ran out of gas. A truck. A white truck. A skinny man with a beard...*

The nausea thundered back. *Fight it!* A hot sour taste climbed up her throat. *Keep your mind working. You can't let this destroy you. For one thing, you're unable to scream.*

She struggled to focus. *He said his name was Johnny O'Brien. He'd mentioned Warren, said he'd seen him somewhere. A software convention at the Marriott. Yes. A clean-cut young man around thirty- -no, he had a beard. A scraggly, funny-looking beard that didn't match his face.*

That should have been your first clue ... why were you so clueless?

I was upset from being stranded, from running, from Warren treating me so badly. Then someone

114

stopped, called my name. Mentioned Warren. My guard was down, and I was so relieved to find help, I tossed caution to the wind.

Stupid!

I walked back to his truck. But he grew nervous as we got closer to the vehicles. Giddy, shaking.

That was the second clue.

Stupid, stupid, stupid!

Then ... someone else came up from behind ... was hiding behind the truck.

The reality of her situation zapped her with the force of an electric charge.

Something very wrong happened. This Johnny, or Tommy, or whatever his name was, hadn't stopped to help me. They must have been following me all along. And when I stopped, they were ready. Oh, my God!

Now, just minutes after consciousness had come back in hot, jagged waves, she lay on her side in total darkness. Totally helpless, trying not to think of what might happen to her. A large warm ball of sourness squirmed up her throat. She swallowed, forcing it back down. *Not the right time. You can't open your mouth.*

Survive. She had to.

Yes. I will. I will survive. Somehow.

***

The cop used the toe of his boot to apply the kickstand, raised a long leg and swung it over the motorcycle.

He adjusted his helmet with a gloved hand, all the while sizing up Hank. In his shiny black leather boots, he was a couple of inches taller than Hank--

six-four, maybe--and beefy around the shoulders and chest, no doubt due to the leather jacket and Kevlar vest. He was about thirty-five, his cheeks dark with five o'clock shadow, even though it was morning. "Both cars yours?" he asked, his strong voice audible over the passing traffic.

"I wish."

The cop pulled out a notepad and fanned it open. He plucked a ballpoint pen from the front pocket of his jacket, but had trouble manipulating it in his heavy glove. He bit the tip of the middle finger, yanked off the glove, and stuffed it under his left arm. "A honey." He nodded at the Mustang, admiring it, but trying to be cool at the same time. Cops always had to display an air of cold dullness. The older ones called it authority, the younger ones probably thought it was being cool or tough. "Don't see too many of 'em. Just at car shows. Know the owner?"

"Maybe." Hank didn't want to say too much. Cops tended to take things the wrong way.

The cop marched back to his motorcycle, probably to check on the plate number. "You don't sound convinced!" he shouted above the roar of a passing logging rig.

Hank waited for a lull in the traffic noise. "An old friend of mine was driving a similar model when I spotted her coming out of a bar last night. This looks like the same car."

The cop's face tightened as he came back. "She have much to drink?"

Sally liked wine or an occasional mixed drink, but always stopped at two. To his knowledge, she

116

hadn't touched the one she'd ordered at Tillie's. She'd been more interested in that phone call. "I don't remember her as being much of a drinker."

The cop tried the driver's door and found it locked. He bent over and peered inside the Mustang, one leather-clad arm shielding the glare of the sun. He straightened, shaking his head.

"Something wrong?"

"There's a woman's purse on the floor."

Hank moved in and had a peek through a corner of the windshield.

A woman would *never* go anywhere without her purse.

"Say you might know her?" The cop was studying Hank again, trying to decide what was going on.

"Maybe."

"That why you're concerned?"

Concern was a strong word, but it seemed appropriate. He knew he shouldn't be--not at all. She belonged to someone else. But he couldn't help it. Even when he thought of those rocks on her fingers, he couldn't help it. "It was a long time ago."

"Got a description?"

Better be subtle about this. If he described her the way he saw her, the cop would definitely be suspicious. "Mid-thirties. Blond hair. Slender."

"Gotcha." The cop marched back to his motorcycle.

Hank quickly recalled the events of the previous night. *She comes into the bar, orders a drink, slips into the ladies' room, runs back outside, and tries*

117

making a phone call. Then slams the receiver down,
jumps back in her car, and tears out of there like a
Kamikaze pilot...

The next morning, her car is still here.

Once again, the image of that damned Dodge truck popped into his head.

"Name Bascomb ring a bell?" The cop scribbled in his notepad.

"Bascomb..." Maybe it wasn't Sally after all.

"Car's registered to a Sally Bascomb. Husband's name is Warren. Orlando address. Bascomb's CEO of Bas-Com, Incorporated. Software conglomerate."

Hank's face grew hot. The cool air from the passing travel trailer did little to diffuse it. "You said ... Sally."

"Knock something loose?"

"Just a feeling."

"This doesn't add up." The cop was frowning again.

"What doesn't?"

"Everyone's got cell phones these days. Hell, my ten-year-old daughter has one. The wife of a CEO would definitely have one. She would've called, had someone pick her up. CEO's make fifty mill a year. That much coming in, you don't put up with inconveniences."

Hank was still trying to absorb all this. If Sally had a cell phone, why'd she try to use the payphone outside Tillie's?

"They'll do an inquiry." The cop snapped his notepad shut and slid it carefully underneath his vest. "GreeneWay folks don't like abandoned vehicles cluttering their roads." He stuck the pen

118

back into its pocket. "We'll wait till we hear from the owner. If not, we'll put a sticker on the windshield. Car will be towed if someone doesn't–"

"Bascomb, eh?"

"Yeah."

Hank struggled to make sense of it.

"Have a good one. And drive safe." The cop straddled the motorcycle. He buckled his helmet, started up the bike, and roared away.

***

Bascomb's old lady hadn't moved.

Bill Landry's gut throbbed like an open wound. *Goddammit.* He sure hoped he hadn't used too much chloroform. Schiller was just blowing smoke. Whining. Doing what he did best. But it was possible. *Shit...*

No. He'd done the research and had given her only as much as was prescribed for a healthy hundred-and-twenty-pound woman. They were both assured that she weighed one-twenty and was determined to stay at that weight the rest of her natural life. "That woman'll spend a month living at Bally if she gets on that scale and it registers anything above one-twenty," Bascomb had told him.

Still, he could've messed it up. Her resistance might've been down. She was scared, wasn't she? All sorts of adrenalin pumping wildly, messing up her system. What if she had a cold? Or some sort of blood malady no one knew about? Or–

Enough of this crap. I did everything right. If anything, a portion of the stuff evaporated when the packet was opened. It could've made the dose

119

weaker during the struggle. She's just sleeping it off.

He had to stop listening to Schiller's hysteria and snap back to reality. Focus on what had to be done. Wake her, then go through the charade of telling her what they wanted, what was expected of her. And above all, keep her calm. They didn't need her going all ballistic and crazy on them while they were supposed to be keeping her on ice. Timing was important. Bascomb had stressed that above all else. Timing and discretion. What would happen to poor Mrs. Bascomb after her time was up was a different matter altogether...

Best get this over with. He couldn't afford to stop and think about what they were doing. Otherwise, he'd never be able to go through with it. But as he eyed the beautiful woman lying helplessly behind the truck's front seats, he caught himself admiring that fine stuff. She was really put together. Genuine eye-candy. And so totally dynamite in those jeans–

Stop it. You're in enough trouble. Don't make this worse.

What the hell could make it worse?

Bascomb, of course. That bastard brought out the worst in everyone. If it weren't for Bascomb, this wouldn't even be happening.

That last meeting had sealed the deal. Bascomb pacing the conference room in his tailored Baroni, his hands clasped behind his back. Studying him and Schiller in that dark, condescending way of his that made you want to strangle the son of a bitch. Then, finally, bringing his hands around, crossing his arms over his chest, and making his

120

announcement. "You two are terminated. Immediately. I could easily have you both prosecuted to the fullest extent of the law, but since I happen to be in a charitable mood at the moment, I might be inclined to overlook your classic blunders–"

"What's wrong, Billy?"

He pulled himself out of replaying that nightmare and came back to the present reality. Schiller. The truck. The construction site just beyond the trees. Bascomb's old lady. Only then did he realize he was scowling. "Just thinking."

"About what?"

He tried to get Bascomb's words, *charitable mood*, out of his head, but each time he thought about it, a clot of heat climbed up his back. No point getting Schiller worked up again. He forced a smile and answered, "Brazil – what else?"

***

Footsteps.

Doors clicked open.

The floor shook.

Sally cringed, her skin popping with gooseflesh. She hadn't prayed in years, hadn't picked up a St. Joseph Sunday Missal since she was a little girl. Back then, things seemed simpler, much easier to comprehend. During the week, she went to school. On Sundays and the other holy days the Catholic Church recognized, she went to Mass with Mom and Dad. She attended Catechism Class and learned about the saints and the apostles and Lucifer and Christ and the angels and their trumpets. If you did something good, you were praised. If you did

121

something bad, you were punished. The world was much simpler and brighter when she was a child. Good and bad were easier to see, love and hate easier to distinguish, God and the Devil easier to identify. And bad guys were scary-looking and always wore black.

She'd learned so much more about life once she'd left the sanctuary of Dad and Mom and their normal middle-class existence, where the meaning of life could be explained simply--going to college, finding a man with a promising career, getting married, having children, bringing them up Catholic, and staying married.

After setting out on her own, she'd learned that many things were seldom as they seemed. Good wasn't always good, bad not always bad. People were many things and as predictable as they were different. They frequently didn't mean what they said or say what they meant. She'd also learned that the world was filled with very bad people much nastier than the monsters depicted in scary books and films. Sally feared she'd just fallen victim of very bad people.

The floor continued to shake. She figured she was lying in some vehicle. Probably a truck, going by the heavy thumping of the doors.

The same truck as last night? She fought hard to visualize it. Light-colored. White? A long bed, maybe? Was it a Dodge? Or a Ford? She couldn't remember.

The reek of cigarette smoke. "Mrs. Bascomb." A man's voice--not the nervous one who had lured her back to the truck last night. This was definitely

122

someone different. The same one who had snuck up behind her? Who had shoved the wet rag in her face?

"Mrs. Bascomb, we'd like to know if you're all right. If you feel sick or nauseous."

His voice was low-pitched and calm, but with an edge to it. She could tell by its slight tremor that he was nervous and trying to hide it. But it didn't tell her how nasty he was. It didn't have to. She knew already. Only someone mean and cold-blooded would do what he'd done last night.

"Nod if you're okay."

Okay? She'd been knocked out, bundled up, and kept like this for God only knows how long. She was nauseous and cramped. Her head ached. Her side had gone numb, and her bladder throbbed. And they wanted to know if she was *okay*.

Just fine, she wanted to say. *I've always enjoyed bondage. And knockout juice has always been a particular turn-on for me. Almost like an aphrodisiac.*

"Mrs. Bascomb?"

Now was not the time to show her temper or lose her composure. *Calm, Sal. Show them what you're made of. You can only find out what this is all about if you're calm and don't upset them.*

Her heart pounding, she nodded.

"Good. Now listen carefully. We want money for your safe return. Once we get it, you're back home, safe and sound. We're not murderers, so don't even go there. It's not even an option. When the transaction's complete, we're all out of here. Understand?"

Again she nodded.

"I'm going to pull the tape from your mouth. If there's something you need, now would be the time to tell us."

Her body stiffened at his touch. The smell of cigarettes and sweat made her want to throw up. She held her breath while the tape was peeled away. Her mouth free, the sour taste returned with a vengeance. She forced it back down. It gushed back up, making her eyes water. She coughed. And coughed again. The sourness dissipated.

"You okay?"

Of course I'm not okay, you idiot! She wanted to throw up on him. It was lucky for him that she hadn't had supper. Nothing down there to throw up. Maybe she could bite off one of his fingers.

"Anything you need?"

A gun would be nice. As long as it's loaded. But that wasn't what concerned her now. This man was lying to her. She was certain of it. She suspected she was in terrible danger. He had already used the word *murder*.

A strange, forbidden thought occurred to her. The other one had mentioned Warren out on the highway. Maybe these two actually knew him ... in a very wrong sort of way.

"Is there anything you need?" he repeated.

Despite what she felt, what she feared, she gathered up what courage she could find and forced herself to think rationally. Survive this moment. This instant. The throbbing urge low in her gut made another protest. And she knew that in this case, modesty was the last thing on her mind. She

124

took a deep breath. "I ... have to pee."

CHAPTER TEN

Hank parked beside a chocolate-brown Hummer in the gravel parking lot adjacent to the construction site.

The morning, bright and warm, glistened just like any other morning in late May. The sun splashed wavy starbursts onto the tinted windows of the buildings across the street. Exhaust fumes from heavy morning traffic, along with a knot of burnt coffee from the eatery across the street, sauntered over and assaulted him.

At the corner, a group of old women in shorts and baggy shirts crossed at the light. A young Asian couple and their two tiny daughters huddled in front of a tee shirt shop window, an opened map held out in front of them. The construction site buzzed with activity. Men and women wearing hard hats, overalls, and heavy boots hauled toolboxes, lunch pails, and thermoses up the steps of the shanties lining the rear lot. The thumping and grinding of machinery echoed loudly.

Hank's cell phone buzzed. Colleen Moore's number registered on the display. *So much for mellowing before driving to the office.*

He punched in her number. *Busy. Good. Things are looking up.*

He grabbed his hard hat from the passenger seat and crossed the sandy lot. In the first shanty, a gray-haired guy around sixty hunched over a folding table, sipping hot coffee. The hot end of a half-burnt Camel protruded between the fat fingers of his right

126

hand. A burly guy sporting a thick black Buffalo Bill mustache sat across from him, dropping sugar cubes into his thermos. Two younger men, both in their late twenties, squatted on the wooden bench, arguing football.

Hank stuck his head inside. "Anyone see Amos Miller this morning?" A couple of negative grunts. Hank tried the other three shanties, but with no success.

A tall, skinny black man with white whiskers and light-blue eyes passed him on the way out of the last shanty. "Mr. Lee," he said, tipping his hard hat. "Ain't seen you out here in a month of Sundays."

Hank remembered him from a project they'd worked on a couple of years before, in Kissimmee. "Dragon Lady keeps me on a tight leash, Ignatius. Doesn't want me taking a dump anywhere, unless she's there to supervise."

The man chuckled.

"Seen any of the surveyors this morning?"

"Couple, maybe."

"Amos Miller?"

"Don't recall seeing Amos, no suh."

"Thanks."

His cell buzzed again. The number on the display made him grind his teeth. He crossed the street, slipped behind the wheel of the Caddie, and pressed redial on the cell. She answered on the first ring. *Damn.*

"Lee, where the hell are you?"

"And a cheerful and enthusiastic good morning to you, too."

"Why aren't you at the office?"

127

"I'm at the site. Unless they finally swing the deal on human cloning, I can't possibly be in two places–"

"What are you doing *there*?"

"Checking out a few things."

"Did Miller show up?"

"You called me just for *that*?"

"Answer the question."

Amos was probably fighting a hell of a hangover. If he was on his way in, he didn't need Colleen Moore waiting to pounce on him like a hungry cat. "He's here--all right?"

"Wonders never cease."

"That all?"

"You wouldn't by any chance want to put him on the line, would you?"

"Sure. Why not? He's in the one of the Porta-Johns at the moment. I'll just open the door and see if he's got a free hand–"

"You can be really disgusting, Lee."

"You know, that's probably one of the nicest things you've ever–"

"Staff meeting. Nine-thirty. Don't be late." Click.

"And a warm, pleasant and enthusiastic good-bye to you, my vision of loveliness." Hank pocketed the cell. Once again, the notion of strangling the woman registered brightly in his thoughts.

***

Tommy met Billy outside, near the tailgate. Billy had the burn phone in his hand and was ready to dial.

"You ... calling him?" Tommy asked uneasily.

Billy shrugged. "It's the plan, isn't it?"

Tommy had never thought much of the plan. He knew what had to be done, when, and how--he just didn't want to think about any of it. Bad enough they'd kidnapped the lady in the first place. The rest of this was ten times worse. "Yeah," he said, looking at the sand at his feet. "It's the plan."

"If he thinks we blew this, he'll get in touch with the Feds faster than you can fart, and he'll tell them all about our dummy account scheme."

Tommy dreaded that damned phone and didn't want Billy making it. It was a simple message and all, but it made all this real--frighteningly real.

Billy dialed, then waited. A moment later he said, "Everything's fine," then hung up, dropped the phone on the ground at his feet, and stomped on it.

Schiller couldn't bring himself to stare at the smashed phone. It was like looking at what was left of their futures. The worst part of it all was that it meant the job was half finished. The job would be done when Billy made the next call with the second phone that had been provided. Each time he thought about the second call, he felt the strong urge to throw up.

"Something on your mind?" Billy watched him closely, probably waiting for him to say something stupid.

"Nothing."

"Good. Whenever you have shit going on in your head, it makes you go all screwy. Like last night."

"I was nervous, big-time."

"We've gone through all this before. We have to keep our cool. We're running the show. Keep that in mind."

"You really think we are?"

"From this end, we are."

"But ... this wasn't ... our idea."

"Don't you think I know that? I was sitting in that room, too. Remember?"

"I just hope we don't blow this. If something happens tomorrow–"

"Twenty-four hours. Remember? We don't do anything until then. Then–"

"I don't ... want to hear it." Tommy brought up his left hand and jammed his thumb in his mouth. There was nothing to say to that. Nothing in the world would make any of this right.

Billy flicked away his smoke, then pushed sand over the mashed phone and tamped it flat. "Now it's time to let the lady relieve herself. And you're gonna be the one to do it."

"*Me?*"

"We alternate, like we agreed. Just walk her down that path a little ways, find some bushes–"

"I'll fuck up." The thought of standing beside the woman while she squatted in the bushes freaked him out. He didn't want to think of such a classy lady squatting. It just didn't seem right. "Like last night. She looked at me and I just fell apart–"

"Let her have a few minutes to herself, then bring her back to the truck. Just find some bushes and stand clear until she's finished. But make sure you're not far, just in case she tries to bolt."

"What'll *you* be doing?"

"Keeping an eye out to make sure no one comes down the road. We can't have any dickheads from

130

that construction site snooping around. If someone wanders out this way, we'd have to get rid of them. You wanna be the one to do that?"

***

The staff meeting finished quickly, thank God.

As usual, it was a waste of time. Just another of Colleen's time-management talks that did nothing more than interfere with everyone's morning break. Colleen probably just wanted an excuse to show off her new outfit--cream silk blouse, knee-length black skirt, and black open-toed spikes. The outfit gave her the dangerously sexy appearance she constantly sought to achieve. The spikes looked like they came straight from Lenore's House of Pain.

When she opened the conference room door, everyone scattered. Hank didn't have a chance to escape. She'd already closed the door long before he could reach it.

"We need to talk." The sparkle in her big dark-brown eyes suggested something was up. She'd probably called the site right after she'd talked to Hank and heard Amos hadn't come in. "Miller gonna be a problem?" she asked, standing in front of the door.

"Nope."

"You're sure?"

"Yep."

"Your Gary Cooper isn't very amusing."

"The situation calls for it."

"You said Miller was at the site."

"Yep. I did."

A deep sigh. "He wasn't there, was he?"

No sense taking this any further. "Not while I

"was there."

"Why lie to me, Lee? Is he worth sticking your neck out for?"

"He had a few last night. He probably feels like hell this morning."

"He deserves to feel like hell. I have very little tolerance for drunks."

"I drink."

"I've never seen you drunk or hung over, Lee. You're always sober and alert."

"I'll only use my powers for the good of all mankind."

She didn't smile. He shrugged.

"What's the difference with you and Miller?"

"I'm not hung up over a stripper young enough to be my daughter."

"Miller's washed up." The defiance oozed from her.

"Just because of the stripper thing?"

"Actually, I meant the young-enough-to-be-my-daughter thing."

"Hey, if a guy's lucky enough to find one of those—"

"Typical." Her eyes flashed.

"You're not too wild about the male gender, are you?"

"What is it that bothers you?" She crossed her arms. "The fact that I'm a woman running a big company?"

"That's not quite it, actually."

"Men resent women in power. I've encountered tons of them all through my career. They didn't make my trip very pleasant, nor did they make it

132

easy. I succeeded, so I guess the experience helped me appreciate the end-result. But I didn't realize until now that you're actually one of those narrow-minded, bullheaded Neanderthal's women therapists write about."

He felt sorry for her. Someone so intelligent being so off-base and naive.

"Nothing to say?"

"I might have a comment or two, but I don't think you'll like it."

"Try me. I didn't trap you in this room just to stare at you."

"I thought it might be my aftershave."

Her expression didn't change.

"In a nutshell, you expect me to trash Amos Miller because he's going through a personal crisis. And when I give you a hard time about it, you tell me it's because I'm a Neanderthal."

"Miller's a liability. Parker's a multi-million-dollar project. That's entirely too much investment to risk on employees we can't count on."

"Give him time. I'll vouch for him."

"You already have. He's made you look like an idiot." She approached the tinted window. "My project engineers are due to visit the site at eleven." She consulted her Rolex. "That's roughly an hour from now. If Miller's there, he'll have his last chance. Otherwise..." She shrugged.

Hank didn't like this at all. Now he had to go looking for Amos and cart his sorry ass back to the site. "That's your only proposition?"

"Take it or leave it."

Hank quickly focused on the door and pulled it

open. "I'll let you know."

"Eleven o'clock, Lee," she called after him.

***

Two pairs of cold hands eased Sally out of the truck.

She was carried only a few feet before her legs were lowered. The sudden shift in her position made her nauseous. She forced it away and tried to ignore the heavy tingling gathering on her right side.

Her kidnappers held her up, preventing her from falling. One of them stood close behind her, the other in front. The one behind her held her arms while the other peeled the tape binding her ankles.

A hot flare of sharp pain danced up her legs, making them buckle and forcing one of her abductors to grasp her around the waist so she wouldn't fall. His right hand pressed against her right side, which burned as if it had been tapped with a hot skillet. A flurry of jagged pain galloped up her back. The tape over her mouth kept her from screaming.

After what seemed an eternity, the numbness left her legs. A stinging sensation started at her hips, moving downward. With difficulty she slowly raised each foot. They felt like they weighed a ton, but she forced them up, setting them gently back down. She had to restore the circulation in them. A strange tickling started in her feet, spreading fanlike to her toes. The sudden queasiness made her feel faint.

Fight it, Sal. You're tough--remember?

"Here's the itinerary." The familiar reek of cigarettes enveloped her. The one who'd spoken

134

earlier peeled the tape from her mouth. "My partner will lead you into the woods. We're miles from anything, so screaming won't do you much good. You'll have a couple of minutes, then we've got to put you back in the truck."

With her upper arms held firmly, Sally was guided carefully through the brush. Moving was awkward. The blindfold prevented her from watching for exposed roots or uneven ground. She was forced to lift her tingling feet to keep from stumbling. Part of her wanted to come out of her skin and just disappear.

Take things one at a time. Her top priority: her bursting bladder.

The man guiding her was obviously the redhead. She suspected there were only two of them. The one doing the talking appeared calmer, surer of himself.

For a second she wanted to throttle both of them, but she wasn't violent--even hated arguing. She'd been walking away from unpleasantness, from complications, ever since she could remember. Confrontations made her queasy. It made her physically ill to know she'd done or said something to cause someone enough anger or hurt to want to retaliate. Walking away always seemed the easiest solution. Arguing caused so much hostility, harsh feelings, hatred, and hurt. She'd gone off by herself whenever Mom or Dad scolded her for something, or if she did or said something stupid or ridiculous in school. She'd also walked out of a wonderful man's life when it became too painful and complicated to be with him any longer. Only the night before, she'd dashed out of her own house to avoid a stupid, pointless argument with her husband.

Well, like it or not, you've just encountered a situation where you can't walk away. You've got to stay and face it. Senseless terror has just invaded your life, and you're the only one who can find a way to deal with it.

She had to make headway. The little voice inside her said it would require working this from another perspective. *You're aware of one very important thing. You've known it ever since you first realized what it meant to be female. It's the most important thing a girl can learn. It's your legacy.*

You're still a fine-looking woman, even though you're on the wrong side of thirty-five. Your hair is as thick as ever, your breasts haven't yet discovered gravity, and you look just as nice in jeans as you did fifteen years ago. As much as you hate these men and want them both dead, you have to put that aside and let your soft side show. Use it. It might just save your life.

"It's wonderful, getting my blood flowing again," she said with a deep sigh.

No response.

"My legs ... really hurt. They're burning inside, like pins and needles."

He still didn't speak.

"I hope I don't cramp. If I do, *please* don't let me fall."

Ten more steps. Their pace slowed, and things in the ground--palmettos or other bushes--rubbed her jeans. The hands gripping her pulled her back. Sally and her abductor stood still. Her heart pounded. He

136

stood close behind her, his face inches away, his breath coming out in short bursts. The mere thought of him being so close, in total control, brought back the fear. She heard him swallow only a moment before his hands unwrapped the tape binding her wrists.

"How much money ... do you want ... for my release?" she asked in a soft voice.

No response.

"I'd really like to know."

Her hands were freed. She let them drop to her sides, then shook them gently. They were as warm and as tingly as her legs. She massaged them while he fiddled with the blindfold. Despite the numbness in her hands, she felt her fingers curling, tensing, becoming rigid. *Relax. Don't come apart.*

The blindfold was pulled away. She kept her eyes closed for a few seconds before easing them open. Her darkness instantly exploded with tiny piercing triangles of harsh light from the morning sun penetrating the branches of the trees around her. Squinting, she brought up an arm. It took nearly a minute to acclimate herself.

"Pl-Please hurry," he blurted out. "We haven't got ... much time."

She fought the urge to spin around and gouge out his eyes. *No, Sal. You're not that kind of person. Anyway, he might be your size, but you don't know where his partner is ... or how big the other guy is ... or if this jerk is holding another knockout pack. Besides, you'll probably pull back at the last moment and just get everyone upset.*

She rubbed her eyes to get rid of the little black

negative triangles floating across her vision. Then she surveyed her surroundings. Pines, scrubs, Palmettos, Spanish moss. Just like any other wooded area in Florida. It was impossible to tell where they were. But the distant buzz of steady traffic behind her told her they weren't that far from civilization.

"*Please*. Don't ... look around."

She began unbuckling her belt. "Why not?"

"We don't ... want you to ... to see us."

Another lie. The other one had said she'd be taken home safe and sound when they got their money. But last night this one had mentioned the convention at the Marriott. And that they knew Warren. How much of that was the truth? And what about his Johnny O'Brien lie?

"I've already seen you," she said, hoping to keep him talking. "Last night, remember?"

No reply. He was probably thinking up a good answer.

She finished with her belt and unzipped the jeans, wondering if he would watch while she took care of business. Or give her the privacy his partner had promised? She stood perfectly still, her thumbs hooked beneath her jeans and panties. "I guess there's no way I can appeal to your gentlemanly instincts, is there?"

"Wh-What?"

"Would it be possible to give me just a *little* privacy?"

A gulp. "I'm ... not looking."

She could tell by the fading of his voice on that last word that he'd just turned away.

She slid down her jeans and panties. He was probably looking again, but it couldn't be helped. Her urgency outweighed his silly voyeurism. Besides, these two men were calling the shots. If they needed the thrill of peeking at a middle-aged woman squatting amongst the scrubs, they definitely had issues.

"Maybe you f-forgot ... what I ... l-look like," he said softly.

Telling him she had a good memory would not be very bright. Acting the part of the classic dumb blonde could work in her favor. And as nervous as he was--his stuttering said it all--he wouldn't be able to concentrate properly. This would make him screw up--maybe at the perfect moment.

"Please tell me how much you guys want."

No response.

"I'd like to know how much you think I'm worth."

Finally, "A m-million."

Strange. Warren was worth *hundreds* of millions. If they actually *did* know Warren, they knew he was filthy rich. So why a paltry million, when they could easily get ten times that?

"Is that all?"

Another pause. "L-Listen, lady–"

"Please call me Sally."

She'd learned from TV and crime stories that it was essential for you to do whatever it took to have your kidnapper 'humanize' you. The first rule was to make sure he knew your name. That way you ceased being a 'package' or 'merchandise.' It made you more difficult to be discarded or murdered.

139

She decided to try a gamble. "Actually, I have five million in my own savings. Not to mention my shares of Bas-Com. I've got ten thousand shares. At fifty dollars a share, there's half a million just in stock."

No reply.

She straightened, pulling up her jeans. At least now she had him thinking. As she buckled her belt she said, "I'll tell you something else." She had to get him thinking even harder. "I can personally get you the five million if–"

The tape was quickly slapped over her mouth.

"Gotta go back." The blindfold was awkwardly replaced. His hands shook so badly, it took him several tries to get it knotted right. Then the tape was quickly slapped over her mouth. He gathered her arms behind her and clumsily wrapped tape around her wrists, yanking it from a roll he'd brought with him.

The smell of his sweat overwhelmed the warm air.

***

The stifling afternoon heat singed Hank's sensitive skin as soon as he left the building.

Normally, he preferred the hot outside air to the cold, recycled stuff engorging the offices. But not now. Escaping Colleen's offices was a nice respite, but he wasn't looking forward to going out after Amos Miller and hauling his pitiful butt back to the Parker site.

His first inclination was to say hell with it and head for the beach. Stripping off the confining suit, walking around barefoot on the hot sand, and taking in the heavy salt air sounded like a great idea. Right now he didn't care what Colleen did to Amos. At the moment he didn't care much about anything.

But he couldn't abandon Amos. It would be like ignoring an injured dog lying beside the road. Despite his hatred for bullshit and his distaste for taking orders from Colleen, he was going to drive back to Amos's apartment, pour hot coffee down the old fool's throat, and drag him back to the site.

But just ten minutes after he'd left the parking garage and turned onto the GreeneWay, his plan changed drastically. The abandoned GT-350 came into view. And he quickly found he couldn't think of anything else.

If Sally had stopped on the highway, it was for a good reason. If she was having engine problems, her CEO hubby wouldn't wait too long before sending someone for her. But would he know something was wrong? He'd be in his office, running his empire, and much too busy to care what was going on at the home front. Unless, of course, he'd already called the home front.

If he did, he'd know Sally wasn't there. If she was the typical trophy wife, she'd be required to be at her husband's beck and call. And if she wasn't, Bascomb would find out immediately. CEO's had resources ordinary people could only dream about--attorneys, accountants, drivers, bodyguards, mechanics, pool guys, lawn maintenance people. And if the big man's wife was in trouble, the militia would be summoned in a heartbeat.

If Sally had her cell phone, why'd she use the payphone at Tillie's? From what he saw, the only reason she went to Tillie's was to use the phone. And going by her reaction, whoever she was trying to call wasn't there. Otherwise, she would've been at the phone longer and might not have been so angry when she hung up.

Using a payphone was not a very pleasant experience nowadays. Not many of them even worked anymore. And since mostly everyone carried cell phones, payphones were much harder to find. When you found one, you faced the immediate dilemma of having to actually touch it. Punks and druggies puked on them and broke them open for the change. It was a wonder *any* of them worked. Even more of a wonder that anyone should try using them.

And as far as stopping along the road... Too many weirdoes were out there. Kidnappers, serial killers, stalkers, all sorts of crazies out on the prowl. Dregs the likes of Ted Bundy. Harvey Glatman. John Wayne Gacy ... the list was endless.

What self-respecting fiend would pass up the chance to make a meal out of someone like Sally? What if something bad happened back there? Would he be able to live with himself if he didn't try to find out?

His thoughts in a loop, he got off the GreeneWay, then got back on, and sped through the E-Pass lane, in the opposite direction. Several minutes later, he sat staring at the abandoned car, his nerves making his limbs tremble. He couldn't shake the bad vibes generating from the discarded purse.

Braving the spiraling exhaust fumes from

passing traffic, he got out of the Caddie. The GT's dash was impossible to read. So was the gas gauge. Out of gas? Engine trouble? Would someone pull over and help?

Sally had on a pair of seriously tight jeans. Her sexy appearance would definitely make the situation tense if she got out of the car. The jeans. The rocks on her fingers. The blonde hair.

Each time the scene in front of Tillie's Tavern drifted back into Hank's mind, the white pickup also popped up. His scalp itched. Something was very wrong... Sally, irritated and angry, trying to make a phone call, leaving the bar in a hurry, but stopping two miles later, on a lonely stretch of highway not very far from the nearest exit.

He squatted behind the Mustang. Concrete. Gravel. Skid marks. Cigarette butts. A pull-ring from a beer can. Then he saw it. A patch of mashed grass just a few feet from the Mustang's rear bumper. Tire treads. Big ones.

He hurried back to the Cadillac. *Sorry, Amos, but this could be slightly more serious than hauling your ass out of bed, dressing you, and pouring hot coffee down your throat.*

He snatched up his cell.

CHAPTER ELEVEN

The blindfold was strangely comforting as Sally lay on her side while the vibration of the truck lulled her toward sleep.

She fought the urge to succumb to slumber. It was important to stay alert so she could concentrate on her strategy. Confusion was her most effective tool. If her abductors were confused, they'd screw up. Someone might notice, suspect something.

She didn't quite believe what the nervous one had told her about their ransom demand. If they knew Warren, they'd surely know how much money could be gained by this. A million dollars wouldn't hurt her husband at all. He'd barely feel the sting.

Would the nervous one tell his partner about the five million she'd mentioned? Or would they consider it nothing more than a simple ruse by a desperate woman? If they believed her, would they try to get it? And if Warren knew what she'd told them, would he hold it against her?

Why should Warren care how much they wanted, if it meant getting her back? How important was money anyway? Why quibble about such a tiny portion of your worth if your wife's life hung in the balance?

Their argument earlier that evening drifted back. This time, the situation felt different. He'd come into the house, poured his drink, and immediately turned defensive. Looked at it in this new perspective, it all seemed planned.

No. Not possible. It was chance--nothing more.

She paid so little attention to the gas gauge, he'd reminded her time and time again to check it. How could Warren plan something on the off-chance that a stupid mistake she'd made three or four times in the past would happen again?

It was possible, wasn't it? If you wanted to get rid of someone, wouldn't it be logical to let nature take its course? "Go take your walk," he'd said. Not once, but twice. Once, she could forgive. But not twice. Twice made it feel as if he actually wanted her to leave. But how would he know she'd leave without her cell phone? Even if he did, why would he want her gone? Just because they were going through a bad spell in their marriage didn't mean he wanted something to happen to her, did it?

Did these two know Warren? Bits of conversation from their talk earlier picked at her. *Options. Program. Transaction. Itinerary.* They talked like computer people. And if they worked with computers, they might indeed be associated with her husband. It also meant they were white collar.

They'd said they weren't murderers, hadn't they? White collar people committed white collar crimes. Non-violent undertakings. Although this was a kidnapping, it didn't necessarily mean they wanted her dead. The fact that she was blindfolded told her they were being careful. They didn't want her to see their faces. That could mean they intended to release her unharmed.

Sally, you really can be stupid sometimes. These two knocked you out, taped you up, and tossed you

145

in the back of a truck ... and you think it's good that they're computer people?

She fought down the anger and forced herself to focus on something else. The gas tank seemed a good place to start. If she went over it in her head, it would take her mind off Warren and the two who'd kidnapped her. And if she could keep her mind busy, she might stay sane--at least for the time being.

When had she filled it last? Three days ago? Four? It was probably last Friday morning, while on her way to Bally. After her workout, she'd stopped at the grocery before returning home. Five, maybe six miles to Bally. Three to the mall, another mile to the grocery. Then back to Bally again on Monday. *And don't forget that trip to Sanford Saturday morning to look for glassware. That's twenty miles, one way.*

Too many things to think about. Mileage. Stop-start in-town traffic. The way her foot liked that gas pedal, especially on the toll roads. And it sure didn't help, highballing it last night.

It was your own fault. Admit it. And stop blaming Warren.

***

Tommy couldn't believe they'd just pulled into a Wendy's.

What was Billy thinking? Driving to a crowded eatery with a woman trussed up in back would probably earn them a Darwin Award.

This only happened because Tommy hadn't been paying attention to where they were going. He was deciding exactly when he should tell Billy about

146

Mrs. Bascomb's proposition. He wanted to be sure to get everything straight before hitting Billy with it. Otherwise, he'd sound like a shithead. Billy had a nasty habit of asking questions you hadn't thought about yet. And Billy was bound to ask all sorts of questions, considering how much was at stake--five million smackeroos.

It was a lot to think about. A *huge* chunk of change. Bascomb's million would set them up in Brazil for a few years, but five times that would give them a much classier ride on the merry-go-round. It would be the difference between driving a first-class machine like a Porsche rather than some clunker they'd find in the junkyard.

Billy coaxed the truck behind the big building and chose a place in the vacant rear lot about two hundred feet from the dumpsters, behind some untrimmed hedges. It was quiet here, and isolated ... but it was still a *fast food place*, for Chrissakes.

Tommy had never really cared for the fast-food culture. Too many weirdoes fighting with their kids, yelling orders at takeout, revving engines in the back, playing bumper-car in the front, messing up the rest rooms. Too much noise and confusion. Tommy hated noise and confusion. *"Fast food?"* He couldn't help sounding hysterical even though he was whispering.

"Aren't you hungry?"

"Starved ... but *here*?"

"What's the problem?"

"*Jeez* ... why don'tcha just pull up to the takeout window?"

Billy glared. "Want a fancy sit-down place?

147

We'll just leave the engine running so the air-conditioning keeps her cool. Inside, we can sit at a table and wait twenty minutes for our snooty waitress to notice us. Sound better?"

"But *jeez* ... all these *people* around?"

"Chill, okay?" Billy put the truck in park. "Be back in fifteen."

"What if ... what if someone looks in?"

"Windows are tinted, brainiac."

"What if one of these stupid tourists comes over to ask for directions? Tourists always ask for directions. I know a guy who was taking a piss and a stupid tourist walked right over to the urinal and asked him the best way to get to Disney."

"Like I said, *tinted windows*. Got it? If you sit back and keep away from the windshield, nobody'll even see you. We're a hundred yards away, dammit. You still like those greasy onion rings?"

Tommy knew better than argue when Billy's mind was made up.

Billy pushed open the door, climbed down, slammed the door and wandered casually toward the building, not a care in the world, damn him. Tommy wiped his moist brow with the back of his hand. Weird that he was sweating with the air-conditioning on full blast. *You're just nervous. Chill – you'll be fine.*

He hoped Billy was right about the tinted windows. As a precaution, Tommy lowered both visors.

***

"How the hell's it hanging, Henry?" asked the familiar voice. "I thought maybe you'd dropped off the face of the earth."

"Sometimes I think I have," Hank said to his cell. He knew Pete Hayes from Saudi, where they'd both been sent to guard several hundred dark-skinned natives with bad teeth and terrible hygiene. When their tour was over, Hank returned to Orlando to finish college at UCF while Pete resumed his career at the *Sentinel*, where he'd been a reporter since graduating from Journalism School.

Hank could visualize his old buddy at his desk, those size twelves propped up, the long dirty-brown hair as unkempt as always, that scraggly beard stained gray from too many Marlboros.

"Whatever happened to that poker game?" Pete asked. "That was over a year ago."

"Got busy doing something else."

"Too busy for *poker*?"

"I know that's hard to believe, but yeah, something else did come up..."

"Who was she? And did you name it after me?"

"As we speak, there's a little girl named Petie running around, wondering who her daddy is."

"I'll bet she's cute as a button."

"Her beard is already coming in pretty good."

"Glad to hear it. So how have you been?"

"All right, I guess."

"Those crotchety hard-hats getting to you?"

"They're a rowdy crew, all right. But it's actually the crotchety ball-buster in the executive office who's been giving me the ulcers."

"Ah. A woman in power. Every man's dream."

"Nightmare, actually."

"You've been doing that for what? Ten years

now?"

"At least."

"From here it sounds like burnout."

"Sounds like that here, as well. Lately I've been considering a much less dangerous line of work-- maybe with the bomb squad or looking for terrorist cells."

"I can sympathize. Sometimes this paper makes me want to try the Tibetan monk bit just for the peace and quiet. Why the call? Poker game back on?"

"Does the name Warren Bascomb ring a bell?"

"Bascomb." A pause. "Of course. Big money and connections." Hank heard him punching keys. "Yep, owns a software corporation based here in Orlando. What about him?"

"You got anything on his wife?"

Pete punched more keys. "If my memory serves me, he's been married a few times."

"His latest."

More punched keys. A pause. "Here it is. Sally."

"Anything else? Maiden name?"

Another punched key. "Burns."

Damn. It was her. A knot of heat swelled between his shoulder blades, then popped, turning ice-cold as it slid down his back.

"Hank? Still there?"

He took a deep breath, rubbed the back of his neck, and told himself to snap out of it. "I need an address. And anything else you can find."

"What's going on?"

"I think his old lady is in trouble, and I'd like to find out for sure."

150

"Why?"

"Why what?"

"Why would you think she's in trouble? And why should you care?"

"I saw her last night in a bar. She was all bent out of shape about something. She seems to have disappeared."

"You're meeting married women in bars again? I thought you gave that up for Lent."

"Lent's over, last I checked."

"What's this old lady look like?"

"Blonde, with a great figure. She's about our age."

"Thought so."

"Can you help me out here? Or do you plan on acting like a shithead the rest of your life?"

"You want answers to *both* questions?"

Hank sighed. He should've known Pete would give him a rough time. "Just the first. I already know the answer to the second."

"Oh hell. Why not? I really shouldn't be surprised. You always were a sucker for a pretty face. Remember that Iraqi hooker you shacked up with? The one with the sliced-up face?"

"What does she have to do with this?"

"You gave her your wallet and your watch--even your Good Conduct medal."

"She made off with my stuff while I was sleeping one off. Besides, I never even had a Good Conduct medal. And the only thing I actually *gave* her was--"

"We both know what that was. Then what's the story with the divine Mrs. B?"

"If I knew that, I wouldn't need *you*, would I?"

"That's cold, Henry. So tell me what this is about. Are you really worried about someone else's trophy wife? Or have you got ulterior motives?"

"Can't I just be neighborly?"

"I can tell when there's more to something when I hear it. It comes from twenty-odd years of digging into dirty laundry and getting on people's nerves."

"Sally and I ... well, we knew each other a while back."

"Was this before she married Bascomb?"

"Of course."

"Before Saudi?"

"After."

"After Heidi?"

"Right after."

"This have anything to do with why our poker game was canceled?"

"Fuck that damned poker game."

"You *are* cold, Henry."

"Only when I have to be."

"Sorry if I said anything offensive. Sometimes I shoot my mouth off. You know me."

"Yeah, I know you. You're a reporter. But I can still tolerate you."

"I don't get *that* very often."

"So how about it? Can you help me?"

"You will owe me."

"How bad?"

"That poker game I've been waiting for the last year or so."

Hank sighed. "What about it?"

"We need to reschedule."

"No problem."

"And I need to win. Big."

"Does that mean you want me to bring the marked deck again?"

"How else am I gonna win?"

***

The truck slowed, then stopped.

Sally lay there, listening. The two up front were whispering, but even with the air-conditioning, she still could make out a few words. *Takeout window. Sit-down place. Greasy onion-rings.*

My God. They just stopped at a fast-food place...

It made perfect sense, didn't it? You're hungry, so you stop somewhere. The fact that you were carrying around a woman you've kidnapped and tied up in back shouldn't matter at all.

She forced down the waves of heat. *Think rationally.* She had to remain in control. It was the only way she could fight them.

The skinny one was probably the weak link in the equation. He was nervous, flighty. The typical computer geek who wasn't happy unless he was popping speed or snorting cocaine. His partner was all business. He liked giving orders and calling the shots. Flighty was definitely the follower. He did whatever Business said. Business had probably masterminded this nightmare. To get to Business, she needed to bond with Flighty.

She'd taken several courses in college, settling on psychology but dropping out after three years when an amateur photographer saw her walking along the beach at Cocoa one hot summer weekend and offered to set her up for a photo session. It didn't amount to much--just a couple of perfume and hair ads in the local mag--but the exposure earned her steady work with JC Penney for five years, doing swimwear and underwear until the latest batch of anorexic young cokeheads came out of the woodwork and took all the high-paying jobs.

She'd chosen psychology because she wanted to learn how to communicate with people better. To see what made them tick. To understand their flaws, their moods. She knew she needed to break out of her shell once she was living on her own. She also knew there would be times she'd have to deal with problems without just turning her back on them. If she could understand the motives and desires of people, this would help her immensely. Under the current frightening conditions, things she'd learned in college were coming back very quickly.

One of her kidnappers had just left the truck-- probably to get the food. Since Business was the one who'd asked about the greasy onion rings, this could possibly mean Flighty was left to watch her. Sally geared herself up to apply one or two things she'd learned in college, as well as one or two things she'd learned as a young woman.

***

Cypress Lake Estates.

Villas, mansions, and bungalows proudly displayed fountains, trimmed hedges, and fancy gazebos.

Porsches, Corvettes, Mercedes, and Ferraris sat comfortably in the shade of palm trees. Neighborhood Watch signs appeared at each block. *Keep off the grass. Private property. No trespassing*. Hank expected to see a sign at the intersection that said: *Rich, important people live here--keep out*.

The Bascomb estate sprawled lavishly in its tree-lined kingdom, arrogant and fat with its stucco walls, Spanish tile roof, four-car garage, and ornate stone fountain spewing water in front of the main entrance.

A black wrought-iron fence spanned the front of the property. The gates were open, probably to accommodate the groundskeepers, landscapers and delivery people. But beyond the climbing ivy and the well-tended flowers and bushes, no signs of life interrupted the serenity of the man's extravagant sanctuary.

Pete Hayes had done some quick investigating, using the *Sentinel's* databanks. It didn't take him long to discover Bas-Com was the parent company of Venture, Limited, and CellWorldVue.

"WorldVue is the Dow's current hottie," Pete had told him. "When it first started up, it was a miniscule hole-in-the-wall business--a three-man operation working out of someone's home. You could've bought out the complete portfolio for less than a hundred K. But since it went public last year, it's literally exploded. Its stock originally sold for pennies a share. Now it's hovering around thirty and two-thirds."

"What made it rip?" Hank asked.

"The grapevine says a merger's in the works. The folks I talked to said this one's big."

"How big?"

"It could involve International Computer

Services."

"I might've heard of it. One of the largest computer companies in the country, right?

"The *world*, Henry. Offices in Paris, London, and Madrid. Not to mention New York City and Los Angeles, of course."

"What's it worth?"

"Tens of billions, apparently."

"And they want to merge with a hole-in-the–wall outfit like CellWorldVue?"

"That's the poop."

"What's your take on this?"

"It's hard enough getting these stories out, let alone understanding them. I dabble in the market, but when it involves corporate dealings, forget it. I don't even know enough to be considered dangerous."

"Makes two of us," Hank said.

"Maybe they want a piece of Central Florida."

"By hooking up with a nickel-and-dime setup?"

"They might want their eggs in as many baskets as possible. There's obviously more to this than meets the eye."

"What else did you find out?"

"Bascomb's a genius when it comes to making money. He has a sixth sense, good timing and ridiculous good luck. A man with the Midas touch."

"A real-life Auric Goldfinger."

"Much bigger, it seems. And when dealing with people, he's a bastard. Uses them, then trashes them."

According to Pete, Bas-Com had a turnover rate that would rival the average supermarket chain.

Bascomb paid top dollar but demanded so much from his employees, he could barely be tolerated. Once his employees had earned enough money through cash buyouts, bonuses, or personal investments, or bought enough stock through the company's option plan to build up a sizeable savings, they left. The typical Bas-Com employee stayed an average of six months. Those remaining longer were contractors or consultants.

Sally had been married to Bascomb nearly seven years. Sources said she owned portions of Bas-Com, but exactly how much was not commonly known.

Married nearly seven years. That was the part of this equation Hank couldn't dismiss. Coincidental? Not important now. He had to find out if Sally was okay. If this meant stepping on important toes, then so be it. He'd stepped on important toes before, and it had never bothered him. In fact, he enjoyed it. In his view, the only toes worth stepping on *were* the important ones.

The tension within him increased, forcing him to grip the wheel as he guided the Caddie up the winding paved drive.

***

Loud moaning behind the front seats shattered the tense silence.

Tommy's arms broke out in gooseflesh as he twisted sharply around. Mrs. Bascomb lay on her side, her head up, her blindfolded face pointed in his direction. He glanced toward the eatery. No sign of Billy. Probably standing in line or taking his time in the crapper. *Bummer.*

More moaning. *Jeez ... what should I do? Find*

157

out what she wants? Or wait for Billy to come back? Can't go inside and get him. And can't let her use the ladies' room if she has to pee again. I don't want her to wet her pants ... but I sure *don't want to screw up again.*

Have to wait. When Billy comes back, we'll figure out something.

Maybe she wanted to talk more about that five million. He thought about removing the tape from her mouth. But what if she screamed? What if someone heard her?

He quickly scanned the premises. No one walking around. The closest car was fifty yards away, near the corner of the building. People milled around their vehicles in front of the place. One of them, a skinny guy in red shorts and a sleeveless blue tank top, stood in front of the dumpster, picking his nose.

What harm could it do, letting her talk? If she freaked, he could always put the tape back on.

He bent over the console, gently peeled the tape away from her mouth, and let it dangle. She moved her lips around, getting her mouth muscles working again. But she didn't say anything. Maybe she just wanted to get the blood moving around in her cheeks for a little while. He couldn't blame her. It probably wasn't pleasant at all, having your mouth taped all day.

Just then she said, "I'd like to know if you're considering my offer."

He didn't reply. Not at first. He was expecting the lady to ask to relieve herself, and he wasn't at all prepared when she said something totally

158

different. But this wasn't bad. Not at all. Talking about five million bucks was a good thing. A real good thing.

But, what to say? He didn't want to tell too much and give something away that Billy would get pissed about. *Bluff.* Couldn't hurt, could it? It might get her to say more. "So ... what if we have?"

Mrs. Bascomb smiled. She looked nice even with the scarf hiding her eyes. The tiny dimples at the corners of her mouth made her look like a little girl. He wondered if her eyes were as blue as the ocean. Her hair was that color naturally. Billy had said so. Most blondes had blue eyes.

Incredibly--as if it had a mind of its own--his left hand reached out for the scarf. *Just a glimpse, then I'll slide it back down and--*

Idiot!

He jerked his hand back. *That was close. You almost did it again, you moron. Good thing something in your head's still working.*

"Does that mean you have?" she asked.

"M-Maybe."

"I'm glad." She smiled again.

He began trembling. Billy had told him all about ladies like her. They had their special magic and knew how to use it. When they wanted something, they knew how to get it. This lady had tricked Bascomb, of all people. Even got him to marry her. She probably dictated what clothes she wanted, what shoes ... and when she wanted jewelry, she probably drove to the store in her classic Mustang and used Bascomb's card. At home, she decided which furniture to buy, where to put it, what colors

159

to paint the walls. Bascomb called the shots at the office, but at home this lady did what she wanted.

Tommy had seen classic Mustangs like hers at car shows. *Jeez,* some of those babies went for six figures. This lady could be driving one of those Italian sports cars if she wanted to. The long, sloped-hooded ones, really low to the ground, only came up to your waist but cost half a million. All she had to do was tell Bascomb. *Get me one of those, darling. I have to have one.* The fool would just pull out his cell phone and order one right from the plant.

Getting five million from Bascomb wouldn't even take much. All she had to do was give him some once in a while. The bastard could get anything with tits and a decent set of legs. This lady had to be totally on the ball to hold on this long. Her smile probably did him in. And those titties sure didn't hurt.

"Please ... do me a large favor?" she asked.

His pulse raced. "I .... guess it depends on–"

"Please help me up. My side's totally numb. It would be nice if I could sit up for a change."

Billy wouldn't like this. *Why'd you do it?* he'd say. *Couldn't you be cool for fifteen lousy minutes?*

"I-I don't think–"

"*Please*? Just for a couple of minutes?"

She tensed on the floor, her face grimacing, the smile going away. Obviously in pain but keeping quiet about it.

He didn't want her smile to go away, even though it was so sweet, it made him feel like a jerk.

What would it hurt, helping her up? She wasn't

160

asking him to untie her. His gaze shifted to the jeans hugging her hips ... the swell of her titties under the blouse. *Jeez ... how can I help her up without ... without touching her ... without grabbing something and losing my nut ... without getting the shakes?*

There had to be a way. He could close his eyes and grab her shoulders, then pull her up. That way he wouldn't have to touch anything else.

"I'd *really* appreciate it." She shifted a shoulder, moving it in a nice way.

He risked another glance toward the building. Still no sign of Billy.

He climbed over the console and lowered himself carefully onto the floor, almost touching her. As soon as he caught himself staring, he forced himself to focus. *Stop it. You want to risk five million by being stupid?* He reached underneath her right shoulder and placed his free hand on her left arm, closing his eyes tightly. *Now ... just pull her.*

He took a deep breath and held it in, then pushed it back out. He took another breath and pulled her upright, letting her shoulder blades rest against the padding of the folded-up back seat. He let out his breath slowly so she wouldn't think he was up to something. The vanilla scent of her hair made him suck it back in and, in spite of himself, he opened his eyes. Her face was only a few inches away, her lips moist and parted.

Then he lowered his eyes. Her left tittie ... it was pressing against his ribcage. *Oh shit ... oh shit... Stop it, you moron. She doesn't even notice it.*

He shook himself out of it and backed up a little, until he was no longer touching her. *There. Much better. No harm done. She didn't notice. Just make sure you don't give yourself away.*

He felt the sudden stirrings and looked down at himself. *Shit. Shit. That little bit of contact and I'm hard... As long as you don't do anything stupid.*

Five million, dammit. Brazil. Bikini babes who can't speak English. For Chrissakes, pull yourself out of it!

Mrs. Bascomb sighed, smiling again. She moved her head, turning it gently from right to left and rolling her shoulders. Loosening up--and in doing so, made those titties move at the same time.

He couldn't help wondering what they looked like under that shirt--

"This is so much better," she said softly, and he could tell she meant it. "Thank you."

"No problem." He scrambled over the console, relieved he wasn't so close to her anymore. *Jeez ...* if all he had to do was bump against her to get his mind all screwy, he'd better not do it again. It really frightened him how women like her could do their number on a guy without even trying. The dimples. The pouty lips. The smile. The jeans. The fact that she was so *nice* ... so *soft*...

And she'd let him *touch* her. She'd actually let him touch her without freaking or acting like she knew he'd done it. That made things much, much worse for later.

He didn't want to think about that. It just didn't make any sense, no matter how much money was at stake.

Denial again. Turning your back on your problems. Close your eyes, turn around and presto!

162

Problem's gone. That's why he had the drug addiction in the first place. There were too many things he didn't want to think about. When you're high, problems vanish. Unpleasant people disappear. Everything turns mellow.

When he was mellow, nothing could bring him down. Daddy, the vicious and vengeful Bible-thumper, just faded away. Momma also faded away, gin bottle and all. Uncle Jimmy, who came over to play his 'touch-and-tickle' games with little ten-year-old Tommy when they were alone, turned into a big, ugly roach, scuttling for safety under the closest rock.

Without thinking, Tommy reached for his tranquilizers. Just one, and he wouldn't have to worry about saying the wrong thing. One would mellow him out. He might even take a short nap before Billy—

The sight straight ahead made his hand freeze. Billy, carrying three large white bags, crossed the pavement, heading toward the truck.

"I really would like to mention something."

Mrs. Bascomb's voice made him jump.

"I was thinking that maybe you might want to—"

Tommy spun around. He slapped the tape clumsily over the woman's surprised mouth.

Billy opened the door, climbed in and set the bags carefully on the console as he pulled the door shut. He glanced at Mrs. Bascomb. His gaze stayed on her. Then he turned and raised a brow at Tommy.

"She ... asked me if she could sit up," Tommy whispered nervously. "It's okay, isn't it? She said

163

her side was numb–"

"How'd she ask?"

"She moaned." Tommy swallowed, wiping his forehead. "I ... I thought maybe she ... maybe she had to pee, so I ... I let her talk. It's all right, isn't it? I mean ... I didn't do anything else, Billy. I swear."

Billy reached for a bag. "That all she said?"

"That's all. Nothing else. Zilch. *Nada*."

Billy's eyes stayed on him as he opened the bag.

***

The huge, stained mahogany door cracked open.

A short matronly woman poked her broad, grim bulldoggish face through the slim opening. A dark-blue maid's uniform and white lacy apron also showed in the ten-inch gap. Hank guessed there would be a large bow in back.

"Yes?" Her small, blinking black eyes regarded him curiously but disapprovingly. She obviously didn't like visitors. He figured he'd interrupted her in her work. Or while she was watching her soaps.

"The Bascomb's at home?"

"Mr. Bascomb at work."

"What about Mrs. Bascomb?"

The woman blinked again. "She ... not home."

"Where is she?"

The black brows mashed together--two fat caterpillars bumping heads.

"I'm an old friend," Hank said, trying to be tactful.

The maid continued frowning. "The lady ... she not home."

He could tell he wouldn't get anywhere with this woman. He could also tell she knew something was

164

wrong but was probably afraid to say anything--
especially to a stranger. Best try working this from a
more logical angle. "How can I get in touch with
Mr. Bascomb?"

"He's in his office--like I say."

"The one on South Orange and Church Street?"

"*Si*--yes."

"I can visit him there?"

"*Si*."

"Getting back to Mrs. Bascomb." It was worth
one last try. "When was the last time–"

"Have nice day." She backed up and nudged the
big door shut.

Hank frowned at the ornate brass knob.

***

Crouched in the back, Billy fed Mrs. Bascomb
some fries and a little ice-cold Sprite. He offered
her a bite of cheeseburger, but she said she wasn't
very hungry.

Tommy couldn't blame her. She'd asked Billy to
untie her and was real nice about it. Said she needed
to get the blood flowing again, just for a minute or
so. She wouldn't try anything, just wanted to move
around a little. But he said he couldn't--not yet. The
blindfold and the tape stayed on. He was nice about
it, too, but firm. Tommy could tell he felt bad about
keeping her like that. That's probably why he
volunteered to slip into the back and hold a napkin
under her chin while offering her fries and sips of
the drink through a straw. Tommy felt sorry for her,
too.

"We gotta talk," he said when Billy got back
behind the wheel.

"Later." Billy sat back and closed his eyes. Tommy could tell the two burgers, fries, and chocolate shake had made Billy sleepy.

But he couldn't let this go. They needed to discuss this. "We have to talk *now*."

Billy stared at him, trying to read his face. He must've seen something important, because he jerked a thumb at the door.

Outside, they lowered the tailgate and sat down facing the empty back lot and the subdivision on the other side of the sliver of woods that hadn't been cleared yet. Traffic roared down the six-lane stretch. The drive-thru lanes at Mickey Dee's across the street hustled with hungry customers. Next to it, four cars sat in front of the liquor store in the small strip mall. At the corner, an E-Z-Stop, three gas stations, and a 7-Eleven struggled to keep up with the constant flow.

Tommy was barely able to light his cigarette. His hands shook from all the neat stuff going on in his head.

"What's so damned important?" Billy asked.

Get it out right. Otherwise he'll think you're being a shithead again and won't take you seriously. "She's worth five ... million ... bucks." Tommy said the words slowly so he could savor them again, and so Billy could concentrate on them.

Billy said nothing. Probably didn't believe him.

"*Five million*, Billy."

"How do you know?"

"She told me."

"When?"

"This morning. In the woods."

166

You could tell Billy didn't like that, the way he pulled back. "Why didn't you tell me before now?"

"I ... had to think it out first. I was waiting for the right time."

Billy stared across the street, where a skinny brunette in a red convertible Toyota picked up her order from the takeout window at Mickey Dee's.

"Know what we can do with five million bucks, Billy?"

Darkness had drifted across Billy's face. Tommy had seen it before. Billy was about to get what he called 'objective.' When Billy was 'objective,' he said a lot of things Tommy didn't like. "Before you get your panties in a wad, just listen."

Tommy waited patiently.

"First of all, she could be feeding us a crock. And so what if she does have that much? It's not gonna do *us* any good."

"Why not?"

"It's not the original plan."

"So what?"

"We've got to go with the original plan, Tommy."

"Because he said so?"

"Why else?"

"Maybe if we do this our way, we might luck out for once."

Billy didn't reply.

"He's been dictating our every move. I know he's got us by the balls, but who says we have to keep letting him do it? Five million, Billy."

"We've got no choice. If we do this his way, we'll be in the clear. Once he gets our money ready

167

and waits for our call tomorrow morning, we're all set. He makes his call to the cops. Then we do what we have to and—"

"Don't wanna hear that."

Billy sighed. Tommy knew that sigh well but didn't care. He didn't want to go over the gory details again. Hearing it always made him want to puke.

"What I'm trying to say is this. Once this is done, he deposits the money. We pick it up and it's all over. We head off to Brazil."

"Why can't we just take her money and let her go?"

"Listen…and try to understand. We fuck Bascomb, Brazil's out of the picture. We'd better be trucking our asses off the damned planet. He's worth half a bill. A million to him is like twenty bucks to us. He's probably been planning this for a while now and was just waiting for the right suckers to come along and do it."

"Lucky us."

"That's beside the point. He won't even miss the million. He spends that much on cigars and suits. We do this his way, we're off the hook."

"We'll be off the hook anyway, once we're in Brazil."

"What makes you think he won't send people after us?"

"It's her money, Billy."

"That doesn't matter. She'll still be walking around. He doesn't want her doing that. That's why he planned this in the first place. Get it?"

Tommy got it, all right. He just didn't like it. "I

still like my idea better. We end up with five million, we're out of the country, and we won't have to work anymore. We can change our names and everything. Five million's a lot of bread."

Billy sighed and rubbed the back of his neck. "I know it, dammit."

"Then why can't we just kick this around a little and–"

"Because of Bascomb, like I just said. That dude's so bright, he's scary. He knows all the angles and can sniff out something wrong in a heartbeat. How do you think he caught us working those bogus accounts in the first place?"

"Plain luck. Bascomb's always had good luck. But that doesn't change the fact that his lady's got five million bucks and wants to hand it over. I don't know about you, but *I'll* let her go for five million."

"We can't."

"Why not? Because we're afraid of what he'll do if we split and leave her still walking around?"

"Yeah, dammit. Because of that."

"Not our problem."

"How the hell can you say that?"

"Because we'll be out of the country. And because we'll have enough money to stay out. We won't have to worry about him anymore."

"Why the hell not?"

"Because he'll be much too busy with other things."

"Like what?"

"Like having to deal with her still being alive. And if she suspects he was behind all this, he's *really* gonna have a hard time dealing with her."

Billy stroked his beard. Tommy could tell he liked the idea but was fighting it. Billy could be awfully stubborn at times. Almost as stubborn as Tommy's old man when you did something he didn't like. Then he shoved Scripture down your throat for the next couple of hours. Good thing Billy wasn't a Scripture kind of guy. "We can do this," he told Billy.

"What if she doesn't even have it?"

"What if she *does*?"

Billy didn't say anything. Tommy kept on. "Shoot, once we get it, we can dump her somewhere, so it takes her a while to get to a phone. We'll already have the fake ID's and the disguises. We can get away. I *know* we can."

"Sounds like it could actually work."

"We'll be taking *her* money. Bascomb won't even be able to make calls to his bank to freeze anything because he won't know what we're doing."

"What about the deadline?"

"He's not gonna call the cops and report her missing until after we call him, right? That'll give us enough time to find out about getting her money and deciding where to leave her. Bascomb gave us forty-eight hours for ... for us to ... to–"

"Yeah. Forty-eight hours. That gives us another day to get all this done."

"Plenty of time, Billy. This way makes more sense. And we won't have to waste her. It's not like she's seen us."

Billy didn't say anything. Tommy hoped he'd agree about not wanting to waste her, either. But he didn't--which was unsettling, because Billy hadn't said too much about doing the rest of this. Not that Billy actually *wanted* to do it, of course. He probably just didn't want to say much about it, either.

"We ought to just take the money and run," Tommy said. "At least there won't be a murder they can pin on us. The only thing they can get us for is kidnapping--if they can find us. And like I said, if the lady suspects Bascomb planned this, the FBI might be more interested in him than us."

Billy didn't say anything right off, but Tommy could tell he was figuring. His dark eyes got all squinty when he went inside his own head. He seemed to be staring at something far away, but he wasn't really looking at anything in particular.

"This could change the whole ballgame," he finally said. "Our motivation has been to do exactly as Bascomb says to get him off our backs. For good."

"Five million bucks will make us forget all about Bascomb."

"But there's still one very large problem."

"What's that?"

"Getting our hands on it."

"Isn't it worth a try? We've got enough time to do it."

Billy inhaled a thick wad of smoke and forced it back out in a puffy cloud. "Before we do anything, we need to find out if she even *has* that much jack."

CHAPTER TWELVE

The offices of Bas-Com, Software Specialists & Analysts, Inc., occupied two floors of the massive building facing Orange Avenue.

Hank got off the elevator on the tenth floor, where the fancy lobby directory said the company's executive offices were located.

A slender, fine-featured redhead around twenty-five years old graced a desk among the plants in the reception area, directing calls from the complex unit covering nearly half of her desk blotter. Between calls, she smiled at him and asked what he wanted. When he told her, she jabbed a long-nailed index finger at the door on his right.

An endless maze of cubes, aisles and glass offices spanned the floor. The room oozed with a potent mixture of perfumes, colognes and strong Colombian coffee. Neatly dressed men and women engaged in frantic conversations behind desks, in isolated corners, and on cell phones. A thin, well-dressed guy around thirty, reeking of Stetson, shot out of the rest room, a phone buried in his left ear. A tall, slender blonde in a loose black sleeveless blouse, red skirt and shiny black spikes stared impatiently at the wall clock while gripping the fax machine in front of her.

He moved in a little closer and tried to keep his mind on the purpose of his visit. "Excuse me. Where can I find Warren Bascomb?"

She extended a shiny red nail to his left. A generous cloud of *Tabu* floated over. Her deep blue eyes took him in instantly. "End of the aisle, his office is marked." A sheet of paper whispered softly from the fax machine. She plucked it out and marched quickly down the hall.

Bascomb's office was marked, simply, *WARREN BASCOMB, C.E.O.* in bold black lettering on a shiny brass strip nailed to the cedar door. Huddled behind a desk around the corner, a woman typed on a computer keyboard while answering calls. She was about forty-five--old in comparison to everyone else--but just as attractive and sharply dressed. She looked up. "May I help you?"

"I'd like to see your boss."

"Do you have an appointment?"

"Nope."

"Your name, please?"

"Hank Lee."

"Whom do you represent, Mr. Lee?"

Bascomb's wife, he wanted to say, but decided diplomacy would probably work best in this case. "Myself."

"One moment." She picked up the phone and spoke very softly into it, then replaced the receiver. Sympathy clouded her face. "I'm sorry, Mr. Lee. Mr. Bascomb's very busy. He told me to take your name and number and said he'll get back with you at the first opportunity–"

"You might want to tell him this actually concerns his wife." So much for diplomacy.

The secretary saw something in his face that made her blink. "One moment, please." She grabbed the phone again. This conversation took longer. Her face reddened. She carefully replaced the receiver. Bascomb's door opened abruptly.

Bascomb filled the doorway, a flushed expression on his broad, leathery face. Hank guessed him at least fifty and around six feet tall, with broad shoulders and forty-some pounds of extra flesh settled around his middle--no doubt from too many martinis and Porterhouse steaks. The tailor-made Italian suit could only hide so much of it. Bascomb's dark-brown hair, thinning a little in front, was combed back from the broad, lined forehead. Bushy black brows hovered above the piercing dark-brown eyes. A reddish nose--probably the result of the martinis--hung over a severe bloodless mouth. The soft jawline extended to a double chin nearly covering the knot of his red striped silk tie.

Hank was disappointed. Bascomb didn't look like the sort of man who could attract someone like Sally. But he knew better. Rich men didn't have to be good-looking, attractive, or even well-mannered to snag the best women.

"Hank Lee?" The voice was rough and loud. Bascomb gave the impression of someone who was interrupted in the middle of something important because of something stupid.

Hank nodded rather than spouting his usual, *That's what it says on my birth certificate.* Now was not the time for droll levity.

Bascomb raised his left forearm and read the glittering Rolex on his hairy wrist. "I really don't have much time--"

"This won't take long."

The bastard continued studying his Rolex. He

174

seemed genuinely engrossed in what it said. Hank Lee wanted to grab him by the collar and drag him into the office.

"I might be able to spare a couple of minutes. I have a conference–"

"I could be finished with this by the time it's taken you to dazzle me with your Rolex and your hectic schedule."

Bascomb lowered his arm. Slowly. He acted as if he'd just been slapped.

Hank felt the secretary's eyes on him. The tall blonde rushed by, trying not to be obvious. Her tangy trail of *Tabu* didn't distract him as it had before.

"Follow me." Bascomb tossed a brash, "No calls," over his shoulder.

Hank followed him into the office. Bascomb closed the door and circled the big mahogany desk in front of the large tinted window. The blotter was cluttered with piles of papers. They looked like contracts and legal forms. Others were memos and phone numbers. "Say what's on your mind, don't you, Lee?"

"When I have to."

"Sit." Bascomb produced a small cigar and carefully lit it. The room instantly grew pungent with the sweet aroma. "Haven't I seen you somewhere before?" He seemed curious.

"I think I'd remember you."

Bascomb flinched. He could tell he hadn't been complimented. "What do you do, Lee?"

"Do?"

Bascomb shrugged. "How do you make your

175

living?"

"I'm a field administrator with Anderson & Associates." He found it strange that Bascomb hadn't asked about Sally.

"Of course. A&A. You build high-rises and skyscrapers."

"Not me, personally. I've got people who do that for me so I don't have to get my hands dirty."

Bascomb used the red tip of his cigar to jab at the window behind him. "The building across the street?"

"Yeah. That one."

Whatever did Sally see in this jerk?

"I don't know Anderson personally–"

"Where's your wife, Mr. Bascomb?"

Bascomb pushed a slim plume of gray smoke in Hank's direction. "What do you *mean*, where's my wife?"

"That was a simple question. Pretty self-explanatory, actually."

"Now why the hell would you want to know about–"

"Her car's on the GreeneWay, sitting on the shoulder. Between Aloma and Red Bug. It's been there since–"

"How do you know it's my wife's car?"

"I asked around."

Bascomb scowled. "And just why would you want to do that?"

"It's a beautiful car. A classic. Not exactly the kind of vehicle someone abandons."

Bascomb focused on the center of Hank's forehead. Probably trying to penetrate it, see what

176

he could find in there. "You've been asking around because you like my wife's car?"

"A cop pulled up when I was checking it out."

Bascomb blinked. "Cop?"

"One of those big, burly guys dressed in blue? Wears a badge, helmet? Rides a motorcycle?" Hank nearly smiled. "He called it in. DMV gave him her name. He told me the GreeneWay people don't like abandoned cars cluttering up their roads. Not even classics."

Bascomb crushed his cigar in the big glass ashtray on the desk. "Lee, if my wife abandoned her car, don't you think she would've called me about it?"

Hank sat up. "You didn't say she called you."

"I didn't, did I?" Bascomb got to his feet and waited for Hank to follow suit.

Reluctantly, Hank stood. His eyes didn't leave Bascomb's.

Sally hadn't called him. If she had, he would have mentioned it right off--especially if he was so busy. It would have ended the interruption. She could have met up with a serial killer, and this high-priced piece of trash acted like he'd been yanked off the crapper in the middle of a dump. Hank felt his insides starting to simmer.

"Listen, Lee. I appreciate your concern, I really do. But my wife is a very independent lady. If you knew her, you'd agree."

Hank almost smiled again. "I understand. And I usually mind my own business. Hell, I *never* get between a man and his wife. But her car's ditched. I think something's happened. I don't think she'd

177

deliberately—"

"As a matter of fact, I know about the car."

Hank waited for the rest of the lie.

"She called. Last night, in fact. Asked me to send someone out. I sent a limo for her." Bascomb consulted that damned Rolex again. "I'm grateful you've come to tell me about the car." Bascomb circled his desk, coaxing Hank with an open hand. "I should've had someone pick it up last night, but I didn't think of it. Too busy. As I just said, I have to get on with this conference, hash out this project we've all been working on. But I do appreciate your concern." Bascomb opened the door. "I'm sure you have better things to do."

You cold-hearted bastard...

They moved out into the aisle. People rushed past, carefully avoiding eye contact. Hank's thoughts slipped into overload. He wanted to nail Bascomb with one good zinger before the bastard could slam the door in his face.

Bascomb held out his hand. "Thanks again, Lee. It was—"

"How'd your wife get in touch with you?"

Bascomb's features tightened. His hand dropped abruptly.

Hank knew he'd hit pay dirt. Now was the perfect time to bait him. "Did she call from the GreeneWay?"

Bascomb's features relaxed. "Used her cell. She didn't even have to get out of the car." Bascomb spun around and retreated back into his office.

The door slammed shut. The large sailboat print trembled on the wall above the secretary's head.

178

Hank trudged back to the elevators, the dark thoughts pounding at him. *If Sally had a cell phone, why did she stop at a bar and use a payphone? And if she was picked up in a limo, why wasn't she home when I asked the maid about her? And why did she leave her purse in the Mustang?*

***

Alone again, Sally managed to tug her wedding ring off her finger.

With her wrists taped together behind her back, such a simple action was rough going. But the tension and the fear brought on by her situation helped her persevere.

She carefully slipped the band onto the tip of her right thumb and held it in place with her first two fingers. Keeping the stone pointed upward, she began rubbing it back and forth against the tape-- awkwardly, since the angle prevented even a moderate range of movement.

It was a large, beautiful stone set in platinum-- chosen by Warren the summer he'd swept her off her feet. She'd forgotten how many carets the ring was. Such details had never been important to her. But at one time she'd liked how it looked and what it meant, so she wore it.

She'd learned since then that it was important to Warren only because of his obsession for her to look perfect. A CEO's wife always had to be dazzling. A vision of loveliness. The sort of woman who enters a room, confident every man in the room desires her.

Concentrate on what you're doing.

Her efforts quickly turned arduous. The tape was

179

looped around her wrists several times, making even the smallest movement difficult. But after a hundred or so short, deliberate strokes, she could feel the friction warm on her skin underneath the tape. It probably wouldn't be long before she could initiate a slight tear.

As she worked, she considered ways to outwit the two who'd nabbed her--to gain time, earn their trust. Confuse them, pit them against each other. Keeping them distracted was the best idea she could think of. Baiting Flighty had made them leave the truck, possibly to discuss her proposition. And it gave her the time she needed alone to free herself.

Her five-million-dollar story proved ingenious. It put things in a whole new perspective. Made everything much more exciting. Right now, they were probably discussing how they should spend the money.

Once again, the possibility of her husband's involvement in this drifted into her thoughts. Even worse--if he had planned it, agreed to it.

Warren? Wanting her dead? *No. Not possible.* The idea was inconceivable. But it made her blood boil, nonetheless.

***

Hank stared at his angry reflection in the distorted metal door of the elevator.

As he did, he agonized once again over Sally's deserted Mustang. Her purse on the floor. Her brief appearance at Tillie's. Her attempt to use the payphone.

"Used her cell..."

Hank got off the elevator and went down the

180

wide aisle, where he'd parked the Caddie. He couldn't stop the anger from taking hold. If he didn't cool it, he'd probably end up doing something stupid, like punching something, or kicking someone's fender. But he couldn't stop the images flashing by. Bascomb's arrogance, his smugness. Plus the fact that he might have done something awful to Sally and thought he could actually get away with it.

Loud taps echoed on the concrete floor behind him, growing louder. Hank spun around. It was the tall blonde. The babe with the big blue eyes who'd made an ordinary fax machine look deliciously sexy. She kept glancing behind her but didn't lose a step. "We need to talk."

"No problem," he said, instantly noticing the tension tugging at her delicate features.

"You can spare a minute, can't you?"

"Sure."

She passed him and crossed the aisle.

He followed her over to a shiny maroon Camaro. He watched how she moved but was much too curious about her sudden appearance to properly focus on her fine ass.

Her keys and a remote appeared magically from her leather bag. She darted her head around, her frosted locks splashing her shoulders. Both doors chirped simultaneously, unlocking.

Her *Tabu* scent instantly turned overwhelming in the confines of the car. So did a reek of coffee and cigarettes. From her bag she removed a pack of Winston Lites. She tried lighting one but couldn't work the yellow Bic lighter. Hank took it and held it steady. When the cigarette fired up, she took the lighter from him and dropped it in her bag but kept it open in her lap. She risked another quick glance behind them.

"What's your name?" he asked.

"No names." She puffed busily on her cigarette. *This is getting interesting.* "Okay..." he said.

The interior quickly filled with heavy ropes of gray smoke. Hank coughed.

She lowered the windows a few inches and held her cigarette close to the gap. "I saw you upstairs with Bascomb." She squinted, probably from the smoke. "You're hard to miss."

"It was kind of impossible to skip over you, too."

She looked surprised.

He shrugged. "A skirt like that rarely gets past me."

She focused hard on his face. "What were you two ... talking about?"

"A personal matter."

"It didn't look that way."

"How'd it look?"

"Kind of scary, actually."

"Personal matters aren't usually pleasant."

"Are you ... a friend ... of Bascomb's?"

It was time to find out what this babe wanted. And why she was so nervous. "You his girlfriend?"

"No. No. It's not ... like that."

"How is it?"

"I overheard some of ... of what you were saying. I happened to be walking by."

"I know. I happened to be watching."

She turned away. This was apparently difficult

182

for her. "You were discussing ... his wife."

"And you care because...?"

She glanced out her window. "I need to know why ... you were talking about ... Sally."

This was getting more interesting by the second. But he wasn't about to make this easy. "And *I* need to know why *you* want to know."

"I ... can't say."

He sat back and sighed. This was going nowhere. "Please, I need to know."

He glared at her. "Don't tell me you're in love with that jerk."

"*No.*" She lit another cigarette from the hot end of the first and tossed the spent one out her window. "At least ... not anymore."

"Tell me about it."

She shifted awkwardly in the seat. Those long legs kept getting caught under the steering wheel. It took him quite a while to determine if her skirt was interfering with her movements, or if her legs were just too long for the confined space.

"He pays well and he's got contacts all over the world. If you stick with him, you'll make out. But he's a snake."

"How long ago were you two involved?"

"Last year."

That didn't make sense. "And you're still working for him?"

A nervous nod. "Can't afford to leave. Not yet."

"How bad was it?"

"We'd do it in his office. On his desk. The floor. His private bathroom. Whenever he wanted it, he buzzed me. His favorite game was having me do

183

him underneath his desk. He liked it while he was on the phone. He'd spank me later on if I made him giggle. Then he'd spank me if I didn't. When he was finished, he told me to get out." She looked down at her purse. "I meant nothing to him."

"Then this is about revenge?"

"No. Not … not that…"

"What, then?"

"I met Sally one day when she came to the offices. She was very, very nice. We got along as if we'd known each other for years. And of course I felt horrible for doing her husband behind her back. But not long after that, Bascomb decided he didn't want me anymore, so I was off the hook."

"You couldn't break it off?"

"You don't break off with Warren Bascomb. Unless you don't care if you work or not."

"Why'd *he* break it off?"

"Why do you think?"

"Someone working here?"

"Another company. This one's higher up. Near the top, most likely. Everyone thinks she's with ICS, but nobody really knows. The scuttlebutt says she's got something to do with the merger."

"With WorldVue and ICS?"

"The word is out that WorldVue might be going away. We think Bascomb's turning it into another junk subsidiary to use as a write-off."

"I thought it sounded phony."

"We think Bascomb started it himself."

"Why?"

"Don't know. But if he started it, it was for a good reason."

Hank rubbed his eyes. Bascomb certainly was one busy asshole. No wonder he didn't want to talk about Sally. If he was involved with someone else, his wife was low on his priorities. But it might just explain the ditched Mustang, and why he was less than candid about her whereabouts.

"Please tell me why you were discussing Sally," she insisted. "You asked how she got in touch with him last night."

He wondered if she was telling the truth--or sent by Bascomb to get the real story. But her frightened look said it all. "I think Sally's in danger, but I don't think he cares."

Her fine features crinkled up. "I was afraid of that."

"What makes you say that?"

"We've all heard that two guys at Venture were pulling a scam, but Bascomb caught them and got rid of them."

"What's this have to do with Sally?"

"Bascomb uses people and discards them when he's finished. And if you try and get back at him, he turns nasty. No one's ever tried that yet--and lived to tell about it."

"You think someone might use Sally to get back at Bascomb?"

"If you couldn't get back at someone, wouldn't you go after his family?"

"I've never hated anyone that much."

"Bascomb has tons of enemies."

"I've seen how his employees tiptoe around, trying to be invisible. Like a swimming scene in *Jaws*."

185

"So what do you think? About Sally, I mean."

"My gut tells me she's in trouble. Who's behind it doesn't matter--for now, anyway."

"Do you think *he* might have done something to her?"

He shrugged. "It's possible."

"Sure you want to find out?"

"I don't seem to have much of anything else to do right now, so..."

"Have you met him before?"

"The first time I saw him was half an hour ago."

"Then why bother? You haven't told me how you figure in this."

This girl was awfully nice and extremely easy on the eyes. She even smelled good. But she didn't need to know the details. If this turned nasty, he didn't want anyone knowing what was going on. "I saw Sally last night at a bar on Colonial. The way she was acting, I knew something was wrong."

"Did you talk to her?"

"She was in no mood to talk."

"She ignored you?"

"I don't think she saw me. She didn't seem to notice anyone."

"Did you know her before? Or were you just looking for a pickup?"

"You don't have to be insulting."

"Er, sorry..." She looked down at her lap.

He sighed. "I'm kidding, all right?"

The big baby-blues studied him. "Then it *wasn't* a pickup thing?"

"I knew her before she married Bascomb."

She tilted her head, as all women do when they

186

hear something interesting. "How well?"

"You're pretty damned bright," he said.

She smiled. "I'm a woman."

"Why's that relevant?"

"Women instinctively know certain things that have to be explained over and over to men."

"Like putting the toilet seat back down?"

She laughed. "Among other things."

***

The truck shook. Sally's heart fluttered, and she stopped her frantic efforts to cut through the tape.

Her abductors piled into the truck and slammed the doors. She could hear them doing something to their seats. A moment later, one of them shifted on the floor directly in front of her face. It was Business. The cigarette reek clinging to him brushed her face and rapidly grew more intense. The tape was peeled away from her mouth, making her skin tingle.

"That five million you discussed with my partner," he said. "Why didn't you pitch it to me?"

"It's hard to pitch anything with your mouth taped shut." She'd said it bluntly, hoping they could both read the irritation in her voice.

After a moment's pause, he said, "That's a big chunk of change." He'd obviously decided to change the subject rather than apologize. "We just aren't one hundred percent sure you've got that much in the kitty."

"My husband's very rich."

"It's his money."

She knew what he meant but also knew how important it was to keep them talking. The longer she could hold their interest, the better her chances. "Are you saying you don't believe I have money of my own?"

"No offense, but you're not his first wife."

They did know Warren. But they couldn't possibly know everything about him. This would work in her favor. "He's made most of his money during the last five years. I've been his wife for nearly seven. Do the math."

A pause. She suspected they were both thinking that over.

"He was rich when you met him."

"Maybe, but nowhere near what he's worth now."

"Lady, your husband didn't exactly come from the wrong end of town." Business sounded tired, bored. "He began his corporate career as one of AT&T's youngest district managers, starting up one of their data processing companies in Orlando a few years after the divestiture, when the shit hit the fan with Judge Green. The companies downsized, then split up. Bascomb was one of the big boys on their hit list. He was slated to move to Denver when AT&T spun off Lucent but saw his big chance and chose their buyout instead. The package, from what we all heard, was close to eight figures, including three years' salary, bonuses, stock options, and a boatload of other perks. He quickly bought up half a dozen small software outfits with his winnings. Then, after snatching up a couple of dozen top-notch programmers who'd been given the royal shaft by the Bell System, he incorporated and went public. He started up Bas-Com about ten years ago.

Word is, he had more than fifty million to get it going. So let's just say we know more about your husband than you think."

"Then tell me what's on your mind."

"We're just not too sure about your claim of five million."

"But it's true. I do have that much."

Their silence was reassuring. Get them thinking. They might know all about Warren but couldn't possibly know how much she had socked away.

"How'd you get it?" Business asked.

She'd had most of this worked out but telling it just right would be tricky. If they'd worked for Warren, they were both very bright. Warren hired only the best people in the field. "I had money before I married Warren."

"Go on."

"My parents split their estate into thirds during their divorce, which left me slightly less than a million by the time I turned twenty-one. It sat in a trust fund, accruing compound interest for years. It more than doubled before I even met Warren. Since I haven't had to touch it, it's been growing steadily. In fact, when I received my quarterly statement last month, the balance was just under five million dollars."

A pause. "You can touch it now, right?"

"It's not something I think about very much. I have an arrangement with Warren that'll keep me living well even if the marriage dissolves."

"What ... arrangement?"

"Warren gave me papers to sign right after we were married. This happened when he was buying

189

up some small independent companies. He said it would be safer if most of his assets were in my name. He could work freely without worrying about judgments being slapped against him and his assets. No one could touch him."

This pause was much longer. She could feel them staring at one another.

"Remember which companies you signed for?"

"There were close to a dozen."

Business leaned closer. She could smell the cheeseburger and cigarettes on his breath. "If I named one, would you recognize it?"

"It was a long time ago, and I didn't have time to go through the papers or read them like I'd wanted to. Warren didn't give me a chance to–"

"WorldVue ring a bell?"

Her pulse began to flutter. "Some of the papers had the WorldVue logo on the top of the page. But Warren said I'm not supposed to–"

The tape was hastily slapped over her mouth. The truck shook as Flighty and Business scrambled outside.

CHAPTER THIRTEEN

After that ridiculous intrusion by Hank Lee, Warren Bascomb found it impossible to concentrate on business.

He was forced to cut short two phone calls and postpone an important international conference call with half a dozen of his field reps.

He hated people who didn't mind their own business. And he hated it even worse when someone put a kink in the works.

This couldn't come at a worse time. He checked his voicemail on his private line just half an hour ago and listened to the message he'd been waiting for. Those two idiots had actually pulled it off. They had Sally and were going to do what they were supposed to do. Without anyone else entering the picture, this would be nothing more than a cakewalk.

Blackmailing an employee facing Federal prosecution always proved a most profitable venture. But dealing with someone you couldn't entirely trust involved a very large risk. Someone with his back to the wall was usually the best man to have around when you needed something unpleasant and dirty done. He had nothing to lose and would always do as he was told. And when money and freedom were his reward, he'd do his job eagerly.

With Landry and Schiller doing the dirty work, there should be very little to worry about. But since Landry was a hopeless drunk and Schiller a neurotic cokehead, Warren knew he couldn't take anything for granted. Still, even though Landry and Schiller weren't the tightest knots in the loop, he couldn't see them double-crossing him. Not with what they had to lose.

The present crisis revolved around the man calling himself Hank Lee. Why would a total stranger show up out of the blue and ask about Sally's car? And why the hell was that damned Mustang parked off the GreeneWay in the first place? Warren was desperate to get to the bottom of all this. He didn't like loose ends. Loose ends had a habit of coming back to create major problems when a person least expected it or wanted it. Now was not the time for surprises of any kind.

He'd start with Lee, of course. The man's sudden appearance had raised entirely too many red flags. He wore a decent suit, but his belligerent attitude couldn't disguise his true character. Good clothes and a weekly visit to the local hair stylist couldn't hide a rough upbringing. Lee was the type you expected to see getting into scraps in cheap dives. His arrogance oozed prominently from the steel-gray eyes. His broken nose probably got that way from sticking it where it didn't belong.

He asked too many questions and asked them much too loudly. His looks and presence tended to attract a crowd. People grew curious and nosy. They came over to listen when they were supposed to be working. Like that bimbo Alicia Tate. She hadn't even been subtle about it, stopping to pick up a piece of paper, then forgetting something and coming back to look for it. And that needless trip to the copier... Only an idiot would fail to notice. Stupid twit. He should've fired her last year, when he was finished with her. *Another loose end.*

Warren rested his elbows on the desk blotter and rubbed his temples.

That damned Mustang. It stuck out like a sore thumb. Why couldn't Sally have taken her nightly walk around the block and made things easy? But dealing with females was like playing with dynamite. She'd left the house in a huff, taken the Mustang to the GreeneWay, and now an idiot was snooping around.

Where the hell was she going? Didn't matter. What mattered was that her classic car was pulled over on one of the heaviest-traveled roads in Orlando and would probably be stolen if he didn't call someone and have it picked up shortly. Damned woman probably ran the tank dry again. She'd done this same thing before--why should he expect her to start developing brain cells at this late date?

Some females just didn't get it. Buy them an expensive classic machine, and they're too stupid to keep gas in it. Last night would've been a perfect time to run it dry again. She'd probably been upset enough to hightail it and use up what gas she had much quicker.

So, what the hell happened last night? She hightailed it, ran it dry, pulled over, and ... what? Called for a tow? Or was she helped by a Good Samaritan?

Unlikely. Sally had probably called someone from her cell. Her friend Paul George, possibly. She knew better than call home. She'd already been read the riot act about running the tank empty.

Hopefully Landry and Schiller had intercepted her when they were supposed to. If things had gone right, Sally might have gotten in touch with George, but had been kidnapped before the attorney could pick her up. If so, George would be suspicious and might call the police.

Not likely. If George had heard from Sally, the cops would have called by now. But since they hadn't, he had to assume Sally hadn't had the opportunity to call anyone before Landry and Schiller grabbed her.

Getting back to Hank Lee...

The man just didn't look like a field rep. He looked more like an errand boy. The way things were going, Lee probably worked for Donaldson. That sounded more reasonable. Donaldson had paid Lee to sniff around, get every bit of dirt he could find. Lee might have been paid to watch the estate. And when Sally took off last night, he tailed her.

But why? Donaldson wasn't interested in Sally-- why would he even care what she was up to? This could be Lee's idea. He might have seen Sally, liked the way she looked in those jeans, and decided to see what she was up to. Maybe he thought she was going to meet someone and decided to stay close. Such a scandal would upset everything if the *Sentinel* got wind of it, or CNN.

But if Lee was following Sally, why wouldn't he help her when the car ran out of gas? Lee seemed the type to offer help to a lady in distress--especially someone looking like Sally. Lee looked the part of the arrogant stud--he'd jump at the chance to come to a woman's aid. So why didn't he?

Lee had probably been ordered to stay back and make something out of this. Some added pressure might cause Bascomb to get his mind off the merger. Warren's concentration shifts, and the merger suffers. Donaldson finally wins.

Who else but Donaldson had more of an ax to grind? Donaldson had been a nuisance from the beginning. His decision to notify Florida's attorney general, asking him to meet with U.S. and European Commission regulators to investigate Bas-Com, nearly proved disastrous. It was also common knowledge that Donaldson planned a quick trip to Tallahassee to discuss the matter in detail.

Donaldson's main gripe was that the merging of two corporations such as Bas-Com and ICS would create unnecessary stock manipulations and sizeable disturbances in the Dow. And with the Dow's questionable activity over Enron, Nine-Eleven, and AIG, not to mention other more recent dips, such as the tanking of the auto industry, the economy didn't need a scandal of this magnitude.

It was nothing but jealousy. Donaldson's brother-in-law headed Macro Industrial Computers. Donaldson was stupid enough to think that by dissolving or delaying the merger, he'd nudge MIC a couple of notches higher in the industry.

But even though Donaldson was a meddlesome idiot and had no basis for a legitimate complaint, this wasn't the time for fuckups. Warren had to find out what was going on. But it had to be done delicately. It also had to be done quickly. Everything had to be in place before he called OPD to report Sally missing.

Warren opened his bottom drawer to select a suitable burn phone from the pile.

***

After talking to the blonde at Bascomb's office, Hank found the Caddie two aisles down from her Camaro. It was sandwiched between a silver Corvette and a shiny black BMW with a personalized Florida plate that said CALSRYD.

His cell buzzed. The screen showed Colleen Moore's number. Dandy. After sparring with a loud, pompous dickhead, Hank wasn't quite in the mood for a ball-buster.

He picked up his cell phone, then stopped and wondered what he was doing. Why was he putting up with this crap?

He started with A&A right after college, just a few years after he'd come back from Saudi. A tall, middle-aged guy with thick white hair and a winning smile named Bill Solberg ran the show back then. Solberg got along with everyone. He made you feel good about yourself and glad you were part of the team. He organized social events that lifted team spirit, resulting in higher company performance and very little turnover.

Things took a sudden nosedive when Anderson Senior, the horny old fart, met Colleen in an Orlando bar and liked the way she filled out a skirt. In no time at all, Solberg was offered a fabulous buyout package that enabled him to retire at fifty-five and spend as much time on the golf course as he wished.

When Solberg left, Anderson & Associates

196

began its steady decline. Colleen, a results junkie, didn't care about employee morale. She'd fired more people in her three-year reign than Solberg had in his entire thirty-year-career.

The cell buzzed again. This time, he took a deep breath and clicked her on.

"Where the hell *are* you, Lee? It's almost three o'clock and you're not in the office. And Miller's a no-show. I fired him, of course."

"Of course."

"I had no choice."

"Hey, the man's his own worst enemy." He knew he should feel bad for Amos, but for some reason, he no longer cared.

"So where *are* you?"

"I'm working on something."

"We have to talk."

"Now?"

"In my office."

"Where are you now?"

"In my office."

"So talk."

"I'd rather do this in person."

"I'll get there when I get there, all right?"

A pause. "Are you in some sort of trouble?"

"It's too complicated to discuss on the phone."

"What did you do, Lee?"

"About what?"

He heard her sighing. "Lee, if you're in some sort of trouble, I wish you'd just come right out and–"

"It isn't about me."

"What's it about, then?"

197

"An old friend."

A long pause. He could tell she wanted to ask questions. But in Colleen's world, maintaining her superiority cancelled out everything else. "So you'd like to ask me for some time off?"

He hadn't even thought of that, but since she brought it up, it sounded like a good idea. "If you don't mind."

"Why didn't you ask before?"

"It just came up."

"Lee, if you're in some kind of jam–"

"It's not me, like I said."

"How much time do you need?"

"I've got no idea."

"All right."

He waited, but she said nothing else. "All right, what?"

"Handle it." *Click.*

***

"She owns WorldVue, Billy. Can you believe that? WorldVue!"

Schiller stood still, facing the passing traffic. His eyes were glazed over. He looked like he'd just gone inside his head again. It was a little frightening. Bill wanted to slap him out of it. "You in there somewhere, Tommy?"

Schiller didn't seem to hear him. He remained lost in his own little fantasy world. If Bill didn't know better, he'd think Schiller was standing in someone's living room, staring at a Christmas tree on Christmas morning, wondering what was wrapped in the presents stacked beneath it.

Bill wanted to knock some sense into him but

198

had to be careful, what with people all over the damned place. Maybe he could just lead him back to the truck and get the hell out of here. The lunch hour had passed, but Wendy's still handled an impressive crowd. With shitloads of people close by, you never knew when somebody was looking. And since everyone had cell phones, any one of them would pull it out in a heartbeat if they saw something suspicious.

"Tommy. Snap out of it."

"She owns WorldVue, Billy. You got any idea what that means?" Schiller's glazed blue eyes made him appear stoned, even though he hadn't done a line recently.

"Listen and try to keep calm, all right?"

"I'm calm, Billy. Cool, too."

"We can't be sure about anything right now. The woman's been roughed up, chloroformed, and stuck in the back of a truck. She's uncomfortable and exhausted. She might seem okay, but her mind's got to be in serious overload right now."

"Billy ... what if she *does* own WorldVue?"

"She probably does. Why else would Bascomb want her gone?"

"I don't know, Billy. Everyone's talking about that merger."

"Maybe she's dragging her feet on signing it back over. He'd need total control over it if he wanted to do anything with it."

"Would he want her *dead* because of that, Billy?"

"She's causing him aggravation, isn't she? He's a CEO. He's rich. He doesn't put up with aggravation like the rest of us. And why should he? Would *you* put up with aggravation if you were worth half a bill? In other words, he's special. And when someone upsets his boat, he'd want them out of the way."

"That seems awfully rough."

"Not for a ruthless bastard."

Schiller was silent for a little while. Then he crossed his arms in front of him, turned, and grinned. "I think we ought to cause him even more aggravation by letting his wife go, Billy."

"You're not serious."

"Yes, I am."

"We'll be in uncharted waters. Bascomb's scheme was one thing. Small potatoes. Something that goes away in a couple of days. People are always wandering off and going missing--especially women. A million bucks barely gets people riled anymore. Even the five million would go away in a few weeks, maybe a month. But holding those papers for ransom to stymie a billion-dollar merger? That's front page. CNN stuff."

"We'll still be able to get away and leave the country. Think Brazil."

"Fuck Brazil." He was growing tired. Schiller's little-boy mentality had worn thin. He wanted to get this crazy mess over with. "If this thing gets full-blown--which will definitely happen with any international merger--Bascomb will want our heads on his wall. Trust me on this. We really should pass on it."

Schiller sat down on the tailgate. He was clearly exhausted, but his eyes were no longer glazed over.

"Don't you see, Billy? We've got nothing to lose."

Bill could tell by Schiller's calm, steady voice that he was thinking clearly. And he was right. They did have nothing to lose. And they were pulled into this against their will. Bascomb's plan of having them snatch his wife, holding her for twenty-four hours, then killing her, dumping her body in a lake, and sending Bascomb her index finger for proof, had never set well with either of them. Schiller was the last person in the world who could do this sort of thing. He was a total mess and would rather OD on downers than hurt another human being.

Bill, on the other hand, had had more than his fill of princesses. He'd always been attracted to the type--he just couldn't help it. Toss him a pretty face, a tight little body, fancy clothes, and an uppity air-- and he was in heaven. He let them lead him around by his dick and didn't care--not as long as they used it once in a while. But he did care that their free hand stayed buried deep in his pocket. He cared quite a bit. But by the time he realized just how much he cared, they'd already stomped on him on their way out the door. He seldom realized the actual extent of their actions until it was all over, and he found himself lying in the gutter, his pockets picked clean.

Trudi did quite a job on him. It only took her a couple of years to totally destroy him, clean him out, and drive him halfway to the nuthouse.

Sally Bascomb was a princess and acted just like all the others. The classic Mustang was a dead giveaway. So were the clothes, the hair, the shoes, and the rings she always wore. He hadn't seen her rings while taping her up, but figured she only wore them to fancy shindigs. Trudi was the same way. Whenever a princess was going out for the evening, she spent hours shopping for a new outfit and new shoes--even spending megabucks on her hair. Then makeup. Then jewelry--rings, necklaces, bracelets. The works.

Bascomb, like Bill Landry, asked for everything he got. However, Bascomb definitely had an edge. He was too damned rich and too damned bright to let anyone clean him out. He made legal provisions for everything he did and stuck to them. His babes agreed to these provisions or found themselves in deep trouble. They obviously went along with whatever he dictated and were able to walk away-- possibly because they hadn't stuck around as long as Sally. Otherwise, they, too, might have forced Bascomb into extreme measures.

Bill had no qualms about doing in a princess, then dumping her precious body in a lake. No qualms at all. He'd wanted to do in Trudi and had thought about it dozens of times in the two years they'd lived together. He often wondered if murdering Trudi--or any other cold, pampered bitch--might help balance the scales and establish an order to the Universe.

He wouldn't tell Schiller any of this, of course. The boy would freak and turn useless for the rest of this job. Best keep his views to himself.

But WorldVue entering the picture made things different. This was bigger than anything. Bigger than Sally Bascomb. Bigger than Bill Landry getting his due.

The merger of WorldVue and ICS meant *billions*. And if a stumbling block could halt it, not only would Bascomb be screwed out of a ton of money, he'd be forced to shell out millions just to break even.

But could they pull this off without really *doing* it?

Maybe they didn't have to. Maybe all they had to do was reach a certain point--say, grabbing the five million from Bascomb's old lady, snatching all the WorldVue papers they could find, and hightailing it to Brazil. Bascomb would shit if he thought the merger might be compromised.

"Tell me what you're thinking, Billy."

He stared at his friend but saw only the image of Bascomb slamming his head into his office wall. It brought an easy grin. "We need to tell Bascomb's old lady there's been a serious change in plans."

CHAPTER FOURTEEN

Sam Cole hated it when one of his bouncers suddenly turned stupid.

Damn that Lenny Ray. Too bad his brain cells weren't as strong and as developed as the rest of him.

Lenny Ray was one of those morons who pumped iron for two hours, drove to the closest restaurant, gobbled up a side of beef, then went back to the gym to push more tonnage for two more hours. Boy was six-three, weighed in at around two-fifty, and had a waist that was smaller than some of Sam's strippers.

Lenny Ray did his job. No one gave him any shit. You don't go to a bar and upset the ladies with a human tank following you around.

Shame he couldn't leave the girls alone, though. Sam was gonna have to give him *The Talk* again. He'd given it to him before--just as he did to all his employees. It was how Sam operated, why his businesses ran so smoothly. They *had* to run smoothly. Otherwise, you got used to the fuzz showing up and closing down your operation with all types of legal bullshit.

Sam Cole, formerly Santino Colissimo--former bagman, runner and part-time shooter for the Manfredos in Lauderdale--had been respectable for several years. He ran three high-class clubs--Good Guys in Altamonte, Heavenly Dolls in Maitland, and Moulin Rouge in Winter Springs. Sam employed more than a hundred people and made enough from his clubs to enable him to live in a large, comfortable estate in an exclusive lakefront section not far from Sable Point.

His association with the Manfredos had long passed. Back then Sam was a shave-tail--a smart-assed kid with big ideas and the knack for attracting the right people. Since the Cubans, Jamaicans, Haitians, Puerto Ricans, Dominicans, and Colombians had swarmed into South Florida like hordes of fire ants, the Manfredos pulled up stakes and headed for the Mississippi coast, buying up the casinos, a large portion of the fishing industry, and some of the fanciest eateries in the French Quarter of New Orleans.

Sam severed ties with Old Man Manfredo and moved to Central Florida. He preferred it for the weather. His sinuses rarely acted up as they had in South Florida, with the salt air from the ocean constantly clogging him up. Using funds he'd saved up, he bought up some vacant buildings, revamped them, and turned them into clubs. He hired only the best dancers and the best bartenders in the city. Muscle was plentiful--you could find walking slabs of beef at any of the beaches.

Good drinks and sweet ladies. If you couldn't get filthy rich with that combo, something was wrong. It was easy staying respectable these days. Nowadays the Feds had their hands full keeping tabs on the Arabs, with the Russian gangs and the illegals making things even more complicated. Feds didn't waste their time bird-dogging Dagos for penny-ante games when Muslim terrorists were bringing down planes and blowing up buses. Since those crazies kept Sam and his cronies out of the limelight, he was able to operate his clubs, enjoy the *dolce vita,* and stay fat and happy.

Too bad Lenny Ray turned *stupido* and let his dick take over. The boy definitely needed to hear The Talk once again. Occasionally someone would forget--which was to be expected, since the girls were red-hot and could make any normal guy forget his own name.

The Talk was simple and direct. It took less than a minute and stuck with you. It went like this: "Don't drink, smoke, or fuck around in my place. You want your ashes dusted? Find a hooker and do it on your own time. You don't like it? There's the fucking door."

Lenny Ray had obviously forgotten. Two of the girls had complained recently. Nothing serious, just some flirting outside the dressing rooms--*Hey, baby, how's about coming over to the gym, watch me move half a ton*? It couldn't be helped, Lenny Ray being a young buck, his hormones *tumulto*. This happened when you tossed around so much iron in the gym during the day, then worked around so much sweet-smelling stuff at night. But business was business. If you couldn't work around sweet-smelling stuff without wanting samples, your ass would soon be on the other side of the door.

The phone on his big walnut desk rang. The display said unknown name, unknown number. Sam rubbed his jaw. A fucking telemarketer? Or someone using a disposable phone? No way to find out without answering.

"Sam Cole here. Who's this?"

"Sammy? This is Warren Bascomb. How goes it?"

The familiar voice brought a broad grin. Warren Bascomb. Mr. Money and Connections. "What can I do you for, Mr. B.?"

"I need a favor, Sammy boy."

Ah. Sam's biorhythm was working full swing this afternoon. Life was good. "Just name it."

"There's an asshole sniffing around my short curlies. His name is Lee. Hank Lee. Big guy, late thirties, maybe forty. He's a smartass but looks tough."

Sam had encountered a slew of so-called 'tough guys' in his forty-six years. One thing he'd learned was that no matter how tough a jerk thought he was, things quickly changed when you shoved a gun barrel down his throat. "What else do I need to know about this *sfachim*?"

"He told me he works for Anderson & Associates in town as a field rep. I think he was shitting me. Do what you can to find out, all right?"

"How soon you need this?"

"Give me something by tomorrow morning."

"That's kinda pushing it."

"The job pays five K if you want it."

"We might as well start right now, then." Sam knew who he could give this to. Things went considerably smoother when you had the right contacts.

"One other thing," Mr. B. added. "This has to be kept *quiet*."

***

The truck doors opened.

207

The floor shook.

The smell of sweat overwhelmed the interior of the cab. Sally paused in her tape-cutting efforts.

Business's familiar cigarette breath drew very close. The tape was peeled away gently from Sally's mouth, and he said, "We've got something to tell you. You might even like it."

The tension in his voice was unmistakable. The squeaking in the passenger seat told her Flighty was fidgeting, possibly moving around to get a better view.

They'd probably discussed her proposition and had figured something out. This would change their plans considerably. They'd need her help in getting the money. "You're going to consider my proposition?"

"Well, yeah, that would be our most important item."

"Are you going to untie me?"

A pause. "Uh, not yet."

She could tell they were looking at one another. The fidgeting in the passenger seat had stopped. Business said, "First of all, we've got to find out a few things."

"What kind of things?"

"If WorldVue's in your name. But we'll need time to do this right."

"Time?" She didn't like the sound of that.

"We have to wait till morning. In other words, we'll have to park you somewhere. Can't get any of this done with you tied up in the truck, can we?"

"I wouldn't want to make this harder for you," she said flatly. She was in no mood to be nice.

Being taped and blindfolded all night and most of the afternoon tended to take the nice out of a girl. Being told this was going to go on even longer was not something she wanted to hear. But she knew she'd done the right thing about baiting them. It had already upset their equilibrium.

"Got anything to tell us you might have forgotten?" Business asked.

She decided to toss them a bone. "The papers I signed are in Warren's home safe."

"What else does he keep in there?"

"His valuables. Papers, mostly."

"Stocks? Bonds? Ready cash?"

"I've only seen glimpses of what he's got in there, but it's a pretty large safe. He's got a lot of stuff in there--stacks of cash, and I'm certain he keeps all his stocks in it."

"We'll have to figure out something. We'll need to find out if your hubby pulled something when you weren't looking. Like forging your signature. He might've done that to retrieve ownership."

"If you can open his safe, I'm sure you'll find everything you'll need."

"We'll talk this over later." Business replaced the tape and climbed back behind the wheel. The truck began moving.

Sally resumed her frantic efforts on the tape binding her wrists.

***

Just before four, Hank stopped for gas at a 7-Eleven on East Colonial, about a block east of the Trail.

He filled the tank, replaced the nozzle, and got

209

back in the Caddie. Once he returned to his apartment, he would fix a drink and call Pete. To find out what happened to Sally, he would probably have to lean a little harder on Bascomb. From what he'd already observed, Bascomb carried around a short fuse. It wouldn't take much at all to light him up.

His cell phone buzzed. He didn't recognize the number, then remembered giving the blonde at Bascomb's office his number, in case she heard anything about Sally. He answered.

"I've got some news for you," the voice whispered. It was indeed the blonde from the parking garage.

"I'm listening."

Silence.

"Still there?"

"Got to be careful."

"This sounds mysterious."

He heard her sigh. "I'm in the bathroom."

He reluctantly pushed aside the delicious images. "Talk when you can."

"Those guys I told you about at Venture?"

"Vaguely."

"Not too long ago, Bascomb caught them putting dummy accounts in the computer to filter funds into them later on."

"Go on."

"They're both programmers."

"I suppose they were fired."

"They haven't been to work for a couple of weeks."

"Got any names?"

210

"Bill Landry and Tom Schiller."

"How'd you find out about the dummy accounts?"

"Things like that can't stay quiet with two hundred people working in close quarters."

The sound of a flush. About twenty seconds of silence. Then, "I talked to a friend of mine about it. We take software classes together at Rollins. He said Schiller was freaking over it. Schiller's a mess anyway. Does coke and used to freebase until it almost blew him away. He was so hooked that he had to deal so he could afford the stuff. He was bringing it to work and snorting in the bathroom. Apparently one of the execs caught him, and that was that. No one knows what really happened. My friend seems to think someone hushed it. Otherwise, we would have heard more about it."

"Bascomb?"

"Like I said, no one knows for sure."

"Maybe he didn't want anything to sour the merger."

"Possibly. Anyway, Schiller never could keep his mouth shut. When he's high, he rambles. He must've told someone what happened, because my friend heard through one of the programmers that Bascomb brought Schiller and Landry into his office and yelled at them. A few minutes later, they bolted out of the office and practically ran out of the building. No one's seen them since."

"They left of their own accord?"

"That's the rumor."

"Isn't Security supposed to escort them off the premises for certain offenses?"

211

"That's what's so screwy about this whole thing."

"Yeah, it definitely sounds like a serious hush job. Know anyone in Personnel?"

"No one who'll risk his job."

"Any idea what Schiller or Landry drives?"

"Sorry."

"Well, at least now I've got names."

"Let me know what you find out."

"How do I get in touch? Is this cell number you're calling from good to use? And I don't even know your name. I promise I won't write it on the bathroom wall where I work."

She laughed. "I guess I can trust you. I really liked the way you stood up to Bascomb. My name's Alicia. Alicia Tate."

***

His feet propped up, Sam Cole sipped a small glass of Johnny Walker Red while enjoying one of the five potent Italian cigarettes he allowed himself daily.

Moderation was important when you were looking the big Five-O full in the face and had cancer in your family. Control was also very important. If you couldn't manage yourself, you had no business being your own boss.

He'd learned these old-fashioned mores from his grandfather. The old man worked in the fields of Sicily as a youngster and saved every penny so he could come to America. He settled in New York, doing repair work in the Italian neighborhoods until he retired just a couple of years after Sam was born.

Little Santino was the apple of Grandpap

212

Giorgio's eye. He'd plant his favorite grandson on his knee and tell about the old days, when self-respect meant everything and your word was all a man really needed.

Sam could imagine how badly Grandpap would react now--kids dissing their elders, using foul language, young girls getting pregnant, angry punks carrying guns to school and shooting their classmates. No order in the home no more. No sense of morality, of honor. It was a cold, scary world now.

Sam wondered what the old man would think if he returned from the Great Beyond and saw his beloved grandson at his desk, waiting for a colleague to discuss an arrangement that sounded suspiciously like something the mob boys from Palermo would set up. *They badda people*, Grandpap would say in his limited English. *You no mess with the stronzoni, the Black-a Hand.*

Grandpap, sometimes you got to deal with Satan himself to survive nowadays...

Warren Bascomb was a respected CEO running one of the largest corporations in the country. Grandpap would consider him an *animale*. He wouldn't care that Bascomb was a good man to have for an associate. And even though this big shot was no better than the scum Sam had dealt with when Pops Manfredo was showing him the ropes, he knew how vital it was to play the man's tune. Warren Bascomb had just as many connections as Manfredo, but these guys were respectable, and more powerful than Manfredo ever was.

The phone rang, and he answered.

213

"Sammy?" It was Ricco Arragon, right on schedule.

Ricco had been a personal friend for years. Sam turned to him whenever he needed something done right. Arragon had connections with the Orlando Police Department, Department of Motor Vehicles, and the Orange County Sheriff's Department. All sorts of friends in interesting places, mostly from the old days when the Mob was more heavily into political corruption.

"Find out anything?"

"Henry John Lee. Thirty-nine, born in Pittsburgh."

This was getting better already. Pittsburgh still had some good men, despite the fucking mayor's persistent efforts to clean it up just a few decades earlier. "LaRocco boy?" Sam asked.

"Figured the same thing, but no dice, Lee's not into *famiglia* stuff."

"The name ain't shortened? Liani, maybe? Leonetti? I heard he's got dark hair, looks Italian."

"Nothing that I found."

"Go on, then."

"Left college after a year and enlisted in the Marines. He was deployed to Saudi."

"Lee work for A&A?"

"One phone call and they say he's on their payroll."

"Married?"

"He was married to a Heidi Weller, but she divorced him eight years ago."

"Where's she now?"

"Airline stewardess, does the international

214

flights."

"Divorce nasty?"

"Apparently Lee didn't give her a rough time."

"Maybe he didn't wanna be married no more. Or maybe he was working something else. He got a girlfriend?"

"No."

"Kids?"

"Nope."

"Shit." Loners were much harder to deal with. "I have to squeeze this boy's *cojones*, I got to do it hard. Can't use nobody for leverage. He ain't close to no one. Got any parents?"

"Both dead."

"Brothers? Sisters?"

"One brother, died a year or so back."

This was definitely gonna be a ball-buster. Loners usually didn't care if they lived or died. "Lee's made to order if you want someone to cap the fucking President. What else you got?"

"Lee's old service records. The boy didn't make a very good soldier."

This sounded interesting. "You telling me he freezes up under fire?"

"He don't like to be told what to do. Coupla insubords, an Article-Fifteen, and some field-grade bullshit. Lost a stripe coupla times."

"Tell me more."

"He told a Second Looey, then a Captain, to kiss his ass. Nobody stepped outside with him 'cause he's big and tough. Officers ain't by nature scrappers and won't risk losing their bars."

"How about that field-grade?"

215

"AWOL. Looks like he was set up. Lee's captain had it in for him. Caught Lee coming back late from a three-day drunk, dumped him in the tank, then wrote him up for not being where he shoulda been. A full bird conducted the hearing. Seems Lee pissed off the right people that time."

"Mickey Mouse shit. Got an address?"

"One-bedroom apartment in Orlando, South Conway area."

"Go on over there, check his setup. Do it quiet. Make sure there's nothing else we need to know--*capisc*?"

"Now's a good time. Lee's at work. A&A says his hours are from nine to six."

"How close are you?"

"We're on Maguire, about a mile from Curry Ford Road. Had to feed Big Al. Boy needs food every coupla hours. Otherwise, he's liable to rip one of my arms outa the socket and suck it down."

"Go nose around, then. You've got over an hour."

"Consider it done."

"But like I said--quiet."

"Like fucking church mice."

CHAPTER FIFTEEN

After her last talk with Business, Sally stopped slicing at the tape binding her wrists.

She expected to have time alone to get free – assuming he was telling the truth about dropping her off somewhere for a while. She knew if she managed to tear through the tape too soon, she'd meet with certain disaster. Even if she could get free, she couldn't run very well. Her right side had gone totally numb. She could hardly feel her feet, legs, or arms. If it weren't for her frantic tape-slicing efforts, she would've lost all sensation in her hands.

Hopefully they'd park her without tying her up. They couldn't keep her tied up like this forever, could they? Only a fiend would do that. They weren't fiends. They were white collar workers. Computer people. College grads. Professionals. They had class. Education. Intelligence–

There you go again, being incurably optimistic...

She *had* to be. She had to remain positive. Think clearly. Logically. Couldn't let doom defeat her right now, could she?

Remember the blindfold. You don't blindfold someone you intend to murder.

Right now they kept quiet, whispering intermittently as the truck did its erratic stop-and-go routine through the heavy traffic. She thought she heard one of them utter the word 'camp.'

Was that where they were taking her? One of those remote shacks men went on weekends to get away from their wives? One of those places guys could escape to when they could get roaring drunk and act like total idiots?

Wherever they were taking her had to be secluded. They couldn't let anyone see her. And if that was the case, the isolation would be just as good for her as it would be for them. And if they left her alone again, Sally could free herself.

But what if the seclusion is for some other reason? What if they want the isolation so they can question me more thoroughly?

She'd have to revise her escape plan and use the time for careful bargaining. Nothing could be left to chance.

During the last few minutes, she carefully combed her memory for details she might've forgotten when she'd signed those papers for Warren. She had no problem bringing everything back. The memories were as clear as glass.

Just about a year ago, Warren had summoned her into his home office, where papers were spread out neatly on his desk blotter. His notary stamp sat off to the side. He showed her where to sign, then snatched the papers away, one by one, as soon as she'd finished. Not another word was said, and the issue was never brought up again.

Now that she'd brought the memories back, certain things that hadn't come together before made sense now. What stood out most vividly made the blood pulse hotly through her veins. Their marriage began significantly deteriorating early last June, about the time she'd signed the papers. And that time frame corresponded with talks of the merger.

The merger. Warren's mood swings. What on earth was all this about?

***

Fired up by what Alicia had just told him, Hank phoned Pete Hayes right away, to see if he could find an address for Landry or Schiller.

While Pete was looking up the information, Hank would stop by the apartment just long enough to change his clothes and grab something to eat.

Finding those two in an area the size of Orlando would be difficult. He saw no alternative other than getting the FBI involved. But since Bascomb didn't seem to be very concerned about any of it, Hank didn't even know if this was even a kidnapping. For all he knew, it might just be a marital spat that had gone south. But it didn't matter. Bascomb's attitude, the way he treated people, plus the fact that he didn't seem to care about Sally at all, had made him suspect. It was crucial to find out if Sally was safe.

Hank parked the Caddie beside a small group of palm trees across the street from his apartment.

It had been a long day. There was still a lot to do, but he didn't want to make a move until Pete got back with him. He didn't like waiting around – especially if Sally could be in danger – but there was no point in setting out blindly until he had something to work with.

As early-evening rush hour continued hot and heavy on Conway Road, the sounds of kids splashing and yelling from the complex pool echoed loudly. With keys in hand, Hank trudged up the walk. A glance at the doormat made him stop cold

219

in his tracks. It looked like it had been pulled up, then pushed back down, causing a slender triangle of sand showing at the corner.

The paperboy? Didn't wash. The paper sat in its usual place in his box at the corner. A salesman, maybe? Salesmen usually left their cards shoved in the door jam or wedged beneath the knocker. Upon closer inspection, he discovered that his front door was slightly ajar. Someone had found his spare door key. His scalp began to itch big-time.

His long-barreled 45-caliber Ruger Blackhawk revolver hung from its cowhide holster on the coat tree inside the front door. Well-hidden among his jackets, it wouldn't be discovered by a burglar unless the tree was searched. If he could reach in and grab it, he'd get the jump on whoever had let themselves into his apartment.

His heart sputtering, he edged closer and eased the door open.

Silence.

Holding his breath, he moved his hand through the four-inch gap.

***

The truck doors opened abruptly, then slammed shut.

Once again, the big vehicle shook. Business's foul breath drew closer. "We're all tired and need to crash. We're gonna let you have a shower and rest. Sound okay to you?"

Rest? She was bundled up and tossed in a truck. Now they wanted her to *rest*? She just nodded and waited for them to do whatever they'd planned.

"We'll walk you inside but fix it so it looks like

220

it's your idea. Not many folks are out here, but we have to be careful. You never know when someone might be playing cute with binoculars. Understand?"

Oh my God...

The hole she'd made in the tape. They'd *see* it...

"Understand?"

Her nod was slight.

"The blindfold will have to go. I'll tape your eyes, then let you wear my sunglasses. I'll have to uncover your mouth, but we'll be close in case you try something."

Sally's heart pounded wildly.

"Inside, you can have a hot bath. Then we'll give you something to eat and let you sleep."

She cringed. The tape had quickly become the least of her worries. The idea of them strapping her down--possibly in a bed--brought chills up her spine.

"No need to worry about ... that," Business said. "This is strictly business. A transaction."

She found herself nodding in spite of her fears. No need to anger them--not at this point. But she couldn't help dreading this...

The sound of tape ripping from a roll exploded in her ears.

This is it. If they see that tear...

Flighty held her arms. She hoped it was dark, that they'd be too occupied and nervous to notice the tear.

"Hold still."

She couldn't help the shaking. She guessed where he was slicing, then moved her hands in the

221

appropriate direction. She knew she might accidentally get cut but had to take the chance. Business bumped her wrist with the smooth end of the knife. She flinched, her wrists jerking again. He pulled away quickly, applying the knife again, this time more carefully.

Business was slicing the tape on the other side of her wrists. The area facing them. She'd been working on the area directly above her thumbs. If she was lucky, he might not even see what she'd done.

Though Flighty's cold hands gripped her elbows, she was still able to shift the angle of her hands, if only slightly.

"Don't be nervous," Business said tensely. He pulled the severed strips away from her wrists. Flighty let go of her wrists. Sally thought she heard him squeezing the used tape into a ball and dropping it on the floor beside them. A warm wave of relief flowed down her limbs. *So close...*

One of them helped her up. Once she was upright, they brought her cold, tingly arms in front of her and massaged them. They were trying to ease her discomfort, but the pressure brought on an army of new pain. She moaned.

"Sorry."

Tape was wound loosely around her wrists. Her ankles were freed. Something cold, light, and smooth was draped over her forearms. More tape was ripped from a roll. Her blindfold was pulled off. She had time only to see the blur of a dark beard before a fresh strip of tape was pressed gently over her eyes. A pair of bulky plastic sunglasses was

222

then slipped over that. They were too big for her head and rested low on the bridge of her nose. The tape was peeled from her mouth.

The door beside her opened. She was helped out of the truck. Huge bolts of jarring pain stabbed her legs. Her right leg gave out, and she stumbled. She had no feeling at all in her hip. Gritting her teeth, she let them half-carry her.

She couldn't see a thing, but instantly recognized the sweet scent of honeysuckle. A strong whiff of the woods brought back childhood memories of Aunt Margaret's place. The odor of fish told her they were near water. Wind whooshed through the trees off to her left and behind her. The bumpy dirt path beneath her stumbling feet intensified a feeling of isolation.

The pain in her legs flared hotly as they led her up three squeaky wooden steps. She fought hard to think through the pain and promised her aching body she'd soon be relaxing in a warm bath.

A screen door moaned. A door creaked open. They were walking on a wooden floor. Its echoing loudness told her the room was inadequately furnished and probably rested on blocks. A heavy musty smell assaulted her nose. The door banged shut a few feet to her right. Two hands grabbed her shoulders and pushed her down in a soft chair reeking of mildew and cigarettes.

The two of them worked quickly--one on each side of her. Tape was slapped over her mouth, more ripped from a roll close by. The sunglasses were pulled away. The tape was removed from her eyes, the scarf immediately replaced. Her forearms were uncovered. The tape pinning her wrists was sliced away. She was turned onto her side. Her arms were pulled behind her. Fresh tape was wound around them as well as around her ankles. Something was placed loudly on a harsh surface to her left.

Two pairs of footsteps hurried away. The door closed and latched. Heavy footfalls descended the porch steps. Moments later, the truck doors opened and slammed shut. She heard the roar of the engine as the big vehicle eased away.

Silence.

Relieved she was alone again, Sally sighed tiredly. Just before the two had climbed in back to fix her, she'd slipped her ring into her back pocket. It was still there, waiting anxiously for her to retrieve it. She decided against it. She was too exhausted and needed rest. Despite the heavy tingling in her arms and legs, she felt herself relaxing in the lumpy, musty-smelling chair.

***

His legs weak and unsteady, Tommy carried the plastic ice bucket back to the cabin.

Billy said he'd be gone less than an hour. He said to get lots of ice from the machine outside the lodge office, then make the lady comfortable. "But be careful," he'd warned. "Make sure you don't let her see you."

Easy for him to say. Billy wouldn't be alone with her. The last time that happened, Tommy almost ruined everything. *I actually touched her. And she felt so ... so nice. So firm—*

Stop it.

He'd volunteered to do the errands, but Billy

224

reminded him what a lousy driver he was-- especially when he had too much on his mind. So what if he'd been pulled over half a dozen times in the last year? Two of those times weren't even his fault. Stupid cops even apologized, said they got the vehicles mixed up.

But Billy said everything would be okay. "Just stay focused, and don't take any of those damned pills."

They'd passed a Burger King on the way over. It was no more than three miles down the main road. Billy said he'd stop there and get all the food they needed for the night. They'd also passed a liquor store on that same stretch. Billy would buy a couple of six-packs and some Jack Daniel's. They could kick back with some cool ones before bedtime.

Be cool, Tommy boy. You can do this.

He closed the front door behind him and took a few deep breaths, telling himself he'd be all right. *I'm cool. And I won't fuck up this time.*

He eyed Mrs. Bascomb. She hadn't stirred. She was probably pretty tired after all this. He wondered if she was asleep. "Want me to ... free your ankles?"

She nodded eagerly.

He didn't think Billy would mind. They had to free her so she could freshen up in the bathroom.

He set down the bucket on the counter in the tiny kitchen area. *Take things easy. Focus. Be cool.* "How about your mouth? You're probably too tired to scream anyway."

Another nod.

This wasn't nearly as much trouble as he thought. The WorldVue thing had psyched him up.

He pulled out his pocketknife and carefully sliced through the tape around her ankles. His eyes once again locked onto her titties. *Not this time, moron.* He focused on the tape--pulling it off, wadding it up, tossing it on the floor, all the while watching her titties. How come he couldn't get his mind off them? *You're almost thirty, and you've only seen bare titties in stroke flicks and on the hookers you paid for.*

The hookers' titties were covered with tattoos and cigarette burns. And to top it all off, the three sets he'd seen were pierced with nipple rings. One tit was marked up with a long, jagged red scar where her pimp had sliced her to 'make her behave.'

This lady's were probably perfect. No tattoos, piercings, or scars. What was wrong with wanting to see a perfect pair in the flesh? *It's not like I'm gonna--*

Focus.

He reached out with his free hand. It only shook a little now, the tittie issue shoved to the back of his mind. He took a deep breath, then gently peeled the strip from her mouth.

She sighed, moving her lips around, making it look just as nice as one of those sexy lipstick commercials. "Thank you."

See there? Use your head and you end up doing something smart. Things turn out just fine. Look at her, she's all grateful and everything, even smiling. Not tense anymore, as she was in the truck. "When my partner gets back, we'll have something to eat. Hungry?"

A nod.

"Burger King okay?" He didn't know why he asked. She'd have to eat whatever they brought back. But he wanted to make her more at ease.

"That'd be fine."

"You'll be able to take off your blindfold soon, too."

She stiffened.

Jeez ... what the fuck did I do now?

"You don't *care* if ... if I ... *see* you?"

He sighed. *Jeez ... almost blew it again. Look what you did. Now she's shaking and worried again.* But he couldn't blame her. He hadn't told her the whole story. Everyone knew that if you saw your kidnappers' faces, you were toast.

"We ... brought along disguises."

She nearly smiled. "You had me really scared."

This sucks. This really and truly sucks. Bascomb should be tied up in the chair instead of this lady. They could keep him like that all day long, maybe even knock him on the floor and kick him around whenever they got bored.

Mrs. Bascomb shouldn't even be here. She was real nice. Sweet. The kind of lady you respected. He wanted to let her go just so he could watch her run away. He and Billy had seen her jogging a couple of times near the estate, when they'd first been told to do this. She looked really great in her jogging suit, her nice, firm shape showing through. She even looked good when she was running for the woods in the dark. She really made those jeans look sensational.

But even though she couldn't be set free just yet,

227

at least their plan had changed. Now they wouldn't have to do anything really *bad* to her.

The idea of freeing her made him warm inside. So warm, in fact, that he wasn't nervous any more. Things would turn out okay. A regular happy ending, just like in those sappy old movies they made, years and years ago. Mrs. Bascomb would soon be home again, and he and Billy would be on their way to Brazil.

"Would you like me to untie you?"

She raised her head. "Are you ... serious?"

"The bathroom's straight ahead. It's not sparkly-clean or fancy or anything, but it's got everything it's supposed to. I could let you, you know, do what you need to do."

"I'd *love* that. Thank you *so* much..."

It would be okay. The window had been boarded up and nailed shut long before Billy bought the cabin. It couldn't be forced open, except with a crowbar.

"I'll make sure you have enough towels. And soap. There's even a small tube of toothpaste and a little mouthwash in there. Just as long as you don't come out till we tell you to."

She was smiling again, showing those dimples. He really liked seeing them. It made him feel good all over.

"It would be *so* wonderful. I feel so ... *dirty*..."

"Just don't take off your blindfold till I close the bathroom door, okay? And *please* don't scream or anything."

"Don't worry. I'm so tired, I'll probably fall asleep in the tub."

Tommy found himself staring at those titties again, wondering if there was a mole on one of them. Or maybe a birthmark. *Idiot. Get your mind straight.*

"You promise you won't ... come in?" she asked softly.

Tommy's cheeks flushed. Once again he hated himself and Billy for putting this lady through all this. "Mrs. Bascomb, that's one thing you don't have to worry about. Besides, there's a lock on the door."

She nodded, but he could tell she was still a little scared. He wanted to strangle himself, watching her shake like that. All this because of her bastard husband.

Focusing once again, he took hold of her bound arms and pulled her gently into a standing position. She stumbled, her legs giving out. He held her up and she fell against him, both her titties pressing against him this time. *Jeez. Both of them. How am I gonna–*

"I'm *so* sorry..."

Jeez, she's apologizing for doing that ... for pressing those beauties against me. I'm a real moron. An idiot. "That's ... all right." He wanted her to stay like that. She felt real nice. Warm. *Be cool.*

He forced himself to ignore her warm closeness, the feeling of her body against him, the smell of her hair, the softness of her slender arms trapped in his grip ... his growing excitement ... the tightness gathering quickly between his legs. *Focus. Five million. Brazil.*

He gently pushed her away. After a few stiff,

awkward steps, he coaxed her toward the bathroom.

***

Warm air brushed Hank's face as his apartment door opened abruptly.

A whiff of B.O., cigarettes, and Aqua Velva assaulted him as a huge hand from inside grabbed his wrist and yanked, nearly pulling his arm out of its socket. The door slammed shut behind him. Before he could straighten and pull free, a heavy piece of material – probably one of his lightweight jackets – was shoved roughly over his head, making everything black. The grip on his wrist throbbed like an open wound, and a cluster of white-hot pain danced up his arm.

He was spun around and would have stumbled if the grip on him hadn't been so solid. His captured arm was yanked behind his back, twisted and forced straight up until his hand pressed between his shoulder blades. The move was done perfectly. Hank was large and strong. The last time he'd been handled so easily was years ago, by an eighty-year-old Chinese Kung Fu instructor.

He tried pulling away, but his opponent anticipated his every move. The jacket over his head made it impossible to regain his equilibrium.

A hard fist caught him squarely in the midsection. It was short and well-coordinated, forcing him to his knees. The man behind him dropped with him and delivered a sharp blow to his kidneys. The man facing him was obviously a bone crusher. Judging by the calculated, unhurried method with which the blows were delivered, he was a professional.

Hank tried dropping to the floor, but the ape behind him grabbed his collar and held on. The pro facing him kept up the stomach work. All Hank could do was keep his midsection tensed and wait until they got bored. Each time he tried using his free hand to lash out, Ape Number One delivered a pulverizing blow to the gut. Ape Number Two kept the pressure on Hank's collar, forcing him off-balance.

Something big and hard, shaped like a knee, slammed into the small of his back, sending a flurry of hot rippling pain thundering up his spine. Their coordination was flawless. Soon the punches no longer hurt. His body had decided to protect itself by switching off. He suspected one of them had tapped him on the back of the head, but since everything had become so fuzzy, he might have just imagined it.

The jacket slipped to the floor, but everything remained dark. The grip on his collar vanished. The blackness was oddly comforting.

***

Submerged up to her neck in warm, soapy water, Sally let the lazy waves lull her toward a relaxed state of bliss. The sensation was so wonderful, even though the tub was filthy and smelled of mildew.

Cleaning it out helped. She found some cleanser and a couple of sponges in the tiny plywood cabinet underneath the sink. It took only a few minutes to scrub it down, rinse it with the shower hose, and let it drain. Then she filled it with warm water and, after double-checking the lock on the door, stripped.

She scrubbed her bra, panties and tee shirt with

231

soap and hot water, wrung them out thoroughly, and laid them across the sink, directly beneath the two eighty-watt bulbs over the mirror. While they dried, she lowered herself into the soothing hot pool and leaned back while the steam permeated her pores, gradually easing the pain in her cramped joints and limbs.

After washing and rinsing her hair with the shampoo provided, she covered her face with a wet washrag, which helped relieve the irritations caused by the tape and blindfold.

As she drifted off, someone tapped gently on the door.

Darn. She didn't want to leave the safety of the bathroom so soon.

She didn't know what she should do. Flighty had been reassuring, but she didn't want to take any chances. What if they weren't wearing disguises? What if one of them had it on wrong? What would they do if she stayed in here?

She reluctantly got out of the tub, dried off, and blotted her hair with the towel. The panties were dry, but not the bra or shirt. It didn't matter. She slipped them on anyway.

Once fully dressed, she found the courage to approach the bathroom door. It was her only ally. The only thing keeping her safe. This was her own little sanctuary, and she didn't want to leave it. But if she stayed here and forced their hand, it would change everything. If they thought she was trying to slip out through the boarded-up window, they might break down the door. But if she unlocked the door, opened it and saw their faces, all would be lost.

232

She couldn't stay here forever. And since she couldn't possibly force the window open–

Another tap.

She froze.

"C'mon out," Business said.

"You're sure?"

"We're wearing masks."

She reached for the lock and froze again. What if–

"Food's getting cold."

Her pulse fluttering, she unlocked it and inched it open. Cautiously she eased her head past the door and glanced around. They were sitting at the table in the small living area, their faces covered with those silly President masks you can buy at novelty stores. Both wore baseball caps to cover their heads. One of them appeared as Reagan, the other Nixon. Flighty was Nixon. His skinny red-haired arms poked out from the sleeves of his tee shirt. White bags and wrappings were spread out on the table, along with a six-pack of Coors and three Styrofoam cups of coffee with sugar packets and creamers.

Despite her initial anxiety, she ate ravenously, devouring the lukewarm food as if it had been meticulously prepared by a gourmet chef. No one said anything, which was good. She wasn't in the mood to talk anyway. She tried very hard to keep her eyes from wandering to the door. She didn't want them to guess what she was thinking. But occasionally she did observe portions of the open area. The cracked, peeling walls, lack of furniture, and smallness of the area depressed her even more.

When she finished her meal, Business asked if

she'd like some whiskey to help her relax. She wanted to tell him that the only thing she really wanted was to leave. But she didn't want to anger them. They were in good spirits--no doubt from the new development in their plans. She didn't want to do or say anything to ruin her chances.

To appease them, she accepted a shot of whiskey. It didn't exactly relax her--she loathed the taste--but made her a little less edgy. Without another word, she returned to the bathroom to perform her nightly toilet, then retired to the bedroom for the night.

This door also had a key. She twisted it until she heard the lock slip into its slot, then sighed in relief. The room was only slightly larger than the bathroom, with two boarded-up windows. Though dirty and sparsely furnished, it would serve as another excellent sanctuary. An upright wicker chair sat in a corner. She picked it up and quietly wedged its wooden back beneath the doorknob. That instantly made her feel better.

She spent another minute or so examining both windows and checking the sills, the latches, and the boards nailed to the outside frame. When she was confident she could do nothing without alerting her kidnappers, she lay down on the musty blanket and tried directing her cramped, exhausted body toward sleep.

The mattress was lumpy in spots and hard in other places, but compared to the truck, it was soft and luxurious. The small lamp on the chipped table next to the bed stayed on. It gave her more security than the darkness, which, due to the blindfold, she'd grown to fear.

As she gazed at the jagged strands of plaster dangling from the yellowed ceiling, she wondered if she'd done the right thing by taunting them with WorldVue. From what she'd heard during the last few months, dividends alone from such a merger would generate millions. Latching onto even a small part of it would be to anyone's advantage. But how would the merger benefit her kidnappers? What could they gain by getting their hands on the papers? Leverage? Publicity?

Knowing how Warren treated his employees, Sally could easily see these two scheming to bilk Warren out of much more than what was originally agreed on. But if they wanted to get back at Warren, why punish her? What have I done to deserve this?

The rage came back. She fought it down. It was difficult, but she managed. On impulse, she pulled the wedding ring from her back pocket and slipped it on. Then she closed her eyes and tried focusing her thoughts on sleep.

PART III
The Third Day

CHAPTER SIXTEEN

Wincing at the heavy throbbing in his head, Hank sat on the edge of the hospital bed and tried to concentrate on that last question.

It was extremely difficult. All he could think about was finding whoever had ambushed him in his apartment.

Just a few feet away, the cop scribbled busily into a notebook. Hank figured him not much more than twenty-five, probably still lived with his parents. He wore no wedding ring. His nametag said Donley. He smelled strongly of *Brut* and talcum powder. The faint brown stubble peppering his upper lip made Hank wonder if the boy hadn't shaved for the last three days or was trying to grow a mustache.

Donley stopped writing and looked up. "Sure you didn't get a glimpse of who broke into your place?"

Hank frowned. This kid was either plain stupid or he just wasn't paying attention. "Like I just said, someone tossed one of my jackets over my head as I came through the door."

"Pro?"

"Don't think so. Bastard obviously heard me coming in. He got behind the clothes tree and waited. If I'd seen him, he would've been brought here instead. Or he'd be in the morgue."

Hank had been living in the apartment nearly five years and hadn't seen an ounce of trouble. The complex consisted of mostly retired people and white-collar professionals, and even had a Neighborhood Watch. Though Conway had been filling up with minorities during the last few years, the immediate area had seen very few incidents of drugs or gang activity.

He didn't want to tell the cop his suspicions. When you told cops too much, they kept asking questions. Besides, Hank just wasn't in a chatty mood.

The officer snapped his notebook shut. "When you're released, go back to your place, make a list of what was taken, and notify your insurance company. You'll need to contact us and let us know what we should be looking for. You mentioned firearms."

"I've got three--my Blackhawk and two others, both small autos. I'm pretty sure the moron took the Blackhawk, since I keep it hanging under jackets on my coat tree. I haven't had the chance to see what's still there."

"Small autos?"

"Beretta's. Both pocket models. One's a Bobcat twenty-two, with the skinny four-inch barrel."

The cop shrugged. "Not bad for close work."

"Five yards, max. Strictly up close and personal."

"How about the other?"

"Cheetah three-eighty."

"Good, solid compact." The cop obviously knew

his guns. "Your Blackhawk a forty-five? Or the forty-four model?"

"Forty-five."

"Long-barreled cowboy type?"

"You got it."

"Nice piece. You have a permit?"

"Concealed carry."

The cop reopened his notebook. "Got the serial number somewhere?"

"I'll call it in when I get back."

"You might be a while."

"Don't think so. Just some bruised ribs."

"What about that nasty golf ball growing out of the back of your head?"

"Hell, my ex-wife used to hit harder than this." Hank gingerly touched the bandage. It hurt like a bastard but wasn't too bad. Not enough to keep him here. One of those assholes probably hit him with the Blackhawk. The image made him see red. "I guess everyone's right about my having a hard head."

"I've been telling you that since I've known you, Lee," Colleen Moore tossed in from the doorway.

She was dressed to kill as usual, her black skirt an inch or two shy of the knee. The top two buttons of her white silk blouse, both undone, showed off her gold necklaces. Her four-inch red spikes glittered from the morning sun filtering in through the open blinds. The strong scent of *Obsession* quickly invaded the room. Her leaning against the doorjamb made him think of the sleazy bitch in that Dalmatian story. With a fur coat and cigarette and holder, the look would be complete.

He sighed. *Just what I need right now...*

Donley straightened awkwardly. "I'd better head back. Glad you weren't hurt any worse. But give us a list as soon as you can. Especially the serial number on that Blackhawk and any other guns that might've been taken. We'll need it as soon as possible." He hurried out, tipping his service cap but keeping his distance from Colleen.

"Slumming?" Hank asked. "Or showing off your new spikes to the hospital staff?"

"Funny, Lee. Your head's split open, and you're still cracking jokes."

"I have to entertain myself. They won't let me play with the stuff in the drug cabinets. They're afraid I'll accidentally take something."

"I buzzed your apartment complex." She came in, frowning at everything. Not exactly her kind of room. Not enough lace, glitter, or rich men. "At around eight o'clock, a man answered, said he was your landlord. He told me what happened. I came here and made some inquiries. Since I wasn't family, they didn't tell me much. I went higher until I was given more substantial information."

She'd probably threatened someone's job. Or showed off her talons.

"They said you needed rest, so I left and came back this morning."

He decided not to ask her why she was so concerned. For Colleen, concern usually translated into something selfish. "Don't expect me in today."

Colleen smiled. "With that goose egg, I don't expect to see you for a while." She lowered her perfect ass into the chair nearby and placed her red leather bag on the table in front of a small lamp, white pitcher and glasses. She rested her elbows on the metal arms of the chair and brought her hands together, as if in prayer. "I don't want you back until you're one hundred percent. I need you, Lee. You're my best field man."

"Where do I pick up my award?"

She sighed. "So what happened?"

"Look at my head."

"I see that."

"Didn't you hear what I told that shave-tail in the blue uniform? You were standing right there."

"Your landlord mentioned a van coming into the complex not long before one of your neighbors saw you crawling out of your apartment. He thought they were wearing uniforms and figured they were plumbers."

"My plumbing's fine."

"That's what your landlord said."

"He's good. For a guy pushing eighty, he makes sure everything's up and running—"

"Anyway, you were crawling around on the front slab."

"I don't remember that."

"You were probably barely conscious."

"Plumbers are rough in this part of the state."

Her frown said she was not amused.

"They don't like it when you don't pay your bill."

"*Were* they plumbers, Lee?"

"What else could they be?"

"You're involved in something. You told me earlier, on the phone. Tell me about this old friend."

240

He knew it wouldn't be long before she got personal.

"Lee, if you're in trouble, I'd really like to know. Maybe I can help."

He wasn't listening. He was thinking about the two goons. They'd obviously been paid by Bascomb, but why? To find out who he was? Or why he was asking about Sally? Hank didn't particularly care. The only answers he wanted concerned Sally. Where she was and who she was with. And if she was all right.

***

Even the deep-blue Orlando skyline could not lighten Warren Bascomb's dark mood.

He turned away from the big, tinted window and shot a quick glare at the phone on his desk. It was just as silent now as it was a minute ago.

He'd spent the last half-hour trying to contact Sam Cole. For some reason, no one was answering the damned phone.

Another peek at his watch told him it was after ten. Good Guys opened for their lunch buffet promptly at twelve. Cole would no doubt be there long before that. He needed to supervise, sample the cuisine, see that everyone was present and accounted for. In such a competitive business, organization was paramount. That is, if he was a top-notch businessman. And judging by the number of vehicles parked outside his places on any given day, Cole certainly was. However, being successful in that line of business was a cakewalk. When you hired the hottest babes in the city to lather up the clientele and employed the best chefs and

241

bartenders to wine and dine them, you didn't have to be a genius entrepreneur. Still, there was no excuse for not answering your phone.

Something very strange was going on and should be addressed before too many people became involved. Bad enough one of his Venture employees had just called, asking if Sally's Mustang was parked off the side of the road on the GreeneWay. Naturally, Warren immediately called his mechanic, Stu Evans, to pick it up. Stu always did what he was told and didn't ask questions. When he called back to say the Mustang was simply out of gas, they'd shared a chuckle or two about it, then arranged for Stu to bring it back to the estate after a long-overdue tune-up.

But it bothered him that Stu had told him Sally's purse was in the car. And when Warren had asked him to check it out, Stu said that her credit cards and rings were in the purse.

This could be good news. If Sally had called Paul George and asked him to pick her up, she would have taken her purse with her. But since she hadn't, that could mean Landry and Schiller had picked her up before she'd been able to contact George.

But why were her rings stuffed in her purse? Sally *never* took her rings off.

Maybe Landry and Schiller had taken them off when they snatched Sally because they wanted to hock them. He didn't think they'd do something like that, but you just never knew about people these days. Those rings added up to around fifty grand--it would be a terrific fringe benefit to the million they collected when this was all over. But if they'd taken them off Sally, why put them in her purse?

He couldn't wait. This should all be over in twenty-four hours. He was supposed to call OPD and report her missing, but he didn't want to do it until he knew exactly what was happening. He didn't like surprises.

But first things first. The issue of Hank Lee had to be resolved. He snatched up the throw-away cell phone and punched redial. It rang twice. Then, finally, the familiar voice. "Morning, Mr. B."

"Sammy, I've been trying to get you all fucking morning. What's going on?"

The resulting silence told him the worst. Silence sucked--especially from someone you just paid good money for answers. Silence meant a fuckup. Warren didn't mind fuckups--they were part of life. But not with such high stakes. "I asked you a question, Sammy."

"There was ... some trouble, Mr. B."

Warren's pulse raced. "Define trouble."

"Two of my boys went to Lee's place yesterday around four-thirty. It was a simple snoop job--you know, sneak in quiet, find what you can, then evaporate. No fuss, no muss. Anyway, they get there and start sniffing. Next thing they know, Lee's sneaking in."

Warren's forehead grew warm. "He *saw* them?"

"My boys are good. They got him before he could do anything. Pulled him inside, put him down, then made the apartment look like a burglary. Didn't get much, but--"

"They didn't ... *kill* him, did they?" Warren whispered.

243

"These boys, they ain't hotheads. We're talking pros here. You told me what you wanted done. They did it. Just made him take a nap. Nothing permanent."

"You're sure he'll be all right?"

"He's in ORMC, but yeah, he'll be all right. He's a big boy. They said he was solid."

Warren sat back and rode out the wave of heat. *Imbeciles.* He tried calming himself. *Close your eyes. Think good thoughts. Take deep breaths.* "As long as Lee didn't actually see anyone, I guess we're okay."

"He didn't."

"You're sure."

"Positive."

"So what did you find out?" he asked. "Anything about a man named Donaldson?"

"*Nada.*"

"Anybody check Lee's phone bill activity?"

"My boy's got a contact with the phone company, has access to the Billing Department."

"No calls to Tallahassee? Washington?"

"Nope."

This was getting a little better. "What else?"

"Lee had a gun. A long-barreled Blackhawk .45."

"Revolver?"

"Cowboy model."

"What's he doing with a gun like that?"

"He was a Marine, Mr. B. You know how those boys are. Their juices make them all kinds of whacko. He probably drives to the range on weekends to get rid of some stress. He looks the

244

type."

"Any other toys?"

"None that we found. They said they only found the Blackhawk because one of them was checking out Lee's coat tree. Had some nice jackets hanging there. Then he spotted the .45 mixed in with them."

What was Lee doing with such a large gun? And why hide it on a coat tree? "That Blackhawk was the only gun you found?"

"Like I said, they didn't have enough time to really go through the entire place. Not the way they wanted to, anyway."

"You don't think Lee's some sort of private dick or anything?"

"We checked that out already. If he was, he'd be registered. A call was already made to OPD."

"Then Lee seems to be what he says."

"Going by what A&A said, Lee's a good man. He's conscientious, knows how to motivate the men, and gets things done."

It was good that Lee wasn't a cop--even better that he wasn't a snoop for Donaldson. But Cole's last statement didn't make Warren breathe any easier. Judging by their short meeting yesterday, Lee faced things head-on and didn't back down. He'd stand up to anybody. Based on what Sammy had just told him, and what he already knew by talking with Lee, the man was going to be a major pain in the ass.

***

A few minutes after Colleen left, a short, slight nurse with curly blond hair came in and said in a soft, high-pitched voice, "Mr. Lee, we need to keep you under observation for a couple of hours to make sure everything's okay once the tests are all in."

He smiled politely.

"Is there anything I can get you before I leave to make my rounds?"

"You wouldn't by any chance have a bottle of Jack Daniel's hidden somewhere beneath the folds of that cute little uniform, would you?"

Her cheeks reddened. "Boy, I wish I did..."

"Know any good movies on the cable they pipe in? A guy can get awfully bored, sitting here all morning."

"I'm not really familiar with the channel listings, but–"

"How about something on the order of *Barbarian Babes of Babylon*, or *Vanessa's Voracious Vixens*?"

"I'm sure those channels are blocked, Mr. Lee."

"Can't blame a guy for trying..."

She just sighed and shook her head as she left the room.

So much for humor in poor taste. Makes 'em walk away every time.

He waited a few minutes, then slipped on his clothes and snuck out. Three cabs eagerly awaited a fare outside the front entrance.

His cell phone was ringing when he opened his apartment door. On impulse, he glanced at the coat tree. The empty hook where the Blackhawk holster used to hang sneered at him. He collapsed on the couch and grabbed his ringing cell phone sitting in the middle of the coffee table. It must've fallen out of his jacket pocket in the scuffle. His landlord

246

probably put it there after dialing 911. Once again, the image of being roughed up by those two brutes brought back a rush of heat. He pushed it aside and applied his cell to his ear. "Pete."

"Where the hell have you been? I tried calling half a dozen times. Cell need a recharge?"

"Just got back from the hospital."

"What the hell were you doing there?"

"Two goons attacked me when I came home yesterday afternoon."

"Christ. What happened?"

Suddenly exhausted, Hank let his head fall back and groaned when the goose egg made contact with the back of the couch. He eased his eyes closed. "Some bruised ribs and a bump to the head. Whoever did it knew what they were doing. My favorite gun's missing." He forced himself back up and shuffled down the hall, pausing in the bedroom doorway. The empty space on his nightstand verified his suspicions. "That old watch Heidi brought me for a birthday present. It's not there."

"Robbery?"

"I don't think so."

"You just said they knew what they were doing."

"I'll bet those assholes lifted the watch to make it look like robbery."

"Why bother?"

"Something tells me they know Bascomb. They probably showed up to check me out. If they were asking about me, they expected me to be at the office."

"But why would a CEO risk his reputation to do something like that?"

247

"You don't risk anything when you pay someone else to do your dirty work."

"It still doesn't make sense. Why would Bascomb even bother?"

"I rattled his cage when I asked about Sally's car."

"But you can't prove he was behind it--or *can* you?"

"Not right now. But give me a little time. Just enough for me to find those two and get my Blackhawk back."

CHAPTER SEVENTEEN

Bill Landry climbed the wooden steps of the cabin.

Before stepping inside, he gave the dirt road and the woods one last quick scan. No one wandering around. *Good deal.* The tourists didn't normally clutter up the place till June, when school was out. And most anglers owning cabins only showed for the weekends.

He went inside and found Schiller slouched in the chair near the door. That favorite magazine of his, the one showing the Rio de Janeiro babes lying half-naked on the sand, lay open in his lap.

He hoped Schiller wasn't getting any weird ideas. Schiller was like a teenage kid with his first hard-on. After spending a few minutes gawking at those hot, scantily clad babes, any guy with the usual amount of available hormones would automatically fantasize over the fine-looking babe lying in the bed behind the door.

Good thing Schiller wasn't normal. If he was, they'd be having even more problems.

Bill jabbed a thumb at the bedroom door. "Everything okay?"

"She's probably still asleep."

"See if she wants breakfast." He put the bags on the table, then picked up his Reagan mask. Schiller put on Nixon. The masks had to be pushed out from the bottom so they could eat. Even so, she wouldn't be able to see much.

Schiller knocked lightly on the bedroom door.

249

"Yes?" came the muffled reply.

"Breakfast, Mrs. Bascomb."

"One minute."

"Take your time."

About five minutes later, the door opened.

Sally Bascomb paused in the doorway, watching them warily before joining them at the table. She shot one quick glance at the front door but didn't do anything stupid. Her hair was messed up and mashed on one side, and she had circles under her eyes. Definitely a little rough around the edges without her make-up and usual primping. Most women looked like crap without makeup--especially those Hollywood bimbos. That's why they didn't like to be seen unless they'd put in a few serious hours with their make-up artists and hair stylists. They didn't want their fans knowing they looked no better than everyone else.

Trudi wouldn't leave the house unless she'd spent at least an hour in front of the mirror. It made him crazy, especially when her narcissistic shenanigans caused them to show up late wherever they went.

If Bascomb's old lady was sensitive about her looks, she wasn't showing it. She really had no choice. She had to do whatever they said, whenever they said. It was a damned shame he'd never been able to do something like this with Trudi. Hell, she hadn't even wanted to play any sex slave games when she was in one of her rare playful moods. It would mess up her hair and give people the wrong idea. "Rope-burns, Billy," she'd say. "You want folks to think you're kinky when we go out?"

Sally Bascomb sat across the table, hunched over a little, her hair messed up, red blotches on her face. Not exactly in the position to be uppity now, was she? If they told her to clean up the table, she'd have to do it. And maybe even sweep the floor as well.

Women like her had been dissing him all his life. A babe like Sally Bascomb wouldn't even turn his way when she passed him on the street. Not even if he was having a coronary. In different circumstances, he'd consider this a kind of sweet revenge. *Ignore me all my life, eh? Treat me like the pavement you've been walking on for the last three blocks?*

It would have been easy to try something with her while she was bundled up in the truck. Just remove the tape from her ankles and she was all his. Since they were supposed to kill her and dump her body anyway, a few minutes of rough bondage sex wouldn't have worsened the situation at all. So why didn't he do it? Was it because she belonged to Bascomb? Because he didn't want something Bascomb had already defiled? Or was it something else? Something he didn't want to admit?

I just didn't want to bother. Too many other things to think about at the time. Besides, it would've upset Schiller, made him freak.

"You like sausage biscuits?" He pushed the bag toward her.

She pushed her hair back so she could see what she was doing. "Sounds great." She reached for one while Schiller placed a Styrofoam cup of steaming coffee on the scratched-up surface near her elbow,

251

along with sugar packets and creamers.

Bill watched her eat. She had more of an appetite than before--which was only natural. But now, she definitely seemed a little less depressed. She was probably feeling better about things since they'd decided to take her up on her offer. He wondered if she was already deciding what she was going to do about Bascomb when she got back home.

He almost smiled. *That* would be his revenge. A revenge much sweeter and much more complete than killing her. And it would be something he'd remember fondly for the rest of his life. *Not* killing Sally Bascomb. Sending her back home to her husband. Sending her back so she could bleed him dry, then leave him for the wolves.

***

After a warm shower, three scrambled eggs, two large cups of black coffee, and three Tylenol, Hank was ready to go after the two who attacked him.

He had seen many things in his thirty-nine years that made no sense whatsoever. It made him realize that, despite his suspicions, this could have actually been a random burglary. Or some neighborhood gang members doing this for some sort of initiation. Or even a couple of college kids pledging for a fraternity. But he knew better. College kids didn't work that way. They weren't methodical, and they weren't professional. And they certainly weren't the type to cause a physical altercation. Neither were gang members. And everyone knew gang members were cowards.

The two who'd worked him over did this for a living. They had done it before. It took experienced

252

coordination to handle a fit, two-hundred-and-ten-pound former Marine that easily. Everything about this reeked. Bascomb's reaction to the news about Sally's car. His irritation for the interruption, then his shrugging off the entire matter. But his cell phone lie proved to be the icing on the cake.

Another trip to the estate was in order. There, Hank could decide what course of action had to be played out.

He opened his top dresser drawer and felt beneath the two stacks of underwear. Both pistols lay beneath them in the drawer. He was relieved the two goons hadn't found them. If they'd been snatched as well, he'd be three times madder than he already was. Taking the Blackhawk was bad enough--lifting two small autos worth nearly twelve hundred dollars would make this much more personal.

He picked up the Cheetah .380 and dropped the clip to make sure all ten rounds hadn't been tampered with, then laid it on the bed while he dressed. He put on a tan short-sleeve polo shirt, jeans, and his most comfortable tennis shoes. Then he picked up the Cheetah, grabbed his lightweight jacket from the coat tree, slipped the automatic into the inside pocket, and left the apartment.

The pounding in his head had subsided as soon as he went out into the afternoon heat and got into the Caddie. His ribs had already quit aching. The Tylenol--and breakfast--worked wonders.

Traffic was heavy, but he kept with the steady flow heading north on Semoran Boulevard. In less than half an hour, he turned onto the familiar winding road, made a left, and eased up the hill to the exclusive development of estates partially hidden behind palm trees, well-tended gardens, elaborate fountains, and wrought-iron fences.

A Lutheran church appeared at the knoll beyond the intersection. He pulled in at the side entrance and inched past the huge domed brick building. At the other end of the parking lot, pines and scrub oaks extended down the slope, stopping a few yards shy of the clearing that emptied onto the main road facing the wooded rise. He stopped short of the tree line and put the Caddie in park. Then he pulled his binoculars out from under his seat and removed the lens caps.

A hundred yards beyond the slope, the Bascomb estate shined like a glittering gem behind the bushes and orange blossoms lining the other side of the road.

***

Warren Bascomb sat at his desk, agonizing over what almost happened the night before.

If they accidentally killed Lee, OPD would be coming after me in a heartbeat. It wouldn't take a brain surgeon to put two and two together. Lee comes here to ask about Sally's car, then drives back to his apartment – and gets beaten half to death by two goons who can be traced back to Sam Cole ... who can be traced back to me.

It would ruin everything. And if Landry and Schiller were keeping Sally somewhere and did something stupid, like getting caught committing a minor traffic violation, that would be the ball game.

Once again he wondered if he should make his

call to OPD earlier than scheduled but decided against that. Best stick with the plan. Landry and Schiller had a little less than twenty-four hours to do what they were supposed to--that is, if they wanted their million bucks, free and clear. If they failed, it was their funeral. The call to OPD would already have been made, Sally would already be reported missing, and the Feds would be contacted and told about Landry and Schiller's hacking efforts.

Simple, direct, and virtually foolproof--but much more complicated with a third party like Lee snooping around. Some tweaking was going to be required in this case. Schiller and Landry would be busy with Sally until tomorrow morning. That left several hours to decide what to do about Lee. This wouldn't be a problem. Sammy was a good man--he could get this done properly.

Warren glanced at his watch. Tonya was also due to call at any time. He longed for that call. It would set his mind to rest. Everything else quickly dimmed into the background, almost like magic, whenever she entered the picture.

He'd met her at the National Software Convention in New York City one year ago. She'd recently been promoted to Executive Director of Sales Administration in the Tampa offices of ICS when the company was known as Euro-International Computer Systems. Intelligent, well-educated and very striking, Tonya dressed conservatively the day they met--tan business suit, silk blouse, and brown Oxfords. Her shiny raven hair was pulled back and tied, making every guy in the room wonder how it would look when she let it fall loose.

Over lunch, Tonya demonstrated her marketing skills by giving him a capsulized version of how she'd turned ICS's Tampa offices into one of Florida's top ten branch companies in just a few short months. That evening, after an elegant banquet in the hotel restaurant, she lured him to her room and demonstrated her more personal skills.

Warren quickly decided Tonya was the woman for him. She was the perfect age--twenty-five--with perfect looks and a bedside manner a man could only dream about. But he knew it wouldn't be possible to pursue an active relationship while he was married to Sally. Their affair had to be conducted with total discretion. Any disturbance would make the stockholders freak, causing Bas-Com stock to drop drastically. And if Sally found out, she could get with her friend George to start up the fireworks with that damned prenup they both signed before the wedding.

If only George hadn't conned her into pushing that deal. But Warren had been smitten at the time. He'd been like a teen with a killer hard-on--giddy, infatuated, and as stupid as a post--and couldn't help himself. No one filled a dress like Sally or demonstrated glamour as keenly as she did. And no one looked better on his arm at a convention.

He signed the prenup reluctantly, knowing deep-down it was just a formality. He was certain that, like his three former marriages, this one wouldn't last any longer than three or four years. He had no idea that Sally was so smart or resourceful. The only thing he'd learned from this marriage was that it would be his last. Sally would be far from his last piece of ass, but she'd definitely be the last female to drag him to the altar.

He was confident things would soon be settled and turn out the way they were supposed to. Once Sally was out of the picture, he could go on with his plans with Tonya and ICS. Under the guise of an upcoming merger, he and Tonya could continue their affair without arousing suspicion. He'd decided to unload WorldVue long ago. The company had simply become too expensive to run. It relied too much on highly paid contract workers and had been steadily losing both money and profits during the last fifteen months.

Their plan was perfect. But when Donaldson from the State Business Regulation Board heard about the merger and stuck his big nose into the works, things turned shaky. However, everything would soon be resolved, and Donaldson could just wait until the dust settled before trying to figure out what actually happened.

Warren's personal line buzzed. "Mr. Bascomb?"

The low, breathy whisper instantly made his pulse pound louder and faster. His face hot, he sat back in his chair. "Miss Madison," he said diplomatically. It was a secure line, but he didn't want to take any chances. "And how are you?"

"Just fine. Yourself?"

"I'm doing well." Discussing business had always been second nature to Warren. But with this woman, his natural talents had taken a back seat. Keeping his attention on anything but that wonderful body and those luscious lips proved impossible.

"I'm sorry I didn't call earlier. Something came up. I just got back to my office."

"I understand. Things have been hectic for both of us."

"I was wondering about my trip this weekend. If everything is arranged. There are certain issues that have ... come up ... which should be addressed."

He sighed. "Some problem?"

"Something we've been neglecting. I believe it is something that should be straightened out as quickly as possible."

"Something ... big?"

"Eventually."

Her suggestion, as always, made his entire body throb.

"Still there?"

"Oh, yeah..." He loosened his collar.

"I was just wondering about my arrival time. I know we've discussed it before..."

"No need to worry. My limousine will be ready to pick you up promptly at ten-thirty. I haven't heard of any delays in the works–"

His other line buzzed. Sam Cole's number displayed prominently. It brought him back like a bucket of ice water to the face. "That's my other line," he told Tonya. "I'd better take it."

"I understand."

Hanging up on this woman made him shake with rage. "Sam, this better be important."

"It's about Lee, Mr. B..." Sam sounded tense. "Looks like we're gonna have major problems."

***

258

A skinny Hispanic in his late sixties carefully tended one of the flower gardens on the east side of the Bascomb estate.

There was no sign of anyone else. Hank figured there should be. A man that age wouldn't be able to handle the estate. A landscaping outfit would be required to maintain such a large piece of property. The gardener was probably needed for weekly touch-up work.

Hank lowered the binoculars. He wanted to drive over and pump the old boy with questions. *Not a good idea*. The old man probably didn't even speak English. And he might not respond well to a stranger. It would be different if Hank were Spanish. Latinos generally lowered their guard for other Latinos. But even if the old man did speak English, what would he know about his employer?

Would the maid know what was going on? From their brief conversation previously, Hank couldn't tell if she was hiding something or simply hadn't a clue. Judging by his single encounter with Bascomb, Hank suspected the poor woman was probably so intimidated by her employer that she was afraid to open her mouth.

Movement behind the wrought-iron fence caught his attention, and he brought the binoculars back into play. A battered lime-green station wagon crept down the drive and stopped at the entrance. The gardener sat behind the wheel. The vehicle slowly pulled out, heading west.

Hank put away the binoculars, got his Gators cap from the back seat, and put it on gingerly to hide the bandage on the back of his head. Then he slipped on his sunglasses and stepped out of the Caddie.

***

His solid, hairy forearms resting on the steering wheel of the rented white Ford Super Duty van, Ricco Arragon kept the binoculars trained on the cream-colored Cadillac parked near the woods behind the Lutheran Church across the street.

Their orders were simple: "Stay close, but don't let him see you. Don't move in. And none of that macho shit you *sfachims* pulled yesterday. Stay hidden and let me know everything Lee does."

No problem. Sammy was giving the orders. Sammy paid well and provided a lotta jobs. You pissed him off, he wouldn't ask you to do anything else. Besides, two K apiece for one simple job was nothing to sneeze at.

Al Simon sat beside Ricco in the padded bucket seat, lighting another cigarette. Simon went six-four, three hundred, easy. Like most huge men, he sweated freely. Always splashed those jowls silly with Aqua Velva. He had to, since he needed to shave twice a day. And when he sweated, the scent was strong.

He sat all tensed and bummed-out, chain-smoking. Ricco knew why. Big Al didn't like Lee walking around when he should still be in the hospital. Big Al was a proud man. He was a hitter years ago, growing up in the Bronx. Fought heavy, weighing in at a tight two-ten back then. Fucker had an iron jaw and a killer left that earned him thirty-nine knockouts in forty-four professional bouts. He took it personal when he couldn't get you down fast. He'd always boasted about dropping a guy--

any guy--in two punches, tops. But Lee hadn't gone down.

Ricco could understand Big Al's dilemma. Hitting fifty in just three or four years, Al carried around some heavy shit in his head. Ricco still had twelve years to go for The Big One, so he saw no reason to start sweating it right now. But Al had set himself up with some unreasonable standards. The years were definitely fucking with Big Al. Getting older. Getting soft. Slowing down. Not enough lead in the pencil. Your hair isn't coal-black no more and you can see patches of scalp where there wasn't any before. You don't have the wind you used to have, and every time you turn around, you want to take a nap.

After the ruckus with Lee at the fucker's apartment complex, Big Al mumbled, "Fifteen punches, easy, that stupid fuck's still on his feet." Sounded like a fucking broken record all the way back to their Winter Park condo.

Ricco figured he ought to take this easy. When Simon was upset, he made life miserable. He'd sit there, stewing in his own juices, then out of the blue, slam the dash with a giant fist. Once was bad enough. But when you had to take the rentals back to the shop time and time again to have half the fucking interior replaced, it bit real heavy into your expenses.

"You were off-balance," he'd said, hoping it would pacify the big fuck.

"So was he."

"We were in a hurry. Suck it up."

Lee was tough--no doubt about it. He'd probably

261

also done some time in the ring, going by the busted honker. His machismo shit no doubt had something to do with his old Marine days. Those psychos always pulled Mr. Tough Guy even years after they were mustered out.

There shouldn't have been a scuffle in the first place. Sammy had said look around, find what you can. But nothing about what to do if they got caught. And when they were ready to case the apartment and saw Lee's arm slipping inside to grab something from the coat tree, they knew they had to put the big boy down fast and make tracks.

Right now, Ricco didn't like what the binoculars were telling him. Lee got out of the Caddie and headed straight for the Bascomb estate. Ricco lowered the binoculars. "This don't look good. Lee ain't supposed to be out here, sniffing around."

"He walking funny?" Big Al scratched the black stubble on his prow-like jaw.

"Nope."

"Not even holding his ribs?"

"Not holding anything."

"I shoulda aimed higher."

"He's wearing a baseball cap."

"So?"

"He's trying to hide the goose egg. It's probably a *big* mother."

"Fuck ... *you* did that with the asshole's Blackhawk."

"Just trying to make you feel better."

Big Al grunted. "So how long we gotta sit here?"

"Long as it takes."

Ricco could tell his buddy was thinking of the

old days. They sure made better sense. You leaned on a rival by dropping him, slipping the barrel of your gun into his mouth, then making your proposition while he lay there, shitting his threads. Nowadays you laid low, keeping an eye out and making sure the opposition didn't see you. Then, when you were told to talk, you had a fucking *discussion*. You were *diplomatic*. *Nice*. *Considerate*. The corporate assholes called it being 'businesslike.' *Fuck ... the world's going right down the shitter, and everyone wants to be fucking diplomatic.*

"We ought to show ourselves," Big Al said.

"What for?"

"How can we scare the asshole, he don't see us?"

"We ain't *supposed* to scare him."

"Hey, we scare him, he stops moving around so much."

"Sammy wants us to watch him. Quiet-like. No fuss."

"Don't care much for this modern bullshit. Never know who your enemy is."

"Don't care much for it, neither. But it pays the bills."

"You can get fat and sloppy, whacking off in the car while the dickhead you're getting paid to watch is wandering around."

Ricco frowned. "Be patient. Something'll pop up."

"You think so?"

"Like I said, Lee ain't even supposed to be nosing around out here."

"So?"

"He keeps nosing around, we call Sammy. Sammy might tell us to try something else. Maybe something we used to do in the old days."

Big Al grinned, relaxing in his seat.

CHAPTER EIGHTEEN

Taped and blindfolded once again, Sally lay in her little nook behind the front seats while the big vehicle fought heavy traffic.

Working by feel, she had brought the wedding ring back into action. Once she'd sufficiently weakened her bonds, she was determined to free herself as quickly as possible. Her life depended on it. If they knew she'd been bluffing about everything, she was as good as dead.

Being an only child, she inherited everything when her parents died, but nowhere near the amount she'd told her abductors. Thanks to Paul George's excellent legal work, she'd earned slightly more than two hundred thousand dollars from the sale of her parents' house. Minus Paul's fees and other costs, less than a hundred and forty thousand remained. She'd invested the money and turned it into three hundred thousand in just ten years.

Her only other possible source of income was based on the assumption her marriage to Warren wouldn't last--a kind of divorce insurance. The original clause of her prenuptial agreement with Warren, again due to Paul's watchful eye, stated she would walk away with five million if their marriage dissolved after seven years. If the union ended before that period of time, her entitlement would amount to one million in cash and half a million in Bas-Com preferred but would be forfeited if she contested in any way.

According to Paul, the five-million-dollar

settlement was actually the most sensible way Warren could end a marriage. He was worth half a billion dollars and due to mergers and stock dealings, would easily become a billionaire within the next two or three years.

Sally wondered again about the coincidence of being kidnapped so close to the seven-year limit-- only a few weeks left to go. She wanted to believe that Warren wasn't involved in this at all. If she'd been right in her assumption that these two goons who'd grabbed her were former employees given the shaft by her husband, the million-dollar ransom was strictly their own idea. This could be simply an act of revenge. They knew how little a million dollars mattered to Warren. But in their case, it was more than enough to live on for years. Maybe *that* was their revenge.

It was bad enough being kidnapped, but when she thought about the motivation behind it, chills rushed down her back. She sincerely hoped she was right about this being a coincidence, and totally wrong about Warren's involvement. But she had to examine all the possibilities and thinking about Warren engineering this to save himself some money fed her anger and sense of betrayal. It also made her stronger and more determined to fight back.

She stilled, trying to reason this through. The worst-case scenario ... her seven-year stretch as Warren's wife was almost complete, and a kidnapping before she reached that milestone would save him five million. She couldn't see him planning this without her death being the end result.

Dead, she wouldn't be able to fight the original pre-nup.

Would he really arrange something this dastardly for five million, when he could easily be worth a billion in a few years? And would he actually harbor so little regard for her, to want to cause her harm to save himself some money when he already had more than he could reasonably spend in a lifetime? She forced herself to be objective, truthful. *If it meant having to share his wealth and success with an aging wife whose glamour had worn thin ... maybe ... yes..*

She'd always known Warren was cold-hearted, vicious, and merciless—especially when conducting business. She didn't want to believe he was also a monster. Would five million make him consider going to the extreme of having her killed to get her out of the way? Her heart fluttered at the thought. If he had planned this, he probably not only was having second thoughts about the five million and had decided to choose the cheaper way out, he may have also found someone else to become the center of his sexual attention. Getting rid of his current wife—her--would necessarily have to be done before the seven-year target date.

But if he had somehow engineered this skewed plan, why would he have resorted to having two burned employees do the dirty work? Why wouldn't he hire someone professional to make it look like an accident? The only conclusion she could come up with was that he had something on Flighty and Business, to make them agree to go through with this for an agreed-upon amount. A flat million

267

handed to those two would close the matter forever and ensure their silence about what they had done. He'd never have to worry about them coming back on him, or exposing the truth about what had happened to her. Maybe they were supposed to get rid of her so she'd never be found, or at least be found a long, long time later. She shuddered at the thought.

Your fault, Sal. You brought this on yourself. It's what you get for rushing into a marriage to forget a soured love affair.

When she thought of Hank Lee, she wanted to cry. She felt her throat tighten up and fought the sensation. With her hands tied, she couldn't afford to choke on tears of self-pity.

Hank had swept her off her feet with one look of his gorgeous steel-gray eyes. She could have followed him to the ends of the earth. She'd be with him right now if only–

If only he hadn't gone back to his former love.

She'd never forget the afternoon she'd driven over to his apartment to tell him she wanted to move in with him. They'd been seeing each other for six months, and she was certain that with one last nudge on her part, he'd be over Heidi totally. She'd just gotten over her parents dying a few months apart from one another. With Paul's help, she had recently finished handling the estate and had started working in Orlando as a secretary at an insurance firm. She was anxious to get on with the next phase of her life. Meeting Hank had helped considerably. His mere presence had been a most wonderful distraction, speeding up the mourning process and helping her forge ahead. And she wanted to be with him all the time--not just evenings, or on the weekends. She felt they'd reached the next level and wanted this to be her dream romance. Moving in with him would help him recover from his recent divorce and be good for both of them--or so she thought.

But when she buzzed his apartment door and found herself staring at a near-naked blond vision, his ex-wife, she realized that her dream romance was never meant to be. Tall, statuesque Heidi stood proudly in the doorway, hiding some of her flawless nakedness with a jacket she'd pulled from the coat tree. The message was painfully clear--Heidi had come back and was going to stay, this time for good.

Sally turned right around, got back into her Camaro, which was parked beside Hank's blue Lexus, and drove back to her condo. Upset, humiliated, angry, and horribly heart-broken, she got back in her car and drove ... and drove. In no time at all, she reached the beach, where the brisk salt air and the vast openness of the ocean dried her tears and pulled away the suffocating cloak of hurt and regret, making her breathe easier. She walked in the hot sand for hours, the entire afternoon, until it became night.

The tide came in. Then the sun dropped from the sky and set the ocean aflame. She stayed there that night, sleeping in her car, then drove back to her apartment to move out for good. Her cell phone rang several times that day, but she didn't answer. She didn't want to talk to anyone. If it was Hank, she certainly didn't want to talk to him. The mere thought of hearing Hank's voice--of listening to his excuses, his reasons for going back to his ex-wife-- immediately brought back fresh tears. To avoid what would certainly be very painful, she had ignored the irritating protests of the phone. But she knew it probably wasn't him calling. Heidi was back in his life--why would he need anyone else?

She left Orlando that same weekend, took the Interstate down the coast, and stopped in Miami Beach, where she felt reasonably anonymous among the palm trees, the bright sun, and the endless white sand. She took a job as bartender at a small, bamboo-shrouded shack, where everyone was happy and didn't take life too seriously. She worked there several weeks, until a man came in wearing a straw hat, Bermuda shorts, sandals, and the baggiest Hawaiian shirt she'd ever seen. He plopped down on a stool, flashed a smile in her direction, and told her the oldest bar joke in the world. It was just as awful as it was the first hundred times she'd heard it, but she laughed anyway. Making drinks for people and listening to their problems seemed to agree with her. Oftentimes it made her own problems pale in comparison.

Psyched up by her laugh, her new customer told her another one, this one equally bad. She laughed again and quickly remembered how good it felt to laugh, how natural--and how much she missed it. The man turned out to be witty and bright, and made her laugh constantly the entire weekend. She had no idea that he was rich--she just figured he was one of the many software execs coming to Miami for the conventions. But he'd made her feel good about herself for the first time in ages, and she needed that, craved it, and didn't want it to stop.

The man's name was Warren Bascomb, and for the next several weeks, he treated her like a princess. As a result, the hurt gradually grew smaller. After a while, she no longer felt it. It didn't fully disappear, of course. It didn't matter, because she had no illusions that it ever would. The loss of a love like Hank's would forever leave a tender numbness in her heart. She just hoped that one day the hurt would metamorphose into a fond memory she could occasionally revisit without anger or regret.

But even after seven years, and now a victim of this horrible predicament, she still felt the hurt and the betrayal. And with this frightening suspicion hovering about Warren, a new hurt and betrayal had been born, this one far worse than the one caused by Hank.

She just couldn't understand why the memories of the love she'd shared with Hank--hurt and scarred as they were--remained as strong as ever. Compared to the agony of what she now faced, her six months with Hank had become her happy place. And each time she rushed back to it, a feeling of peace and hope overwhelmed her, warming her broken heart.

She wondered how he was doing all these years, if he'd remarried Heidi, if they were finally happy. Funny how those six wonderful months with Hank had popped into her head more and more frequently--especially as things got steadily worse

271

with Warren. It was only natural. *When your life is headed down the tubes, your mind automatically returns to happier times in an effort to eclipse present troubles.*

Once again she cursed herself for bailing, for walking out. She should've confronted Heidi right then, told her how much she loved Hank and would make him much happier than Heidi ever could. She should've stormed right in, gone down the hall, and confronted Hank too, demanding to know why he'd chosen a woman who'd hurt him so much over a woman who'd never hurt him at all. She should have told Heidi to put on her clothes and get out. Forever. But she hadn't. She'd bailed. Quit. Given up. Turned tail.

The anger and regret rushed back, once again with full force. She almost lost it in a fit of sobs, but again, she knew she couldn't allow herself that kind of release in her current predicament. She shook herself out of it and focused on tearing through the tape binding her wrists.

***

From the sheltered bus stop bench one block down from the estate, Hank saw little activity.

Rich neighborhoods didn't see much traffic. *This was good. You don't want witnesses watching you nose around.*

The sound of an approaching bus made him jump up. He jogged across the street, moving in the same direction as the bus. It approached the stop and slowed, then sped up and disappeared around the next bend. Hank went back to the enclosed bench.

The posted bus schedule was printed boldly on

the bulletin board. A quick glance at his watch told him the next stop would be in half an hour. He could probably stay here and observe undisturbed until then.

The distant roar of an engine reverberated from the paved drive of the estate. Since the plexiglass shelter provided ample protection, he was sufficiently concealed. The walls were covered with schedules, local ads, and folks providing their phone numbers for assorted services. He peeked through the slim space between the bus schedule and an ad for someone posting a grainy black-and-white photo of their beloved lost Pekingese.

A dark-brown Volvo stopped near the wrought-iron gate. Hank turned his back to the estate and remained still. Seconds later, the car slipped into gear, then backed up.

Hank turned. The lid of the mailbox was cracked open. Whoever was driving the Volvo had picked up Bascomb's mail.

A few minutes later, the Volvo crawled back down the drive. It paused at the entrance, eased out onto the main road, turned right, and drove away.

Hank left the seclusion of the shelter.

Just as he reached the driveway, the wrought-iron gates hummed closed.

**

Bill Landry parked the four-door pickup near a liquor store facing six busy lanes of Highway 436. The lot was deserted, but the Winn-Dixie farther down kicked ass. Two discarded shopping carts were shoved together and mashed against a telephone pole just a few spaces from their truck.

A constant stream of cars, trucks, SUVs, and tour buses roared past. Propelled by thick columns of exhaust-laden air, a crumpled Mallo Cup wrapper skittered wildly across the cracked concrete, into the path of passing vehicles.

A slender blonde babe sat behind the wheel of a silver Mercedes convertible at the light, running a hand impatiently through her long tresses. Bill sat on the open tailgate beside Schiller, watching her through his cigarette smoke.

"Why'd we stop here, Billy?" Schiller asked.

"I need a little more time to think this out."

"So what're you thinking?"

The blonde shook her head to free some of the tangles, then shrugged to let them fall down over her shoulders. He sighed. "Right now I'm trying to remember the last time I got laid."

"Keep thinking Brazil, Billy. It won't be long now."

Yeah. Brazil. Sometimes the dream seemed so real, he could almost smell the perfume in their hair and taste the salt of sweaty flesh. Other times, like now, the image was all grainy and out of focus, like a dying TV signal. He knew he should be in a much better mood, but somehow the whole idea seemed so out of reach. "Just wondering what can go wrong."

"I wish you'd stop that. It hexes us."

"It's life, Tommy. Life sucks. You know it."

"She's got the money." Schiller still held that wild-eyed look. But at least he was calm.

"This WorldVue thing's bugging me."

"She said she signed all sorts of papers. She

274

probably owns at least part of it." Schiller shrugged. "And if we can get the papers—"

"Then what? It's not like we'll be able to sell the damned thing. Be like trying to fence the Hope diamond."

"Bascomb's got enemies standing in line. They'll jump at the chance to do him in. Even if we can't do anything with the papers, it'll mess him up. He'll be dead in the water. Whipped."

Dead in the water. Whipped. The mere thought made his dark mood dissolve instantly.

"And we'll still have her five mill," Schiller added.

"That's what's keeping me going." He flicked his cigarette at the curb. "Hell, she's been married to that bastard for years. She'd have to be an idiot not to have a giant nest egg."

"And all we have to do is sneak into the estate and take it."

"The stuff's in a *safe*, Tommy."

"I'm sure she'll help us get to it."

He just couldn't wrap his brain around that one. "Bascomb's too fucking paranoid to let someone else have the combination."

"Even his old lady?"

"Especially her."

"I dunno, Billy. There's something about her. I'd trust her with *my* stash."

"You're not Bascomb. He can have any piece of tail he wants. Look how many of those babes in the exec offices he's nailed. They all hate him, but they spread their legs anyway. Babes love money. Bascomb knows that. You think he'd let any of them get her claws on his personal assets?"

"If she's no different from anyone else, why stick with her for so long?"

"Once they get you to sign papers, you're dog food. And once they sign papers that'll keep your ass out of legal trouble, they've got your balls in their hot little hands. Why else would he want her dead?"

"He must not have fussed about it too much, Billy. Not at first, anyway. Otherwise, it would've ended a long time ago."

Bill lit another cigarette. "She's a smart cookie, obviously. She's got her name on WorldVue. Can't get her to sign it back, can he? She knows how much that paper's worth."

"But why would he turn it over in the first place?"

"It wasn't so damned big when it started up."

"He knew it would grow."

"Damned straight. There's not a damned thing that bastard doesn't know about making money. Something tells me he's been planning this merger for years."

"CEO's are always scheming something."

"Damned straight. Look at AT&T. Hell, those bastards have been socking it to their employees so long, they probably get tax incentives for it. The slobs like us, the ones doing the actual work, get squat. But the company makes billions."

"Good thing we'll be getting out of that mess. Maybe forever."

Bill finished his smoke and flicked it across the pavement. Then he jumped back down onto the pavement. "But first, we need to ask her one or two more important questions."

***

Sally jumped when the tailgate slammed shut.

The doors banged open. The truck rocked. The doors thumped closed. The seats squeaked. Her pulse fluttering, she slid the ring back onto her finger, turned it around to conceal the stone, and closed her hand.

A pair of hands grabbed her gently by the shoulders and pulled her into a sitting position. The familiar scent of cigarettes and B.O. stung her nose. She ignored it as well as the hot tingles rushing up her right side. The upright cushion felt wonderful against her aching back.

"We need to get a few things straight." Business pulled the tape from her mouth. "Do you have your own safe?"

"Yes..."

"What's in it?"

In addition to her shares of Bas-Com, Inc., she'd bought two municipal bonds on her own, which she kept in the safe. Their combined value added up to around twenty-five thousand dollars. She owned some jewelry, along with five thousand dollars in cash--her 'mad money' account--which she intended to use if she was able to get out of this. "Cash, Bas-Com preferred, and jewelry," she told Business.

"Anything about WorldVue?"

"No, unfortunately."

"I take it the papers are in his safe."

"Yes."

277

"And you've got the combination to it."

She nodded and hoped with all her heart that her body language hadn't given her away. Warren refused to let anyone have the combination. As far as she knew, it was stored in a sealed envelope in a safe deposit box, available only to his attorney in the event of his death. But these two couldn't possibly know that.

"Why don't I believe you?"

Undaunted, she focused on getting the next part out just right. "Despite his arrogance, Warren knows he's not going to live forever. And if he can't trust his own wife..."

"And everything's there?"

"He likes keeping important papers close."

"You sure?"

"Positive."

"What else?"

"As I said before, I'm sure he keeps most of his preferred stocks in there, as well as a substantial amount of ready cash." She hoped the prospect of getting their hands on cold cash would spark their interest. "Warren likes to have a lot of cash on hand. I wouldn't be surprised at all if he has two or three hundred thousand--even more--in there."

A pause. "And you're sure you can open his safe."

"I have a piece of paper with its combination written down."

"Where is it?"

"In my safe."

Another pause. "You're gonna help us get the papers. Everything involving WorldVue and the merger. Then we'll let you go."

Sally stared into the darkness of the blindfold, trying to visualize their expressions. If only she could feel their moods, their thoughts...

"What's the combination to your safe?"

"I have it written down in my purse."

"You don't have it memorized?"

"I don't go into it very often."

"Where's your purse?"

"On the coat tree in the hall leading to the back door."

"What's it written on?"

"A piece of yellow paper. A receipt from Home Depot. It's in there behind my driver's license."

"Where's your safe?"

"In my dressing room just off the master bedroom. Behind the little bookcase facing the vanity. The bottom swings out."

It was a good plan. Since everything was kept in a different part of the house, it would keep them busy longer. A couple of minutes for them to get inside and grab the purse. A few more to find the combination, rush upstairs, find the correct bedroom and locate the safe. Another couple of minutes to open it, then maybe five minutes to go through everything and discover there wasn't one scrap of paper with a combination written on it.

Fifteen minutes, easy. But once they opened her safe, time would stop. They'd scoop everything out, drop it on the bed, and sift through it. Everything would be right there--jewelry, bond portfolio, cash, stock portfolios. They'd sort through the stocks, then the jewelry and the cash. This might keep them busy even longer.

Something suddenly occurred to her. "What time is it?"

"Why?"

"Our maid has the afternoon off."

"What time does she leave?"

"Two."

A pause. Rustling. Business checking his watch, no doubt. "It's past that."

"Then the house is empty."

"We saw your gardener a few times. Scrawny old Hispanic."

"Emilio leaves before one."

"Pool maintenance?"

"Saturdays."

"What about a dog?"

"No dogs."

"A place like yours should have dogs. Don't you like them?"

"I love dogs. When I was a little girl, we had this adorable little cocker spaniel named Tinsel. She used to wait near the bus stop for me–"

"Why no dogs now?"

"Dogs don't like Warren."

"I understand. Totally. How about security?"

"It's usually on at night. Too many people around during the day. Repairmen, deliveries. We had it on for a while, but it went off whenever someone came up the drive. The police told us to do something about it or they wouldn't come out again."

"So it's not guarded."

"Not until dark. We have motion sensors."

280

"And the maid returns when?"

"She usually comes back at six to fix supper."

The tape was replaced. Sally was pushed gently back onto her side. The truck fired up and began moving. Sally put her wedding ring right back to work.

***

Bascomb's front gate locked with a soft click.

Except for the gate, which looked to be about eight feet tall, the perimeter fence appeared low enough to climb. Judging by how the properties lined up, the rear of the estate butted up to the next street. If so, Hank might be able to sneak in from the rear. As far as he could see, the woods in the rear of the grounds provided ample concealment. As long as no dogs patrolled the premises, he'd be safe.

The house was a different matter. A working security system would limit access. If the system was silent, he wouldn't know when or how it was activated. Consequently, he wouldn't have time to escape.

He had no idea when the maid would return. She could've gone shopping or on other errands. He'd worry about that when the problem presented itself. Right now, his only concern was getting in.

He'd learned long ago that everyone has something to hide. Keeping secrets was human nature. And the richer the individual, the more secrets he had. His plan was to break in and look around, maybe find something that might tell him about Sally. His first trip would be to the master bedroom, where he could check Sally's closet and dresser drawers. Logically, if there were no clothes

281

missing, and if nothing looked disturbed, this would indicate that she'd been gone two days, and something definitely had happened.

If he couldn't find anything this way, he'd deliberately leave clear evidence of his 'visit.' The evidence didn't have to be extreme--a few opened drawers in Bascomb's home office would suffice. He might even enjoy a quick drink from Bascomb's wet bar. If Bascomb was like others of his stature, he'd have a wet bar. He probably wouldn't appreciate seeing an open bottle and half-empty glass sitting on the counter when he came home. When Bascomb realized someone had invaded his sanctuary, it would shock him into making blunders.

Something caught Hank's eye farther up, at the end of the block--a white Dodge four-door truck parked across the street from the 7-Eleven. *Strange*. Only two nights ago, a similar truck had cut him off, reappearing off the shoulder of the GreeneWay less than a mile up the hill from Sally's ditched Mustang. Was it the same vehicle? If so, what was it doing so close to Bascomb's estate?

It wouldn't hurt to check it out.

***

"Can't you wait?"

"I gotta go. *Now*." Tommy couldn't help it. It had been hours since they left the cabin. His bladder was about to pop.

He didn't know why Billy was making a big deal out of this. They were only a block or so from Bascomb's estate, parked across the street from the 7-Eleven. Just two minutes, tops, and they'd be back on their way.

Two Styrofoam cups sat in a pull-out tray on the dash. Billy grabbed one and held it out. "Use this."

Billy had to be crazy. "I *can't*..."

"Why the hell not?"

He turned toward the lady behind them. His skin flushed--just like that time when he was a kid and Mom and his aunts wanted to see where he'd been kicked by one of the neighborhood bullies. He lowered his voice. "Not with *her* right there..."

"She can't *see* you, dammit..."

"Doesn't matter. I can't. I just can't."

Billy put the cup back. "You realize this isn't the right time for–"

"I'll only be a minute." He grabbed the door handle.

"What if they don't have one?"

"They have to. Where's the cashier go?"

"They'll want you to *buy* something..."

"I'll get some cigarettes."

"Need I remind you that the estate probably has a bathroom or two in it?"

"That won't work either."

"Why not?"

Tommy couldn't get those forensic TV shows out of his head. You could really learn some important stuff from them. "I might ... you know..." He lowered his voice to a whisper. "I might ... well, splash..."

"So?"

"Evidence? DNA?"

Billy went silent. He must have been thinking along the same lines. He sighed. "Make it quick."

"I will." Tommy jumped out of the truck.

283

Bill tapped a rhythm out on the top of the steering wheel with his open palms as he eyed the 7-Eleven.

What the hell is that idiot doing?

Just as Tommy pushed open the store door to come out, Bill saw movement in the side mirror. He spun around. Someone was approaching the truck. A big guy –six-two, two hundred, easy – headed briskly for their truck. Half a dozen more steps, and he'd be able to sneak a peek inside.

Bill felt his heart thumping against his chest. *Goddammit, this could ruin everything! Use your head. Asshole probably just wants directions*. But it wouldn't be very bright to let him get too close.

Bill got out. He hoped this wouldn't turn into something bad. With their luck, this would turn out to be a mugging or something. Didn't feel like one, but you could never tell. "Help you?" Bill offered in a clipped tone.

"Just admiring your truck," the big ape said, and kept coming.

Can't let him get closer. How can we stop him? He hadn't been in a fight in years, and Schiller didn't weigh over one-twenty after a heavy meal. He would probably make like the Road Runner anyway, if this guy made a threatening move. The last time Bill had been in a fight, it turned ugly really fast. He was drunk and couldn't see straight. The other guy got in the first one before Bill realized he was actually in a fight in the first place.

It helps when you have some size on your opponent--especially if you aren't very good with

284

your fists.

This was definitely *not* the case here. The man's shoulders were a yard wide. The arms sticking out of the short-sleeve shirt were cut and corded with muscle. *Great. An iron-pumper. Or just some guy who likes carrying around engine blocks in his spare time.*

"Nice-looking piece of machinery."

"Yeah. Nice. Real nice." He couldn't believe he was able to get the words out coherently.

"I've wanted one of these for quite a while."

Bill forced a smile. *Be cool. Don't make him suspicious.* Things were going okay so far. "They're selling them everywhere."

Ape nodded, thinking it over.

Bill had him pegged at around thirty-eight, maybe forty. He had dark-brown hair sticking out from beneath his Gators cap. The way he moved gave the impression he was fit and could kick serious ass. The deep-set gray eyes stayed dead-steady on Bill and made him wonder if the guy could tell what he was thinking. *Silly. No one can do that. He's just putting the hex on you. Snap out of it. Time to start thinking straight.* He knew he had to do something to get them out of this. He just didn't know what.

Ape turned back to the truck. "These pickups are just as comfortable inside as luxury cars nowadays. What sort of gas mileage have you been getting?"

"I haven't noticed."

"Really? With gas so expensive?"

Bill shrugged. "Everyone needs gas. We all have to pay for it, no matter what it costs."

285

"You got *that* right. I'll bet she rides smooth."

"Like silk." He tried holding onto his smile, but it felt like a ton, keeping it up. Fear did strange things to your facial muscles. Made them uncoordinated and sloppy. He couldn't tough this out much longer.

He glanced around quickly. He had no idea where Schiller was. The passenger door was open, but he couldn't see him. Probably puking his guts on the curb.

Ape stood near the rear tire. Another step or two closer, and he'd make out her outline. The windows were tinted, but it didn't matter. If he got close enough, he would see the blindfold and duct tape.

"This new?" He squatted and inspected the running board.

"Yeah. New."

The man straightened. "Would you mind if I took a quick peek at the interior? I promise I'll be–"

"We're ... in kind of a hurry."

"How fast does she go?"

"Whaddya mean?"

"I'll bet she flies. Have you opened her up on the GreeneWay yet?"

Bill nearly choked. "The GreeneWay?"

"You can do a hundred if you want, and don't have to worry about–"

"Over here!" Schiller yelled.

Ape craned his head toward the back.

Schiller said, "There's something really funky over here behind this bush. It looks like ... a human *hand*."

Bill gaped. Could this really be happening?

286

Could Schiller actually be using a brain cell for a change?

The big man disappeared behind the rear of the truck.

Bill quickly scaled the running board. Schiller was already scrambling back in. Bill pulled the door shut and slammed the truck into gear. Schiller slammed his own door shut as the big vehicle scraped its tires against the curb.

Hands on hips, the big man watched them as they pulled away.

***

Warren Bascomb's conference had not gone well.

Despite his efforts, he could not concentrate on business. He had to find out, once and for all, what was going on before he made his call to OPD the next morning. If something had gone haywire, and Lee was getting too close to the action, the whole thing would have to be scrapped. Warren couldn't possibly be implicated in anything remotely scandalous--especially now.

His mind looped as he rushed back to his office. He needed a strong drink before contacting Sam Cole. If Cole needed more men to handle Lee, then that was what had to be done. There could be no more delays.

The phone rang as soon as he circled his desk. It was Cole. "Complications, Mr. B."

Shit. This is not *what I want to hear right now*. It was time for that drink. Complications always went much better with a drink anyway. He switched to speaker. "Talk to me, Sammy." He poured brandy

287

from the wet bar in front of his private bathroom/dressing area. He downed half, then returned to his desk with the glass and the bottle. "And start from the beginning."

"From what my boys told me, here's what went down. Lee's circling the block–"

"Where?"

"I'm getting to it."

"Just don't take all day."

"Anyway, he spots a white Dodge pickup parked near the 7-Eleven about a block down the street and gets closer for a better look. Two guys get out. Driver talks to Lee while the passenger's on the other side of the truck. Then the passenger yells something, and Lee circles the back of the truck. While Lee's behind the truck, the two jump in and drive away."

He scratched the back of his neck. This made no sense. Cole was obviously leaving something out. "So Lee was talking to two men. This should interest me because...?"

"This happened down the block from *your* place."

A chill trickled down his spine. "*My* place?"

"Yes, sir."

"You mean my *house?* My *neighborhood?*"

"You got it."

More chills. "What was Lee doing *there?* And who the hell were those two in the truck?"

"No idea, Mr. B."

He drained his brandy. Too many things were going on. He had to get to the bottom of this quickly. "Describe them."

"One's got dark hair and a full beard. Five-eleven, maybe six feet, thin, with a beer gut, mid-thirties. Other's shorter and skinny, with frizzy red hair. Like the kid that played Little Orphan Annie, only older and scrawnier."

Jesus Christ. Schiller and Landry. What the fuck are those two idiots doing near my house? The original plan was to pick up Sally when she was halfway into her evening walk, which would have put her at least two blocks away. They'd botched it badly. And now Lee knew about the whole thing.

"Mr. B? Still there?"

The realization made the heat swell beneath his collar. He loosened his tie. His heart thumped loudly. He poured more brandy and took another big swallow. Things popped wildly into his head as he stared at the brandy bottle. *Those morons. They're even dumber than I thought. How the hell could they botch such a simple—*

Lee was now in the picture. Others had even seen him. They'd heard him ask about Sally. For some strange reason, he'd expressed concern about her. *Concern can prove fatal if it's misdirected. Many well-intentioned idiots were now dead because they'd stuck their noses in the wrong place at the wrong time.*

He loosened his collar another inch to ease the pressure. Right now, it was manageable. It always grew manageable when things began clicking. When they clicked, everything was okay. Things had clicked ever since he was a kid. He'd always impressed the right people, said the right thing, came into the picture at the right time. Warren

Bascomb--the golden child. A man forever destined to stand on top of the pyramid.

And now, thanks to a nosy idiot who'd expressed an unhealthy interest in Sally's classic car, Destiny had paid Bascomb another visit, offering him an even better, more foolproof way of getting Sally and the other nuisances out of the picture forever.

"Mr. B?" Sammy's voice. "You still there?"

He sat back in the chair. "I'm just fine, Sammy boy. Just fine."

"You sound ... different."

"Those boys of yours?"

"What about 'em?"

"You said they're good. And that they know how to keep their mouths shut."

"They're the best money can buy, Mr. B."

"Then I've got something else for you to give them," he said in a clear voice.

CHAPTER NINETEEN

"*Jeez*, that was close! *Big*-time!"

Tommy stared wide-eyed at the tiny image in the side mirror. The big ape quickly turned into a slim speck in the bright afternoon sun.

Billy gripped the wheel and kept his eyes fixed on the rearview mirror. His right eyebrow twitched. He didn't say anything.

Tommy could tell Billy was just as tense as he was, so he decided not to talk anymore right now. They'd both be okay in a few minutes.

It was a good thing, shaking off that guy. It was a sign. They were meant to do this. Everything would be okay. Signs floated around all over the place. You had to pay attention, or you'd never spot them. That's what his old man always said. You had to study the Bible to know what to look for. The word of God baffled the unholy. You needed to cleanse yourself to become worthy. The old man knew how to cleanse you. He did it with his belt. It hurt like hell, but if you realized all that pain was the sin leaving your body, you'd understand. Cleansing was necessary. The old man had stressed that, time and time again. Once you were cleansed, the sins would no longer cloud your head and make you blind. Then the signs would be revealed.

The signs were either good or bad. If the Lord wanted you to do something, He made His messages easy. Like the parting of the Red Sea. And that yarn about the Loaves and Fishes. But sometimes God made you think for yourself, and that's when Tommy had trouble--no doubt because he'd never liked studying the Bible. He'd only done it as a kid, with the old man standing over him. It scared him mostly, all those people killing and torturing one another. They obviously had trouble reading the signs, too. But the signs were everywhere. Just a few minutes ago, Tommy had seen one. And it was bigger than shit. When it happened, everything sort of cleared up. An explosion went off in his head, and he realized he was listening to a sign. This one said, *"Distract him,"* and just as he was about to wonder how he could possibly do that, the image lying in a bush flashed before his eyes. Just like that.

It was just a Wendy's wrapper, probably had part of a cheeseburger sitting inside, but when he tilted his head just so, the sun bouncing off the side of the truck cast a bright glare on the wrapper, making it look like a human hand. Weird, to be sure. Especially at that moment. That's when he knew there was more to it than just the sunlight going all nutso. It was God personally flashing a sign at him. It had to be, because Tommy wasn't cleansed and needed a little help seeing things.

Or maybe he *was* cleansed... *How can I be cleansed when we're doing this nasty thing?*

Their new scheme, most likely. They weren't going to hurt her anymore. They were going to take her five million and then let her go. And in taking the WorldVue papers, they were doing good because they were interfering with the plans of a truly cruel, evil man. And everyone knew what God thought of cruel, evil men.

That was it all along. They were about to ruin an evil man, and were also going to free the sweet lady he'd wanted dead. In doing so, they'd cleansed themselves. And once they were cleansed, their minds cleared up instantly.

Tommy could finally see things as they truly were. He and Billy could still be caught, of course ... and if they were, they wouldn't go to Brazil, they'd be tossed in prison instead. But this way, the lady would be returned safe and sound, and her husband would face all sorts of hell in his business ventures.

Brazil, here we come!

***

"Pete? Hank here."

"What's up?"

Hank put his binoculars on the seat beside him and sat back. "I was about to ask you the same thing."

"How'd you know I found something?"

"I didn't."

"Good. For a moment I thought maybe I had a sudden attack of Alzheimer's and totally forgot what I'm doing."

"Did you?"

"Not exactly. I did learn a couple of things about your two boys, but nothing that'll help much."

"Tell me anyway."

"William Landry, age thirty-seven, graduated from Rollins fifteen years ago in Computer Science, then hired on at Lockheed until Venture lured him over about four years ago. The man's good with hardware but has a drinking problem. Been to AA twice but couldn't stay with it. His wife walked out on him, and he went off the deep end, nearly killed himself on I-4 one night. Cops picked him up and put him in the tank."

"Got an address?"

"Lives in an apartment complex off East Colonial. I can give you the exact address if you need it."

"Tell me about the other guy. I'm not in the visiting mood at the moment. Besides, I don't think he's there."

"Thomas Alvin Schiller, age twenty-nine. This boy's bright, but a real fruitcake. A computer whiz. He's the nervous pill-popping type most companies won't hire anymore because of extensive Government drug-testing and the heavy penalties they face losing contracts if it's found out they hire addicts. Schiller's been busted for cocaine, amphetamines, and marijuana."

"I also heard he was caught dealing on-property."

"Like I said, a fruitcake. Bascomb apparently fired both Schiller and Landry a while back, although I couldn't find much else about it."

"They were filtering money into dummy accounts."

"I couldn't find anything about legal prosecution. Any ideas?"

"I'm beginning to think Bascomb wanted them for something later on."

"Kind of stupid for a high-profile CEO to even consider. Anything goes wrong, and you can basically kiss your ass--as well as your assets--bye-

bye."

"Couldn't happen to a nicer guy. I'm getting the distinct impression Bascomb might be using Landry and Schiller to get Sally out of the picture."

"That's cold, even for someone as nasty as Bascomb."

"Why else would he send two goons to my place?"

"But why would someone in Bascomb's position do in his wife? Divorce can be expensive, but it's a helluva lot more pleasant and healthier than sharing a five-by-eight cell with Bubba for the rest of your life."

"CEOs don't go to regular prisons, my learned but naïve friend. They're sent to country club facilities."

"My, we're cynical."

"Just jealous."

"Still, why would Bascomb risk anything right now? He's got entirely too much other stuff going on."

Hank shrugged. "Maybe he figures that doing it right now would be good timing. With so many distractions, people tend to get confused."

"I'd still go the divorce route. If it were me, that is. So, she claims half his assets. He'll recoup that in just a couple of years."

"If that merger goes without a hitch, he'll be a billionaire overnight. That's entirely too much money to risk."

"High-profilers always make their women sign pre-nups. It would be stupid not to. Even athletes, rockers, and movie stars are smart enough not to let themselves fall prey to gold-diggers."

"Sally's not a gold-digger."

"I didn't say she was."

"I'm just telling you she isn't. But just for the sake of argument ... what if there wasn't a prenup?"

Pete chuckled. "Warren Bascomb not drafting up a detailed pre-nup? You don't know the man, do you?"

"Not socially, but I'm coming to grips with it."

"I'd say a much cheaper--and safer--bet would be for Bascomb to pay someone to set her up."

"You mean that old motel room con? With a young, good-looking gigolo? Pictures? Tape? News story at eleven?"

"Pay three people five grand each. One does the wining, the dining, and the seduction. Another works the cameras. The third gets two connecting motel rooms ready--one for the action, one for viewing. He makes sure everything's perfect-- lighting, audio, the works. You're much better off shelling out fifteen K than watching the missus march out the front door with half your blood and sweat all snuggly and warm in her hot little hands."

"I can't see Sally letting herself be suckered. But you could be right. I only met him once, but he made quite an impression. He's not what I'd call nice."

"He's been called worse."

"I'm in a charitable mood. But before I forget, check out this plate for me, okay?" Hank gave him the plate on the Dodge pickup.

"Give me a little time with this. I'm finishing up a piece on a developer buying up an old section of ancient oaks in Winter Springs to build a strip mall."

"Let me guess. He's up for the Citizen of the Year award."

"Actually, it looks like someone's put a price on his head. There have already been two attempts on his life."

"That's promising. I was beginning to lose hope for the human race."

***

The truck slowed before turning, then coasted over bumpy pavement for a few seconds before stopping.

It began moving again, then hit what felt like a pothole before accelerating. Sally felt more bumpy, uneven pavement as they went straight for twenty or thirty feet, then slowed once again and sank into another pothole. The pickup began moving again, stopping about ten seconds later. She heard the shifting of gears, then the vehicle stopped again.

What on earth could they be doing now? Sally raised her head and listened. Silence. They weren't talking or even whispering.

The air-conditioning suddenly stopped when the engine switched off. The doors opened, the truck rocked, and the doors slammed shut. Her mind reeled as she tried to imagine what had happened only minutes earlier.

That third voice haunted her. Who were they talking to? Someone approaching the truck? A would-be rescuer?

She struggled to sit up. Her heart pounded as she dared hope. *Rescue. Someone's interested.*

Someone's seen something. That voice. A man's voice ... so familiar. I need to show myself. Just force myself up and somehow smack my blindfolded face right against the rear window and leave it there until–

But there wasn't enough time. The doors had suddenly pulled open just as she was gathering her strength to sit up. Then her abductors jumped back inside and jammed the truck into gear. The forward thrust of the big vehicle knocked her back down onto the floor.

So close. So very, very close... Forget it, Sal. It's past history. Something almost happened, but didn't, and now you've got to finish this yourself. The cavalry only shows up in movies.

But maybe she wouldn't need the cavalry. She listened, but heard only distant traffic. Ten seconds. Twenty. Thirty. A full minute.

More silence. Alone again.

A swell of heat gathered in her numb arms. *This might be it.*

Her heart thrashed wildly as she worked furiously to finish slicing through the tape binding her wrists.

***

Bill Landry hunched over the dirty sink, dousing his face with cold water.

His pale reflection in the filthy mirror showed the face of someone who'd just gotten too close to a very bad place and barely squeaked out of it. After a couple of cold beers, he'd be back to his normal self.

Schiller came over from the urinal, whistling. If

Bill didn't know better, he'd swear the idiot had just gotten laid. His grin made him look dim-witted. Lucky for them, no one else was in the bathroom. Since it was between lunch and suppertime, the Qwik Stop was experiencing a temporary lull in business.

"I take it you're okay now," Bill said.

"*Much* better, Billy. *Big*-time."

Bill dabbed his face with a clump of paper towels. He was really proud of Schiller for what he'd done back there. It wasn't like him at all to keep his cool in a crisis. Thinking quickly under pressure, outside the computer room, was definitely not his thing. "You did good, Tommy. You were cool. But that sure was close."

"It was a sign, Billy." Schiller leaned against the sink and ran water. "It was a sign we can get through this."

Damn, he hated when Schiller brought up that Bible-thumping shit. Little runt always went back to his childhood whenever something happened he couldn't explain. "It wasn't a fucking sign. We just happened to squeak by because you used that brain of yours for once."

"It worked, didn't it?"

"At first I wondered what the hell you were doing over there."

"A sign, Billy." Schiller wiped his hands, then pushed some stray hair out of his eyes. "Brazil, here we come."

"If you're so damned sure it was a fucking sign, did you happen to see any others along the way? Something telling us what we ought to be doing

299

next, maybe? It sure would come in handy."

Schiller thought that over. "That's right. We can't go back there, can we?"

"Not unless you want to see that big ape again."

"He's probably long gone by now."

"You sure?"

"Why would he still be there? He only came over because he said he liked the truck."

"Came over from where? I didn't see a car."

Schiller went silent.

Bill yanked more paper towels from the metal dispenser on the chipped plaster wall and blotted his forehead, cheeks, and beard. "We'd better come up with some other plan quick. If Bascomb makes his call to OPD in the morning, we still have a few more hours to figure something out. But if he decides to be a shithead and makes it this evening, that woman just became a big jug of nitroglycerin we're hauling around." He tossed the crumpled towels in the trash. "We get stopped at all--for *anything*--our asses are toast."

"Why would he change his mind? The plan–"

"Fuck the plan. We're talking Bascomb. We both know that if he gets a wild hair, he'll jump at the chance to fuck us."

"We can't think about that, Billy. He said he'd make the call tomorrow. We have to go by that. You know we can't second-guess him, of all people."

The mere thought of driving back to the estate made him nauseous. He didn't want to tempt fate. "That fuckup just cost us close to an hour. Might as well go back to our original plan."

"You don't mean ... *his* plan, do you?"

"Nothing else makes sense."

Schiller turned pale.

"You still think we ought to go back there and try for the bastard's safe?"

"I really do, Billy. Anything's better than ... than what he ... wants us to do."

"Well, he won't give us a dime if he knows we didn't do it. And he won't know that until he opens that P.O. Box tomorrow morning and examines that little package he expects from us."

Schiller turned away.

"Face facts, Tommy. We do that, or we drive back to the estate and try the safe. But if that big ape's back there, we might as well kiss our asses good-bye."

Schiller stared at his reflection in the smudged mirror.

"Something bugging you?"

"I've ... seen that guy before, Billy. I know I have."

He blinked. "You sure?"

"This is really weird. Big-time."

Bill leaned against the sink and scratched his beard. It *was* weird. Doubly weird, since the damned idea had drifted into his head as soon as Schiller mentioned it. *Damned straight.* They'd seen the big ape before. In a suit. And without the Gators cap. "Remember where?"

"It wasn't too long ago."

Bill's mind reeled. It *was* a suit. At night. *Tillie's Tavern.* The image jumped out in front of him. The GT-350. The payphone. The cream-colored Caddie.

"That guy in the bar parking lot. We thought he was after Bascomb's old lady, and we cut him off." Images swept past wildly. "He was watching Bascomb's old lady while she was trying to make her call."

Schiller's eyes grew. "I *knew* I remembered him."

This was just too damned coincidental. Why would that same guy be nosing around Bascomb's estate?

"Bascomb's been pulling something all along, Tommy. I know he has."

"You think he knows that guy?"

"No idea. But doesn't it seem odd that's he's been popping up since this damned thing started?"

Schiller suddenly appeared pensive. "Maybe he's not working for *Bascomb*, Billy..."

"Who else would he be–"

"I know we like her and all. But maybe she actually *knows* this guy."

"How?"

Schiller shrugged a shoulder. "You know..."

"You don't honestly think..." The idea was ridiculous. But the more he thought of it, the more he realized anything was possible. Maybe he'd been right about Sally Bascomb all along. She was definitely a princess, and all princesses were basically the same. Demanding. High maintenance. Eye candy. Controlling.

Although Bascomb hadn't told them his reasoning for wanting Sally dead, Bill and Schiller had never really thought too much about it. It didn't matter to them, so why worry about it? They had to

302

do it, or their asses were fried--why quibble about the reason behind it? The job was plain and simple-- snatch the wife, hold her for forty-eight hours, then get rid of her.

But when she told them about the WorldVue papers and all the other companies Bascomb had transferred in her name, they both assumed this was about money. Ownership. Control. Business. But it wasn't. This wasn't about the WorldVue papers at all, but about something else. Something much more basic. The oldest revenge there was.

"She's been playing us, Tommy. All along."

Schiller just shrugged. "You think I'm *right*? I was just thinking out loud."

"I think you're right. About everything."

"But ... how can you think—"

"You know what they say, don'tcha? If someone lies about one thing, everything else coming out of their mouth is also a lie."

"But ... I didn't mean all *that*, Billy. I was just trying to figure out why that big guy's been hanging around."

"I know. But when you did that, you jarred something loose that's been bugging me about her ever since we first started talking to her. Why she's so nice. So sweet. It isn't natural, someone that *pure* grabbing onto Bascomb. You know it as well as I do. She's got him by the balls, and she's been holding on for years. Bascomb's too much of a bastard to let any female do that."

"So you think she met that big guy and started ... *doing* him?"

"Exactly."

303

"But ... the bar ... they didn't seem to know one another."

"They were probably play-acting. For all they knew, someone hired by Bascomb could've been watching from across the road with a high-powered lens."

"So she probably made a date to meet him somewhere else?"

"Could be..."

"And she would have, if we hadn't split them up?"

"Now you're getting it."

"What about that payphone thing?"

"Who knows? She might have been trying to call someone else to give them some bullshit story. For an alibi, maybe. She probably didn't want to use her cell because it could be traced."

"Why didn't he stop on the GreeneWay when she ran out of gas? He could've helped her so she didn't have to get out of her car."

"Same reason why they played it cool at Tillie's. Someone paid by Bascomb could've been watching her. If anyone had seen them together, that would be it for both of them."

"I dunno, Billy. I like her. I don't think she'd do stuff like that. I don't ... I don't know *what* to think now..."

"Well, I happen to think she's just as bad as Bascomb, only in a much more dangerous way."

"How?"

"I intend to find out." He approached the door. He was all tense and hot, and his hands had curled into tight fists. He knew he should settle down, but

304

he didn't like being played--especially by another babe. It was one thing to be played by a babe you were gonna get lucky with, but quite another when you were dealing with some other guy's property. He knew he'd better settle down, or Sally Bascomb would be carrying around some fresh bruises in her final hours.

"Billy? You're wearing your mad face."

"That's probably because I'm madder than hell right now. I have a feeling that bitch deliberately steered us back to the estate so her big bad boy-toy could have a go with us."

"But if she's a liar, as you said–"

"She'll tell us the truth this time, Tommy. I guarantee that."

"How can you guarantee *that*?"

"Just watch me." Landry yanked the heavy door open and bulled his way through the doorway.

CHAPTER TWENTY

As the Beach Boys performed "*I Get Around*" from the dash player, Hank relaxed in the seat and waited patiently for Pete Hayes to return his call.

His CD, tape, and record collection back at the apartment consisted mostly of bands and groups from the sixties. He also owned vintage recordings of Blood, Sweat and Tears, Chicago, Chase, and the Tijuana Brass.

He never liked the stiff canned music that was popular while he was growing up. When he went to Saudi and found himself elbow-to-elbow with guys ten and twenty years older than he was, he was introduced to a higher class of music, and found himself irrevocably hooked. The Beach Boys, Beatles, Stones, Frankie Valli and the Four Seasons, as well as many of the bands and groups that had performed during the Woodstock Festival in '69, had become his biggest source of solace after a hard day at the office. Although he grew up in the seventies, he'd never liked that decade, and found himself transported to an instant happy place whenever he heard something from the sixties, which, in his own personal view, was the greatest decade ever for popular music.

Right now, as he faced the wooded grove behind the Lutheran Church, waiting for Pete's call, he needed something to help him relax. That last encounter with Landry and Schiller had knocked him for a loop. He'd been afraid those idiots would attempt to back into him and had moved as quickly as possible to get out of their way. Fortunately, they were just as anxious to get away from him as he was to dodge the rear bumper of the truck.

His cell phone buzzed.

"Mr. Lee?" The breathy voice conjured up a clear image of blond hair, long, slender legs, and *Tabu*.

He killed the volume on the CD player. "Alicia?"

"Just wondering how you're coming along." Her voice was almost a whisper. She was probably calling from work. "And I have something to tell you. Something else I just found out."

"I was just talking to those two. Which one's the redhead?"

"Schiller." A pause. "You were *talking* to them?"

"I sort of, well, *coaxed* my way into their little world--just as I did with Bascomb."

"Where was this?"

"About a block from Bascomb's estate. What were you going to tell me?"

"Our hush theory turned out to be true. Bascomb spent a full afternoon with Landry and Schiller at Venture. After that, things quieted down. My friend said both Landry's and Schiller's names were taken out of the employees' accounts, and now there's nothing that even mentions them in Personnel. Whatever they did must've been really bad."

"Why didn't he have them arrested?"

"Exactly. Not long before all that happened, Schiller had been bragging to one of his geeky buddies about hacking into AT&T's databanks. He did stuff like that all the time--even developed viruses to prevent anyone from getting into his

307

programs. The viruses automatically deleted files and worked their way into your hard drive if you opened certain attachments. Needless to say, nobody messed with his stuff. Tell me about your talk with them. What were they doing at Bascomb's estate?"

"They were parked about a block away, across the street from a 7-Eleven. I figured they were about to go inside to buy cigarettes or beer. Like I said, I tried talking to them, but they did everything they could to get rid of me, short of running me over with their damned truck."

"Truck?"

"A Dodge four-door pickup. It might be rented."

"This is really weird."

"That's what I thought, especially when Landry got all tense as soon as I got too close. Is that all you wanted to tell me?"

"I also found out from one of the girls Landry dated a couple of years ago that he camps on weekends. He usually brings a couple of friends, lots of beer, and goes out on a small boat."

"Any place in particular?"

"A camp near Lake Maitland. Apparently there's an isolated spot with maybe a dozen cabins there. I think they call it Angler's Corner, or something equally tacky. Landry bought a cabin out there. When his wife divorced him, it was the only thing she wasn't able to steal from him--or so he's told everyone. But he loves to fish and spends most of his spare time out there."

"Got an address?"

"No. But I hear it's not difficult to find."

"You think they might be staying there?"

"I can't think of anything else he'd do if he just lost his job and was forced to move. If he and Schiller are planning something, they'll need a place to hide, right?"

Something about this didn't make sense. "But everyone probably knows about it."

"That's right. It'd be stupid for them to go there."

"Unless they're not planning to be there long."

***

It took Sally forever to undo the tape wrapped around her ankles.

She had to work much faster this time. They turned off the air before leaving the truck. Despite the cracked windows, the interior was already very warm.

Aside from the sounds of distant traffic, she heard nothing familiar. She had no idea where she was, of course. Once she'd freed her wrists and yanked off the irritating blindfold, she did a quick scan while furiously pulling at the tape around her ankles.

The truck was surrounded by trees, tall weeds, and other wild growth. Directly ahead, a small ramshackle building, overcome with weeds and bushes, sat a few feet off the path. Tossed garbage littered the pavement. About a hundred yards or so beyond the bushes, a huge yellow arch hovered behind the trees.

McDonald's. They were probably in a vacant field backing up to it that hadn't yet been slated for development. It was a good place to leave her

309

temporarily. No one would see her or the truck. But it made her wonder where they'd gone. And for how long.

It doesn't matter. All that does matter is that you'll soon be free. Free!

In her excitement, she was all thumbs. She repeatedly groped for the ends of the tape, but her nails just wouldn't cooperate. Her fingertips had gone numb. She eventually got the corner pulled up, then managed to gain a good grip. However, her limbs were too cramped and tingly, and her nerves too jumpy to get everything working properly. Once the last of the tape was wadded up and tossed on the floor, she pushed herself up.

Her hands shook as she grabbed the door handle. Her skin tingled as she opened the rear door and pushed. She straightened, but her legs were stiff and numb. *This isn't the time!* She massaged them furiously--one leg, then the other--then forced herself down onto the cracked pavement.

And collapsed.

No! Not now!

She forced herself up and took a quick survey. The woods would provide ample cover--*if* she could crawl far enough into the brush before Business and Flighty came back. *Do it! Now!*

Dragging her useless legs behind her, she crawled into the wild brush. After crawling about twenty feet, she tried to stand. Her ankle turned, stabbed at her, then went numb, bringing her back down. Then she realized her mistake. *They'll see me if I get up and try to run.*

She resumed her crawl, forgetting all about

310

snakes and poison ivy and anything else her childhood memories and frightened imagination conjured up. Her fears about nature's dangers vanished as soon as she brought herself back into the present, focusing on her predicament. *Move! Crawl! Got to get away!*

A flurry of movement out of the corner of her eye arrested her attention. The sudden rustling behind her made her heart skip a beat. She froze for one second only, then resumed her crawl feverishly, even as the footfalls behind her grew louder.

Something heavy, warm, and tight grabbed her left ankle and pulled. Despite her efforts, she was flipped over on her back. They were right there, standing over her, a fierce expression covering Business's bearded face, one of alarm taking over Flighty's pale, bony features.

Get away! Kick them! Use your feet! They still work, so use them! Panic screamed at her. *Now! Do it!*

The slimy warm lump in her throat went down slowly, like the sinking of a ship. *Do it. Kick them in the face. Scramble to your feet. Run like you've never run before, and you're home free.* She brought her knees back and let them have it.

Her right foot connected, catching Flighty squarely in his skinny chest and knocking him down on his back. Her left nearly caught Business, but he grabbed her foot and twisted, flipping her over. Her face slapped weeds and grass and loose brush. A mashed beer can sticking out of the clump of loose sand caught her shoulder, digging in. Despite the sudden sharp pain rushing down her arm, she began

311

crawling away again, even as Business grabbed her ankles and pulled her back.

Kick him again. Knock him down. Then you can get to your feet and try to run.

Using both feet, she pulled loose, turned on her side, brought her knees back and kicked out at him again. This time her left heel thumped him on the upper part of his arm, knocking him over. He cried out and fell backwards, and soon he and Flighty were both on the ground in the tall brush, pushing one another away so they could regain their footing.

Gritting her teeth, Sally forced herself to her feet. Ignoring the intense pain in her thighs and calves, she made her way deeper into the woods, with the yellow arch beckoning just seventy or eighty yards beyond. If she could just reach it. If she could be seen. If she could wave her arms even before she reached the clearing...

The footfalls behind her once again grew louder. They were gaining on her. She opened her mouth to scream–

And it instantly turned into a sharp, high-pitched squeal when one of them suddenly pushed her between the shoulder blades, forcing her roughly to the ground.

NO!

Sharp sticks and twigs stabbed her, cutting into her arms and sides. *Ignore the pain. Get away.* A blistering spike of sheer terror drove through her. Sharp jabs of hot jagged pain turned her legs into useless slabs of meat. Fighting the serrated pain in her elbows from her fall, she rolled away in an attempt to gain some ground. Then she could get

312

back up and—

They'd caught up to her again.

Get up! Get away! Run!

A heavy bolt of hot pain lashed out in her ankle, tearing a shriek from her throat.

Someone grabbed her arms and pushed her down again. The ground thumped the right side of her face. She opened her mouth for another attempt to scream. It was promptly stifled when something soft was shoved in her mouth. Her arms were pulled behind her and another angry knot of bright pain danced across her shoulders and down her back. A single blade of grass pressed gently against her eyelid. It was warm from the sun, smelling of dirt. A whiff of stale beer told her this was not a good place to be. A smashed Coors can sat near the bush just a few feet away, winking at her.

She lay there, trembling. The jackals hovered over her, preparing her. The wild bushes hid them all from view. The restaurant might have been a hundred miles away. Her killers could work at their leisure. She was much too weak with fear and exhaustion to resist. Her tingling feet were grasped, held together and brought up. Tape screeched from the roll. It was wrapped quickly around her ankles, then ripped free.

The horrible reality slapped her squarely in the face. She'd seen them, could describe them.

The ground quickly moved away. She was picked up and half-dragged, half-carried back through the weeds. Every clump of bush, every dip in the ground, every item of trash, slapped her agonizing ankles, driving jolts of pain rushing up

313

her limbs.

The flight back to the truck seemed endless. Much longer and more unpleasant than the trip out. The last mile. Her walk to the gallows.

She was then shoved into the back of the truck. One last strip of tape was yanked from the roll to seal the wadded scarf in her mouth. Through the terrible humming of the hot pain in her legs, she could tell they were pulling them up and back, fastening them to her taped wrists with rope.

Her blindfold was not replaced. It was now stuffed in her mouth. There was no further need to cover her eyes.

They slammed the doors shut and situated themselves in their seats. The smell of their sweat, thick and foul in the confined space, nauseated her.

The truck quickly backed out of its space. Sally closed her eyes and whimpered softly.

***

Ricco Arragon pocketed the cell phone, put the binoculars back in the console, and flicked on the ignition.

"What the hell we doing now?" Big Al asked.

Ricco pulled out of their spot behind some bushes and took the van down the block. Lee's Caddie was still parked in front of the grove on the other side of the church parking lot. It had been parked there the last hour or so. Ricco hated leaving the area, but orders were orders.

"Got good news." It *was* good, although Ricco didn't feel particularly thrilled at the moment. He didn't like it when a job turned every which way. It suggested the man in charge didn't know what the hell he was doing.

But at least Big Al would like what would be going down.

"I'm listening."

"Those jerks in the white truck? Sammy says we got to cap them."

Big Al's eyes grew. "No shit?"

"No shit."

"What about the other guy? Lee?"

"Him, too. But we do it quiet, then find a good place to dump them."

A broad grin took over Big Al's large features. This stuff really turned him on. "Why the sudden change?"

"Mr. Boss-Man, he don't want Lee around no more. He also don't want those jerks sniffing around his place."

Big Al scratched his massive jaw. It sounded like he was scraping rough sandpaper. "Ricco, what *is* all this shit?"

Ricco lit a cigarette from the dash lighter. "Who knows? It starts out a simple tail. Mr. Boss-Man wants us to watch Lee 'cause he thinks maybe Lee's working for the competition. Next thing you know, there's these two other jerks in the picture, fucking things up. So now we got to get rid of everybody."

"What did they do?"

"The way I understand it, Mr. Boss-Man's old lady's been fucking around with Lee. Mr. Boss-Man thought Lee was working against him when all Lee was doing was banging his woman."

"What about those other two morons?"

"Seems Lee was paying them to keep an eye on

Mr. Boss-Man. Lee don't want him to know what he's been doing, so..."

"Looked like they had a tiff out near the big man's estate."

"They probably wanted to squeeze Lee for more, but Lee told them no, and now those two are pulling something."

"And Mr. Boss-Man found out?"

"He also found out his woman and Lee were planning to bleed him for a couple million. So now we gotta dump all four of them."

Big Al sighed. "That's *low*, Ricco. *Real* low."

"Hey, he's paying the bills."

Big Al turned away. "Don't like dumping old ladies."

"Mr. Boss-Man wanted to just toss her ass out, leave her high and dry, but when he found out about their scam, he upped the stakes. Can't blame him none--not when so much money's involved."

Big Al scowled. "This still sucks."

"Ten K per. That's forty grand. Sammy takes his usual ten percent off the top, we get what's left."

Big Al shook his head.

Ricco sighed. The big boy was a fucking good soldier when that stubborn Sicilian temperament didn't get in the way. But Ricco couldn't blame him. Ricco didn't like wasting females, neither. But sometimes you had to do things you didn't want to do.

"Dunno, Ricco. Never dumped a female before. My momma always told me--"

"You're pushing *fifty*." Sometimes this gorilla worried him.

"Grew up with five sisters and a shitload of aunts. Nuns did a job on me, too, so I guess I should hate females. But I still don't like capping them. It ain't dignified."

"What about that hooker last year? The one Johnny Deuce contracted you for when she split on him in Boca?"

"I'd have done her for free. Bitch gave me the clap."

"You never said nothing about that."

"Too pissed and embarrassed."

"I hear ya."

"But this chick?" Big Al shrugged his massive shoulders. "Maybe she *was* fucking around. Maybe she had a good reason to. Even so, I'll feel *funny*, Ricco."

"We'll work something out, okay?" Ricco pulled out onto the main stretch and headed north on Semoran.

"Where to?"

"Some fish camp. It's about an hour from here. Sammy says one of those assholes has got a cabin."

Big Al's jaw dropped. "A fish camp? The fucking boonies?"

Ricco held back a laugh. Simon could strangle three guys at once, no sweat. But you get his feet wet, and he went all girly on you. You just couldn't take Brooklyn out of the big fuck.

***

Even with the air-conditioning set on ice-cold, Bill Landry sweated freely as he forced the truck through the heavy rush-hour traffic.

With shaky fingers, Schiller tried pulling a

317

cigarette from the pack. Half of them spilled out, rolling onto the floor. He retrieved most of them, thumping his head on the dash while picking them up. He didn't seem to notice. He'd slipped into a kind of weird fit while trying to spark the lighter. It wouldn't work--he was shaking too much. The flame danced erratically in front of him. He watched it as if he had no idea what it was.

Bill yanked the lighter away, thumbed a new flame, and held it as steady as he could, although he was pretty shaky himself. Once it was lit, Schiller leaned back, puffing away.

Bill grabbed one of the three cigarettes still lying in Schiller's lap, lit up, then gave the lighter back. He hardly noticed the road ahead of them. The road or the traffic. Everything had become a blur. A vast emptiness.

Their new reality had delivered a swell of heat plunging down his back like a bucket of razor blades.

Schiller stared straight ahead, puffing steadily on his cigarette. Bill hoped his friend hadn't gone inside his head. When Schiller went inside his head, he wouldn't come back unless you slapped the shit out of him.

"You know what this means?" Landry said quietly. "It means–"

"Bascomb. He ... planned this all along." Schiller's voice was a whisper. He still stared straight ahead. "All along."

"He wants her dead, Tommy. We both know that."

"I know..."

"He wants us to do it."

"We were gonna ... let her go."

"We can't do that now."

"But–"

"She's a *witness*. You know what a witness is, don'tcha?"

"I'm not an idiot."

"That's not what I meant."

"We can't do this. We can't hurt her. The signs–"

"*Fuck* your signs. We *have* to."

"We *can't*."

"You want to let her go just because of that big ape?"

"It's wrong, dammit. Wrong."

"I know..."

"This sucks." Schiller turned. Though his lower lip trembled, his small, pale blue eyes were dead-steady. "Really and truly."

"Stop it."

No need to think about that. Not now. It wasn't their fault the plan had just gone down the shitter. Wasn't their fault the woman tried getting away and ended up seeing their faces. He had planned doing her all along. Schiller didn't know that, but now it didn't matter.

Bill hated doing this--not because he had any reservations about offing a pampered bitch, but because he hated doing anything that would benefit Bascomb. Bascomb was a bastard. *He* was the one who deserved to die. Bill couldn't blame this woman for cheating. The bastard deserved every damned thing he ever got. He deserved losing *something*. It would be much better if he lost something he really loved--his fortune, most likely--but that was out of the question now. A lot of things were out of the question now.

That dismal day at Venture, when Bascomb had summoned them into his private office, then stood over them as they sat trembling in the soft padded chairs, had sealed their doom. Hardcopy printouts covered the surface of the massive desk in front of them. Printouts of detailed transactions, totaling more than a million dollars, that could be directly traced to consoles accessible only to Tom Schiller and Bill Landry.

He should've just had us popped. We should've let him do it. Told him to do it. Begged him.

But they hadn't. They'd been afraid to open their mouths that day. Both he and Schiller had sat in that room, listening to the man's threats. His promises. Worst of all, his proposition. And because of it, they both now faced something much worse than death or imprisonment.

320

CHAPTER TWENTY-ONE

After leaving the Caddie in the side lot of the car rental agency, Hank squeezed carefully behind the wheel of the dark-brown Saturn two-door sedan.

Based on what had happened at his apartment, he guessed too many people had seen the Caddie. He had to make the switch while he still had time. He didn't want anyone to know he was coming.

He got right back on Semoran, driving north in the heavy late afternoon traffic. He wasn't worried about the traffic at all. In fact, he barely noticed the solid three-lane wall roaring around him. He was thinking about what had to be done. Hopefully, he could find the fishing camp. Then, maybe, he could find Landry's cabin. And maybe even Sally, if they were holding her there.

He also hoped she was still alive and unhurt. He hoped that for several reasons, one of which was that Warren Bascomb's future depended on it.

About half an hour later, he slipped into a 7-Eleven on Highway 1792, just a few miles outside Sanford.

The store was nearly deserted, the tang of burnt coffee a heavy mist filling every corner in the bright cluttered room. He found a payphone near the door marked *OFFICE* and opened the Yellow Pages. The section marked *Camps, Recreational* displayed a short list in the immediate area, all but one on the other side of the lake.

The short white-haired clerk had just finished ringing up purchases for a stocky guy in Bermuda shorts, tee shirt, and flip-flops buying gas, Lotto tickets, and a six-pack of Bud Lite. The bell above the door jingled as the customer left. The clerk popped a cherry Life Saver into his mouth and adjusted his thick glasses.

Hank leaned over the counter. "Where's the closest fish camp around here?"

The clerk coughed wetly, nearly swallowing his Life Saver. "There's only one, you wanna call it that. Glen Haven. Two dirt roads out there, maybe a dozen cabins, but the locals like it. Fish and Game guys stock it once in a while, mostly catfish and mullet, but the locals head out there just to get away. Need a license?"

"No, thanks. I just—"

"Don't have your license?" His thick white brows bumped together. "You could be in for trouble." He sucked noisily on his Life Saver while sizing up Hank. "Fish and Game guys out here? They mean business. Those danged tourists." He quickly lowered his voice. "Come down here and clutter up the highways. They—"

"Where's the camp?"

He jabbed a fat red thumb at the large tinted window behind him. "Down the road, maybe a mile, take the first right."

"Ever hear of Angler's Corner?"

"It's down there toward the end. Road turns to sand, then forks. Angler's butts up to the lake. Take a left, keep going straight."

"Thanks." Hank headed for the door.

"Need a license? We do those here, you know."

"I never would've guessed."

"Get you started in just a few minutes. No problem."

"You do marriage licenses, too?"

The clerk squinted. "You serious, Mister?"

Hank winked. "Not that time."

The clerk studied him a few seconds, then grinned. "I get it. A joke, right?"

"Can't fool you, can we?"

The clerk chuckled. "A good one." He turned serious. "You sure about the fishing license? Only takes a couple minutes—"

"Some other time. Thanks." Hank pushed open the door.

"Watch out for those Fish and Game guys. They're all over. And they mean business."

***

Bill Landry's hands shook badly as he tied Sally Bascomb securely to a kitchen chair.

Twice he'd gotten his thumb caught in a knot and was forced to redo it. Schiller had already scurried back outside. He'd made tracks as soon as he and Landry had half-carried her in and set her down in the chair. The little twerp acted like he was about to throw up.

Concentrate on the job, dammit. Get the knots pulled tight. Then you can get the hell outside and inhale some fresh air...

But ignoring the long blond hair, as well as the fine figure, instantly proved difficult, making the process quite a painful ordeal.

Once he'd finished tying her bound wrists to the back of the chair, he hurried back outside as well.

He desperately needed a drink. Not beer,

whiskey. As he trudged unsteadily down the overgrown path to the dirt road, shaking, his guts throbbing, he craved a full bottle to help him through this.

Schiller shuffled up and down the road, kicking sand and mumbling to himself. Glints of orange peeked through the gnarled branches of the scrubs from the lake reflecting the sunset. The water was mirror-still. He longed to be in his boat right now, dozing after polishing off a bottle of whiskey.

Schiller began kicking sand with much more force. Ready to freak, obviously. But Bill couldn't let that happen. Not now. They had to finish this quietly, salvage what was left of the original plan. If it worked, fine. If not, they had to find some place to go where they could start all over. The beard had to go. Probably the hair as well. No biggie. The buzz cut was popular nowadays. And it made everyone look alike.

"She won't suffer," he told Schiller, knowing damned well how stupid that sounded.

"I already told you, Billy ... we don't need to *do* this."

"She's *seen* us." That fact alone made this necessary.

"This is crazy. *We're* crazy. *Everything's* crazy."

"It's been this way since the beginning."

"That big ape. It's his fault, Billy."

"It doesn't matter whose fault it is."

"If he hadn't been there–"

"Drop it." Talking about this wasn't working. Schiller didn't need to be here right now, complicating things. "There's that liquor store two

324

miles down. Go get us a couple bottles."

"You ... don't want me driving."

"Two miles down, two miles back. What can happen? This is more important. By the time we're finished, she won't feel a thing."

Schiller's eyes grew. "You mean ... you're gonna do it while–"

"No other choice."

"She'll *suspect* something, Billy..."

"She'll be out of it. Trust me."

Schiller turned away.

"I still have some chloroform left. After I get her drunk, I'll cover her face. Then we can cut off her–"

"Don't want to *hear* that!" Schiller covered his ears.

He pulled Schiller's arms down to his sides. The little runt needed a good hard slap right now. But that wouldn't work any better than talking. Schiller would withdraw and wouldn't come back--possibly for weeks.

He forced himself to ignore his quivering nerves, his aching gut. "Once it's done," he said in a softer voice, "we'll get out of here and spend the night closer to town. I'll drop the package in the post office box, then make the call. We should be able to pick up the money tomorrow night."

Schiller went right back to watching the lake. He was beginning to withdraw. "I like her, Billy." His voice sounded far away. "She's nice. Sweet. And really–"

"Stop it." He pulled some bills from the dwindling wad in his pants pocket. "Buy a bottle of Jack's and some cognac. Go get the stuff while I

325

start her up with what's left of that pint from the glove box."

Schiller took the bills and studied them.

"What's wrong?"

"Can't we just ... leave her here and–"

"I told you to stop it. You're pissing me off."

"Billy, this is *wrong*. *Big*-time."

"I know it's wrong, dammit. But we've been penned into a corner. This is the only way I know to get out of it."

"It's just so *wrong*... "

"You still want to go back to the estate and try to get that money? After she's seen our faces? What if we run into that big ape again? What if Bascomb's there this time? What if he gave up waiting to hear from us and has the cops out looking for us?"

Schiller was staring at the sand at their feet. "Billy..."

The more they prolonged this, the harder it would be. "Shut the fuck up and get the damned whiskey!"

Head still lowered, Schiller circled the truck and climbed in.

Bill opened the passenger door, dropped the glove box lid, and pulled out the half-empty bottle. He slammed the door shut, unscrewed the cap, and quickly sucked down an inch or so.

As Schiller inched the big truck down the sandy path, Bill faced the cabin and had another stiff belt to give him courage. Hopefully, two or three more belts would be all he needed to get through this.

***

The bumpy road went straight for about two

hundred yards before veering off.

The wooded terrain revealed nothing. No lights flickered beyond the trees to indicate occupied cabins. The dark desolation of the woods caused an eerie effect. The hair on the back of Hank's neck bristled. *A perfect place to hold a captive woman.*

He coaxed the Saturn into a small clearing amidst some overgrown bushes. A narrow, twisted sandy path branched off to the right, leading to a dark cabin sleeping in a grove of scrubs about fifty yards from the road. A crumbling wooden shed beside it housed a small motorboat, a junk TransAm, and an old freezer chest stacked with magazines.

Hank parked in front of the TransAm. From here, he couldn't see the main road. This seemed like a safe place to hide the Saturn. There were no signs of life coming from the cabin.

He opened the console, pulled out the .380 Cheetah he'd brought with him, and checked the clip. Hopefully, he wouldn't have to use it. But if he did, he could get it out in a hurry.

He pocketed the gun and quietly got out of the car.

It was past eight. The approaching darkness cloaked the woods in a thin gray shroud. The pines whispered with the warm breeze brushing through them. Mosquitoes had already tainted the muggy night air.

A square wooden structure sat in a loose cocoon of scrubs on the other side of the bend. The black oblong windows suggested the place was closed. A sign marked *BAIT & TACKLE*, scribbled sloppily in black paint, hung over the cedar entrance. Also, advertised was 'fishing licenses, bait, tackle, smokes, chewing tobacco, adult movie rentals. And at the bottom, scrawled in the same slapdash manner on the peeled surface of the door, was the proclamation: ENGLISH *ONLY* SPOKE HERE! ESPANOL NO COMPRENDO! A coke machine and an ice chest hummed and clicked against the far wall on the concrete slab.

Hank crept silently down the dirt path.

***

A Honda Accord, a Toyota Sienna, and a silver Dodge Charger sat in front of the liquor store at the corner.

A young, black-haired Barbie doll wearing sprayed-on jeans and a yellow sleeveless tank top trotted out, carrying a bag. She slid her fine ass into the Charger, backed up, and pulled out into the heavy evening traffic.

From his spot facing the store, Ricco watched her disappear in the stream. He'd enjoy nailing that. Sure were tons of high-quality stuff down here. One of the many things he loved about Florida. Babes strutting around, lots of tanned flesh showing, with no cold months to keep them bundled up.

But not much action here--not even with the weekend coming up. The store should be thumping, folks gearing up to get wasted. Sammy told him this place did a lot of business with the weekend fishermen and the tourists. He didn't know where Sammy got his information. Going by the near-empty parking lot, their boss had been slightly misinformed.

"Whatta we doing here?" Big Al yawned and rubbed his eyes. He spotted the liquor store straight ahead. "Buying some *vino*?"

"No booze till after the job."

"So why we here?"

"I'm gonna go inside and ask directions, make sure we know where the fuck we are. That cabin ain't far, but I'm not sure which road to get on."

"Take your time."

"You saying that 'cause you like it here? Or 'cause you wanna take another nap?"

"Love it here. Always wanted to retire to the fucking boonies."

Ricco snickered. "Maybe we'll find a vacant shack out there by the lake."

"Funny." Big Al leaned back, squirmed into a comfortable position, and closed his eyes. "Wake me when the shit starts."

A white pickup pulled into the lot and parked in front of the store beside the Toyota. It was the same rig they'd seen near Mr. Boss-Man's estate. The same truck Lee had been sniffing around. Ricco remembered the plate number. It started with a 7 and ended with two 7's. It stood out because Ricco's lucky number was 7.

The taillights darkened. A skinny redheaded dude climbed down. He nearly stumbled, using the side of the truck for support. Once he was upright, he shuffled inside.

Dude looked like one of the two jerks Lee was talking to. He was also one of the four they were being paid to cap.

Funny thing, though. He didn't seem the type to

have the 'nads necessary to squeeze money from a guy as tough as Lee. But hell, you just never knew what turned an asshole's crank these days.

Skinny appeared slightly wasted. And he was going into a liquor store.

Ricco chuckled. This evening might turn out to be entertaining.

***

Tommy didn't think that downer would *ever* start working.

It usually took a little while. Had to dissolve first, didn't it? It would've probably started working sooner if he'd washed it down with something.

At least he managed to make it to the liquor store in one piece. *Nothing to worry about when you're mellow.* He had a little trouble jumping down--his feet did a weird number on him, kind of went away for a second. Good thing he was able to grab the door.

How come your feet did so many crazy things when you were mellow? No matter. Everything's cool...

He even picked up what he was looking for, brought it over, and put it on the counter without knocking it over or dropping it. *Cool.* Pulled out Billy's money. *Here. Thanks. No, I'm okay, really. Just a little clumsy tonight. You have a good weekend, too, my man...*

Tommy left the store and climbed back up into the truck. No feet trouble this time. *Mellow. Cool.* Got behind the wheel, sat back and closed his eyes. Then opened them and found he was staring at the lighted store window just beyond the windshield.

No one in there now but the tall, skinny clerk talking to two middle-aged ladies about something on the shelves.

Why am I here? How'd I get here?

Then he noticed the bags in his lap. Billy wanted booze. Jack's and some cognac.

More neat waves of mellow drifted down his limbs.

He laid the bag carefully in the seat beside him. *Should I prop them up? Or put them down? Put 'em down. Wouldn't want them tipping onto the floor and crashing, would we? Now ... drive back to the cabin, where Billy and the lady–*

For a moment he'd forgotten. Booze. For Billy and the lady. To get her drunk. Then Billy could–

No need to think of *that*. No reason for it. None at all. She was a nice lady, with dimples and the brightest blue eyes he'd ever seen. Like the ocean. Or the sky on a sunny day. She was sweet. They should let her go.

I'll be nice and relaxed when I get back. I'll calmly tell Billy we're going to set the nice lady free.

They needed to be in Brazil. And the lady needed to be back home, making Bascomb pay for what he'd put her through.

But hurry. Gotta get there quick. Billy was already feeding her booze. *If I don't get back in time, it might be too late.*

"Got to get back." He fumbled with the keys. "Got to get back *fast*."

The fucking key wouldn't go in the ignition. *Bummer--where was it? Try again. Too fucking*

331

dark in the cab.

Both hands now, then—

Mellow. Plenty of time. Be cool.

Damn ... one last jolt of tension whizzed right past his mellow on its way out. *Good riddance.* He took a deep breath, and the tension was gone. The mellow came right back. *Much better.*

Billy would probably finish that bottle himself, then sack out on the bed and doze off.

Tommy chuckled, thinking of walking in and finding Billy sacked out in the bed. That would be *so* cool... *I'll just untie her, drive her back to the liquor store, and let her call for a cab. I don't care what Billy says--it won't matter that she's seen us. She won't tell anyone as long as she gets back home safely. I could even get money from Billy for her fare. He won't mind. He'll be sacked out. And when Billy's sleeping one off, you couldn't wake him.*

He tried the key again. It turned. The truck fired up. Tommy grinned. *When you're mellow, things work out.*

CHAPTER TWENTY-TWO

Bill Landry pulled out a kitchen chair and collapsed heavily into it.

He rubbed his eyes. When his vision cleared, he found himself staring at the scuffed linoleum at his feet. *Damned floor's filthy. When was the last time I swept it? Last month? Longer. Way longer. It's all covered with dirt, sand, and mashed butts. All sorts of crap. Maybe I should give it a quick–*

Damn. I'm talking to myself like a fucking idiot.

What did he expect? He was sitting in a chair, four feet away from a trussed-up woman. And he couldn't even look at her.

Was it any wonder? How could anyone with a conscience look at someone you're about to get drunk, then chloroform to death?

I'm a goddamned idiot. Worse, I'm gonna be a goddamned idiot who's also a murderer. No. Just a guy with bad luck. I'm not violent. I never belted Trudi--not even when she started pulling her swift moves with my bank account.

How hard can it be? Just make believe it's Trudi sitting here. Then I'll be able to do it like a champ. Just feed her a few shots. It wouldn't take much. Then hold the packet over her face for about a minute. No fuss, no muss. She'd go to sleep. Forever.

But the first thing you need to do is suck it up and look at her. Easier said than done. Now that she wasn't wearing the blindfold, he'd have to look right into those big blue eyes.

He'd have to get past that, somehow. Otherwise, he might as well just haul his ass out of here and find some place to hide. That's what a loser would do.

He'd been called that before. Many times. Grade school, high school--even college. After a while it stuck, put a hex on whatever he did. Once the hex squirmed into his head and set up shop, he couldn't change things no matter how hard he tried.

This was supposed to change that, turn his life around. Schiller's, too. They'd screwed up and got caught, but Bascomb's proposition would make everything right. They'd have money. And property. And women. Just like the big boys.

Not a loser. *There's no reason why you can't raise your head and look her right in the eye. It's Trudi sitting there, and she's about to bite the big one because of what she did to you. She ruined you, then walked right out the door. Last you heard, she was doing the same damned thing to some other poor, unsuspecting slob. She has to be stopped, and the only way to do that is to get her drunk, then feed her the chloroform.*

He forced himself to raise his head. He did it by inches--first gazing at her bound ankles beneath the table, then the table itself. Then the bottle of Jack's and the rope wrapped around her tits. Then, finally, her face–

Not Trudi. No way could he visualize Trudi sitting there. There was no way he could change Sally Bascomb into Trudi. But was she any better than Trudi? What about her sneaking around with that big ape behind Bascomb's back? Didn't that make her just as trashy as Trudi and every other two-timing, gold-digging bitch in creation?

No. Despite his reservations, his prejudices, he knew she was cut from a much better mold. She was classy. As far as he could tell, she didn't possess a trashy bone in her body. Both he and Schiller could tell that by the way she'd acted in her captivity. Sure, she'd married Bascomb. She'd been living with him for years--who could blame her for stepping out with another guy to have a little fun? Bascomb had been bonking the very best stuff at Venture and Bas-Com as far back as Bill could remember--didn't the jerk deserve a little comeuppance of his own?

Revenge or no revenge, this woman didn't deserve any of this. There was just no point. Even though he'd been lying to himself, thinking she was no different from any other princess he'd ever known, and that it would be no trouble at all for him to kill her and cut off her finger, he found that he had no desire to hurt her at all. He didn't know when this first started happening or why, just that it had. It came to a head when they'd wrestled with her out in the open field. At first he didn't realize what was going on. He'd suspected it was because of her struggles, her frantic attempt to escape, even though she didn't have a prayer of getting away. And when he finally realized how he actually felt, he didn't believe it. He thought he was just upset, frightened, and hurting from where she'd clipped him with her foot.

But now that he actually faced the reality of having to make the final decision, he knew. And what his brain just told him frightened him more than anything else. *I can't visualize Trudi when I look at her, but I sure as hell can visualize myself. And Schiller.* Right now, he felt just as trapped as she undoubtedly did. Despite the circumstances, all three of them were victims of Warren Bascomb. They had all become hapless casualties of Bascomb's wrath.

But I've got to do it. I've got no choice. If I don't do this, I might just as well find a gun and blow my brains out.

She sat still, her wide-open eyes dead-steady on him. The heavy throbbing in his gut made this *so* much worse. Another belt or two of Jack's might help things along. He raised the bottle and had a swig. She stared at him as he drank. *Dammit. She's doing a number on me.* He turned away and had another swig. *She knows. She damned well knows what I plan to do.*

Woman was bright. She knew they were going to clean her clock. But she wasn't coming apart, not at all. She kept her gaze steady on him--as if she thought she could psyche him out. Her mouth was taped shut but she was still able to work her magic. Women didn't have to talk to bust your balls.

The only way he could do this successfully was to start feeding her the booze right now, before he could talk himself out of it. He leaned forward. His fingers shook, but he managed to peel the tape away and let it dangle from her cheekbone. He yanked the soaked cloth out of her mouth and dropped it on the table.

"This ... isn't our idea," he said, his voice weak

and sort of raspy. But it had to be said. She had to know. "It's not like we *want* to do it, understand?"

She just watched him.

"You ... saw us. You can ... identify us."

She said nothing.

"You understand, don'tcha?"

Still no reply, but those big baby blues stayed on him.

Loser, they said. *I tried to run but you and your partner caught me, and now here I am, tied to this chair and forced to listen to your bullshit.*

His hand shook as he grabbed the bottle.

***

Only one cabin was lit.

The three others along the path formed square black blocks among the trees. The lit one rested on a grassy knoll where the dirt road ended just a few yards shy of the woods.

No sign of the Dodge truck. That meant someone was missing.

The cabin was small--maybe five hundred square feet. It had one door and a shuttered window facing the front. The tiny backyard ran down a weed-choked slope to the dock, where an aluminum canoe tied to a post bobbed lazily in the water.

Hank disappeared in the bushes on the far side of the cabin. To his left, a broken rectangle of hazy barred light brushed the top of the overgrown bush rubbing the plywood wall. He crept silently toward the building, hunkering in the weeds a couple of feet from the peeling wooden shutter. With the help of the inside lighting, it was easy to see through the snagged and dingy sheer curtains.

Sally sat in a chair, her arms bound behind her back, her ankles taped. She was watching her captor. A strip of duct tape dangled from her right cheek.

Landry sat facing her, drinking from a small bottle.

Hank's pulse hastened. Should I call 911? Was there time? He didn't want to take the chance. Not yet, anyway. Once he took down Landry, then he could get the cops here.

The front door was his best bet. But could he rush on in without putting Sally in jeopardy? He didn't see a gun, but that didn't mean Landry wasn't armed. Hopefully, the door wasn't locked. Since Schiller was probably somewhere with the truck, Hank had no idea how long he would be, or when he was due back. Hank had to act fast.

***

Ricco Arragon parked the van in some bushes, doused the lights, and killed the engine.

"Cabin's on the other side of those trees," he told Big Al. "Road forks to the left. See a light over there. That's where Skinny took the truck. We'll just sneak through, surprise everyone."

"Yeah. Surprise the fuckers." Big Al was not amused.

Ricco wanted to laugh. "Don't worry. Snakes and bugs are probably all fast asleep in the trees."

Al's big black eyes blinked. "I thought they came out at night to look for food."

Ricco shrugged. "Figure I'd give you a line of bullshit, make you feel better."

"It sounded like bullshit."

"I'll go first--how's that?"

"It sucks."

"Howzat?"

"You go first, step on a fucking snake. It gets all pissed off, curls up and catches *my* ass as I walk by. I'm feeling much better."

"*You* wanna go first?"

"You fucking crazy? I step on the fucking snake, piss it off, and it catches my ass anyway?"

"Thought I'd ask." Ricco pulled out his Llama 9 from the holster in his waistband. Nice gun for the money. Cheap, light, efficient, and untraceable with the numbers filed off. "We check out the layout first, see what happens. We try and get everyone rounded up, then loaded in the back of the van."

"Can't we use the road?"

"Don't know where the hell it goes. It might take us back to Seventeen-ninety-two."

Big Al shivered. "I was afraid you'd say something like that."

"We do this one step at a time. I go first, move real careful. You stay close behind. I hear something rattle, you'll hear it, too. You'll have more time to get away than I will. That ought to make you feel better."

"Yeah. Hearing a fucking rattle. Makes me wanna do a cartwheel."

"We'll be all right, *paisano*. You'll see."

"What'll you do when you see a fucking snake?"

"I'll say, Mr. Snake, please go away. My big buddy here, he don't like critters that slither."

"Funny, Ricco. Real funny."

Ricco suddenly went dead serious. "Don't forget.

339

No guns. We use 'em only to keep everybody quiet." He patted his jacket pocket. "That's why we brought along the duct tape."

***

Business raised the whiskey bottle to his lips, swallowed, then lowered it and stared blankly at her.

This is it. The end. They brought me here to kill me. Just how, she didn't know. She only knew she was going to die.

Business had drunk from the bottle at least three times since he'd come back inside. He obviously wanted to get drunk. He probably wanted to be numb and relaxed.

Sally closed her eyes and suddenly felt calm. It was strange how peaceful everything was when you knew the end was near. There would be no more empty years, no more struggling. No more worrying about losing your mind. Or wondering how you'll get around, who'll take care of you.

Business stared at the bottle for the longest time. Gathering courage? Or debating whether to take another sip?

He suddenly sighed, bent forward, and moved the mouth of the bottle toward her lips.

Despite her effort to pull away, he tilted it just right. A splash of the fiery whiskey slid across her tongue and plunged down her throat. Once her gag reflex forced her to gulp it down, he pulled away.

She closed her eyes. It slid down hotly, causing a sizzling eruption in her gut. Twin rivulets fell down her chin and dropped onto her shirt. Only then did she realize how long it had been since she'd last

340

eaten. She tried remembering the details, but her brain grew cloudy. Too much stress, pain and discomfort.

How horrible. She'd forgotten her last meal.

"Your husband," Business said softly. "This is ... all because of him."

The stinging subsided. She swallowed. Her throat burned. "Please ... do me a favor."

"What's that?"

"Stop that. I'm ... not in the mood."

It was surprising how easily the anger gushed out. But there was no reason for it not to. She had no time left. Her adrenaline trudged along on all eight cylinders. She was determined to fight them however she could. "Excuses don't work where I'm sitting," she said. "Telling me this is all because of my husband." Her cheeks grew hotter. "Don't bother. It makes you look even more like a stupid jerk."

He cringed. She could tell her statement had hurt, but she had no intention of letting up. If he was going to kill her, he needed to suffer through every inch of it.

He sat up. "You just don't know–"

"I don't *care* what I know or don't know. Don't sit there and try to con me into believing it was all Warren's fault."

"Lady, it *was*. He–"

"Oh, please. If you had any brains, you would have told my husband where to stick it. Others have. Others with backbone."

Business stiffened at the insult. "He caught us ... doing things ... that could put us away."

341

"And what do you think will happen for what you're about to do?"

"You weren't supposed to ... see us."

"Can you actually blame me for trying to escape?"

No reply.

Suddenly the most important question of all needed to be asked. And answered. "Tell me. Was this ... his idea?"

A nod.

The rage rushed down her bound limbs, making her tremble. It was Warren all along. He'd planned this. Engineered it. *My God. I did marry a monster.* She took a deep breath--two deep breaths. *Collect yourself, Sal. Don't lose it now.* "And what's supposed to happen?"

"You're ... supposed to ... disappear."

"Then what?"

"No one's supposed to find you. He's going to report you missing."

She ignored that grisly thought. She didn't want to think any more about this. "So all this ... it's because he caught you doing things?"

A nod.

"Worked out really well for *me*, didn't it?"

He turned away.

"What happened to my five-million-dollar proposal? It was enough, wasn't it?"

Business scowled. "It would've been--if that big ape hadn't showed up. Your boyfriend. We could've got what we wanted from your safe, then dropped you off somewhere. That would have been the end of it."

342

Big ape? My boyfriend? Sally's pulse sputtered. "Who ... are you talking about?"

"He wanted to have a peek at the truck. If we'd been able to get to the safe, none of this would've happened."

A witness, maybe? That third voice? The one that sounded so familiar? But why did they think he was her boyfriend?

"Who ... was this man?" Sally asked softly.

He raised the bottle and sucked down more whiskey. When he lowered the bottle, he scowled. "We know what you've been doing, lady. So does your husband. That's why he's making us do this."

She had no idea what he was talking about. Her mind had apparently switched off. Her pulse raced. All she could do was watch him in silence. He kept shifting the bottle from one hand to the other, then turning around to gape at the door. Avoiding eye contact.

He obviously hated this. He was a lowlife, but certainly no killer. He was so nervous, he'd come apart.

But someone else was out there. Someone they thought was her boyfriend. *We know what you've been doing*... What on earth was he talking about? What did Warren think she was doing?

It didn't matter. Not now, anyway. If someone was looking for her, stalling might help. As long as she could gain time, she had hope. But she had to stay sober. The effects of that first swallow had already registered, relaxing her.

"It might interest you to know that my husband has lied, cheated, and destroyed people's careers.

343

He's obviously lying about me as well. He's lying to get you to do this. Why? I've got no idea. But if you let him put you in this position, you're making the worst mistake you'll ever make. You're letting him make you commit murder."

Business fidgeted and stared at the bottle in his hands. Just a couple of swallows left in it. If she could get him to finish the bottle before Flighty came back...

"But that doesn't mean you should *let* him, does it? If you kill me, the rest of your life will be ruined, and it'll be Warren's fault."

He cleared his throat. "It doesn't matter..."

"Kidnapping is one thing. It's serious, yes, but nothing near what you'll get if you kill me. That's the needle, no questions asked. Do you honestly want to be strapped down in a room while Warren's sitting behind the window, watching you?"

He still didn't reply.

"And another thing." The rage threatened to take over. "If he wants me dead–"

The bottle returned to her lips, this time with much more determination. Pressing his free hand against the back of her head, he coaxed her head gently back. Then stopped.

The hum of an approaching vehicle made the floor vibrate slightly.

***

His hand trembling, Bill Landry carefully pulled back a corner of the drape covering the front window.

Lights off, the truck stopped along the sandy path, then went silent. He took in a giant gulp of air.

344

He should've expected Schiller coming back. Who else knew they were here? *You're being paranoid. Relax.*

Schiller pushed open the door of the truck. Before climbing down, he grabbed the brown bag from the passenger seat.

Bill walked up just as Schiller was slamming the door. "Anyone follow you?"

Schiller jumped, nearly dropping the bag. Then he sighed and grinned sheepishly. Even in the darkness, his eyes sparkled like flickering candles.

Bill couldn't believe it. This was the worst possible time for either of them to zone out. "You stupid fuck. You took something, didn't you?" Bad enough that he himself had polished off most of that pint, instead of using it to get Bascomb's old lady drunk.

"Billy, we've got to talk." Schiller swayed a little, gripping the bag as though he was holding a baby.

"Goddammit, I told you—"

"I'm all right, Billy, I just needed a little mellow. You know how I get."

"We'll deal with that later. Right now I want you to get your head on straight." He grabbed Schiller's shoulders and shook him.

"B-Billy? I'm ... g-gonna ... throw up—"

He let go and backed up.

Schiller leaned against the truck. "I'm okay now. But we need to—"

"Were you followed?"

"Nope."

"You're sure."

345

"Yep."

He wanted to belt the silly fuck, but now was not a good time to lose it. Couldn't go back inside half-cocked, could he? He owed it to that woman to keep his head on straight, even though he was a little drunk.

"Billy, we need to talk."

"We've got to get this done."

"We shouldn't *do* this."

"We've been through this before. It has to be done. She's seen our faces."

"I don't care, Billy. I don't want us doing it."

"*We're* not doing it--*I* am."

"I don't want it done *at all!*"

He couldn't believe how obstinate Schiller was acting. He wasn't his usual wimpy self. "What's gotten into you? What the hell did you take?"

"I just had one--to kill the shakes. And this has nothing to do with that."

"There's obviously something wild growing up your ass."

"She's a nice lady, Billy. She doesn't need to be *dead!*"

He snatched the bag. "Stay out here."

"*Please* don't." Schiller didn't look stoned even with the glaze in his eyes. He actually appeared calmer than Bill had ever seen him. He wondered if Schiller had gotten hold of some bad stuff.

"What's with you?" He turned for the cabin.

Schiller grabbed his arm. "Billy, don't go in there."

He yanked free. "God dammit. Go take another one of your damned mellows. And stay the hell

346

away from me."

"Billy?"

He stomped back up the grassy path.

"Billy!"

He turned around one last time. Schiller was standing in front of the truck, a pitiful expression on his face. Looked like he was just about to be sent off to a death camp, almost.

Fuck him. This has to be done.

***

Hank crouched on the other side of the bush, watching Landry and Schiller through an opening in the branches.

After their argument, Landry broke free of Schiller and stomped up the hill toward the cabin, carrying a brown paper bag. The door eased shut.

Schiller staggered back to the pickup, climbed the running board, and knelt on the driver's seat. His scrawny ass faced outward. He was obviously searching for something inside the cab.

Hank could easily grab Schiller by the belt and yank him out of the truck. A chop to the back of the neck would do. It wouldn't even have to be hard-- just sharp enough to knock him out of commission.

Schiller climbed back down and closed the door. He was gripping something in his right hand--a hammer. He stood there, shaking, staring at the cabin. Then he took a deep breath and started up the hill.

Hank kept close to the bush. It was going to be tricky to get behind Schiller, but he had to get that hammer. He couldn't let him take it inside. He had no idea what his intentions were. He only knew that

Schiller was upset--and Sally was inside, tied to a chair.

Best wait until Schiller reached the front porch. Hank could sneak around the bush, trip him, and knock him out. Then dial 911, slip inside, and take on Landry. Hank fished inside his trouser pocket for his cell.

A flurry of movement emerged behind the pickup. Shadows appeared, rushing straight for Schiller.

CHAPTER TWENTY-THREE

Business pulled a fresh bottle of Jack Daniel's and a small bottle of cognac from the brown bag and set them on the table.

Sally eyed the bottles and the grim expression on Business's face. He avoided her eyes as he picked up the Jack's, broke the tab, and unscrewed the cap. The bottle moved in her direction.

She turned away. "Why don't you just kill me? Why must we go through this stupid charade? I *hate* whiskey."

He lowered the bottle. "I thought it would be easier ... for you ... if you were drunk–"

"Easier for *you*, maybe." It was lucky for him she was tied to the chair. She wanted to claw his eyes out. She would have, too, if she'd had the chance. If she wasn't so furious, she would've smiled at the thought of her former self--meek, non-confrontational, and humble--clawing someone's eyes out.

Business did not reply. He could see her fury.

"You can't look me in the eye, so you're going to do the big nasty after I black out. Is that your lame plan?"

"Like I already said–"

"I know. It's because of Warren. You and your stupid friend are caught up in the middle of this. There's no way out." A harsh breath fumed from her lungs. She sucked in another. "You want to know something? This is getting really old, and I'm not so sure I believe you anymore."

"It's true."

"Even if it is, it's still *way* over the line. No matter how bad you say you feel about it, most of this is your own making. Warren wouldn't have nailed you if you hadn't been doing something wrong in the first place." She hoped she was getting through to him. If even some of it registered, he might start thinking about what he was really doing. "I don't believe anything either of you have to say–"

"But it's all *true*. Every damned word."

She had to keep him upset ... off-balance ... thinking. She needed to gain time. "Tell me something. If I hadn't seen your faces, would you have let me go?"

After a pause, a slight nod.

"So ... you're saying it's really *my* fault you're going to kill me?"

No reply.

"And if I hadn't tried to escape, you would've deposited me safely on my doorstep?"

Silence.

"You *really* expect me to believe that?"

"Listen, lady–"

"You're both losers. You were caught doing something stupid, so you did something else a hundred times stupider in retaliation. And neither of you can own up to it." Her anger, a hot coil in the pit of her stomach, made her quiver in the chair. "I really wish you'd realize just how pitiful both of you really are."

"Stop it, lady."

"Or what? You'll kill me?" She forced out a

350

laugh. "Please! Just go ahead and feed me the whiskey. Then get your lame courage up to–"

The bottle shot out, knocking against her teeth.

***

Skinny went down without a sound.

One chop to the back of the head with the butt of the Llama dropped him.

Ricco squatted, felt for a pulse. "Fucker's dead."

Big Al pocketed the roll of duct tape. "How hard you belt him?"

"Don't matter. One less to worry about."

Big Al bent and picked up Skinny's hammer. "What's this for?"

"Who knows? Maybe they wanna fight over the woman."

Big Al pulled out a hankie and wiped the hammer down. He tossed it in the tall grass across the sandy path. "You think maybe they're doing something nasty in there?"

Ricco shrugged. "Anything's possible. They obviously snatched her to squeeze Lee's balls. Let's get this finished. I need to get home and have a little *vino*, watch my Extreme Fighting on the tube."

Big Al turned toward the road. Ricco could tell the big guy was using his special killer's instinct, listening and smelling the air. "No one around." He sounded disappointed.

"He'll show--trust me. They have his woman."

"You don't think he's here already, do you?"

"Didn't see that Caddie parked out here anywhere, did you?"

"What makes you think he'll even find this place?"

351

"Found these two before, didn't he?"

"They were fucking around near Mr. Boss-Man's estate. Lee just staked it out and waited. Any asshole could do that."

"Maybe."

"Hard, being lucky twice in a row."

"Just stick to the plan. I go inside, get the others ready. You stay out here, hidden. You see Lee, take him down quick. Then one of us waits here while the other gets the van. We toss 'em all in back, then find a nifty place out here to dump 'em. Got it?"

***

Gasping, Sally tried pulling away, but Business's free hand grabbed the back of her head, holding her fast.

She forced her eyes shut. The whiskey plunged down her throat with the force of a blowtorch. Despite the grip on her, she yanked her head to the side and choked violently. A mixture of spittle and booze dribbled down her chin, gathering in large spots on her shirt. Her eyes burned. She sniffed, still hacking away.

"You okay?" The jerk actually sounded concerned.

She squinted at him through her tears. *Of course I'm not okay, you moron.* A wave of dizziness caused the wadded-up heat inside her to subside.

"I didn't mean to ... do that. What you said ... it hurt." He had a swallow of whiskey and put down the bottle.

"I ... meant it to hurt. Something tells me you and your friend are above all this."

"We're losers. You had us pegged right."

352

It sounded like he really wanted out of this. She might be able to build on that. Some guys puffed up easily. These two showed all the signs of being beaten down. She hated them for what they'd done, but felt a strange kinship with them. Maybe it was because she herself was a victim--Warren's as well as theirs.

"Your husband had us pegged, too."

"Don't bring him into this." The anger trickled back, filling her limbs and heating her flesh. It was important not to give in to it.

Business stared at the bottle of cognac on the table, then had another swallow of whiskey.

"Why didn't you ... take your walk the other night?" he asked. "Why'd you take off in the GT?"

What a strange question to ask right now... The images floated back darkly, like some old movie that hadn't been properly preserved. Everything came back in hazy puffs. The wild look in Warren's eyes. How he'd slipped quietly through the archway, like some mysterious phantom. The coldness in the air that had turned the room almost foul. Her sudden strange feeling that nothing could ever be the same again. "We ... had a fight. I was ... escaping."

"Escaping?"

"Warren's very difficult. He can also be very mean. You've got to ignore most of what he says and does."

"He makes you feel trapped?"

"Yes."

"His property?"

She nodded.

353

Business stared at the whiskey bottle the longest time. She suspected he was going to make her drink more, but he didn't. He slowly stood, looked at her, and said, "Lady, you're absolutely right. About everything."

"Wh-What are you—"

"Your husband. He gets away with everything. He can't get away with this. We can't let him."

Sally's heart skipped a beat. Had he said what she thought he said? Did this mean he was going to let her go? "What do you ... plan to do?" she asked in a soft voice.

"I plan to let you go. My partner was right all along. We need to send you back to him. It's the only way. The only way we can get him. You're the only one who can."

She had no idea what he was talking about, but that didn't matter. It didn't even matter if he was drunk or just on his way to losing his sanity. What mattered was that they were going to set her free.

She tried to say something, but her voice caught in her throat. She cleared her throat and tried again. This time, it came out. "Are you sure? I mean, are you really—"

"We'll take you back to the main drag." He pulled out his chair and started circling the table. "You can use a payphone at the liquor store, or one of the eateries. All I ask is that you give us half an hour to—"

Footsteps on the front porch stopped him mid-sentence.

***

After tossing Skinny into the truck, Big Al

crossed the dirt path, staying just inside the tree line.

Hopefully, the critters and slimy things would want to stay closer to the lake, where it was cooler.

Rustling in the bushes not far from him made him still. *The breeze scattering leaves, maybe?* He knew better. Not much of a breeze, and this sounded more like a twig being snapped about twenty feet to his left, in the woods. *Something fell onto a pile of leaves? A pine cone? Or a squirrel leaping from a branch?* He looked around cautiously. *Why the hell would something fall from one of the trees right at that moment? Unless ... it was intentionally dropped--or tossed?*

He recalled a tactic they'd taught him in jungle training in his old Army days. Distraction. You want somebody to turn in a certain direction, just chuck something in that direction. Then–

The realization took too damn long. And rightly so. Thirty years does serious damage to your reflexes. Your memory, too--especially if you don't keep things up there or go back to them from time to time to make sure they're still there. Even if you remembered your training, it still took a damn long time to register.

He swiveled sharply to his right. His hand dove beneath his jacket, groping clumsily for the Blackhawk in its oversized holster. Then he remembered. *Madre. That long fucking barrel! Why the fuck am I going for* this *monster?* He reached down instead for his Llama--smaller, lighter, more compact, and much easier to handle. He'd decided to try an ankle holster for the Llama after commandeering the Blackhawk from Lee's apartment. The Blackhawk was a mother of a gun, and he felt beefed toting it under his jacket--until now. He fumbled with his trouser hem. *Stupid! On a job, you came prepared, and didn't fuck around with a–*

Something hard cracked him on the back of the head. A beautiful shimmering starburst raced across his vision before fading to nothing.

***

Ricco kicked the door open.

Beard stood beside the kitchen table in the center of the room. He had turned at the intrusion and nearly dropped the bottle of Jack Daniel's he held. His eyes filled the sockets, his mouth frozen in a giant 'O.'

Boss-Man's old lady was tied to a chair, her arms pinned behind her, her ankles also fastened. A strip of duct tape dangled from her right cheek. Shame she had to be capped. She sure was a looker.

Beard probably thought the same damned thing. They'd brought her here to squeeze Lee's nuts, but no doubt developed other ideas along the way. Feeding her some booze, getting her drunk, then taking her off to bed for a real party. These two really had some 'nads to be doing this to Mr. Boss-Man's lady. Didn't they know that if Lee didn't tear them apart, Mr. Boss-Man would really do a number on them? Some guys didn't have the brains it took to outsmart a slug.

Didn't matter. This gig had quickly turned into a sleeper--Skinny out of the way already, the woman all wrapped up. And Beard at a huge disadvantage. Ricco couldn't remember *any* job being so damn

356

easy.

"Hope there's room for one more here." Ricco nudged the door shut with his left foot. With his right hand, he kept the Llama pointed directly at Beard's face.

"L-Listen, mister..."

"Plant your ass back down and maybe I won't blow your fucking head off."

Beard backed up and sank back onto the seat. It creaked beneath his weight.

"Grab the bottle, index finger and thumb only, by the neck. Put it on the table. Nice and slow."

Beard did as he was told.

Ricco took two steps into the room and gave it a quick scan. The bedroom and bathroom doors were open. A small light lit up each room. Obviously, no one else was here.

He gestured to the woman. "Put that tape back where it belongs."

With a shaky hand, Beard covered the woman's mouth. She whimpered softly and lowered her head.

"Put your hands behind your back."

Beard opened his mouth to protest, but Ricco jerked the gun. "Don't fuck with me. I'd just as soon splatter your brains right here and now. I really wouldn't mind burning this dump to the ground, but that's not what's s'posed to happen. I were you, I'd do every damn thing I was told. Get it?"

Beard nodded.

Ricco produced a small roll of duct tape from his jacket pocket.

***

Hank dropped the hammer he had found in the

grass and bent to check the big man lying on his stomach at his feet. Probably every bit of six-six and weighed in at three hundred, easy. Not all of it fat, either.

The breeze shifted. He caught a whiff of Aqua Velva. Yep. Definitely the idiot who'd suckered him in the apartment.

He went through the gorilla's pockets and found a roll of tape. "You're making this really easy." He ripped off several feet and tied the massive wrists together behind the broad back. More went around the ankles, with a final piece slapped over the big boy's mouth.

Hank opened the man's jacket. His Blackhawk. A lucky break. He also found a small auto strapped to the big boy's ankle. Looked like a Llama 9 mil. It was light and easy to handle. *Why didn't he keep it in his jacket and leave the Blackhawk in their vehicle?* Hank shook his head. The big gun digging into his pit probably made the big jerk feel powerful. *Dumb bastard.* His ego--as well as the Blackhawk--had saved Hank's life.

Hank pocketed the Llama, did a quick check of the Blackhawk, then crossed the dirt road.

Before he snuck up to the front porch, he pulled out his cell, dialed 911, and made his call. They told him to stay on the line. *No time for that.* He left the cell lying in the grass just a few feet from the Dodge pickup.

***

Ricco admired his work.

The two sat wrapped up just as nice as you pleased. It would make the job simpler if he did

358

them both before sticking them in the van. Just a simple snapping of the neck would do. He was an expert at that.

The chick would be easy. It wouldn't take much. She seemed half out of it, anyway. Probably a little drunk from the booze Beard had been feeding her.

Big Al would want to do Beard. He'd been on the rag since they'd suckered Lee at his pad. When the big ape carried around the taste of blood, there wasn't much you could do but toss him something to munch on.

"Sorry, you two, but we're getting paid a nice chunk of cash for this. I promise it'll be painless, and when I promise something, you can take it to the bank."

He removed a cotton handkerchief from his pants pocket. He'd stand behind the chick and hold it against her temple. Since her trap was taped, she wouldn't make much noise. The handkerchief would cover her nostrils in case she was still breathing once he'd snapped her neck.

He'd done this before. The technique worked just fine, but he'd need both hands--one for the handkerchief, the other for bracing his forearm under her neck. Since Beard was now harmless, Ricco no longer needed the gun. Big Al was outside; no one would get by the big galoot.

Ricco pocketed the Llama. "Okay, sister. Just close your eyes. It'll be nice and quick."

***

In her half-drunken state, Sally tried to think clearly, but everything had turned blurry, moving in slow motion.

359

Nothing made any sense.

He was going to let me go. I was going to be free. Then–

It was the whiskey. She had only had a couple of swallows, but on an empty stomach, it was more than she could tolerate.

The dark, thickset, scary-eyed man moved toward her, circling her chair. He stood behind her, his chest pressing against the back of her head. His forearm slipped under her chin. A whiff of B.O. entered her nostrils. Some sort of cloth was pressed snugly against the side of her head.

With a muffled sob, Sally began to pray. *Our Father, Who Art in heaven...*

The hand against her temple increased its pressure.

... Hallowed be Thy name ...

Sally shut her eyes and gritted her teeth.

A loud crash wrenched her out of her daze. The pressure eased up. She opened her eyes.

A tall, broad-shouldered man filled the doorway, a huge black gun in his right hand, its barrel aimed in her direction. *Oh, God ... now someone's going to shoot me?* She blinked her tear-blurred eyes. *Hank?*

She let out a shuddering breath. *You're dreaming. You're about to die. Your mind has already jumped ship. You're seeing things. Wishing ... dreaming...*

A blanket of darkness swept down on her.

***

"Get away from her."

Hank could barely keep his finger from pulling the trigger. The fact that the hood's dark face was close behind Sally's head made the decision a no-brainer. Hank had been a candidate for Sniper's School before being sent to Saudi. His aim was close to perfect, but he just didn't have the heart for what the job meant. Right now he did, but he was twenty years older, hadn't fired a weapon in months, and didn't want to take the chance--not with Sally being so close to his target.

Thank God she'd passed out. The goon relaxed his grip. But something in his deep-set eyes conveyed the message that he wasn't about to give in.

"Guess I shoulda locked the door, huh, Jack?"

"The name ain't Jack, and yeah, that was way past every conceivable kind of stupid. Now move away from the chair."

A strange look of victory covered the other man's pockmarked face. "Funny, but you're the one who loses at this party, pal."

"I don't think so. And I'm not your pal." Hank pulled back the hammer of the Blackhawk and steadied it with both hands.

The other man straightened a little, inadvertently putting Sally a little more out of the range of fire. He eyed the Blackhawk. "I see you met my buddy Al. That's his gun."

"That sloppy side of beef who wears too much Aqua Velva? He's lying in the woods, taking a nap. And the gun's actually mine."

"You must've got him from behind. Otherwise, you'd be dead meat."

"Just shut up and move away from her."

"This is business, asshole. I do what I'm told."

361

"Good idea. Now do what you're told and move away from her."

"I have a better suggestion. Drop that gun, or I'll break her neck before you can even squeeze off a round. Believe me, I can do it."

Hank kept his arm dead steady. As long as the other guy didn't squat down, Sally was basically out of the line of fire. But it would still be close. Like most long-barrel guns, the Blackhawk shot a hair low. But this wasn't the time to break his concentration and switch to the Cheetah. "You don't seem to understand. I'm the one with the gun."

"And I'm the pro here, hotshot. You're what ... a fucking field rep at a construction site?" He laughed. "I done six, maybe seven, just this year. How many assholes you wasted lately?" His grip tightened beneath Sally's chin. Fortunately, she was still out of it.

Hank sighed. This jerk was obviously a psycho hitter. Anyone who didn't mind breaking a helpless woman's neck was not the type to be taken alive. Hank carefully steadied the gun. "Just one," he said, and calmly squeezed the trigger.

PART IV
The Last Day

CHAPTER TWENTY-FOUR

Sally lay in the hospital bed, slightly groggy from the meds they'd given her for her aches and pains.

Hank stood just three feet away, watching her closely. Except for a few grays around the temples, he was just as handsome and as fit as ever. The glow from those steel-gray eyes, something that had always excited her in the past, made her just as warm as ever. Despite the anger and hurt still consuming her from their breakup, she couldn't help feeling warm and relieved that he'd somehow returned to her life.

This had played out like some sort of modern-day fairy tale. She'd never believed in fairy tales--not even as a young girl--but she couldn't help feeling this way, nonetheless. After seven years, her prince had returned, saving her from the evil forces that had almost destroyed her. He'd returned out of the blue--as if some sort of strange magical chant had told him she was in danger. It was almost as if fate itself had dictated that she needed him.

"How're you feeling?"

"I feel pretty good right now." She was surprised her voice sounded reasonably normal. The meds were still working. This was probably why everything seemed like a fairy tale, why the world had turned surreal. She felt as if she'd been dreaming, but even though she'd awakened, the dream continued.

"In spite of being kidnapped and hauled around town for three days in the back of a truck? Then nearly murdered by a mob punk?"

"In spite of all that."

Sally just sighed and enjoyed the realization that the lovely man standing there, smiling at her, was not just a hallucination.

"They must've given you some good drugs."

"I think your visit's helping more than the drugs."

He didn't say anything, but the sudden flush to his cheeks told her what she wanted to know. Despite this strange situation, she had to force her mind on more logical things--such as the mystery plaguing her since Hank burst into Landry's cabin. The little girl still lingering inside her wanted to keep the fairy tale going. She wanted to think Hank had actually picked up on her dilemma. Maybe he was in the area or thinking about her at the time. Just because he married someone else didn't mean he never thought about her anymore, did it? He might have been driving by when Business and Flighty were chloroforming her. Stranger things had happened. Where did it say that, once you grew up, you had to abandon your childhood fantasies?

The little girl in her who'd experienced cold fear for the first time in the woods behind Aunt Margaret's country place would always exist, alert for similar childhood fears. And now, as that same little girl stared up at the prince who'd saved her

364

from the evil monsters, the big girl in her--the mature woman who'd stared death in the face more than once during the last few days--realized she needed answers. "How'd you know what was happening to me? Those two had me bundled up in the back of that truck, then kept me hidden away at that stupid fish camp. No one could have possibly–"

"I saw you at Tillie's Tavern."

Tillie's. Strange. She'd blocked out that part of the nightmare. Even now, it remained a blur. A big, dark emptiness, like a long-forgotten dream. Something you knew you'd dreamed, but just couldn't remember what it was. "I ... didn't see you there."

"I didn't think you saw anyone."

The dark images wafted past, like smoke from a dying fire. "That was the night I left the house. The night Warren showed me just how little he really cared about me. The night my life turned upside-down."

"I could tell you had a lot on your mind."

"Is that why you didn't come over and talk to me?"

"I wasn't sure it was you--not at first. It was too dark. Besides, I was pretty preoccupied that night as well."

More images, these not quite as dark, floated past, making her wonder about the voice she'd heard outside the truck that day her kidnappers planned to break into the estate, just hours before she'd nearly escaped. "That was *you* outside the truck? Talking to those two?"

"Let me guess. You were in the truck."

She nodded. This *was* turning into a fairy tale. A very strange one. Hank had been tracking her ever since he'd seen her at Tillie's. Even though she'd thought she'd be killed, he'd been out there, hunting for her. He'd walked out of her life seven years before, but fate had brought him back. Business had called him her 'boyfriend.' What would make him think that? And what would make him think Warren knew about Hank in the first place?

But despite all that, she found there were more pressing things she wanted to know about. "How's ... Heidi?" She was surprised she was able to say the name at all without choking. She knew what opening up all this could mean, but it was necessary. Seven years of hurt and frustration was a long time to be kept in the dark.

"Heidi?" His look of confusion shimmered through her.

"Your wife..."

He shrugged. "We're divorced. I ... thought you knew that."

"I thought I did, too. Until..." Now the words *wouldn't* come out. They stayed down in her gut, where they'd been hiding the last seven years.

"Until what?" he asked.

She couldn't look at him.

"Sally? Why didn't I ever hear from you again?"

She forced herself to look at him. Confusion--as well as hurt--covered his features. Then, finally, the words came out. "She was there ... when I came to see you ... that Saturday. That day we were–"

"She was where?"

"In your apartment--where else?"

366

He didn't speak. The confusion remained, but the hurt was suddenly replaced by a glint in his eyes that looked like anger.

"I figured you'd decided to go back with her. I–"

"I wanted *you*, Sally. I was over Heidi. You helped me through it. I wouldn't have gotten through it without you."

Oh my God. My dear God. "I went there ... to your place ... to see you..."

"I ... didn't know."

"You were there, weren't you?"

He shook his head.

Icy-cold rivulets trickled down her back, between her shoulder blades. Something had gone terribly wrong. "You ... *weren't* there?"

"I got home late that day. Probably close to seven that night."

She ignored the pain in her limbs and forced herself to sit up. Things weren't making sense. Not at all. But she knew him. He wasn't a man who lied. "But ... your car. It was–"

"If it was the Saturday I remember, I was called in to work that morning, just for a few hours. I intended to call you, but I didn't get the chance. Some idiots fell from a girder two stories up, and the site was in total chaos for quite a while. When I finally was able to get away, I called. And kept calling. I never heard from you again."

"But ... your car. The Lexus. It was in your space–"

"Heidi and I drove the same kind of vehicle in those days. She liked my Lexus, so naturally I had to buy her one. When she wanted something, she

367

got it, or life turned into instant misery. It had to be the same color, too, since she liked that shade of blue." He put his face in his hands. "I don't believe this."

"She answered your door naked."

He just shook his head.

"Well, practically. She held one of your jackets in front of her."

"She never was subtle about some things. Her body was one of them."

"Why'd she answer the door like that? And how'd she get in? Don't tell me you gave her a key..."

"She probably thought it was me coming in. Anyway, Heidi doesn't need a key."

"Then ... how could she get in?"

"The motel manager at the time was around seventy. How many seventy-year-old men do you know who'll turn down a woman looking like her?"

He was so right. Women like Heidi could get anything they wanted. From just about anyone. And it didn't matter what they wanted. "But ... what was she doing there in the first place?"

"She wanted to get back together. I got a call from her that morning, just as I was getting to the construction site. She said she wanted to get together again, but I said I didn't want to. She wouldn't take no for an answer. I had no idea she was at my place when she called."

"She wasn't there when you got home?"

"Not a sign. I did notice two wet towels lying in heaps on the bathroom floor. Heidi was a lot of things, but neat wasn't one of them. I should've figured things out at the time, but I was too distracted."

"Distracted?"

He sighed. "I couldn't get in touch with you. I must've called you a hundred times that day. I thought something happened, that maybe you'd been in an accident. I went over to your place the next day, but they said you'd moved out."

She lay back and closed her eyes. The tears had already started. "I actually thought you'd gone back with her."

"You were wrong."

"I didn't know that, obviously."

"Where did you go?"

"Miami."

"Why?"

"I had to get away."

"You did that, all right."

She smiled at him through her tears. Once the shock of it had swept through her, she couldn't deny the irony of the situation. Seven years without this man because of a crazy mix-up. Seven years gone because she hadn't wanted a confrontation. Because she was so upset that she didn't want to hear this man's voice. *And now I feel like the world's stupidest human...*

"Let me guess," Hank said in a soft voice. "You're not okay now."

She sniffed. "I'm ... really glad you decided to come looking for me," she whispered, the words coming out heavily again.

"Once I realized it was actually you, there was no decision to be made."

369

"I'm also glad you're back in my life."

He just stared at her. She tried reading the steel-gray eyes, but they told her nothing.

"You *are* back in my life, aren't you?"

"If you want me to be."

She grabbed his hand. She had almost forgotten how safe and warm she felt when he held her. "What do *you* think?"

***

As Warren Bascomb gazed out his office window, he tried to shake the doom that had unexpectedly slipped a black shroud over his world.

Why the hell had so many things gone so badly? Once Landry and Schiller had picked up Sally, things went steadily down the tubes. That asshole Lee showed up. Then Sam Cole, using only his best people, stepped in. And within twenty-four hours, the whole thing had gone right down the crapper.

How could a couple of well-seasoned pros mess up such a simple job? How could a big-mouthed moron like Hank Lee possibly get the drop on two professional wet-boys?

And why did Sally refuse to see him at the hospital? Landry and Schiller weren't stupid enough to tell her what was going on, were they? Telling your victim anything, especially in a case like this, would seal your doom. Schiller was dead, of course, so he was no longer a problem. However, Landry was still walking around. He was on ice at the moment, cooling his heels while the Feds sorted this all out. Even though he'd made a mess of all this, he knew how it would look if he opened his mouth and started pointing fingers.

Sally couldn't possibly believe *he* had anything to do with this. The way it played out, Warren presented the perfect picture--a victim of a vengeful plot against him, engineered by two disgruntled employees. Sammy's boy wouldn't open his mouth. And even if Landry broke under pressure, who would believe him?

His intercom buzzed. "Mr. Bascomb? Mr. Wright would like to see you."

"Have him come right in."

His attorney hustled in and closed the door behind him. He dropped his leather briefcase on the walnut table beside the chair, unbuttoned his silk imported jacket, and eagerly lowered his large butt. "I want to know exactly what happened, Warren." Ken's baritone voice, normally loud and powerful, sounded anxious.

It was time to send up the smoke screen. Ken Wright was kept on retainer, but he was also a friend of sorts--and he liked Sally. If there was a way to squeeze out of this mess unscathed, it had to be done convincingly, and Warren knew he would need Ken's help.

He shrugged. "Sally was kidnapped. That's about all I can say now. I tried visiting her at the hospital to get to the bottom of this, but she wouldn't let me in her room. Still traumatized, obviously. Can't say as I blame her. She was, after all, snatched right off the GreeneWay, bundled up, and driven all over town for several days."

Ken rested his hands in his ample lap. Warren didn't like the man's frown. "This is *me*, Warren. Your friend as well as your attorney."

"I'm aware of that."

Ken sighed tiredly. "My phone's been ringing off the hook. People I've never heard of are asking for my version of the story. They've been asking me if I need an agent. And what about television rights and movie rights and book rights. This is the big time, and you have to level with me."

"I just *told* you what happened. Sally was kidnapped by two former employees who have been nothing but trouble. Drugs, of all things. Dummy accounts. Hacking. You know all about that mess."

"So you're saying this was some sort of revenge thing?"

"Those two obviously decided to get even by snatching Sally and squeezing money from me."

"And you knew nothing about this?"

"I don't believe you've just asked me such a question."

"I'd feel better if you'd answer it."

Warren had known Ken more than twenty years. How could a drinking buddy as well as a long-time business associate even think along these lines? "I wasn't even in town when it happened."

Ken sat forward. "Sally was abducted a couple of hours after suppertime last Wednesday night. You were in town then. She was held for two days before she was found Friday night. It was just before nine-thirty when Hank Lee made the nine-one-one call from his cell phone at Landry's Lake Monroe cabin. Where were you then?"

"Disney Village. I was there that afternoon, a little past four. I received a call on my personal line and learned about the kidnapping shortly after I reached the hotel. I had business there–"

"You were with the Madison woman."

He stiffened. "Miss Madison happens to be handling my–"

"I *know* what she's handling." His attorney's broad face grew tense.

"I don't like your tone."

"What *I* don't like is the fact that you've done something despicable, and you're trying to cover it up."

"What makes you think I had anything to do with this?"

"Hank Lee visited your offices Thursday morning. He told you Sally's car was abandoned on the GreeneWay."

A lump gathered in Warren's throat. "What the hell does that have to do with anything?"

"The fact that you were given information indicating your wife could be in grave danger makes you suspect, Warren."

"I'd never laid eyes on Lee before. What makes you think he told me about Sally in the first place?"

"Lee was overheard telling you about Sally's abandoned car."

He and Lee weren't talking loud enough to be heard in such a large, busy area. Everyone else was working. Everyone except Alicia Tate. He made a mental note to fire or transfer her at the first opportunity. "Whoever claims to have overheard what was said, heard it wrong," he told Ken.

"There's more than one witness. Your own employees are corroborating one another."

The room grew warmer. He loosened his tie. He

373

was going to have to do some serious housecleaning when this was over. "Even so, what proof did I have that Lee was feeding me the truth? Like I said, I didn't know him from Adam."

"You could have checked it out."

"I was much too busy."

"You weren't too busy to have Sally's car picked up and hauled off to the garage."

"That took one quick phone call. The car's a classic. I couldn't risk leaving it abandoned."

"What about Sally?"

"We'd ... had sort of a tiff that night. She left the house with her feathers ruffled. I assumed she'd gone for a ride to cool off."

"When Lee told you about her car, didn't it occur to you that the rest of what he said might actually be true?"

"If I believed every jerk who gave me some kind of cock and bull story, I'd be out of business in a week."

"The fact that you did absolutely nothing implicates you. It also suggests you either masterminded the kidnapping or acted as an accessory–"

"As soon as I got the call, I drove back to Orlando. I even tried to visit Sally at the hospital. But like I said, I was sent away."

"This doesn't look good, Warren."

"There's no way I can be charged with this. It's a matter of record that Landry and Schiller were fired for various offenses."

"I've just seen their files. There's definitely something going on."

374

He blinked. "What were you doing at Personnel?"

"I'm your attorney. When something like this comes up, I go into action. One of your personnel managers gave me access. Want to know what I found in their files?"

"I know what you found. I was the one who fired them, wasn't I?"

"Yes."

"Then what's the problem?"

"The files had obviously been filled out hastily."

"Hastily?"

"I could also tell they were copies. And when I asked the manager about them, he said he wasn't supposed to say anything."

"I'm sure you're aware of our proprietary policies, Ken."

"Don't give me that shit. You altered the files. Admit it."

Wright was getting a little too close to this. He wasn't behaving in his usual protective way. Warren suspected his good friend had suddenly turned into an enemy. "I admit nothing."

"Landry and Schiller should've been prosecuted for what they did. Anyone else would've been. You know this as well as I do."

"Maybe."

"But you merely fired them."

Warren shrugged. "I was being charitable."

Wright frowned. "I'm concerned about what was in those files before they were altered."

"Why should you be concerned about that?"

"Because this makes you look guilty."

"I just don't understand how you could think for one instant that I'd be instrumental in having someone kidnap my wife."

"You and Sally were having problems."

"All married couples have problems."

"But not all married couples are facing a billion-dollar merger."

Warren's pulse hastened. "Are you saying I'd deliberately let something terrible happen to Sally because of a merger?"

"It might make you drag your feet a little at the right time."

"That's ridiculous. It's also nothing anyone can prove in a court of law."

"You used them, Warren. You used Landry and Schiller."

"That's ridiculous. I had absolutely nothing to do with this. If I'd honestly believed Sally had been kidnapped, I wouldn't have left town at all."

Wright sat forward. "I like Sally, Warren. I've always liked her. And when I think of what she went through–"

"I had nothing to do with this!"

"You're about to be hit hard. Even if you do manage to squeeze out of it, it's going to cost you."

"It's my word over Landry's. And with his record–"

"Landry's the least of your problems. The evidence will be enough to hurt you."

"*What* evidence?"

"The courts will no doubt want to see everything involving the Bas-Com/ICS merger. And, of course, WorldVue."

376

Warren wiped his palms on his trousers beneath the desk. "What does the merger have to do with this?"

"They'll want to see the entire picture."

"Speak plain, dammit."

"I'm talking about how the picture changed when Tonya Madison made her grand entrance."

Warren took a deep breath.

"Anyone can find out all about Miss Madison by making a couple of phone calls, Warren. I made a call to ICS's personnel offices, told them who I was, and they told me she's been doing very well at ICS the last two years. I then made another phone call, this time to their legal staff, and found out that one of my old buddies from my alma mater is one of their top men. He had a few choice things to say about Miss Madison. He said she's intelligent, resourceful, cunning, and got her present position by nailing the CEO of ICS in his New York office."

"Watch it, now..."

"I have one question. It's very important, and it'll definitely shed much light on this issue. Why would such an aggressive, intelligent, self-motivated woman with a nose for power and a sixth sense about company futures even bother with WorldVue?"

"It's come a long way since its old CellFonics days."

"Compared to the average corporation, it's still a nickel-and-dime operation. Why would Madison bother with something so small, when she's got such a sweet setup with ICS?"

Warren didn't speak. Wright was getting entirely

too close to the bone.

"There *is* no merger, is there?" Wright asked. "Madison isn't interested in WorldVue, she's interested in Bas-Com."

Chills raced down Warren's spine.

"Bas-Com's got contacts all over the world. In just a few years it'll be even bigger than ICS. Madison's as high up as she can go with ICS--that is, short of taking over. But she can't. Too many men running the show. With Bas-Com, she could be in an even sweeter position. And all she has to do to is use her well-known weapons to get you exactly where she wants you."

"Don't even go there."

"Admit it, Warren. Sally's used goods. An old toy you no longer like playing with. Madison's got years before she sees thirty. She's got looks, brains, and sex appeal, and knows how to run things. You probably told her you'd let her head your European branch from Paris, but it would have to be kept secret for the time being, because there are two good men who might squawk loudly if someone of the female persuasion suddenly cuts in line."

Warren took another deep breath. Wright was getting even closer, but he was still blowing smoke.

"Someone obviously let it leak that WorldVue would be involved in a merger. People are closely monitoring WorldVue while you're playing Madison. You've also been secretly manipulating the appropriate stocks all along, using programs designed by your employees to sell certain stocks short just before the close of the Bell. With the right program, a sub-program pops up automatically, triggering an instant call-in to adjust Venture International as well as Bas-Com Preferred. As a result? You've increased your wealth by millions in one business day. Isn't that about the size of it, Warren?"

Wright had no proof. Tonya was much too bright to let anything slip. And Warren was much too bright to let her know anything she shouldn't. He'd been dangling the carrot in front of her for a full year. She had no idea Sam Randolph had already taken over Euro-Bas-Com, Inc. in a temporary capacity.

Warren pulled a slim cigar from his jacket pocket. "All conjecture," he said calmly.

"It's true, isn't it?"

"Now why should I admit something like that? Confessing to such ridiculous trash can get a man in serious trouble."

"So, I guess, once again you're in the clear."

Warren sniffed his cigar. "Actually, Miss Madison and I have been considering a merger for some time. She's got some sound ideas for incorporating a branch or two of ICS into Euro-Bas-Com, but it isn't workable just yet. Maybe next year--provided the market cooperates, of course."

"You've got everything covered, don't you?"

"You don't get where I am by being careless." Warren lit his cigar and pushed a billow of blue smoke at the ceiling fan.

"Warren, even if you didn't engineer Sally's kidnapping, you dragged your ass on it. I won't risk my career for you, and I won't leave myself open to the wrath of the Florida Bar, as I've done too many times before."

"Sorry you feel that way, Ken."

"Don't underestimate everyone. It won't take a rocket scientist to put two and two together."

"Proving it is something else, isn't it?"

"I was the one who worked with Paul George when drafting up your prenuptial. I clearly remember every last detail. Just one week from now, you'll owe Sally five million dollars. But God help you if one shred of evidence ties you with another woman."

"Adultery has nothing to do with property distribution. You know that."

"Marital misconduct could nullify the original pre-nup. No-fault will no longer apply. Florida's an equitable distribution state, but it also happens to be a charter member of the Bible Belt. It frowns on extramarital affairs. And since everyone knows Sally was being a faithful wife while you were amassing your fortune, many will think she should be entitled to half of all marital property. They'll go back seven years and consider splitting everything right down the middle. From what I've figured, your earnings for the last seven years could easily top three hundred million dollars." Ken Wright sat back. His broad grin quickly covered his face. "What's half of *that*, Warren?"

EPILOGUE

A New Beginning

Although it had been nearly two weeks since she was released from the hospital, Sally still suffered considerable back pain from her ordeal.

She also experienced sporadic circulation problems, such as tingling sensations in her toes and fingers. The doctors said the circulation would eventually come back, and that there had been no permanent damage. They'd also assured her the spinal compression from grappling with her assailants wasn't severe – no doubt due to her highly-toned condition – and would improve greatly with three or four weekly visits with her chiropractor.

Sally's physical condition wasn't foremost in her mind as she entered the dark, half-empty hotel bar, where'd they'd agreed to meet. The only thing that mattered now was the man sitting in the corner booth, waiting for her. Hank immediately slid out of the booth. His warm smile instantly made the lingering memories of horrible events in the last few weeks disappear.

Even though he came to visit her every day in the hospital, Sally ran to him as if she hadn't seen him in years. Aside from the sudden twinge in her back and a slight tingling in her right foot, she made the short trip without incident. She rushed into his arms, pressing against him, her cheek mashed against his chest. She closed her eyes and listened to the heavy thumping of his heart while his powerful arms wrapped around her. She felt safe and warm – more content than she'd felt in years. She could stay like this forever. But long before she wanted their embrace to end, he sighed and slowly released her.

Had she really and truly walked away from this man? Had she married someone else – someone she never really loved? Had she forced herself to believe she was even remotely happy the last seven years? That living in a mansion and having all she ever could want substituted for true love?

She focused on Hank's rugged face and the sweetness of his cologne. And when she took in the delicious nearness of him, she realized, after those years of blindly telling herself she was happy, her real life could finally resume.

"How's your back?"

"Actually, it doesn't hurt at all right now." She snapped out of her dream world and slid into the booth. He joined her, pressing his thigh against hers and draping an arm around her shoulders. She felt her heart pounding wildly, then pressed even harder against him. His hand closed over her left shoulder. For a moment she forgot what she'd wanted to say. Then she closed her eyes, took a deep breath, and it came right back. Focus. It was important to talk this out. Then she could think about getting him to the hotel room. "It was our anniversary last week. Mine and Warren's. Our seventh – and last."

"The divorce is official?"

"Paul pushed it through. I should be getting the final papers in just a few weeks."

"So, what was the verdict?"

382

"Believe it or not, Warren didn't quibble about anything."

"I didn't know he had it in him."

"He's going through so much with the corporation right now. A five-million-dollar divorce settlement is the least of his worries. When you're about to lose something worth nearly half a billion, your priorities change drastically."

The waitress took their orders and vanished.

"Warren was the luckiest person I've ever known," Sally said. "Everything always fell into his lap. But when this happened, it seemed as if the bad luck he's avoided all his life finally caught up."

"Couldn't happen to a nicer fella."

"His few loyal friends are gone. Ken Wright was Warren's attorney and best friend, but he jumped ship when the FBI started questioning Warren about the kidnapping."

"Smart man."

"Warren's new lawyer, Ed Springfield, was just too inexperienced for this kind of thing. He wasn't performing the way Warren wanted him to. Warren fired him and hired a Miami-based law firm that handles high-profile clients."

"Judging by what I've seen on the news, Bas-Com isn't doing well, either."

"It's downsizing, but this time it isn't Warren's idea. The stock has dropped more than twenty percent in the last week. Thank God I dumped my shares before it took a dive. When Warren's new girlfriend found out what he'd been doing, she not only dumped him, she started making phone calls. CNN was among them."

"I love it when someone mean and nasty loses everything. It kind of puts a sense of order to the universe."

Sally smiled blandly, then frowned and met Hank's serene gray eyes. "I never told you why I married him, did I?"

Hank looked like he wanted to say something, but he kept quiet and let her continue.

"I'm sure a lot of people assumed I was a gold-digger, but I didn't even know he was rich when I met him. I was working at a bar in Miami, and he came in with a group of other guys attending a software conference, and they took one of the banquet tables."

"Any of them try hitting on you?"

"Just about all of them. Actually, Warren was the most subtle of them all."

"That certainly says a lot."

"It did to me, but I wasn't myself. I was pretty depressed at the time, and he managed to joke me out of it."

"Bascomb? With a sense of humor? That's hard to picture."

"The jokes were pretty bad, and I could tell he was using them to hit on me. Some women like it when a guy falls flat on his face trying to hit on you. I'd been hit on before with bad jokes."

"I remember. I tried one or two on you when I first saw you."

"Yours weren't that bad."

"That's not what you said at the time."

She laughed. "I was so taken in by your beautiful gray eyes, I barely heard what you said. Your smile

384

did quite a job to me, too."

"Does Bascomb ever smile?"

"He did when I first met him. Maybe that was why those horrible jokes worked."

"You must've been at rock-bottom."

She shrugged, trying not to let her mind visit that place in her memories where her future looked so bleak after splitting with Hank. It was not a place she ever wanted to visit again. "Warren told me he ran a few companies, but he never said how much he was worth. I only found that out when we were planning the wedding. My lawyer friend Paul Gregorhoff heard about it and paid me a quick visit. That's when I really learned how rich Warren was."

"Was Bascomb divorced at the time? Or separated?"

"He told me he was separated and in the process of getting divorced. That was a lie, but I didn't find that out until much later. He didn't tell me his wife was really fighting the divorce. He also didn't tell me he was married twice before that. If I'd known, I wouldn't have agreed to marry him. But he was a dazzler, and when Paul told me about his past, I was already caught up in Warren's plans. He swept me off my feet. That was easy because I was heartbroken over losing you. Warren set me up in a mansion. I was so busy getting used to things and my new way of life, I didn't have the time to feel sorry for myself."

"I'll bet that was hard to take."

"I actually didn't like the new lifestyle. Not at first. Dressing up all the time, meeting slews of well-dressed people smiling at you for no reason and telling you all sorts of bizarre things. But I kept telling myself the increased activity might help me cope."

"Did it?"

"Warren gave me everything but what I really needed. Love. Respect. Companionship. He just couldn't understand how anyone could prefer that over material things. As rich as he was, Warren couldn't afford to give me what I really wanted and needed."

"But ... they're all free."

Sally shook her head. "That's the really sad part. Warren never understood that. I think he simply didn't have the capacity to genuinely care about anyone."

Hank said nothing, but she could see the hurt in his eyes.

"I know how lame all this sounds, especially now, but I was so upset and hurt by what happened between us, that I decided to hook up with the next man who showed any interest in me."

"You didn't love him at all?"

"I told myself that would come later. When a woman is over thirty and loses the man she loves most, she does some really stupid things."

Telling him about this hadn't made her feel better. It brought back the ache she'd suffered from wasting too many years with the wrong man.

The waitress brought their drinks.

"What'll we toast to?" Sally said.

"Your divorce?"

"I'd rather toast to something more important."

"What could be more important than that?"

"Guess."

He smiled. "Us, maybe?"

"No maybes."

They clinked glasses.

She put down her glass. "I hope you realize how stupid I feel about walking out on you. If I'd only stuck around, or at least picked up the phone when you'd called–"

"You were hurt. And angry."

"I wasted seven years, Hank..."

"*We* wasted seven years."

"Even worse." She wanted to slap herself.

"There is a good thing about wasting that much time."

"If there is, I'd really like to hear it."

"It feels so good when it's all over."

She finally smiled. He was right. As bad as it was, it was all over. Good times lay ahead. She only hoped he felt just as she did. "Something like this had to happen. Otherwise, we wouldn't be back together. And it's all because of Warren. He provided the perfect escape clause for me to walk away from our marriage. It was dangerous, of course – but it worked."

"Next time I see him, I'll thank him."

"I think he already knows what he's lost."

Hank started to reply, but Sally gave him a long, passionate kiss. It was even better than she remembered. She hadn't been kissed like that in seven years. It was the kind of kiss that made her tingly and hot all over – the kind that reminded her what a good kiss was supposed to be.

When her mind finally began working again, she

placed her hand on Hank's thigh and instantly felt the heat coming from him. "Heidi really wasn't at your place when you went home that day?"

"Nope. She'd taken a shower, though. I think she wanted to take a shower, then greet me at the door naked. She'd done that dozens of times before – usually when she wanted something."

"She must've taken a lot of showers."

"Heidi had an obsession for being clean. She used to take at least three showers a day. But I obviously pissed her off when I told her about you."

"How do you know?"

"Remember that picture I took of you that time we went to Vegas for that spur-of-the-moment three-day vacation?"

"Of course."

"I kept it in that collage of us on my pegboard in the kitchen. A day or so after you left, I noticed someone had taken two thumbtacks and shoved them through your eyes. That always bothered me, because I knew I didn't do it."

She laughed. "You think she did that?"

"Heidi was a lot of things, but nice wasn't among them. Like she told me many times, a woman who looks like her doesn't have to be nice."

"I felt uneasy as soon as I met her. She seemed ... cold. Even when she smiled at me."

"She was cold."

"But she sure was beautiful."

"She always was breathtaking. Almost as beautiful as you."

Sally's eyes suddenly brimmed with tears, but she told herself not to cry. This wasn't the time.

"That's something I wanted to hear seven years ago."

They kissed again. The dizziness and the warmth billowing down her limbs overwhelmed her. When the kiss ended, she took a deep breath and looked into his eyes. "When I left your place that day, I hated you. I hoped I'd never see you again."

"I'd say you changed your mind since then."

"What gave me away?"

He shrugged. "You're here. Sitting beside me. Rubbing my leg." He studied her mouth. "And that glint of drool on your lower lip is also giving off messages."

"You're a natural-born profiler."

"I have to be. There are some crazy females out there these days."

"I could be one of them."

"Is that why you're gripping my thigh like a cat hugging a tree?"

"Maybe I just don't want you to get away again."

"I honestly don't think you'll ever have to worry about that."

She searched his eyes. They told her he meant what he said. "That's a promise. Right?"

"If you still want me."

"You're not serious."

"Me? Serious?"

"I know, I know. But just to set the record straight, let me think about this for a second." She put her index finger to her chin and rolled her eyes, faking deep thought. With a little hum, she said, "Yeah. I want you."

"You don't want to think about it some more?"

389

She gripped his thigh even harder.

He grimaced. "I guess that means no."

"You always did know how to read a woman." She smiled, trying to be coy despite her eagerness.

"Should I get us a room? Or am I being a tad presumptuous?"

A tingle went through her body as she looked up at him, smiling wider. "A tad. But I already took care of it." She opened her purse, pulled out the key, and slid it across the tabletop toward him.

He stared at it, then at her, his eyes twinkling. She shrugged. "I didn't want to waste any more time."

With his arm already around her shoulders, he hugged her and bent down, giving her a lingering kiss. "I love you, Sally ... never stopped loving you."

Tears flooded her eyes. A lot of men carelessly tossed the word 'love' around, but when she heard Hank say he loved her, she knew he really meant it. "I love you too, Hank. And..." She gulped back the sudden urge to sob with relief and joy. Gripping his hand, she felt his strength and warmth imbuing her with calm reassurance. "I want to thank you."

"You mean for rescuing you?"

She focused on her drink as tears continued to trickle down her cheeks. She was on such an emotional high, she didn't trust herself to say anything else for a moment. She grabbed her drink and gulped the last of it, then set her glass down. She took a deep breath and faced him, tears and all. "For saving my life. For giving my life back to me. For the first time in seven years, I actually feel

390

alive."

He bent down and kissed her again, on both cheeks and then on the lips. This time his mouth sought hers passionately, and the urgency took her breath away. "I know exactly how you feel," he murmured. "I should thank you for saving me, too. Because you did – seven years ago, and now."

He slid out of the booth seat and held out his hand to her. "Let's go."

As he pulled her up, she straightened, and her legs suddenly felt like limp noodles. They were strong and toned, but as unsteady as they felt right now, she wondered if they would get her to the room without her collapsing. But if she couldn't make it all the way on her own, she knew she could depend on Hank's strength and love to carry her the rest of the way.

THE END

OTHER WORKS BY
DAVID BERARDELLI:

THE APPRENTICE
THE WAGON DRIVER
STEPPING OUT OF MY GRAVE
ESCAPE CLAUSE
FATAL INNOCENCE
COLORS
IN ANOTHER REALM
BEYOND RECOGNITION
THE NIGHTMARE COLLECTOR
HIDDEN
BEYOND GUILT
A RIPPLE IN TIME
YESTERDAY'S JOURNEY
ENLIGHTENMENT
REDEMPTION
AWAKENED

Titles available through:
Fiction4All